Alanna Knight is a novelist, biographer and playwright. *Enter Second Murderer*, *Blood Line* and *Deadly Beloved* are her first three novels to feature Inspector Faro; Alanna Knight is now working on the ninth. She is a committee member of the Crime Writers' Association and Secretary of the Society of Authors in Scotland, and she lectures in the Scottish Arts Council's Writers in Public scheme. She is an authority on Robert Louis Stevenson. Married with two sons and a granddaughter, Alanna Knight lives in Edinburgh.

Alanna Knight

INSPECTOR FARO
AND THE
EDINBURGH MYSTERIES

ENTER SECOND MURDERER
BLOOD LINE
DEADLY BELOVED

PAN BOOKS
IN ASSOCIATION WITH MACMILLAN LONDON

Enter Second Murderer first published 1988 by Macmillan London Limited
First published by Pan Books Limited in this edition

Blood Line first published 1989 by Macmillan London Limited
First published by Pan Books Limited in this edition

Deadly Beloved first published 1989 by Macmillan London Limited
First published by Pan Books Limited in this edition

This omnibus edition published 1994 by Pan Books
a division of Macmillan General Books
Cavaye Place London SW10 9PG
and Basingstoke
in association with Macmillan London

Associated companies throughout the world

ISBN 0 330 33943 5

Printed and bound in Great Britain by
Cox & Wyman Ltd, Reading, Berkshire

INSPECTOR FARO

AND THE

EDINBURGH MYSTERIES

ENTER SECOND MURDERER

In memory of Maw

CHAPTER ONE

Patrick Hymes was tried and convicted at the High Court of Justiciary in Edinburgh for the murders of Sarah Gibson (or Hymes) and Lily Goldie. He made his exit from the world on 11 May 1870, a day that promised to be bright and cheerful for everyone but him. With the noose about his neck, to the accompaniment of a single blackbird's tumultuous song and without a single human tear as requiem, he went into eternity protesting his innocence of the second murder.

There was little known about Patrick Hymes, an Irish labourer whose pretty young wife had abandoned him and their two small children to make a new life for herself as maidservant in an Edinburgh convent. There the nuns were ignorant of her moral lapses, for Sarah Hymes was, in the parlance of the day, no better than she should be.

Patrick Hymes, a simple uneducated man, showed remarkable industry and ingenuity in tracking down his runaway wife, and luring her out for an evening stroll on the pretext of a reconciliation gift. He knew that baubles were the one way to Sarey's grasping heart. When his attentions threatened to become more familiar, as was his right, they quarrelled. His manly pride insulted, his role of husband and father belittled, Patrick dispatched Sarey by strangulation on the highest ridge of Salisbury Crags.

Hymes had, according to evidence at the trial, hoped to escape justice by her demise being classified as an unfortunate accident on a narrow path in an area notoriously prone to landslides. Even a cursory post-mortem examination, however, revealed suspicious marks of violence upon her person and bruises about her throat.

There was enough evidence in the subsequent murder of Lily Goldie, in similar circumstances, to convince everyone that she had also been the victim of Patrick Hymes. According to the newspapers, townsfolk were afraid to sleep in their beds at night.

'GRUESOME CONVENT MURDERS' ran the headlines, promising an epidemic of horrible strangulations. The police were assisted in their enquiries from a totally unexpected quarter: the troubled conscience of Patrick Hymes, who appeared all atremble at the Central Office of Edinburgh City Police and dramatically confessed to his late wife's murder. On producing proof of identity and evidence to link him with the murdered woman, there were sighs of relief all round. But even as the report was being hastily written in the Central Office, came the assassin's vehement denial.

'Lily Goldie? Who's Lily Goldie? Never heard of *her*.'

The evidence was read to him. Only two days earlier, the body of Lily Goldie had been discovered at the foot of Salisbury Crags, some hundred yards from the spot where Sarah Hymes was murdered. A remarkable coincidence made even more remarkable by the fact that she too had been strangled, not manually but with a scarf knotted about her neck. And stretching coincidence to its utmost: Lily Goldie was also employed, as a teacher, at the Convent of the Sisters of St Anthony in the Newington area.

Hymes was now eagerly accepted as Lily Goldie's slayer and sternly advised to admit to both murders and thereby make it easier for himself. Hymes continued to be outraged by the suggestion, expressing himself in violent language which was subsequently monitored for the ears and eyes of those with more sheltered upbringing as, 'I don't care what she was or who she was. I never heard of her. You find out who done her in – it weren't me.'

Resisting pleas that another confession would make a lot of people happy, and ignoring assurances that swinging for two murders was no more painful than swinging for one, he shouted, 'Easier for meself, you mean easier for yous. Ties it up all neatly.' And stabbing a finger at the unfortunate constable taking down his statement, 'You can write that in your — evidence.'

Refusing to be cajoled or threatened, Hymes remained stubborn on the matter of Lily Goldie.

For Detective Inspector Jeremy Faro, the case of Patrick Hymes, double murderer, meant a few less illusions about a depraved humanity, one more in the annals of sordid domestic crimes he had investigated during his twenty years with the Edinburgh Police Force.

On the eve of Hymes's dramatic confession Faro unfortunately had been struck down by a typhus-like illness, not altogether rare in Edinburgh City and with consequences fatal for those of less robust constitution than his own.

His stepson, newly graduated Dr Vincent Beaumarcher Laurie, had returned home to find him lying on the floor writhing with pain. The most cursory examination revealed a condition too advanced to respond to home treatment. Hailing a passing gig, he rushed Faro into hospital for immediate and drastic treatment.

Faro was grateful. He knew that he owed his life to Vince's presence of mind and the great good fortune of his leaving Dr Kellar's surgery earlier than usual that afternoon.

Vince had watched over him until he was out of danger, and as soon as he was able to return home again had questioned him closely. Had any of his colleagues suffered in a similar fashion?

That had been Faro's first question to his visitors from the Central Office. Heads were shaken, but Vince refused to be convinced.

9

'It is as I suspected, Stepfather. Someone was trying to get rid of you. Someone who had it in for you.'

'What an idea. I am hardly that important.' Faro laughed weakly. 'More likely one of Mrs Mallet's mutton pies, from the shop we patronise at the Central Office, was the culprit.'

The illness left him weak in body, depressed in spirits. Much as he disliked leaving a case before the trial, he felt too sick to protest. Suddenly the detective's long hours, where strong legs and stronger stomachs were absolute necessities, palled on him. Vince insisted that he must go away and convalesce, a suggestion received by Superinten-dent Mackintosh of the Edinburgh City Police with more than his usual warmth. Patting Faro's shoulder heavily, he said, 'You are too valuable to lose, Faro. Take a holiday, you deserve it. Why not go home for a while – as long as you like,' he added, with unaccustomed generosity.

Home was Kirkwall, in the Orkney Isles, where his two little daughters, Rose and Emily, aged eight and six, had lived with their grandmother since Lizzie died.

'Absolutely not,' said Vince. 'Much too far for you to travel – and a rough crossing is the last thing you need in your condition. Don't even consider it. Besides, you know how Grandmama fusses. How about your Aunt Isa? Her nursing experience would be admirable.'

Aunt Isa, nanny to several generations of middle-class children, had married a gardener at Balmoral Castle. A widow for many years, she lived in an estate cottage at Crathie, where Deeside's fresh air and some excellent fishing aided Faro's recovery better than the abundant good food, which still revolted him. Edinburgh and the existence of violent murder seemed remote as the moon and stars, impossible among those peaceful hills, and he hoped all would be resolved before his return.

He found instead that Hymes, his execution imminent, had made a last request to speak to Inspector Faro.

Faro went reluctantly, arriving at the cell as the priest was leaving. He had never overcome his distaste for the barbaric biblical law of an eye for an eye, a tooth for a tooth and a life for a life, especially in the case of a man who, far from being an habitual criminal, for one instant in his life lost control over man's most primitive emotion.

As he sat opposite Hymes, he felt sure he was right. There was something about a killer's eyes, a destroyer who kills wantonly, a quality that defied words but which his intuition told him was lacking in the man before him.

'You're a fair-minded peeler, I'm told. And as sure as God is me witness, I am no cold-blooded killer of innocent women,' said Hymes desperately. 'I killed my Sarey. That I freely admit and am willing to swing for the faithless whore that she was. The world is well rid of her. But that other lass – whatever they say, I never even laid eyes on her, much less a hand. Sure, it's a pack of lies they're pinnin' on me. Someone's made it look as if I done her in too. They needn't have bothered – I swing tomorrow – I've made my confession, I've received absolution for my crime and I'm not sorry to be quit of this world. I loved my Sarey and I'll love her with my dying breath – aye, and curse her in it too. But I'd never killed that other one.' He looked around the tiny cell, wild-eyed.

'Listen to me, Inspector. What I'm saying is the truth. Sarey would be alive if I hadn't a temper on me, always in me nature to be a violent man but only with her on account of her wicked nature. When we went out walking, so peaceful and agreeable like it started, I thought I could talk her round to coming home with me, back to our two poor bairns. But, Jezebel that she was, she laughed at me, scorned and cursed me, and when I tried to shake some sense into her, no different than I've done a score of times afore, I ended up with me hands around her throat, throttling the bitch.'

11

Hymes paused, looking at his hands spread out before him on the table as if he could not believe that they had performed the monstrous task. 'I don't remember anything till I heard her choking – the next moment she'd gone such a funny colour. Dear Mother of God, be merciful to me,' he whispered, and, laying his head on his folded arms, he sobbed.

'I didn't know she was dead, I swear it. It's just like I told you the first time when I gave meself up. I was that shocked I let go of her, as God's me witness, we were that near the edge of the path, she just went limp and rolled over the cliff on her own account. I've told them over and over. I never meant to kill Sarey, it was just an accident that could happen to any man on that narrow path.

'Not like that Lily, that strangling her with her scarf – now that was deliberate murder,' he added self-righteously as he waited, eager for some response from Faro, who could think of no words of comfort that were not either trite or inappropriate to the occasion. Faro could always put himself, however uncomfortably, into the criminal's shoes. What, he thought, if it had been my Lizzie? Would I not have experienced the same murderous rage of a husband and father betrayed, the same impulse to destroy? Since the labouring classes most frequently indulged in the pastime of wife-beating, murder often became violent chastisement that went too far. Such murders, Faro firmly believed, constituted no threat to the community, but the society who would share his humanitarian views was not yet born.

If the public who, ten years earlier, had rushed to see public executions, had seen and heard this pathetic emaciated wife-slayer (who bore little resemblance to the police-court drawings of a robust, fresh-faced labourer), they could never for a moment have believed that every female in Newington was in danger from such a creature.

Faro's silence was misunderstood. 'I see you don't believe

me, Inspector, either,' he said sadly, shaking his head. 'It doesn't matter for, even if you did, it can't change anything now. But God will believe me. He knows that murder's not in me nature and that I'm a peace-loving God-fearing man. Ask anyone who knows me two bairns, the good father that I am to them, denying them nothing, patient as a saint. Sure an' I know I'll go to hell for the cruel thing I did to Sarey and all the saints' prayers can't save me from the gallows tomorrow. But better to die than let Sarey destroy other happy homes and spoil men's lives like she did mine.'

There was an Othello-like dignity about the shabby little Irishman who had killed for love gone wrong, and despite the evidence of that second murder Faro had an unhappy feeling that he had listened to the truth and was assisting a miscarriage of justice, as well as ignoring the important and very disquieting implication raised by Hymes's protestations of innocence: the existence of a second murderer.

Returning to the Central Office, he took down the remarkably small packet which contained an account of the trial, and found that in retrospect the case made very curious reading. There were too many coincidences by far. From his long association with criminals, Faro suspected that the solution with Hymes as the double murderer was just a shade too convenient.

Superintendent Mackintosh, a man of large proportions with a voice like an army sergeant major, looked up from his desk. 'Seen him, have you? Still protesting, is he?'

'Yes. Frankly, I'm a bit uneasy about the whole thing. Doesn't it seem strangely out of character that Hymes should have murdered Lily Goldie? I mean, it was quite motiveless.'

'Motiveless? Of course it wasn't motiveless. The man's a damned villain. Totally unreliable. Can't expect people of that class to reason things out. Blood lust, that's what it was. His wife was a whore, so it follows that any woman

13

like her is a whore. Simple for anyone to understand that.'
And at Faro's doubtful expression, he thundered, 'Do you
know what you're suggesting, man?'

'I'm only suggesting further enquiries.'

'Further enquiries? You must be mad. Authority has to be
appeased and the public's demand for justice satisfied with
a hanging. And in the very unlikely event that Hymes didn't
murder Goldie, he still has to hang for the self-confessed
murder of his wife.'

'He claims it was an accident – manslaughter rather than
murder.'

Mackintosh banged his fist on the desk. 'Ridiculous,
Faro, the case has been tried and he's proved guilty and
that will have to satisfy you as well as everyone else.' He
paused. 'Are you suggesting that in your absence there
has been a miscarriage of justice?' When Faro was silent,
he said, 'You'll have to produce a second murderer.' And
jabbing a finger at Faro, he said, 'And you'll have a mighty
hard job doing that, I fancy. You won't get much help
from the police either, quite frankly, because any idea that
Hymes didn't kill Goldie puts forward the nasty suggestion
that we have failed in our duty and there's a murderer
still on the loose, roaming the streets of Edinburgh, with
other innocent lives – particularly young female lives – in
danger.'

With a clumsy attempt at placating Faro, he said, 'Be
reasonable, man. A public investigation, an admission of
what you suspect in the newspapers and there would be
chaos. You've been very ill, I realise. And you've had your
holidays. The High Court is almost into summer recess.
Sheriffs have families and domestic obligations too,' he
added plaintively.

Faro suppressed a smile, remembering that Mrs Mackintosh, though pint-sized, was a Tartar, who would not
hesitate to resort to husband-beating and similar violence
upon her husband, should he dare suggest cancelling or

delaying the annual family holiday at North Berwick.

Faro sighed. It was fairly obvious that such events, in the absence of the senior detective, had led to a hasty conviction which assumed that Hymes, in common with most murderers, was a consummate liar, who wished only to embarrass and perturb the police further and hamper their investigations.

'It's all there for you to read, Faro.'

Faro glanced at the papers. 'He doesn't bear much likeness now to the drawings. Did he ever look like this?'

Mackintosh shifted uncomfortably. 'Oh yes. But he was determined not to eat until he could get someone to believe his fantastic story. We didn't think force-feeding was called for in the circumstances – I mean, once he had been found guilty.' He smirked awkwardly. 'Seemed quite set on dying, although we tried to tell him that hanging's easier for a heavy man – takes a shorter time than for a light one.'

Faro cut short these unsavoury explanations. 'If, as you tried to prove, Lily Goldie was murdered because she had seen Hymes visiting the kitchen and had been a witness to the pair departing together for that last ill-fated walk on Salisbury Crags, why didn't she inform the police during the routine questioning which I conducted myself? She seemed baffled and shocked as everyone else at St Anthony's, her statement made no mention of lurking strangers.'

'Oh for heaven's sake, Faro. The man was found guilty. The case is closed. And you take my advice if you know what's good for you. Let sleeping dogs – and hanged murderers – lie.'

CHAPTER TWO

Faro walked briskly down the High Street, its eight-storeyed 'lands' looming above his head. This was market day and the noise of vendors, the yelling of fishwives in from Newhaven, the jostling of the crowds and the smell of hot, unwashed flesh were too much for him. Aware only that he was badly in need of some air, fresh and bracing, he hurried down past the Palace of Holyroodhouse. The romance and stormy passions lost for ever behind those grey walls never failed to move him, associated as they were with the story of his beloved Mary, Queen of Scots, beset by villains, tricked and cheated, betrayed. He often wished he had lived in those turbulent days and had been able to wield a sword in her name.

The noise of raucous bustling Edinburgh faded. Salisbury Crags, the distressing scene of the two murders, seemed to stare down at him reproachfully from its lofty heights. Quickening his steps beneath its grim shadow, he walked up the ancient Gibbet Lane towards his new home.

After Lizzie's death he had decided to remove himself from the more convenient house they had occupied in Cockburn Street. He needed a new beginning, and one day, walking in King's Park, he decided to take a look at Newington, which was rapidly developing as a popular suburb on the south side of Edinburgh.

The recently built villas lacked the splendid proportions and classical character of the New Town's Georgian architecture and the house in Sheridan Place was too large and altogether too modern for his taste, having just managed to evade the gross exaggerations of the presently fashionable Gothic style, upon which curlicues and turrets ran rampant.

Faro had been captivated by the views from its windows. Arthur's Seat, Edinburgh's dramatic extinct volcano, filled the eastern skyline, the Pentland Hills, with their ever-changing light, drowsed in the west. By coincidence, the house's first tenant had been an elderly doctor, recently deceased. The fully equipped surgery on the ground floor suggested the benign workings of fate, that this would be the perfect home for Vince and himself. He considered himself unlikely to remarry and enjoyed the most harmonious relationship with his stepson, who would soon be setting up his own brass plate, once he had served his term as assistant to the police surgeon, Dr Kellar.

The house had the added attraction of a nearby gig-hiring establishment, in addition to one of the new horse-drawn omnibus services, very convenient for the Central Office in Parliament Square.

Perhaps most tempting of all, he had acquired with the house a modest but ready-made domestic staff: two kitchen-maids, who he decided were not at all necessary, and a housekeeper, Mrs Brook, who would be a great asset, especially as she had long and faithfully served the deceased doctor and was well acquainted with the rapidly growing Newington area.

Mrs Brook agreed with him on the matter of living-in maids and seemed anxious to dispense with this additional expense. Thus Faro settled happily in 9 Sheridan Place, a move he most urgently needed as a lifeline back into some semblance of lost family life.

'Ah, Inspector sir, the doctor was a widower, just like yourself.' And with a vigorous nod. 'Ye ken what it's like then, all too well. My late sir was right pleased wi' ma

17

services. Came to him when the paint was just dry on the house – his poor wife was an invalid and I saw her through to the very end.' She sighed deeply. 'A melancholy life for a well-set-up gentleman like yourself,' she added with a slyly admiring glance, 'and that bonny young lad, too. Both of you surrounded by so many corpses. At least your last landlady didna' die on you, and that's a mercy.'

Faro was amazed that she knew so much of his history already and guessed that she had wheedled the story out of Vince, always eager for a gossip in her kitchen – an unfortunate trait which he would have to overcome in his chosen profession.

Mrs Brook had regarded him sympathetically. Not that she could blame any woman taking a fancy to the Inspector. Although she would have found it difficult to describe his features or his bearing exactly, beyond saying that he was tall and strong-looking, youngish still, with a good head of fairish hair and good features. 'Stern he is, but he can make a body laugh sometimes. Mind, ye'd no want to get on his bad side. He's no' the kind of man ye'd care to cross. He'd make a terrible enemy, that he would,' she whispered with an expressive shudder to her cronies, eager for more details.

And, flicking away invisible dust from the photographs on the mantelshelf, 'Have you no' thought of having these bonny wee lasses here with you?' And, with a sly look, 'Perhaps wi' them to take care of, we may expect another lady-wife in God's good time.' At Faro's expression, she realised she had gone too far and continued hastily, 'There are some nice schools . . .'

He hoped she wasn't about to recommend the convent school with its unhappy association with two recent murders.

'It's a weary life for those of us who lose a loved one. My own dear man has been gone these twenty years, but I still remember him in my prayers. We who have been spared should stick together.'

18

And stick together was quite plainly Mrs Brook's earnest intention. She talked too much and too often for Faro, who was of a somewhat taciturn disposition, but otherwise he hadn't any real objections. She was an excellent cook and an admirable housekeeper.

After Lizzie died, in those terrible weeks of disbelief and anguish that followed, he had been easily persuaded by his mother to let Rose and Emily remain with her in Kirkwall, in far-off Orkney. Mary Faro was a sensible woman. She had recognised her son's helplessness confronted by grief and the bewildering demands of two children under ten years old. Indeed, he seemed little more than a shocked child himself, this big strong man who could cope with violent crimes but when death knocked at his own door was found totally unprepared. His wounds must be allowed to heal before he was strong enough to resume the role of parenthood, and so he had moved into Leith with a remote cousin, a middle-aged spinster who ran a boarding-house. Her intentions were soon apparent. After the observation of the requisite period of mourning, she had expected to become the second Mrs Faro, a revelation which involved Faro in speedily removing himself to a safe distance.

Mrs Brook met him in the hall as he picked up his mail. 'Another wee postcard I see from Kirkwall,' she said with a sigh. 'Those bairns must miss their Da.' And, with a return to her favourite theme of absent daughters, 'There are always gentlefolk willing to act as governesses hereabouts.'

'My salary won't rise to private teaching,' said Faro, promptly disabusing Mrs Brook of any idea that detectives belonged to the wealthy classes. 'They are happy enough at their school mean time.'

'They have proper schools up yonder?'

Faro laughed. 'Indeed – and very good ones. I was educated there myself.'

Mrs Brook regarded this miracle with new respect. 'Well I never, Inspector sir, who would have ever thought that. You have come a long way, haven't you? Like that hamper—'

'Hamper?'

'Yes, Inspector sir. It arrived this morning by the carter and I got them to put it in your study.'

Faro recognised the hamper, which had belonged to his father. As Mrs Brook put it, Inspector Faro had come a long way. But perhaps not as far as Constable Magnus Faro, the Orkney-born policeman who had served with the Edinburgh Police Force in its earlier days. He had died in an accident, which his wife refused to believe was anything else but deliberate murder. Mary Faro had taken their only son back to her own people, never having got used to living in the city and wishing only to leave behind Edinburgh, which had held out so much promise for their future and had brought only bitter grief and sad memories.

Memories of his father for young Jeremy were far from sad. Possessed of remarkable and almost total recall, which was to prove invaluable in his profession, he could remember in vivid detail the father who had gone out of the house one morning, waving him goodbye, and had returned, carried into the house, cold and still on a bloodied stretcher that evening.

Jeremy had been four years old. But he was never to forget his father's stories of crimes solved and other baffling mysteries unexplained. These had so stimulated his childish imagination that, to his mother's surprise and much against her wishes, he had resolved early in life to make the police force his career. Later, he sometimes wondered whether hero-worship and stories from his mother had built an image that did not exist beyond the silhouette of the handsome policeman on the mantelshelf.

'There's the young doctor now,' said Mrs Brook, 'with another load for the washtub, I see. It's a good job I'm not queasy by nature, being as how I'm used to doctors. All that blood, turns a body's stomach.'

Faro watched Vince striding down the street. Corn-bright curls, deep blue eyes framed by black eyebrows and eyelashes, it was little wonder that the boy's presence was such a comfort, when his sweet Lizzie haunted him every day from out of her son's face. Vince was twenty-one. Lizzie had been but four years older, mother of a nine-year-old son, when they first met. Faro thought wistfully of the future and of his strange fancy that if Vince and he stayed together in this house until they too were old, then his dear wife too would remain with him, never lost, through the years.

The lad had inherited his mother's beauty without her gentle nature. In childhood, he had exhibited a will of iron combined with a violent temper. A nasty, truculent child, difficult for anyone to love, let alone a prospective stepfather. From the beginning Vince had made evident his dislike and disgust at his mother's choice of husband – and Lizzie had made many excuses, certain that being born with the stigma of bastardy had been the cause of it all. For her lapse, Lizzie had not been made to suffer in Skye as she might have done in a more Calvinistic city environment. Islands had sympathy for girls who got into trouble, especially fifteen-year-old servants in the laird's house who were seduced, or, more often, found themselves helpless against what amounted to rape, by rich callous guests.

Since the death of Lizzie and their newborn son, he had needed Vince, as all that remained to him of his beloved wife. From the unlikely spring of dislike and resentment, tolerance and friendship had sprung up between bereaved husband and son, as they sought forgetfulness in agreeable leisure activities, walking in the hills and canoeing on the River Forth. The only echoes of Vince's early rebel-lion shone forth in occasional lively and ill-timed student

21

pranks, which gave his policeman stepfather a somewhat red face. But Faro was proud indeed of the boy he now regarded as his own son in every way except the accident of conception.

Having made his escape from Mrs Brook, he retreated to his study upstairs, reproached by the loving message from Rose and Emily – saying that they had not had a letter from dear Papa for some time. Resolving to write immediately, he opened the other letter and drew out a head-and-shoulders photograph of a handsome young man: 'To my lovely Lily, Ever your T.'

The note enclosed was from the Mother Superior at the Convent of St Anthony.

This photograph was found by one of the nuns when she was clearing out the room which had been occupied by the unfortunate Lily Goldie. It had presumably slipped down behind the skirting-board and had been overlooked during the police search. I realise that the case is closed but I thought you might like to add it to the unhappy girl's possessions which I understand are in police-keeping awaiting a claimant.

There had been no mention of 'T.' in the report on Lily Goldie's murder, of that he was certain. Was this new evidence in the case? With a sense of growing excitement, Faro carried the card to the window and was re-reading the letter from the Mother Superior when Vince's conversation with Mrs Brook in the hall announced his imminent appearance.

'Good-day, Stepfather. Caught any criminals today?'

Faro smiled at the boy's usual greeting. 'Not today, lad. I've just had a last interview with Hymes.'

'New evidence?'

Faro shook his head. 'No. Just the same old story, that he didn't murder Lily Goldie. I'm inclined to believe him, dammit.'

Vince was silent for a moment. 'You know my feelings, Stepfather. I think – although the good Doctor Kellar nearly had a fit when I suggested such a thing – I think that Lily Goldie was killed by the fall – doubtless she was pushed, and that scarf was tied around her neck, afterwards, to make it look like murder.'

'That's precisely what Hymes maintains.'

'Ah, but how do we prove it?'

'We can't, unless we produce a second murderer.'

'Or unless our second murderer strikes again. Talking of which, the Pleasance Theatre are putting on *Macbeth* this week. Shall I get you a ticket?'

'I don't know that I'm strong enough to see the Immortal Bard murdered by amateurs just now.'

Vince laughed. 'Don't be such a snob, Stepfather. They are professional actors: Mr Topaz Trelawney's Thespians. You've missed a very popular season and there are only two weeks left. You must see them, some of the actors are very good indeed, particularly the leading lady. She's an absolute stunner, probably Mrs T.,' he added regretfully.

Faro smiled. His stepson had a penchant for actresses, but usually of the more frivolous variety.

'Oh, talking of "T."— '

'What an outrageous pun, Stepfather.'

'I mean the initial "T." – have a look at this.'

Faro handed him the photograph and the note.

'Good Lord, I know who this is.'

'You do? Could this be our missing man – our second murderer?'

Vince shook his head. 'The likeness flatters him, but I'd swear it's Timothy Ferris. He was in my year at medical school.'

'Did he know Lily?'

'Oh yes, indeed. He met her in January when we all went skating together on Duddingston Loch. He was quite infatuated— '

23

'A missing suitor, by God. Now we're getting somewhere,' said Faro excitedly.

'Only on the road that leads to the grave,' said Vince solemnly.

'What do you mean?'

'I mean that Tim is dead, Stepfather. By his own hand. Committed suicide, walked under a railway train.'

Faro remembered vaguely the case as just another of the tragic suicides that were encountered almost every day at the Central Office, routine investigations in which he wasn't concerned. Except to thank God it wasn't his son – or stepson – that had been driven to such an end. The association with Lily Goldie put the matter of Timothy Ferris into new perspective. But the time-factor was wrong.

Vince nodded. 'Yes, he died two weeks before Lily's murder. Remember, I told you? He failed his last qualifying exams and was thrown out at the beginning of the term. He wasn't a particular friend of mine, but rumour had it that he was deeply involved with some girl who was leading him on.' And, picking up the photograph, 'That would fit the character of Lily.'

'What about his family?'

'Didn't have any. He was an orphan. However, he always had plenty of cash to spend on wine and gambling. Bit of a waster, was Tim. And there was a rumour of some rich relative supporting him through medical school.'

'I seem to remember you went to the funeral?'

A look of pain crossed Vince's face. 'It was at Greyfriars, Stepfather,' he said, trying to sound casual as for a moment they fell silent, remembering that other beloved grave, the mother and wife who was gone from them. 'I steeled myself,' Vince continued. 'Matter of courtesy, you know, from his year, when he had no relatives. We were the only mourners. No girls that I noticed. And I would have remembered Lily Goldie, especially as I had to assist at the post-mortem, one of my first cases,' he added with a shudder. 'Bad enough having to deal with the corpse of a total stranger, but to encounter a pretty girl one has met before, even on the slightest acquaintance ... I had nightmares.'

'Tell me again – about the post-mortem.'

'Nothing much to tell – a lot of bruising, a broken wrist and pelvis, and contusions which would be the case for anyone falling from a steep crag – either falling naturally or grappling with an assailant wouldn't make much difference by the time she reached ground-level. Those marks about her neck were very different from what you'd expect of a labourer's strong hands.'

'You suspected that the murderer followed her down to ... ?'

'Exactly. And tied the scarf about her neck afterwards to make it look like Hymes's work. Unfortunately Doctor Kellar is a pig-headed gentleman and he laughed my idea to scorn. "Enthusiastic young amateur doctors mustn't let their personal interest in cases take precedence over good sense. One must learn to be dispassionate."

'I think he rather gauged by my reactions – since I was very sick at one point – that I had been infatuated with her.' Vince smiled grimly. 'Poor Lily, in life we had the most superficial acquaintance which would hardly have justified the intimacy of a post-mortem. Ironically, I found myself remembering her effect on the more susceptible of my year. Not that she wanted penniless students, she had her sights set well above the likes of us.'

He looked at Faro thoughtfully. 'You know, her tragedy was being born in the wrong age. She should have been a Nell Gwyn or a Pompadour, a courtesan, who knows no allegiance except to her own ambition. She must have been desperate indeed to seek employment in a convent. By the way, I've kept all the newspaper accounts about Hymes that you wanted.'

From behind the clock on the mantelpiece, Vince withdrew a small sheaf of newsprint. 'Let's see. "GRUESOME CONVENT MURDERS",' he read in mock sepulchral tones. '"Chills of horror are being experienced in the respectable modern Edinburgh environs of Newington and Grange where the brutal murders of two innocent female victims from the Catholic Orphanage of St Anthony have thrown a blight of fear and foreboding over sisters and pupils alike at the school whose activities are seriously affected."' He paused before continuing. '"Sufferings of extreme ill-health prevented the well-known and exceedingly brilliant Detective Inspector Faro from solving these interesting and diabolically wicked crimes."'

'Give it here – it doesn't say that.'

'Well, it should.'

'This one solved itself – thanks to Hymes's confession.' Faro sighed, with a shake of his head. 'Nothing more to do.'

Vince regarded him narrowly, very much the doctor. 'Feeling all right today, Stepfather? No more nasty griping pains? Appetite getting better?'

'I'm still a bit shaky, more easily tired than I should be, but with a kind of typhus that isn't surprising.'

Vince scratched his cheek thoughtfully. 'I still wonder, you know.'

'Wonder?'

'Yes. About your illness. I think you were deliberately poisoned.' Even when Patrick Hymes gave himself up, Vince stoutly defended his theory of a sinister plot to poison his stepfather. 'I must say, though, you're looking better every day. Still rather too thin, I fear. By the way, I met Constable McQuinn in Rutherford's howff – he was very solicitous about your health. When were you coming back? Were you fully recovered? Etcetera, etcetera.'

Faro felt annoyance return, the distaste for anything connected with Constable McQuinn, who had taken over

26

the Hymes case when Faro took ill and there was no other senior officer available. Now he felt as if being ill had played into Constable McQuinn's hands and a little responsibility had increased his bumptiousness and made him more know-all than ever.

Faro grunted and Vince smiled. 'You don't like the amiable constable much, do you?'

'No. He smiles too much and too often. Even when he's talking about a sudden death, you'd think he was laughing at a secret joke. And I get a nasty feeling that it's not so much my health as my job he's after. And he should have found that photograph of Timothy Ferris, too, in the final routine search of Lily Goldie's room. It was evidence, after all.'

'You're not going to complain about that, I hope,' said Vince anxiously.

'I'm not – but I'd be within my rights.'

'Come, Stepfather, you're being too hard on him.' Vince smiled. 'Don't worry. He's got a long way to go before he's had enough experience to be a threat to the job of detective inspector. Can't be much older than I am.'

Ignoring this plea to be reasonable, Faro decided that the photograph of Ferris presented an irresistible opportunity of putting the unctuous young policeman in his place.

Next morning he found Constable McQuinn sitting at his desk, smiling and whistling to himself, in a manner that suggested life was being very good to him. He yawned and shook his shoulders with a grin. Was he reliving the night's conquests, the unsuspecting serving girls and shop assistants who seemed to be his prey?

And approaching his desk, Faro wondered if he was seeing in the handsome young constable the youth he had never been. Was envy the root-cause of his irritation whenever he met McQuinn off-duty in Princes Street Gardens or listening to the band in the park, strutting like a pouter pigeon with a different giggling young female on his arm?

At Faro's approach, he stood up, straightened his tunic and saluted his superior officer politely. 'A pleasure to have you back with us, Inspector. I trust you are fully restored to health again— '

'Never mind about that,' interrupted Faro ungraciously, and held out the photograph, carefully concealing the inscription. 'Have you ever seen this before?'

McQuinn looked thoughtful. 'Can't say as how I have, Inspector. Should I have seen it?' he added, smiling gently.

'Since it was discovered by one of the nuns in Lily Goldie's room, of which you were supposed to have conducted a thorough search, one would, in the normal way, have expected it to be produced along with any other evidence,' said Faro heavily, his temper rising.

McQuinn, refusing to be ruffled, held out his hand. 'May I?'

'Well, do you know who it is?'

McQuinn's smile was condescending to the point of insolence. 'Of course I know who it is. Everyone knows who that is, Inspector.'

'Then perhaps you'll oblige me— '

'It's Timothy Ferris, a suitor of Lily's.'

'Is that so? Then why wasn't this information produced in your report?' barked Faro, ashamed to hear echoes in his own voice of the bullying manner he so despised in Superintendent Mackintosh.

McQuinn sighed wearily. 'Inspector sir, seeing that the unfortunate young gentleman had committed suicide two weeks before Lily was murdered, even if we had found his photograph, such information would not have lent any relevance to the case.'

Looking at his superior officer's angry face, he continued, 'If you're in any doubt, all the details relating to Ferris's death are on file. Would you like me to fetch them out?'

'No, no.'

McQuinn nodded. 'May I suggest that you talk to your stepson? Ferris was in his year at medical school. Vince probably knows a great deal about his activities – by personal contact or hearsay from their fellow-students— '

Faro cut him short. 'Yes, yes.' And, somewhat angrily, he went over to the cupboard, unlocked it and, taking out the file on Lily Goldie, he threw in Ferris's photograph.

McQuinn watched him. 'So the case of Lily Goldie is finally closed, Inspector.' He sounded relieved.

'Is it? I wonder, McQuinn, I wonder.' And with that enigmatic reply Faro stalked out of the office and slammed the door behind him, harder than was completely necessary. In the corridor he stopped. Was that McQuinn's suppressed laughter he heard following him, or was it only his over-sensitive imagination?

CHAPTER THREE

The case of Hymes and the Gruesome Convent Murders was forgotten as an uncommonly hot dry spell of weather brought a spate of stomach upsets. There were people who complained that the weather was to blame, and mark their words there would be an outbreak of typhus if it continued. The same folk belonged to the order of gloomy prophets who foretold that every winter chill would also carry off half the population to the kirkyard.

No rain came, the skies remained obstinately blue and cloudless as handkerchiefs were pressed to noses by those forced to encounter the noxious odours emanating from narrow crowded city streets. An Edinburgh without rain was a phenomenon, especially as the mired stinking cobblestones relied upon frequent and heavy showers as Nature's way of keeping them fresh and clean.

Meanwhile, in Faro's garden, the lilacs had their day, to be replaced by an abundance of June roses. He could not fail to notice that their perfume competed with a distinct smell of faulty drains. He also observed, with considerable delight, a great deal of domestic activity in his back garden, where blackbirds and thrushes had nested, the proud male parent easing the wearisome egg incubation of a mate with a dawn and eventide song of joyous exultation.

Faro had little time to enjoy this novelty of his new home, happily distant from the city, for he was once again involved in the sordid crimes that lay behind the façade of city life.

Thefts, embezzlements, sexual assaults, child prostitution – such were mere scrapings on the surface which respectable, prosperous middle-class Edinburgh was at pains to present to the world. Deaths there were too, in drunken fights and street accidents, but none that bore any resemblance to the murders of Lily Goldie or Sarah Hymes.

At the end of a long day on a routine smuggling case at Leith Docks, Faro decided that, compared with the gruesome details of murder cases, there was something almost wholesome about cheating the revenue. Returning to the city, he saw that the radiant summer had temporarily disappeared in swirling mists which hid Arthur's Seat entirely and blotted out the Pentland Hills, but he felt strangely content as the omnibus set him down at the end of his street.

Glad to be returning home, he put his latchkey in the door and found Mrs Brook eagerly awaiting his arrival in order to announce a visitor.

'A lady to see you. I put her in the drawing-room. Said it was urgent, poor soul. I just couldn't turn her away.'

Faro swore silently, his elation suddenly abated. Tonight, for the first time since illness had deprived him of all appetite and interest in food, he was feeling hungry, looking forward to the evening meal as appetising smells of cooking drifted up from the kitchen. Dear God, a visitor was the last thing he wanted.

'Couldn't you have told her to come back tomorrow, got her to leave a message or something?' he demanded irritably.

'I hadn't the heart to send the poor lady away, Inspector sir. She'd come all the way from Glasgow on the train. And in a terrible state, poor thing. I don't know when she last had a good meal.' She lowered her voice with a glance towards the stairhead. 'Very ill, she is, Inspector sir, if I'm not mistaken. Fair wrung my heart just to look at her.'

31

Mrs Brook eyed his stony face reproachfully. 'I took the liberty of reviving her with a wee sup of your brandy, sir.' Leaning forward, she whispered confidentially, 'Have no fears, Inspector sir. A proper lady, she is. You know I would never let the other sort in – I mean to say, any person in who wasn't a gentlewoman.'

Faro tried to conceal his annoyance. As far as he was concerned, the good Mrs Brook had behaved like the busy-body she was proving to be, well-meaning, but a bit of a nuisance. In normal circumstances, he realised, he might have applauded her thoughtfulness, but not tonight, on the occasion of the resurrection of his lost appetite. He knew perfectly well that he was being selfish but the prospect of a stranger to deal with made him feel suddenly old and tired again, conscious of being footsore and with a childish need to be cosseted.

As if aware of her employer's conflicting thoughts, Mrs Brook began, 'I hope what I did was for the best— '

'Wait a minute – what did she want anyway that couldn't wait?'

At this sharp rejoinder, Mrs Brook gave him an almost tearful glance. 'I see I did wrong asking her in, sir. I'm sorry and I won't do it again. But – well, see for yourself. She's just lost her only brother, poor lady.'

'I don't see what I can do about that, Mrs Brook. This is a case for missing persons. Did you not tell her to go to the police?'

'She asked to see you personally.' Mrs Brook sounded offended. 'I expect she read about you in the newspapers. She said you were the only one who could help her.'

Faro sighed. 'What else did she tell you?'

'Nothing else. She was that upset, and I'm not one to pry,' Mrs Brook added, tightening her lips self-righteously.

A lost only brother? Cynically Faro thought that usually meant the brother or cousin was the polite term for a lover. If the woman upstairs was upset, that meant they had been living together and he had run off with someone else and most likely taken her money with him. So why ask for him? Thanks to Mrs Brook's compassion he'd have to listen to the whole wearisome story, utter platitudes of comfort and then get rid of her with some plausible excuse.

Mrs Brook took his rather curt nod as approval and beamed upon him. 'I'm glad I did right, Inspector sir.' She watched him walk upstairs, little guessing that where her employer was concerned her kind heart was likely to be her undoing. If it continued to interfere with her efficiency then she would have to go, Faro decided. He must make it plain to her that being housekeeper to a policeman needed sterner qualities than those for dealing with sick patients. After all, policemen were known to have strange callers, criminals, avengers, informers, and God only knew who she might let into the house through her ever-open, ever-welcoming kitchen door.

He opened the drawing-room door. At the bay window a woman reclined against the sofa cushions. At first he thought she slept, and his entrance did not disturb her. For a big man, Faro could move both swiftly and noiselessly. When he looked down on her, she opened her eyes and sat up with considerable effort.

One glance told Faro the reason for Mrs Brook's concern. The woman's face was pale, emaciated, exhausted-looking and ill beyond the mere travel-worn. Faro's quick eye for detail took in the shabby gentility of dress, the unmistakable badge of the lady's maid.

He closed the door behind him with the well-worn words, 'What can I do for you?'

As she tried to rise, both hands propelling herself forward, a fit of coughing took her.

As she struggled, trying to apologise, Faro said:

'Please, remain seated. My housekeeper tells me you have been ill. May I get you some refreshment to help?

My stepson is due home soon, he is a doctor – he may be able to offer you some restorative medicine.'

'No medicine can help me now, Inspector. But it is good of you to concern yourself.' She gave him a sad smile. 'I am quite beyond the reach of medicines now, I fear.'

Faro did not doubt that she spoke the truth, observing the two bright spots upon her cheeks, the bright eyes and flushed countenance of one far gone in consumption.

'I know I have taken an unpardonable liberty in visiting your home, instead of waiting to see you at the police office tomorrow. I was desperate, I thought you might be able to help me, for when I enquired they told me that the case is now closed.'

Faro was aware of a sick feeling that marked the return of his illness as observation of that skeletal face struck a chord: the emaciated Hymes in his prison cell. He asked what he already knew: 'What case is this?'

'I'm Maureen Hymes, Patrick's sister. I came over from New York hoping to see him. They let me see him, five minutes – five minutes, after all these years. Five minutes – before— ' Her voice ended on a sob, quickly controlled.

'Miss Hymes – er, that was a month ago.' He had not the heart to add, what was the point of coming to him now, whatever her reason.

'I know. I was ill. Afterwards – afterwards I went back to Glasgow. Pat had friends there. I collapsed.' She threw her hands wide. 'You can see the state I'm in, Inspector. They didn't want me to come to you, but I promised Pat. "If it's the very last thing I do, I'll prove that you didn't murder that Goldie woman," I told him at that last meeting. You see, Inspector, we were more than brother and sister, Pat and I were twins. Here's our birth certificate, if you're still doubtful.'

Born Cork, thirty-six years ago, Patrick and Maureen Hymes, he read.

'Things were bad in Ireland when we were children. The potato famine in forty-five, and then both our parents died. Patrick came over to Glasgow, eleven years old he was and he worked anywhere, at any kind of child labour that would pay well, to buy me a passage to America where we had an uncle. He thought I'd be safe there, have a decent life. One day he promised he'd save enough money to come over. When I got to New York, Uncle Paddy had died and his widow didn't want another mouth to feed.'

She stopped with a dismissive gesture. 'I won't be troubling you with the rest, Inspector, except to say that I went into service, bettered myself. Twice I made enough money to send to Patrick to fulfil his dream. Twice that money was stolen. God didn't intend us to meet again, but we wrote letters. I knew Sarah was a bad lot – he hinted at things in letters. He once said if anything happened to him, would I take care of his two little girls.'

She smiled wanly, looking out of the window, where the great bulk of Arthur's Seat glowed in a reflected sunset. 'I never told him how ill I was. I didn't want him to know. And then, when I heard – this terrible business – I sold everything I owned in the world to come and see my brother and fulfil my promise. Those two children have no one else in the world now. I have to see them provided for – find them good homes before I – before I die,' she ended firmly.

Faro was aware that, as she spoke, the Irish accent predominated the American. He was also increasingly aware of how strong the likeness must have been when the Hymes' were children, before the world's grosser sins took over her twin brother.

'I don't doubt that Sarah deserved to die,' she said. 'But I know that it was manslaughter rather than murder. And my Pat never killed that other girl. He's no deliberate murderer, that I do know, as God is my witness. You see, he never lied to me once in his whole life.'

She smiled. 'You might find this hard to believe, but Pat's great dream was to be a priest. That's what he was saving so hard for – and then he met Sarah. I suspect she seduced him and stole the money I sent. Anyway, he had to marry her with a bairn on the way. But he never lost his faith, he still lived by it.'

She paused, exhausted, breathing heavily. 'Inspector, you must take my word for it, someone else murdered that other girl and let Pat take the blame. I've got to find out the truth to save his immortal soul. And you've got to help me. You've got to – you're my last hope on earth of clearing my brother's name.' And she began to cry.

Faro stared at her, incredulous. And you've got to help me, she said. Just like that. What was she asking? That he had to prove a dead man innocent. And he wasn't even a Catholic. He was a lapsed Presbyterian. Maureen Hymes wasn't only sick, but mad, poor creature.

In his profession Faro found it a disadvantage to be susceptible to women's tears. Most men found them embarrassing, throat-clearing occasions, whereas Jeremy Faro, trained to the tears and supplications of two small daughters, had a natural inclination to enfold this delicate, child-like woman to his shoulder and comfort her.

'Do you believe in miracles, Inspector? I should, but I can't. But I do believe in dreams. And my brother haunts mine. You may be like all the others and reckon that a man who murders once will do so again, that he might as well hang for two as for one. But I know I'll be haunted to all eternity unless I can free him from the stigma of that other woman's murder.'

She stood up, faced him squarely. 'Now I must go. Thank you for listening to me so patiently, sir, and for giving me your precious time.' She paused, then shook her head. 'I'm sorry. I see I've failed to convince you.' She cut short his protests with a sudden dignity that again reminded him forcibly of the condemned man in his prison cell.

'Good evening, Stepfather. Oh – my apologies, I did not realise you had a visitor.'

It was Vince. Faro had forgotten that he too would be impatiently awaiting his supper, at the end of a long day in Dr Kellar's surgery.

Faro gave him a hard look, knowing that Mrs Brook, agog with curiosity about the mysterious woman who had suddenly appeared, must have sent him up post-haste to report on what was now taking place in the drawing-room.

As Faro made the introductions, Vince's eyebrows shot upwards at the name Hymes.

'This lady is his twin sister.'

Vince bowed over her hand, holding it now with an anxious, searching glance into her countenance that betrayed the doctor's interest.

'I have been a great nuisance,' she said, 'burdening the Inspector with my troubles. Your stepfather is a kind man and a very good listener.'

Vince's quizzical glance demanded explanation.

'Miss Hymes does not believe that her brother murdered Lily Goldie.'

'Indeed? Then if there was someone else, I can assure you, madam, my stepfather is just the man to hunt him down. He is marvellously clever, you know. No one could ever escape him for ever— '

'Steady on, Vince, I'm not infallible – and I cannot allow you to give Miss Hymes false hopes. The case is closed officially, remember.'

Vince made an impatient gesture. 'But if he does exist – this other murderer – then this is the very man for the job.' He pointed dramatically at Faro, the lamplight glinting on his pale hair, suddenly the picture of an avenging angel. 'Come now, there must be clues, Stepfather, and you are quite excellent on clues.'

Faro's reply was modest and non-committal. He was amazed amd moved that this boy, once so sneering, so wilful, even cruel on occasion, had vanished and left a gallant, caring and suddenly frighteningly vulnerable individual. Vulnerable – was that the word? Was this dropping of the scales from his eyes conditioned by familiarity, familiarity that had blinded him to the qualities of the man emerging from the chrysalis of youth, a man who would some day make a fine doctor – unless some day his vulnerability to defenceless womankind seriously affected his good sense?

'Where are you living in Edinburgh?'

'Nowhere. But I return to Glasgow to my – friends.' A bout of coughing cut her short again. She stood breathless, and Vince's solemn shake of the head in Faro's direction confirmed his worst fears.

'Then I will get a cab and see you safely to the railway station.'

'No – you are too kind, Doctor.'

'Not kind, Miss Hymes. It is my pleasure. I will be back directly.'

As Vince dashed downstairs and out into the street, Faro assisted his visitor to the front door. 'I should not have let him go to all this trouble. Please persuade him that I am perfectly capable of making my own – way.' Again she was shaken by the coughing that the slightest exertion seemed to bring about.

'Please give me your address.'

There was hope in her eyes as she opened her reticule and took out a slip of paper. 'I have it here. You will let me know . . .?'

The sound of wheels on the cobbled street announced the arrival of Vince and the cab. Together they assisted her inside, and Faro's last sight of Maureen Hymes was a frail hand raised in his direction, and lips forming the word, 'Promise . . . promise . . .'

As he closed the front door and walked slowly upstairs again, Faro realised that he had never before seen how his stepson reacted to a woman in distress, even a female long past thirty. He had rarely seen him in young female company, except as a boy at parties, bullying and tormenting small girls into screaming fits. Handsome he was, even then, but under that angelic appearance a frightful bully, who had never been asked to parties a second time. After all, few children are little angels, and he included his own dear Rose and Emily.

As he sat down and penned a loving response to their postcard, he was glad they had each other as comfort in their bereavement. Strange, although they adored each other now, Rose had been an extremely jealous two-year-old. When Emily lay newly born and rather raw-looking in her mother's arms, Rose had studied her carefully. 'She's not very pretty, is she? I like my dolls better than her. Can we send her back now, Mama?'

At least his daughters were the product of a happy and secure life. One day they would recover from the shattering grief of losing their mother. Born of their parents' wedded love, they had not suffered the stigma of bastardy which Vince had doubtless endured most painfully in his childhood. Even though his mother's little lapse was overlooked by the adult population, he imagined that the crofter children would not be ready to forgive so easily when they had the opportunity to hurt so cruelly. Doubtless Vince's difficult childhood had its roots in an ill-treatment he would be too proud to discuss with his mother.

When Vince returned, Faro looked at him gratefully. Thank God his fears – and Lizzie's – about the way the lad would turn out were ended. He only wished she could see her son now. How proud she would be of the man he had become.

'That was very good of you, lad,' he said as Vince followed him across the hall.

'It was the least I could do for a dying woman. Her life is now measured in days, hours, even, and I doubt exceedingly if she will reach Glasgow alive. She will certainly never return to Edinburgh.' He stood with his back to the blaze, since dining in a fireless room at the height of summer was unthinkable to Mrs Brook. 'A good blaze is as nourishing as a good meal' was one of her most frequent quotations.

The furniture which Faro had inherited with the house was handsome and mellowed with age and usage, in keeping with an elderly doctor's establishment, and the massive Sheraton sideboard had once accommodated an army of chafing dishes. For convenience, he and Vince sat together, easing Mrs Brook's serving arrangements and also the discomfort of being isolated at either end of a very long and exceedingly well-polished table intended to seat members of the large family Faro knew he was unlikely now to produce.

Mrs Brook stood by the sideboard, waiting impatiently to serve Scotch broth and a saddle of roast lamb.

Faro's hunger pangs suddenly vanished at the sight of food in such large quantities. 'We should have invited Miss Hymes to dine with us.'

'In that case she would never have boarded the Glasgow train. Besides, I fancy that she is also well beyond consuming solid food. The journey must have cost her dearly, Stepfather. As a matter of fact, I suspect that she sealed her own death warrant.'

While Vince ate his second helping of rice pudding with boyish relish and delight, and Mrs Brook closed the shutters against the dangerous vapours of the night, Faro told Vince the purpose of Maureen Hymes's visit – a sorry tale that was quite at odds with this peaceful domestic setting, enhanced by candlelight whose flickering light in the mantelpiece mirror gave shimmering life to the landscapes in their gilt-framed oil paintings. A bowl of red roses added their sweet perfume to wax polish and cracking logs.

'So, Stepfather, what are you going to do?'

Faro swore under his breath, suddenly resentful of being thrust into a situation he felt was growing rapidly out of his control. It was upon such occasions that he paused to wonder what God-forsaken destiny had led him to the Edinburgh City Police instead of a farmer's life in Orkney, which his mother would have dearly loved.

He shook his head. 'I don't know, but sometimes I think I chose the wrong job. Or maybe I'm just getting too old for it.'

Vince smiled. 'Now, Stepfather, that's not like you. You're just tired. Tomorrow and a good night's rest, and everything will look quite different. Believe me.'

CHAPTER FOUR

Two days later a letter addressed to 'Inspector Faro' arrived from Glasgow. It said briefly that Maureen Hymes had died that same night she returned from Edinburgh. 'Her last words were for you. "Tell the Inspector to remember his promise."'

Faro thrust it across the breakfast table. 'Seems you were right in your diagnosis, lad.'

'Poor creature,' said Vince as he read. 'You know, it often happens like that with twins, particularly identical more than fraternal ones. Curiously, their life-span is the same, and when one dies the other does not long survive.' Handing the letter back, he said, 'Well, Stepfather, what are you going to do now?'

'I don't see what I can do.'

Vince smiled. 'Come now, a promise is a promise, Stepfather.'

'The poor woman is dead.'

Vince shook his head. 'That is beside the point. Where, may I ask, is your chivalry?'

'Killed stone dead by twenty years with the police, I expect.' Faro sighed. 'You do talk nonsense sometimes, lad. Can you imagine me persuading the Superintendent that I want to reopen the Hymes murder case – on the dying wish of his sister?'

Vince pushed aside his breakfast egg before replying. 'Has the thought not struck you that there might be some

42

other clue that wasn't followed up in the evidence? After all, they did miss Ferris's photograph when you were off the case. Shall we have a shot at it, Stepfather?'

'We?'

'Of course.' Vince took a piece of toast and buttered it thoughtfully. 'Of course. I intend to lend a hand whenever available on the assumption – begging your pardon – that two heads are better than one. With my still somewhat scanty medical knowledge and your powers of deduction, I think we might make the perfect team. You know, Stepfather, I've always had a fancy to play policeman.' He grinned. 'Frankly, I didn't care for you when you came courting Mama— '

'I did notice,' said Faro.

Vince nodded. 'Actually, it was my secret pride at having a policeman in our family that completely converted me to having you as stepfather. How I bragged to everyone at school!'

Faro smiled. 'I'm glad there was something to redeem me in your eyes. You were far from the easiest of children.'

'I was an absolute horror,' Vince admitted cheerfully. 'So – you will let me help. Between us, we might even produce a second murderer, and wouldn't that make your policemen jolly uncomfortable!'

'I shouldn't entertain too many hopes there, lad. If he existed, and if he's wise, he will have disappeared long since. The trail is cold and whatever we find it can't help Hymes or his sister now.'

'Hymes was an idiot. You have to admit that, Stepfather.'

Faro shook his head sadly. 'You're young yet. The *crime passionnel* is the most brutal of murders to our civilised minds, the one we are least likely to excuse or forgive, of love gone sour. It is also the most frequent in the annals of crime. You haven't any idea yet what savagery can arouse even the most timid of husbands when he feels that he has been betrayed by the wife he loves.'

43

'Nor have I any intention of finding out. Marriage is not for ambitious young doctors with an eye to becoming Queen's Physician one day.'

'You might well do both, given time, and the right woman.'

'The right woman, Stepfather? I doubt if any such creature exists except between the covers of romantic novelettes – certainly not between wedded bedcovers, at any rate.'

When Faro smiled wryly, Vince continued, 'I see you don't believe me, but I mean it, Stepfather. As for Hymes, can you credit any man being fool enough to be hanged because of his conscience – and all for a worthless whore? He could have taken ship from Leith and been a hundred miles away. Now, the clever murderer, who uses his head and not his heart, and plans the perfect crime, I'd have respect for such a man – respect and admiration, too.'

'There's no such thing as a clever murderer, lad. They always give themselves away in the end.'

'That I don't believe. The police can be absurdly simple – not all detectives are as clever or infallible as my respected stepfather.'

'I'm far from infallible. In every eye there is a blind spot.'

'But not in yours.'

'Oh yes, in mine too.'

'Perhaps you'll meet him some day, then, this murderer who is clever enough to find your blind spot.'

'If he exists, then I hope that neither of us ever have that misfortune.'

Vince smiled. 'Come now, Stepfather, could you resist such a challenge? A man who pits his wits against all the odds, in a tricky game of life – to the death,' he added dramatically, slashing the air with an imaginary sabre.

Faro regarded him doubtfully. With all the reckless enthusiasm of youth, Vince regarded the whole idea as no end of a lark.

'Splendid. You won't forget, by the way, that we have tickets for *Othello* on Wednesday. I've told Rob and Walter that it's your favourite play, and they agree with me that you need cheering up.'

Faro thanked him bleakly. *Othello* would hardly be a cheering experience. In the hands of bungling amateurs it would probably depress him unutterably, but Vince and his friends meant well.

'Has it occurred to you, Stepfather, that there is a great deal of similarity between Othello and Hymes?'

Faro gave him a sharp look. How odd that the same idea had occurred to him at that last melancholy interview.

'Othello, you must admit,' Vince continued, 'was even more stupid than Hymes. Can you imagine any man gullible as the Moor rising to illustrious heights as Shakespeare tells us? A man who would murder his lovely young Desdemona on Iago's testimony? People don't behave like that in real life. Othello would have had a shocking row with her and then all would have been tearfully revealed.'

'Leaving no tragedy for Shakespeare to write and enthral countless generations.'

'Point to you, Stepfather.' Vince laughed and, from the desk, produced paper and pen. 'Now, back to the main business. Let us see. Are there any parallels between the murders of Mrs Hymes and Lily Goldie that might offer us some clues, besides both being employed at the convent?'

Faro considered for a moment. 'They were both young and pretty. They were even somewhat similar in appearance.'

'Indeed, the same physical types.'

'What else do we know?'

'From the post-mortem, that neither had been sexually assaulted,' said Vince. 'And Lily Goldie was not virgo intacta, but she had never borne a child.'

45

'We know that Sarah Hymes had run away from her husband. He suspected her of infidelity, which was not proven, except on hearsay.'

'A flirt who enjoyed teasing men and getting as much as she could from her admirers, at the same time giving as little as possible. What do we know about Goldie?'

'From your description of her at Duddingston Loch and her behaviour with the unfortunate Tim Ferris, wouldn't you say there was a very strong likeness there?'

'Exactly. If not ladies of easy virtue, then trembling on the very threshold. Goldie's background?'

'Quite respectable. An orphan, brought up by her great-aunt as companion in Galloway, which one can also interpret as an unpaid maid of all work. When the aunt, who had presumably seen that Lily was educated, died, then Lily came to Edinburgh and got a situation teaching at the convent.'

'Was it coincidence that led them both to seek employment there at the same time? In view of their flighty characters, a convent does seem a remarkable choice.'

'It isn't much to go on, but I think we might begin by calling upon the Reverend Mother, using Ferris's photograph as an excuse.' Faro looked out of the window. 'I think I'll take a walk to Greyfriars. Are you coming?'

Vince shook his head. 'No, not this time, if you don't mind. I'm going to Cramond with Rob and Walter.' He sighed and added, 'I took flowers to Mama all the time you were away . . .' He regarded Faro, sad-eyed. 'You know, I can't believe she's there – or anywhere, any more. I wish I was small again, like Rose and Emily, and could believe that dear Mama had gone to heaven and was waiting there smiling in a white robe to greet us in due course. For me, she's just – lost.'

Faro laid a sympathetic hand on his shoulder, a gesture that needed no words.

★   ★   ★

A grey colourless summer's day, with a high wind that turned the leaves inside out, added its melancholy to the deserted churchyard. Normally he came on Sundays, when his visit coincided with the emergence of churchgoers, but today he was glad that Vince had decided not to come. The atmosphere was oppressive, a day when it was difficult for anyone to believe that the dead were well and happy, patiently waiting in Paradise.

This was his first visit for several weeks and his path led him past a new marble stone: 'Timothy Ferris, born 1849 died 1870. Erected by his fellow students in tribute to his memory.'

That was a fine gesture for a poor lad who had no others to mourn him, Faro thought as he went on his way to that other almost new headstone which marked Lizzie's grave. Against a sombre background of urns and skulls and florid emblems of mortality, it stood out white and shining and simple.

He knelt down, attending to the flowers. He was not used to being so alone. Sunday afternoons normally saw many similarly employed in this most modern part of the burial ground. He missed the black-clad figures whose sombre attire turned the bright green summer grass into an irreverent frivolity, the widows' weeds, the men with their crêpe-draped tall-hats, the children wearing armbands.

He closed his eyes for a moment, trying to conjure up a picture of Lizzie, not as he had last seen her in those terrible hours of agony before she died, but as she would most wish to be rememberd – the smiling girl he had courted, the young and happy mother playing with Rose and Emily. Bending forward, he laid his right hand on the moulded earth in the region of her heart. He prayed, and then, as always, talked to her a little.

'What shall I do, Lizzie love? How does a fellow keep a promise to a dead woman, and one he only knew for half an hour?' Only the twittering birds answered him. 'You don't know and neither do I. Your boy thinks I should do it – as a matter of honour, he says. He's a fine clever young man. You would be proud of him. And what's more, he's your image, Lizzie love, growing more and more like you every day. And that's a great comfort to me.'

Dusting his knees, he kissed his fingers and laid them against her name so coldly upon the stone. Beset by a feeling of loneliness almost too great to be borne, he hurried back down the path, head down, jostled by the brisk wind.

Suddenly his attention was drawn to the grave of Tim Ferris, where a woman clad in grey, her face hidden in voluminous veils, stood alone. He saw that she wept. The wind fluttered a handkerchief, seized upon the swirling folds of her cape. The next moment she clutched her bonnet with its veils as both were swept from her hair to become entangled high in the shrubbery behind.

Gallantly, Faro dashed to her assistance and a delicate violet perfume assailed him. No sooner had he reached her side than her own fierce struggles released her. There was a final rending of cloth, and a moment later hat and veils were being firmly re-anchored.

But not before Faro had glimpsed a face of haunting beauty. He knew that he had met few truly beautiful women in his life. Now he and this stranger looked into each other's faces for a split second of time; the next instant, she turned away. He hovered still. Was he dismissed without one word of thanks? Sadly, that was the case. But there was more. He recognised the gesture as oddly furtive too. She did not wish to be recognised or remembered.

Turning on his heel, he walked away from that back so rigidly turned from him. He was a man in a dream, his heart thudding against his ribs, with a picture of red-gold curls, eyes of cerulean blue and a warmly seductive mouth sketched indelibly on his mind. Afterwards, trying to describe her to Vince, he could find no adequate words beyond: 'Beautiful – exquisite.'

'Young or old?' was the practical response.

'Neither. I mean, she could have been any age.'

'Could she have been one of Tim's lady-friends?'

'Perhaps.'

Vince sighed. 'You aren't a great deal of help, Stepfather. Where are all those remarkable powers of observation.'

'Blown to the four winds, I'm afraid.'

'And taken your wits with them, if I might say so. Why, you're positively besotted. Exit bereaved husband, enter lovesick swain,' he added cynically.

'That is hardly fair, Vince. I don't suppose I shall ever see her again—'

'I certainly hope not, if that was her effect upon you. How long did you say you stared at her?'

'Seconds only – a mere tantalising glimpse. But to use one of your modern terms, she was an absolute stunner.'

'Well, there's another little mystery for us. What a pity we have no excuse for including this lovely lady in our investigations. I don't suppose you'll ever find out who she was, unless you're prepared to spend a considerable time in Greyfriars Kirkyard.'

'It stands to reason that she must return to her unhappy vigil,' said Faro firmly. 'I shall go back next week at the same time, try and strike up an acquaintance.'

Vince's heavenward glance clearly indicated what he thought of his stepfather's infatuation.

The mysterious woman haunted Faro's dreams. He pursued her through the kirkyard, but when he seized her veil it was poor dying Maureen Hymes who clung to him, weeping, murmuring over and over, 'Promise . . . promise . . .' Even as he supported her, the flesh melted from her skull and he found himself holding his dead wife. 'You wept, begging me not to die. Begging me to return to you. Now you have your wish.' The nightmare continued with

Faro's bizarre reasoning as to how he was to reintroduce the decaying corpse of his dead wife to Mrs Brook and, worst of all, wondering if her son would notice how his mother had changed.

Mercifully he awoke at that moment of horror. He was sweating, he felt sick and ill as he had done so long ago in Orkney when he knew that he had seen beyond the veil of death. His grandmother had been recovered from the sea at Orkney, by repute a 'seal' woman, and his own family were endowed – or perhaps the better word was tainted – with that unhappy gift of second sight she had brought them. The dreadful nightmare from Greyfriars could neither be dismissed nor forgotten. It belonged to that unearthly no-time between sleeping and waking. And it could only be interpreted as a warning.

But of what?

CHAPTER FIVE

The Convent of the Sisters of St Anthony belonged to an earlier age than the newly sprouting villas on Edinburgh's undeveloped south side. As the sixteenth-century Babington House it had enjoyed notoriety. Belonging to a scion of the Catholic family whose ill-fated plot for the escape of Mary, Queen of Scots had cost Anthony Babington a cruel death and had signed the death warrant of his queen, the Scottish Babingtons had managed to keep clear of the scandal. They had remained staunchly but secretly Catholic and had served the Stuart cause as best they could as secret agents, while managing to avoid any public declaration which would have meant sequestration after the Forty-five.

When the last member of the family, an elderly spinster, died in the early years of the century, the house and its park was willed to the Roman Catholic Church for use as a religious house. The Sisters of St Anthony were a teaching Order, their school financed by selling the parkland as highly coveted building lots.

The ancient house had been, as Faro put it, 'somewhat freely restored', with Queen Anne and Georgian wings added to the original tower. They entered by the modern extension, bristling with turrets and gargoyles on the outside and dark panelling and marble on the inside.

A lapsed Presbyterian and non-churchgoer, Faro found embarrassing such evidence of papacy as was exhibited by religious statues and a marble fresco of the Stations of the

Cross. The faint smell of incense assailed their nostrils not unpleasantly, as they waited in the hall outside the newly built chapel.

The Reverend Mother's quick steps were almost inaudible on the marble floor as she came towards them, and over her normally immobile countenance flickered a look of distaste as she recognised the Inspector. She chose to ignore Vince's smile and proffered hand as Faro introduced them.

'Follow me.' In the tiny, sparsely furnished ante-room, she did not invite them to sit down. Faro's immediate reaction was that their impromptu visit was an intrusion and that his presence, and what it implied, had upset her.

'We were hoping that you might be able to help us.'

'In what way?' she asked coldly.

'In regard to Lily Goldie.'

'I see,' she said, in the tones of one who clearly did not. 'Perhaps I should point out that it is in the best interests of our girls that their normal routine is not interrupted. I need hardly tell you, Inspector, that they were all very upset – as were the sisters.' A note of annoyance shattered that calm face, pale as the wimple she wore. 'Our pupils' work and our own meditations have been seriously affected by these disruptions. May one ask what you can hope to gain from these enquiries, since the unfortunate man has paid his debt to society?'

'If you would allow me to explain. We have no intention of publicly reopening the case. This is merely a routine enquiry following your letter and the discovery of the photograph in Miss Goldie's room. I wish to check certain facts – that is all. You may rely on my discretion to disturb your establishment as little as possible.'

'Am I then to understand that you are acting in a private capacity?'

'Entirely.'

'I see.' The bloodless hands took on a supplicant's role, fingertips pressed together. 'Very well. I will do what I can to help you.'

'Were both girls of your faith?'

She looked at Vince coldly as if aware of his presence for the first time. 'Naturally. We do not knowingly take heretics into our establishment. We employ only good Catholic girls.'

'Am I correct in understanding that, though both were engaged at the same time, they were strangers to each other?' asked Faro.

The Reverend Mother shrugged. 'There was no evidence of previous acquaintance. Besides, it is extremely unlikely since they were from completely different backgrounds; one a servant, one a teacher.'

'I only asked because it did occur to me there might be some kinship.'

'Kinship?'

'Yes, they looked alike.'

'A coincidence.' She thought for a moment. 'Interesting that you should mention it though. I had on occasion mistaken each for the other – in outdoor dress that is – and out of uniform.'

Vince's triumphant glance at his stepfather said: There you are.

'May I ask you something personal?' said Faro.

The Reverend Mother hesitated for a moment. 'If it's something I can answer, then I will.'

'What were your own feelings about these murders? I'm not sure what I'm looking for,' he added frankly.

'I think I know.' She smiled thinly. 'Even nuns, Inspector, are not free from occasional flashes of what you might be tempted to call a woman's intuition. I'm afraid most of such feelings in my case relate to spiritual matters. Sarah Hymes was reluctant to go to Mass – now I understand the reason, since she had tainted her immortal soul with adultery and a tissue of lies. Lily, on the other hand, I felt was not what she pretended to be, by no means a good docile Catholic girl. I felt instinctively that she had not been reared true to the faith. I can almost,' she added, with a delicate shudder, and a veiled glance at the Inspector and Vince, 'detect in the air the presence of non-Catholics. And Lily seemed to be totally ignorant of many basic matters of our religion, which made me suspect she had lied in order to obtain the situation.'

Somewhere outside a bell tolled and the Reverend Mother rose to her feet. 'I cannot help you any further and I am relying on your discretion when you make your enquiries, Inspector. Our school has suffered considerably in prospective pupils since this unfortunate scandal. I have learned one thing, and that is in future never to recruit any staff, either servants or teachers, from outside. Bear this in mind, Inspector, if you feel obliged to speak again to Sister Theresa, who found the photograph.'

There was a tap on the door, and with obvious impatience the Reverend Mother opened it. A whispered conversation. 'A moment, if you please.'

As the door closed, Vince said, 'Bless me if I can see any reason why the two women were Catholic or non-Catholic, or lied about it, should have any bearing on the case.'

'It might seem a good reason for the Reverend Mother, perhaps easier for her to understand than the *crime passionnel*.'

'I say, Stepfather, do you think we should be looking for a mad priest or a fanatical nun?' he whispered as the Reverend Mother re-entered.

Faro said, 'I should like to speak to the other teachers who were not of your Order.'

The Reverend Mother eyed him balefully as he consulted his notes. 'There were only two, besides Miss Goldie. Miss McDermot – and Miss Burnleigh, whom you interviewed during the Hymes investigations.'

'Correct.'

'As I remember, Miss Burnleigh was as baffled and shocked as the rest of us.'

'True, she couldn't help much then, but perhaps she might remember something about Miss Goldie. And I'd like to speak to Miss McDermot.'

'Then I'm afraid you are too late, Inspector.'

'Too late?'

'They are no longer with us. Miss McDermot left several weeks before the . . . er . . . first incident. She was intending to emigrate to Canada with her parents and she may have already left the country.'

'And Miss Burnleigh?'

The Reverend Mother's sigh indicated that she was becoming exasperated. 'She left us the day of the murder, I'm afraid. She had word that her mother was taken seriously ill and her presence was urgently required at home.'

'Perhaps you have her home address?'

The Reverend Mother gave him a look of ill-concealed disapproval as she unlocked a drawer in the desk. 'I have the addresses of both Miss McDermot and Miss Burnleigh.'

Faro held out his hand. 'If you please. You have been most helpful. And now, might I see Sister Theresa, if you have no objections?'

'I have made myself clear on the subject of objections, Inspector, and you must please yourself and attend the dictates of your conscience.' Accompanying them to the door, she said, 'Tell me, Inspector, how is Constable McQuinn?'

Faro remembered his first visit, how the young and very presentable constable had been greeted like an old friend by the sisters. McQuinn was well known to them and to St Anthony's, their orphan lad who had made good, and who had 'by some manner of chance' (his own vague description) come to join the Edinburgh Police Force two years earlier.

'A splendid young man,' said the Reverend Mother, and actually beamed at the Inspector, who thought sourly that McQuinn was just the kind of young man to ingratiate himself with nuns, or any other female between eighteen and eighty. Efficient and smooth, Faro should have considered him admirable. Was his unaccountable dislike based quite irrationally on a smile that was a shade too eager and a grin just a wee bit wolfish?

In the corridor, the Reverend Mother waved a hand towards the little formal garden with its arches and flower-beds and rambling roses. 'We have Danny McQuinn to thank for that. This dates from long before his police days, when he was a mere boy. He had a natural way with plants and herbs. If you would care to look around the garden, you will find that he had a hand in most of it. A very gifted boy, Inspector,' she added sternly as if reading his thoughts on the subject of McQuinn.

As they turned to leave, she said, 'A moment, Inspector. There is one question you have not asked, but one that I am quite prepared to answer.'

'And what would that be?'

'One that might or might not help. We talked earlier about woman's intuition, did we not?'

'We did.'

'Then I would be quite prepared to swear on the Holy Book that Hymes was not guilty of Lily Goldie's murder.'

'For what reason?' demanded Faro sharply.

She shook her head. 'Nothing I can lay my finger on, nothing that would be accepted in a court of law, except . . .'

'Except?'

She made a dismissive gesture with her hand. 'Except that it is all wrong somehow. Hymes was a devout Catholic, he knew all too well the consequences of endangering his immortal soul. That is precisely why he gave himself up for the murder of Sarah. Had he also murdered Lily

56

Goldie, there is not the slightest doubt in my mind that, far from denying it, he would have been most eager to make his confession and receive absolution on both accounts. After all, he had nothing to lose, his life was forfeit anyway.'

Faro and Vince exchanged glances, since this theory coincided remarkably with their own, even leaving out Hymes's religious convictions.

'There is,' continued the Reverend Mother, 'only one way it could have happened. And that is, if Lily's had been the first murder, instead of the second.'

'Murdered by mistake, you mean?'

'Yes, if in the dusk Hymes had mistaken Lily for Sarah, as I sometimes did,' she added, putting out a hand to the bell on her desk.

Sister Theresa remembered the Inspector and greeted Vince with a smile. She was stout and jolly, a *religieuse* of the Friar Tuck school, thought Faro. In complete contrast to the Reverend Mother, she was eager for a gossip about the 'unfortunate happenings' as she led the way to the room once occupied by Lily Goldie.

'This is where we found the photograph, Inspector. It had fallen from the mantelpiece here, and slipped down this loose skirting-board.'

As they were leaving, a marmalade cat sidled round the door and, finding the sister's ankles made inaccessible by her long gown, transferred his ingratiating activities to the tall Inspector.

Faro stroked the sleek coat. 'Hello, young fellow. What's your name?'

'That's Brutus – poor Brutus, we might call him now,' said Sister Theresa with a sigh. 'He belonged to Miss Goldie. Pets aren't strictly allowed by Reverend Mother, but we had a plague of mice – it's all this new building around us brings them in, I'm afraid. And Miss Goldie got him for us from Solomon's Tower.'

'Solomon's Tower? You mean the old gentleman gave the cat to her?'

'Oh, yes. She was on very friendly terms with him.'

As they followed her directions to the kitchen, Vince said, 'That was an interesting piece of information about the Mad Bart, don't you think? "Very friendly terms." Now that might be significant.'

Bet and Tina were to be found, red of face and forearms, washing sheets in the laundry. They were eager, even gleeful, at this excuse to leave their labours to talk to the Inspector, especially when he was accompanied by a handsome young gentleman. Their remarks about Lily Goldie were punctuated by coy giggles in Vince's direction. Yes, they recognised the photograph of Ferris as a sweetheart of Miss Goldie's.

'Treated him something cruel, she did.'

'That's why he fell under the train, poor soul.'

'Did Miss Goldie have any other – sweethearts – that you knew about?'

Heads were shaken. 'No.'

'There was yon wee laddie from the school at St Leonard's,' said Tina with a giggle. 'Used to skulk about waiting for her, out there by the gate.'

'You can't count him,' said Bet indignantly. 'He was no more than fourteen or fifteen.'

'What made you think he was a schoolboy then?' asked Faro.

'He was too well dressed to be an errand lad.'

'Aye, too well fed.'

'What exactly did he look like?'

'Never saw him close to. Always wore one of those big caps the school laddies wear.'

'Remember how he kept on coming to the gate, waiting for her, for days after . . .?' said Tina with a shudder.

Bet sighed. 'Aye, the poor laddie.'

'As if he couldn't believe that she wasn't coming back.'

Faro thanked them for their help and they looked yearningly at Vince, who gave them a gracious bow, which brought about more giggles.

'If you're going back to the station,' said Tina, the bolder of the two, 'remember us to Danny.'

'Danny? Oh, Constable McQuinn.'

'He used to do the gardens here before he joined the police.'

'Danny was very upset about Miss Goldie. She was always his favourite.'

'Quite sweet on her, he was,' said Tina spitefully.

'He liked all of us,' cried Bet, suddenly remembering Christian charity. 'A nice lad is Danny.'

'For a policeman,' added Tina doubtfully.

Vince's wry look in Faro's direction indicated that McQuinn had obviously ingratiated himself with an entire convent. No mean feat for a mere male, who was also a policeman.

Their road home took them past Salisbury Crags, the scene of both crimes. Aflame with the yellow gorse of summer, it was devoid long since of anything that might provide a clue.

'What about the well–dressed school laddie?' asked Vince.

'Some poor wretch that took a fancy to an older woman.'

'Thing it's worth a visit to St Leonard's School.'

'I do not,' Faro laughed. 'First a convent and then a boys' school. Bring in the whole wide world,' he sighed. 'Can you imagine how the pupils would react to a policeman's visit, or my Superintendent when he found out? Think of the fear and trembling in every heart, remembering stolen apples and other minor misdemeanours. You wouldn't get any one of them admitting to hanging about near the convent, although I dare say it happens regularly.'

'The fascination of the forbidden?'

59

'Exactly. Lily Goldie must have been a remarkable woman.'

'She was, Stepfather. Even on my small acquaintance with the lady, I'd say she appealed to all ages and conditions of men,' said Vince, poking at the gorse with a stick as if the answer might lie hidden there. Then he pointed dramatically towards Solomon's Tower, grey and ancient far below them. 'And what about the Mad Bart? Do you think he might be included in our list of suspects?'

Faro laughed. 'As a possible murderer, you mean? You're not serious, surely.'

Sir Hedley Marsh, known to locals as the Mad Bart, was the scion of a noble family who, according to legend, had abandoned society after some family scandal, and now lived a hermit-like existence.

'You'll have to do better than that, lad. A harmless old eccentric with a life devoted to cats.'

'But think of the opportunity. She did visit him. Surely that was in your file?'

'It was not. Another of McQuinn's curious omissions,' he said shortly. 'There was no mention of the school laddie, either.'

Vince laughed. 'Surely you wouldn't consider that a serious piece of evidence?'

'Nothing is too trivial to be included. And it's often the most innocent-seeming incidents that lead to a conviction.' He shrugged. 'I'd be more anxious to interview our infatuated school laddie, however, if his visits had ceased at the time of Goldie's murder rather than several days afterwards. Obviously, he didn't know she was dead.' Frowning, he looked towards Solomon's Tower. 'It was remarkably slipshod of McQuinn not to include a visit to our Mad Bart as a matter of routine.'

'Maybe he was misled by the harmless devotion to cats. Seriously, though, consider the proximity to both the convent and the Crags here. Don't you think—?'

'That we would be wasting our time. It's no good, Vince lad, I sometimes get the feeling that Lily Goldie is going to remain a mystery unsolved and that we'll have to settle for Hymes after all . . .'

'What? I can't believe my ears – give up so soon?' was the indignant response.

Faro sighed wearily. 'Well, we might as well see the teachers. This Miss McDermot.' He looked at the addresses. 'She's in Corstorphine. Miss Burnleigh's in Fairmilehead.'

'I'll take Corstorphine, Stepfather. One of my colleagues lives out there and he has been asking me to dine and visit the old church. That's capital. I can combine both activities.'

As he waited for dinner that evening, Faro had another look at the statements from the sisters. Brief indeed, they all expressed shock and bewilderment at the monstrous crimes, at this invasion of the cloister with violence from a world they had long since relinquished. But their overall opinions never wavered: 'Miss Goldie seemed such a nice, well-behaved young lady. Not the kind who would get herself murdered.'

But get herself murdered she had. And Faro had an instinctive feeling that it would serve no useful purpose interviewing all the inmates of the convent a second time. There was little hope of the nuns producing any new clues to Lily's possible life outside the convent walls, and he wished to steer clear of the Reverend Mother's wrath.

He sighed. Only in a convent could two women have lived for months and made so little impression. Obviously religious ladies also gave up the natural curiosity associated with their sex, along with other worldly pleasures, when they took their final vows.

And for once, realising the magnitude of his self-appointed task, he understood why his colleagues had been so anxious to settle for Hymes as a double-murderer.

About the teachers they had still to interview, he felt more hopeful. People suffering from shock have unreliable memories, and some fact or observation forgotten about, or dismissed as too trivial, when they were first questioned might, in retrospect, assume more significant proportions.

He would begin by hiring a gig tomorrow and driving out to Fairmilehead village to see Miss Burnleigh. But tonight . . .

'Tonight we have the Pleasance Theatre, Stepfather. Shakespeare will be a capital opportunity for you to relax. A nice murder, on stage for a change, that you can watch and enjoy, without having to solve.'

CHAPTER SIX

The Pleasance Theatre was already crowded and the curtain about to rise on *Othello* when Faro and Vince arrived. Vince had been delayed by Dr Kellar and Faro secretly hoped they might not be expected to go after all, if the performance had already begun.

To his annoyance, he found his stepson in no way perturbed and quite ready to sacrifice his dinner, much to Mrs Brook's indignation.

'Put it in the oven, indeed. What sort of way is that for a young doctor to treat his stomach, or my rib of roast lamb?'

They arrived breathless, and Vince seized the only seats available in the back row. 'Rob and Walter won't be allowed to keep seats for us as late as this, I'm afraid. That would create ill-feeling, not to say a riot, among the other students who have waited for hours.' As the curtain rose, he added, 'They must be down near the front, dammit. Can you see at all?'

'Good job I'm tall.'

Vince grinned. 'At least we can stand up with no one behind us. Sorry, Stepfather. It's all my fault.'

Faro was non-committal, irritated at having been pressed to attend the play and then finding himself in a poor seat. However, he reflected by the end of the first scene, there were some advantages, and if Mr Topaz Trelawney's Thespians hadn't given a better account of themselves by the time the curtain fell at the end of Act I, he would make some excuse and slip out. Vince would not mind; he had his two friends to meet in the green-room for refreshments.

As cat-calls and loud applause from the noisy audience greeted Othello's first appearance, Faro groaned. It seemed that all his fears had been justified. Mr Topaz Trelawney was an actor-manager, a Shakespearean tragedian of the worst kind. He over-acted, leering, gesturing, making asides to the audience, which delighted them but turned Othello into a buffoon. An inch deep in grease-paint, his overweight frame filled the tawdry costume to overflowing as he pranced and strutted across the stage. Rather too often for comfort, he forgot his lines and took a reassuring swig from a tankard placed on a convenient table. These forays, which grew more frequent as the play progressed, affected his posturing with an alarming unsteadiness.

Faro stirred restlessly in his seat. The performance was exactly what he had expected. It was unendurable, and he would leave at the end of Act I. Scene 2 dragged wearily to a close, and as Desdemona's entrance had been well signalled, Faro groaned, expecting the worst. Then, in Scene 3, thunderous applause greeted her first appearance.

A flower-like Desdemona, with long flowing blonde hair, a voice of astonishing beauty and timbre, which she had no need to raise for it carried with a pure, bell-like quality to the back row of the theatre. While she spoke, she held her audience captive and it was as if no one else existed on stage. Her presence turned Iago, Cassio, Emilia – and particularly Othello – into stiff cardboard painted characters.

The audience loved her, they hung upon every word of her three short speeches, her duty to her father Brabantio and to her husband Othello and her plea to accompany him. As Faro too now waited enthralled, trying to remember the

64

play and when she would appear again, he lost all interest in going home. He forgot the discomfort of his seat, the atrocious over-acting of the Thespians, for he recognised that he was in the presence of that exceedingly rare creature, a great natural actress, who could convey without raising her voice, without outrageous posturing or gestures, a child-like innocence, her love and hero-worship of Othello and a desperate vulnerability.

The curtain fell at the end of Act II, and watching his stepfather applaud, Vince added his 'Bravos' to those of the student audience. As they joined the noisy good-natured throng heading for the green-room, where refreshments were served in the interval, Vince said:

'Isn't Alison Aird an absolute wonder? Can't you see why we're all passionately in love with her? Desdemona's just a small role. Wait until you see Alison Aird as Lady Macbeth or Cleopatra.'

Vince's two companions, Rob and Walter, emerged through the crowd, and Faro, who had found a small table, set pints of ale before them.

'Guess what, Stepfather. Walter's cousin Hugo Rich is playing Cassio – joined the company two months ago. This is his first major role and we've been cordially invited to a party back-stage. You'll come with us, of course.'

Normally Faro would have resisted meeting the Trelawney Thespians, but if Desdemona in her real-life role as Mrs Trelawney would be there he felt this was an opportunity not to be missed.

Desdemona's handkerchief scene and Othello's brutality brought storms of protest from the audience, especially as the latter's performance grew more and more outrageous and considerably less steady. Faro spared a thought for that inebriated gentleman, doubtless seeking consolation in the bottle for the fact that he was a dismal failure as an actor. How many performances would it take for Trelawney to recognise that his own future as well as that of his

65

Thespians hung on a slender thread – that the audience came to applaud Mrs Aird, and that the success of every evening belonged to his leading lady.

How Trelawney must hate all that adulation by-passing him each night. Faro tried to picture them as man and wife in a cosy domestic setting, but imagination baulked.

The Willow Song in Act IV was a triumph of under-statement, made all the more moving. The audience was spellbound now and Faro decided that this lovely woman must indeed be bound to the Thespians by ties of loyalty and love, when her talents so obviously belonged in the ranks of the great Shakespearean actors on the stages of London and New York.

'Kill me tomorrow: let me live tonight.' The words, uttered in no more than a whisper, reached every seat in the house, and sent a chill through Faro. For a moment he forgot that this was a play he was watching. Helpless to avert the tragedy, he expected to see Desdemona's lifeless form in Othello's arms.

And at the last, 'Commend me to my kind lord', the silence was broken by an outburst of scuffling as many of the audience began to take their departure before the curtain fell. It also released Faro from his spell. What was coming over him? he wondered. That strange dark moment out-of-time on stage – too many wife-slayers?

He joined the tumultuous applause as the curtain rose on a smiling Desdemona, risen unscathed from her death-bed. She very obviously supported Othello to his curtain-speech, which was clearly not as reverently received as Mr Topaz Trelawney thought proper to the occasion. He made a drunken, threatening gesture to the audience, quickly suppressed by an anxious Desdemona, and the curtain mercifully descended.

The audience surged towards the exits, while Faro and Vince made their way back-stage to the small dressing-room Hugo Rich shared with the other male members of the cast. Topaz Trelawney, Faro noticed, had a room of his own.

Hugo greeted them anxiously. 'How did it look from the front?'

Walter was full of assurances; Rob and Vince were kind and flattering about his Cassio, putting him at his ease. Mark their words, they would be seeing him treading the boards of the London stage one day very soon. He went away, beaming and happy.

The party increased in volume of noise and merriment as they were joined by a troupe of girls who were part of the company. Faro, alert, looked in vain for Desdemona among these young actresses, who made costumes, attended to laundry and more mundane domestic matters when there were no suitable parts for them.

They were polite to him, and attentive, respectful and courteous in a manner that made him conscious of his age, and of the fact that he had lived and experienced a whole lifetime before any of them were born. By the time he was watching Vince with a girl sitting on his knee, he decided that his presence was superfluous and that he should quietly withdraw. Sheridan Place and his bed, only minutes away, seemed a tempting alternative.

Catching Hugo's eye, he made his apologies about work the next morning, adding, 'No, please, don't disturb Vince.'

'I will see you to the door,' said Hugo. 'Yes, I must. It is a rule that everyone is seen out and the door re-locked. There are often unsavoury characters about and once the box office was robbed.'

As they walked along the dimly lit corridor, the door next to Trelawney's opened and a girl emerged and hurried towards the exit ahead of them. She turned, smiling, to let Hugo open the door for her, and Faro found himself staring into the face of the woman he had last seen in Greyfriars Kirkyard, by the grave of Timothy Ferris.

'Goodnight, Hugo,' she said and stepped out into the darkness.

'Who was that?' he asked Hugo. 'Is she a friend of Trelawney's?'

Hugo smiled. 'I suppose you could call her that.' Then he added, with a great roar of laughter, 'Don't tell me, sir, that you don't recognise Desdemona.'

'Desdemona? But . . . but . . .'

'The long blonde hair is a wig.' And seeing the Inspector's astonished face, he said, 'I would have introduced you, but I'm afraid I didn't catch your name. Mrs Aird is in a great hurry as usual, a carriage usually awaits her each night.'

Outside, blinded by the sudden darkness, Faro became aware of the cloaked figure of Alison Aird pacing the pavement.

Raising his hat, expecting a rebuff, he said, 'Forgive this intrusion, ma'am. I should like to say how greatly I enjoyed your performance tonight. May a complete stranger be permitted to find a carriage for you?' As he spoke, he was conscious of her nervous reaction to his approach. It seemed a long time before she said:

'If you would be so good, sir. I fear some misfortune has overtaken the brougham which normally collects me after the performance.' She sighed. 'My departure was delayed tonight with business matters, hence the mix-up.'

'This should not take long. There is a hiring establishment within hailing distance. Stay close to the stage door. If you are in any difficulties, you need just ring the bell.' And Faro set off at top speed, chuckling to himself, delighted at his good fortune in finding his beauty in distress.

Luck was with him and he found a gig almost immediately. Returning with it, panic-stricken, he almost expected her to be gone.

He sighed with relief when her shadowy figure emerged from the stage door. Giving directions to a street a half-mile distant, she turned to Faro. 'You have been very kind. Perhaps I might offer you a lift?'

'I would be delighted,' said Faro, deciding the opportunity of sharing a cab was too great to miss.

Alison Aird settled herself and stared out of the window. It promised to be a silent journey.

'I was quite enthralled by the play tonight,' said Faro desperately.

In the darkness, her voice smiled. 'Why, thank you again.'

'Regrettably, I have been absent from Edinburgh and have missed most of your season here. But I do hope to see others.' Even to himself, he sounded nervous, too anxious to please.

'I trust you will also find them enjoyable,' said Alison Aird, returning her attention to the passing night, the flicker of torches from other carriages.

'How do you find Edinburgh?'

'Beautiful but lonely.'

Faro's mind again presented the melancholy picture of Alison Aird in Greyfriars. What had been her relationship to young Ferris? Were they lovers, or kin? He could see no resemblance to Ferris's photograph and had never seen the young man alive. He also realised that off-stage his Desdemona was older than appeared at first glance.

'Have you been long with the Thespians?'

'Just this season. This is my first time in Scotland for many years. But I am by birth a Scotswoman.'

'Alison Aird would imply that.'

'Indeed, it is my real name.'

'I gather you are not Mrs Topaz Trelawney.'

'Good gracious, no. Whatever gave you that idea?' She laughed. 'Mr Trelawney is merely my employer. He was once a very great actor,' she said in his defence, 'one I admired greatly.'

69

Faro could think of no suitable comment, beyond secret delight that his Desdemona was unmarried. 'Have you ever considered the London stage, Miss Aird?'

There was a pause before she replied, 'It is Mrs Aird. And your name, sir?'

'Faro. Jeremy Faro.'

She looked out of the window, and said, he thought with a certain relief, 'Ah, here is my destination. Thank you for escorting me, Mr Faro.' Handing her down from the carriage, he made a mental note of the house and street number before giving the driver instructions for Sheridan Place.

'The mourning lady from Greyfriars,' said Vince at breakfast next morning. 'Are you absolutely sure? After all, you only had a glimpse of her.'

'A glimpse I will never forget.'

'But what an astonishing coincidence.'

'Is she a widow?'

'No idea. Sometimes actresses use Mrs as a courtesy title. But she isn't Trelawney's wife.'

'I know. She told me so.'

'What about Tim? Did she offer any explanation?'

'There was no time to ask.'

Vince thought for a moment. 'I expect Tim was one of her many admirers. Come to think of it, we used to see him at performances.'

'Alone?'

'Yes, always alone.'

'There must have been some intimate connection, otherwise why dress up in all those ridiculous veils, so that she wouldn't be recognised visiting his grave?'

Vince smiled. 'Really, Stepfather, you are quite an innocent sometimes. The answer is obvious. They were lovers. After all, she can't be more than thirty-five. Maybe we're wrong. Maybe it's she who rejected him, not Lily Goldie.'

'The same thought has just occurred to me, lad.'

'The sense of guilt would appeal to the actress in her, and visiting his grave be a kind of performance of grief.'

'You make it sound very calculated, lad.'

Vince shrugged. 'I know actresses, Stepfather.'

'What are they doing next?'

'Macbeth. Hugo's playing Second Murderer. And Mrs Aird gives a riveting performance as Lady Macbeth.'

CHAPTER SEVEN

Urgent matters concerning a break-in at Holyrood Palace occupied Faro's immediate attention and, much as he chafed at the delays, he realised that he had taken on the case of Lily Goldie as a private investigation. In future, he could expect to devote only his spare time to it, and he was glad indeed of Vince's proposed assistance.

Later that week, with the prospect of a day off, he decided it would be opportune to make the postponed visit to Miss Burnleigh at Fairmilehead.

On his way to the gig-hiring establishment, he saw a figure emerging from the direction of Causewayside. Although she was too distant to recognise her features, his heart's sudden lurch told him this was Mrs Aird. He was quite elated when she smiled and raised her hand in greeting from across the road. He obviously hadn't been forgotten.

'It is Mr Faro, is it not?'

'You are looking well, Mrs Aird,' said Faro, bowing over her hand, wanting to say that she looked divinely adorable, her face flushed and her bonnet a little askew from the stiff breeze blowing down from Arthur's Seat.

Again she smiled at him, her manner relaxed, inviting conversation. Faro's mind had suddenly emptied of social chat and, sounding infernally dull, even to himself, he said, 'I trust your lodgings are comfortable and to your liking?'

She nodded, frowning. Did she think him tight-lipped and unfriendly? Dear God, did he have to sound so stiff and formal?

'This area is no place for a gentlewoman these days.'

'You mistake me, Mr Faro. I am no gentlewoman, just an ordinary actress— '

'But the area is insalubrious – have you not been warned of its dangers?' He pointed to the wooden palisades that divided Minto Street, where they were standing, from Causewayside. 'There is another such at Salisbury Road. What do you think they are for, Mrs Aird? They are to keep thieves and vagabonds, the wild beasts who lurk around Wormwoodhall and the Sciennes from infiltrating into a decent respectable neighbourhood. The rowdies who break the peace are, alas, the New Town puppies from this side and the keelies from Causewayside.' He stopped, breathless, not having meant to indulge in such a long speech.

'Indeed? Does that also account for the lodge gates at both ends of Sheridan Drive? To keep it select?'

Feeling uncomfortably that she was laughing at him, he replied, 'I don't know about select, but I hope you will not be tempted into this area after nightfall.'

'That is highly unlikely.' And she looked away, like someone suddenly bored, as well she might be, he thought desperately. Politely, she said, 'I will bear in mind your good advice. But I am delaying you . . .'

'Not at all. It is a pleasure to talk to you again.'

'Is it really?' There was sincere surprise in her voice and her accompanying smile which made him realise that her first impressions had been far from favourable. She doubtless thought him oafish, a pompous bore.

'I was on my way to hire a gig to go to Fairmilehead tomorrow. Over there,' he pointed, 'on the approaches to the Pentlands.'

'I've been wondering about those hills. They are very tempting, some day I mean to explore them.'

'Why not tomorrow, then? Why not come with me?' The words had burst out of him as if of their own accord as he towered over her, stammering, blushing like a schoolboy.

She put a hand to her mouth. 'Oh, I did not mean to intrude . . .'

'Of course you didn't. But as this is a purely routine matter of business, I would – would enjoy your company.'

Faro walked home, conscious that his step had lightened considerably. He chuckled delightedly, feeling that he had shed twenty years in the past ten minutes.

Mrs Brook met him with a message that Vince was to spend the night at Corstorphine. 'I was to tell you that he would attend to the business you had discussed before returning to Edinburgh.'

So Vince was to call on Miss McDermot. Good lad. And before closing his eyes that night, Faro said, 'God, I know how busy you are and I haven't asked you for anything since you decided to take Lizzie and the wee lad away from me. But, please God, if you can spare the time for this small request, please, let it be a fine day tomorrow. Keep the rain off. That's all I ask.'

His prayer was answered. He collected the gig in the radiant sunshine of early summer. Ten minutes later he was sitting outside Mrs Aird's lodging. Tucking the blanket about her, he was again assailed by that feeling of light-hearted youth. When in recent times had he felt as young as this? As they jogged down the road together, her arm comfortably close to his own, their legs touching as they took a corner, he had to restrain the longing to put an arm about her shoulders and look into that pretty face instead of staring at the road ahead.

She was a convert to the Quaker religion, she told him, and had been visiting the Meeting House at Causewayside. The actress in her brought vividly to life the characters she had met, those who remembered the area as a thriving weaving community, their Edinburgh shawls sought after as far away as New York shops.

Faro was at peace at her side, content to listen, as they climbed past fields and woods and the grey clutter of villages. Then a distant prospect of the castle brooding darkly down upon the smoking chimneys of Edinburgh, justifying Robert Burns's epithet of 'Auld Reekie'.

A train crawled, puffing importantly and thinly along the railway line, and tiny ships were tacking in the Forth. Their passing gig brought forth from every farm the warning bark of dogs, the agitation of barnyard fowls. A curlew swooped, crying, and for Faro the feeling of *déjà vu* persisted. Had his companion not already said those words, laughed like that at a solemn donkey staring over a hedge, exclaimed delightedly at the sight of children feeding a lamb? He looked at her, filling the empty corners of his life with such grace and harmony, amazed anew that fate had given no warning, no allowance for this intrusion into his life.

Alison Aird was a stranger, but already as she spoke each contour of her face shaped itself into a familiar pattern. As each gesture struck a chord of remembrance, he found himself at the mercy of his own background, which he was careful to conceal from public gaze and comment. The second sight his seal-woman grandmother had bequeathed to him had never seen an occasion for rejoicing.

That intuition accounted for perhaps ten per cent of his success as a detective, and had more than once been a factor in putting him in the right direction of vital clues. It did not always work in his private life, alas. He had no warning when his sweet Lizzie bore their son that she and the boy would be dead, lost and gone for ever, in a matter of days.

'And Hugo tells me that the handsome young doctor is your stepson,' Mrs Aird was saying. Could it be that she had been enquiring about him? He was flattered.

'Indeed. I am a widower, with two little girls living up north with their grandmother. What of you – is Mrs Aird a courtesy title only?'

She shook her head and sighed. 'Would that it were so. I am a widow.' She cut short his commiserations. 'It is a long time ago, and I was married for such a short time that I have almost forgotten the experience.' Pausing, she added, 'I was not so fortunate as yourself, my only child also died.' Then, as a tactful indication that the subject was closed, she pointed a gloved hand. 'Over there. Is that our destination?'

Before them lay Fairmilehead, a huddle of roofs and smoking chimneys with two thread-like roads joining beside a wood heavy with summer trees.

'Journey's end.' He wondered, could it be the same for her? The completion of another journey they had begun together in a world whose shadowy confines were long lost to them?

He looked into her eager smiling face. How unbelievable that this feeling of familiarity was all wrong. This was but their third meeting. And he knew already, with painful certainty, that before the day was ended and they returned in the gig, his heart would be lost to her.

Faro's natural reaction was rebellion at the idea of falling in love again, with all that it entailed. Green love-sickness was the last thing a detective needed, especially a man nearly forty. He knew that his powers of detection worked more efficiently without domestic ties. That was his main reason for distancing himself from his young daughters in Orkney. Even happily married, he had known that he would be a better policeman on his own, with the kind of life he lived, with its uncertain hours, its possible dangers.

While delighting in the experience of having her by his side, he groaned inwardly, suddenly cursing himself for his own folly, wishing he had not asked her, or that she had refused to come. Damn it, how could he help this feeling of rapture? He was helpless to escape, rushing headlong into whatever torments lay ahead. He had thought with Lizzie's death that this chapter of his life had closed for ever, that nothing would again interfere with his dedication. Was he yet to discover that love was eternal, that as long as a man breathed it lurked inescapable on that road from birth to death?

'Do you wish me to wait for you here?'

'You may accompany me, if you wish.'

She frowned. 'You mentioned a business engagement – I would not wish to intrude.'

Faro smiled. 'I am a police officer, Mrs Aird – a detective. And this is a mere routine enquiry.'

Mrs Aird looked startled. 'I had no idea, sir. I presumed you were a business man of some sort. You have the look of an advocate.'

'I wish I was as affluent.' Faro smiled.

She gave him a hard look. 'I will remain here, Mr Faro, and wait for you.' She opened the large handbag she carried. 'I have a script to read – my lines, you know.'

'You are sure? I will be as quick as I can.' And tucking the rug around her, Faro started off down the road, where he stopped an old man, bent double over a stick, and asked directions to Hill Cottage, Mill Lane. 'Number fifteen, it says here.'

The answer was a shake of the head. 'There's no cottage of that name hereabouts. The general store'll mebbe know – newcomers, are they?'

'Burnleigh, did you say? Number fifteen?' repeated the woman behind the counter, with a shake of her head. 'People don't go much by numbers here. I don't know the name and my man Jock's the posty. He'd be able to tell you but he's away in the far pasture. But there's Mill Lane, you can see for yourself, across there.'

Mill Lane was old and cobbled, the cottages huddled in antiquity. The numbers ran out at eleven. Faro pondered, and took a chance on number eleven, where a young woman answered the door, obviously in the middle of feeding the crying baby in her arms. No, she had never heard of any Burnleighs. 'Look, there's Jock – see him, he'll know.'

Hurrying back along the lane, Faro once more repeated the story, this time at the top of his voice, as Jock was more than slightly deaf.

'There's no' many folk biding here and I ken them all. Besides, Burnleigh is an unusual name, I would remember a name like that.'

'I was told that she had come back from Edinburgh – she was a teacher at the convent in Newington – to take care of her mother who was ailing and had sent for her.'

Jock shook his head. 'I canna help ye, I'm sorry.'

Faro walked back towards the gig, deep in thought. Here was something odd indeed. Was this what he was waiting for? Why had Miss Burnleigh chosen to disappear at the time of Lily Goldie's murder, leaving a false address?

He felt the familiar twitch of danger alerted. Had he stumbled on a clue to the identity of the second murderer at last?

Alison Aird put away her script as he took his seat beside her in the gig. 'Were your enquiries successful?' she asked, curious as to his preoccupation.

'I am more baffled than ever,' he said, suddenly needing to tell her the real reason for his visit.

'A teacher at the convent, you said. Was that where the recent murders took place?'

'It was.'

'I thought the murderer had been hanged?'

'I thought so too . . .' And Faro went on to tell her of the visit of Maureen Hymes. 'I keep asking myself why Clara Burnleigh left a false address and spun a tissue of lies about going home to a sick mother, when neither mother nor the house exist.'

'It might not be entirely sinister, of course,' said Mrs Aird. 'It might mean only that she preferred not to tell the truth?'

'But why?'

Mrs Aird smiled. 'Well, it's perfectly easy for another woman to understand.'

'Is it indeed?'

'I can see you're a stickler for truth at all times, Inspector, but Miss Burnleigh's deception might be more readily explained.'

'In what way?'

She laughed. 'The most natural of ways. Imagine she had a lover – a married man – and she has gone off with him. She would hardly be likely to wish to confess that to the Reverend Mother. Or, far more likely, she had the offer of a better situation and was too embarrassed to tell the truth – a white lie, a piece of face-saving, so as not to hurt her employer's feelings.'

'I still think Miss Burnleigh's behaviour needs investigating.'

'Ah, but that is because you are looking at it from the point of view of crime being involved, trying to exercise your deductive powers and find a hidden criminal motive when in fact the whole thing is no more than innocent deception.'

'We're back to deception again – and I must once again disagree with you. In my book there is no such thing as innocent deception. Mrs Aird, you are talking in paradoxes.'

Mrs Aird shrugged. 'Paradoxes are all too often a necessary part of a female's survival in this man's world. It is part of our nature to be devious upon occasion.'

Faro could think of no suitable reply, and as they came in sight of the Pleasance again the sun was setting on Arthur's Seat. A tranquil evening in a world where only man – or woman, when occasion demanded, according to

Mrs Aird – was vile. Be that as it may, he was reluctant to let the evening end.

'Shall we continue into Princes Street Gardens, listen to the band for a while?'

Mrs Aird shook her head. 'Forgive me, but I must return to my lodging.'

At least she offered no excuse, no white lie, but Faro found himself wishing that she had, despite their earlier conversation. It was easier for his male pride to accept an excuse than what he must presume: that she had had enough of him and his dour society for one day. Had he thrown away, by his own folly, an excellent chance of further acquaintance? Thinking back over the day, he felt he had not acquitted himself too well. On almost every score he could have done better. Would Mrs Aird consider him worthy of another chance?

While he waited impatiently for Vince's return home that evening, he hoped that the interview with Miss McDermot had been more productive. Whatever Mrs Aird's explanations, he found the disappearance of Miss Burnleigh so near to the murder of Lily Goldie oddly sinister, and felt that somehow the two were connected.

It was late when Vince arrived home. His first question was, 'Well, Stepfather, how was Fairmilehead?'

'Another mystery, lad.'

Vince listened in silence to Faro's story of the missing Miss Burnleigh. 'Well, I hope you did better with Miss McDermot.'

'At least Miss McDermot exists, very prettily, too. I was just in time to find her emigrating to Canada.' He groaned. 'She goes on the next sailing – in two days – I'm quite heartbroken . . .'

'I accept that, but did she tell you anything useful?'

'It seems that Lily Goldie didn't care much for her fellow teachers, or for female company in general. However, she did mention that on two occasions when she was out collecting nature specimens she observed Lily leaving Solomon's Tower.'

'So? We already know that from Sister Theresa. Presumably she was negotiating the transfer of a kitten.'

'You really think that's all?'

'Look, lad, occasionally our Mad Baronet, an ardent Calvinist who hates popery, rains down biblical curses on passing inmates of St Anthony's, calling them the whores of Babylon. And he carries on a war of insults and threats with the boys at St Leonard's School.'

Vince tapped the notes on Faro's desk. 'I imagine they torment him. But he did entertain a young and attractive teacher from the convent. Could he have made some improper advance, been repelled and had a brainstorm?'

'I'll be the most surprised man on the force if you're right, lad. But thanks for all your trouble.'

'No trouble at all, Stepfather. It was a very great pleasure – although, alas, a short-lived one – to meet the delectable Miss McDermot.' He sighed.

'By the way,' said Faro, trying to sound casual, 'I took Mrs Aird with me to Fairmilehead.'

'Mrs Aird?' Vince's eyebrows shot upwards. 'How did you manage that?'

'Met her out walking when I was hiring the gig. She expressed interest in the distant view of the Pentlands and announced herself delighted to accompany me.'

'Well!' Vince was obviously impressed. 'And what did you find out about the delectable Mrs Aird?'

'That she is in fact a widow – husband long dead.'

'Anything about Tim Ferris?' When Faro shook his head, Vince said, 'It's quite possible that she didn't know of his association with Lily Goldie and believed that he had committed suicide because of her.'

'Since you suggested it, I've been thinking along those lines too. Perhaps a closer acquaintance with Mrs Aird will reveal all.'

'Have you another assignation?'

'Not immediately.' When Vince looked disappointed, his stepfather, not wishing to lose face, said hastily, 'She is very involved with her next role for the Thespians.'

'I should have thought she would have them all off by heart by now.'

Faro offered no further comment and left for the Central Office, where he found an urgent message awaiting him. A message which suggested that his forebodings had been right and that they were now dealing with the murder of a third victim.

The body of a young woman had been washed up at Cramond Island.

CHAPTER EIGHT

Faro knew the Cramond area well. He and Vince often spent a pleasant afternoon canoeing on the River Forth and taking a picnic on the island. Constable Danny McQuinn had been off-duty visiting in the area and had been the first on the scene when the alarm was raised.

'A little lad was playing at the water's edge – he made the discovery. They put up the alarm flag for the boatman, since it was high tide and they'd had to drag the body ashore in case it drifted out to sea again.'

Faro sighed. 'Thereby destroying any likely clues.'

'Clues, sir. There weren't many clues. I'd reckon this was a suicide.'

'Oh, and what reasons would you have for that conclusion?'

McQuinn thought for a moment. 'Young she was, fully clothed – at least, she had been when she fell in. Looked as if she might have been in the water for a week or two.'

'Any means of identification?'

'Not any obvious ones. It wasn't my duty to carry out an investigation. That was for the police surgeon,' he reminded Faro. 'Is that all, sir? I believe they are doing the post-mortem now.'

Faro nodded. Vince had accompanied Dr Kellar to the mortuary.

'Before you go – a moment. You didn't by any chance recognise the body, did you, as that of Miss Clara Burnleigh?'

Constable McQuinn stared at him, and then blushed furiously. 'Miss – Miss Burnleigh? You mean from the convent?'

'I mean precisely that.'

'Well ... no. I didn't know Miss Burnleigh was a missing person, sir. I understood she had returned home to take care of a sick parent.'

'She told you that?'

'Why should she? I mean, it was common knowledge in the convent.'

'But you knew her quite well?'

'I did?'

'According to the sisters, you were very friendly with the teachers, so I naturally imagined you would be able to recognise if the dead body belonged to Miss Burnleigh.'

Again a tell-tale flush rose in the region of McQuinn's neck. Faro suppressed a grim smile. What a desperate handicap in his profession. How could anyone take seriously a policeman who blushed like a schoolboy? This time it was anger.

'The body had been in the water some time. It would be very difficult for anyone to recognise her at a passing glance. And I certainly wasn't on those sort of terms with the lady and I certainly wasn't expecting it to be any other than a stranger.' Looking at his superior's stony face, he asked, 'Has something happened to Miss Burnleigh?'

'I wish I knew. I was trying to track her down, some routine enquiries about Lily Goldie's murder— '

'I understood that case was closed, Inspector.'

'It is, it is,' said Faro irritably.

'Oh, I see,' said McQuinn slowly. 'Did you try Fairmilehead?'

'I did indeed, but the address she gave doesn't exist and no one has ever heard of her mother, Mrs Burnleigh.'

'So you think she might have been murdered?'

'I certainly think there is a strong possibility. Tell me,

when you were on friendly terms, did she talk to you about her home?'

'Only that she lived at Fairmilehead and had a widowed mother,' said McQuinn guardedly.

'Well, this body that's been washed up. Was it her?' Faro demanded impatiently.

McQuinn suppressed a shudder of distaste. 'Like I told you, sir. I didn't look very hard.'

'A policeman can't afford such sensitive feelings. For heaven's sake, man, identifying corpses is all part of the routine, or didn't they tell you that when you joined up?'

'It couldn't be Clara Burnleigh, sir. Why should she want to commit suicide?' said McQuinn defiantly.

'That's what we've got to find out. And while we're on the subject, I've been looking at your interviews following Lily Goldie's murder. I find none relating to Sir Hedley Marsh, whom I am told she visited frequently.'

'Seeing that all the evidence pointed to Hymes and he had given himself up, I hardly thought it necessary to disturb the old gentleman. It would have been a mere formality.'

'In a murder enquiry, nothing is a mere formality. Remember that in future.' Faro felt his temper rising. I must watch it, control my emotions where McQuinn is concerned. Or one of these days, I am going to resort to physical violence.

Fortunately for both men, Superintendent Mackintosh came into the office at that moment.

'Well, what are you waiting for, McQuinn?' McQuinn saluted and departed gratefully.

'About this Cramond corpse, sir,' said Faro.

'Positive identification might take some time. Nothing you need concern yourself over at the moment. From Kellar's report, there's no evidence of foul play. But you'd better be ready for anything that comes up.'

Faro realised that patience would be required as the list of fifty missing females notified to the Central Office

85

by anxious relatives was checked. Where the description tallied with the new-found corpse, the unpleasant visit to the mortuary lay ahead for those who had waited, some for days only, some for much longer, for that moment of awful revelation of whether they had at last discovered a missing daughter, sister, wife or friend.

The newspapers would also announce the discovery, and that was always calculated to bring in a fresh crop of enquiries from deserted lovers and husbands. In particular, those who had not considered that the storming out and disappearance after a quarrel was a matter worthy of police investigation. Faro felt impatient of the delays involved, sure that, if this was a murder case, time was of the essence, but he could hardly explain his feelings to Superintendent Mackintosh, who would take a very dim view of one of his detectives carrying out a private investigation into a murder that was officially closed.

As he was leaving the office, the Superintendent called him in. 'There's a ship docking at Leith on the evening tide. And we've been tipped off that there's contraband aboard. This is maybe what we've been waiting for. See to it, will you, Faro.'

The warning had come too late. Faro spent a chilly evening in Leith investigating the ship's papers, talking to her captain while policemen and Excise officers carefully checked over the cargo and every possible hiding place in the ship.

Returning home, Faro realised that in the Pleasance Theatre the curtain had now risen on Alison Aird as Lady Macbeth. Disgruntled and weary, he sat down at his desk and carefully re-read his notes and his new information on Lily Goldie.

As he did so, he realised grimly that if the body at Cramond proved to be Clara Burnleigh, they were in all probability dealing with a multi-murderer, who might even now be stalking his fourth victim.

In the interval, he decided on a further visit to the Reverend Mother at St Anthony's. A daunting prospect, for he would not be welcome, but he was certain that she had the strength, needed in her calling, not to shrink from what she considered her duty, no matter how distressing or distasteful the task – and even if it meant visiting the mortuary and identifying the corpse as that of Miss Burnleigh.

That was tomorrow. Tonight, he felt the stage in his investigations had been reached where he needed to consult his notes, and with his own observations and conclusions draw up a comprehensive account of the suspects and clues to date.

In his neat, precise handwriting, Faro headed the document:

The Convent Murders: Evidence and Clues thus far

1. Post-Mortem Evidence. Neither Hymes nor Goldie, who had described themselves for the convent records as 'spinster' when examined were found to be virgins. (In the case of Hymes only, there was evidence of child-bearing, and she had indeed borne two children.) Although their deaths had been violent, neither woman had been sexually assaulted.

2. Both the Mother Superior of St Anthony's and Hymes's twin sister Maureen had presented very valid arguments against Patrick Hymes having been the murderer of Lily Goldie. According to the Reverend Mother, he was a devout Catholic and remained so to the end, he would have confessed and wished to receive the Church's absolution for, both murders. This testimony had been confirmed by Maureen Hymes, who stated that her brother, this apparently ignorant, ill-educated member of the Irish labouring class, had once been destined for the priesthood.

3. According to the Reverend Mother, the two murdered women were physically similar. Hymes could more likely have been guilty had Goldie been his first victim – that is, if he had mistaken her for his wife in semi-darkness and sprung upon her in murderous rage. This theory does not make sense with Goldie the second victim, especially as by then Hymes had already settled accounts with his erring wife.

4. The two women, servant and teacher, were employed at the convent and arrived about the same time. Was this fact significant when allied to their physical similarity and dubious morals? Could it have some bearing on the subsequent events? Could Goldie's murderer have been a fanatical inmate, a nun, outraged by such behaviour?

5. The Mad Baronet. Were Goldie's visits as innocent as they seemed? Worth investigating.

6. Would an infatuated schoolboy who hung about watching for Goldie be able to throw any light on her last hours, always presuming that he could be tracked down at St Leonard's?

7. Clara Burnleigh. Did the fact that she had given a false address, and was probably using a false name, have some bearing on Goldie's murder? Is she still alive or is she the third victim at present lying in the mortuary? If so, then we are dealing with a serious wave of murders, and we can expect more of them until the assassin is apprehended.

After some thought, Faro added another name:

8. Danny McQuinn. He had an intimate knowledge of the convent, had access as a respected protégé of the Reverend Mother, and was a former gardener and odd-job man. According to the two maids, he was

'sweet' on Goldie. Is his incomplete evidence deliberate, is he hiding something – or someone? The fact that McQuinn is a policeman does not exclude him from a fit of murderous rage.

Faro threw down his pen. Religious houses, he decided, were naturally secretive places, a boon to prospective murderers and the perfect settings for concealing evidence. Secular staff were not permitted gentleman callers. Therefore all social activities of normal young unmarried women who were not in holy orders had to be carried on *sub rosa*, which made tracking down a murderer even more difficult. Boarding schools were just a little behind convents in natural reticence regarding their inmates.

Faro shuddered at the prospect of investigating a boys' school. The headmaster, he expected, would be equally uncooperative as the Reverend Mother – and for good reason. His school might be tainted by association, however obscure, with a murder. If one of his pupils had been in contact with the murdered woman, then the headmaster wouldn't wish to know officially, and would certainly resist, with every means in his power, any attempt to make this insalubrious association public knowledge.

Reading through the account again, Faro underlined the Mad Baronet. He lived within easy access of the convent, and Lily Goldie had been known to visit Solomon's Tower. Unlikely as it seemed at first thought, this line of enquiry, which had not been investigated, thanks to McQuinn's apparent incompetence, might be pursued with profit.

He did not wait up for Vince that night. He did not want to hear all he had missed, and a ravishing account of Alison Aird as Lady Macbeth. He was relieved, too, when Vince did not appear for breakfast, having left a note for Mrs Brook that he had retired very late and wished to sleep on undisturbed.

CHAPTER NINE

On arrival at the Central Office, Faro was handed the description he had been waiting for:

Aged between eighteen and twenty-four. Five-foot-two in height. Curly red hair, several front teeth missing, body in poor condition, shows evidence of under-nourishment, in fourth month of pregnancy. No marks of violence. Death by drowning.

Obviously a suicide, unless she had been taken out in a boat and pushed into the river. Could this poor creature have been Clara Burnleigh, and had pregnancy been her reason for running away?

At the convent, the Reverend Mother received him with even less grace than the first time, if that were possible. Staring out of the window, drumming her fingers impatiently on the desk, she listened tight-lipped to his account of the visit to Fairmilehead.

'I have no other information than what I gave you, Inspector. I am not concealing evidence, if that is what you think, to protect the reputation of the convent, which, alas, thanks to police meddling, seems unlikely to survive these shattering blows.'

Cutting short his apologies, she demanded, 'And now, Inspector, what is it you wish me to do?'

Explaining that the body of a woman had been washed up

at Cramond, he asked, 'Could you identify Miss Burnleigh from this description?'

Reading quickly, she pushed it aside with distaste. 'Whoever this unfortunate creature is, she is certainly not Clara Burnleigh. There is not the slightest resemblance. Miss Burnleigh is very tall, with blonde straight hair, and she has excellent teeth.'

'You are quite sure?'

'Sure, Inspector? I am positive. My eyesight is excellent and Miss Burnleigh was a particular favourite of mine – and, I would add, a girl of the highest moral principles. I cannot imagine that she would have allowed herself to join the ranks of fallen women or to commit the sin of self-destruction.'

There remained the Mad Baronet, or, to give him his proper name, Sir Hedley Marsh. Faro realised that there was much to be gained from an apparently accidental meeting, an informal chat, rather than a rush to the door with all the appearance of officialdom. He decided to keep a close watch on Solomon's Tower and the behaviour of its owner, behaviour that belonged more to the early days of constables patrolling on duty, to 'watching and warding' rather than criminal investigation.

At the local dairy, on pretence of being a cat-lover, he was soon informed that the Mad Baronet received his delivery for his score of cats by six o'clock. Faro suspected that, in common with many old people, the Mad Baronet rose early, and he decided to be passing the gate, on a 'constitutional' himself, when the milk was taken indoors.

As he lingered, the pale morning mist enfolded and chilled him. It brought back memories of his early days on the Force. Suddenly he felt old – too old for the job. Recent illness had so weakened him that it seemed to have destroyed not only his appetite but also his self-confidence. Once upon a time, before Lizzie died, he had been hopeful, believed in the immortal soul of man, and his job of

91

dealing with crimes and criminals had never destroyed his faith in human nature, for he had discovered that, in even the worst of them, the good seed, microscopic perhaps, still flourished and could be encouraged to grow.

When he had said this to Vince, the boy had laughed at him. 'Good heavens, Stepfather, surely those are not the requisites for a good detective. You would have made priest or minister with such feelings – quite Christ-like and forgiving. Well, I never.'

Faro had laughed. 'And you, dear lad, had you not chosen medicine, would have made an admirable detective.'

His thoughts were interrupted by the door of Solomon's Tower being thrown open as an avalanche of cats of all shapes, sizes, ages and conditions descended into the garden in the direction of the large milk churn at the gate. He was banking on the Mad Bart appearing himself. Having no servant was always something of a problem.

If there had been a maid, he thought, I could have enlisted Vince's help and, with an elaborate pretence of admiring her fine eyes, flattered her into giving information. Even a fine sturdy coachman might have been wheedled by flattery – such splendid horses. But a baronet, mad or sane, who is also a hermit – there's a plaguey difficult situation.

He did not have long to wait. The last of the cats were followed by a shambling figure, immensely tall and, despite hooded white hair and beard, Faro got an impression that he was strong still and powerfully built. It was, in fact, thanks to a piece of haddock retrieved from last night's supper that Faro had succeeded in gaining the attention of a handsome ginger tom, who leaped through the railings and bolted down the juicy morsel, giving polite thanks by an immediate caressing of Faro's ankles.

'A fine fellow you have here.'

The hooded figure scowled and pretended not to hear. 'Come in at once, Boxer. At once, sir.'

'Boxer, is that your name?' said Faro, addressing the cat. 'You're a fine chap. And so friendly—'

'Immediately, I said!' was the shout from inside the gate, and Boxer departed somewhat reluctantly.

'I say – sir . . .' shouted Faro, looking through the railings.

'What is it?'

'I don't suppose you'd have a kitten you could spare – to sell, I mean, to a good home?'

The Mad Bart scowled and cast an eye over his brood. 'Depends.'

'My housekeeper is a great cat-lover, and we're smitten with a plague of mice – these new houses, you know.'

'Mice, is it? There hasn't been a mouse inside these walls for more years than I can remember.'

As he considered Faro in the manner of one about to sell a favourite daughter, the latter said hastily, 'I would willingly pay you. I'm sorry if I've offended you by my question but we are at our wits' end, and as I often see your cats in the garden when I'm out walking, I thought . . .'

'I don't need payment,' said the old man huffily. 'Wouldn't consider it. Have plenty of kits to spare, never miss the odd one.' He paused again and stared hard at Faro in the manner of one about to make a momentous decision. 'Er, perhaps you'd care to step inside and look at 'em. Have some in the kitchen ready to leave their mother.'

This was better luck than Faro had hoped for as, leading the way, the old man apologised for the untidiness, which was not immediately evident. Apart from the offensive odour of cat *en masse*, the house was surprisingly clean and tidy for an old man living on his own and lacking servants.

'Can I offer you some refreshment? A dram, perhaps? No?'

Faro watched the old man pour out whisky from a decanter. Lighting his pipe was a lengthy operation, so it

93

was some time before the conversation resumed.

'Only use a couple of rooms these days, one for the cats, one for myself.' Down the long stone corridor lay the kitchen, which smelt rather worse than the rest of the house, and Faro was careful not to breathe too deeply. However, the kittens were exceedingly pretty.

'I don't know how to decide which one,' said Faro in all honesty. 'Perhaps my housekeeper would be better able— '

'Women are no judges of a good mouser. Here, take this one. Comes of a good mouser strain. Take my word for it, you'll have no more trouble.' As Faro put his hand in his pocket, the old man added sternly, 'As a gift – I insist. I want no money. Can't keep 'em all. Have to be cruel to be kind sometimes,' he added. 'Drown a whole litter occasionally. Better that way than putting 'em out to run wild. Place would be overrun . . .'

Faro could see no valid reason for refusing the offer, and hoped he had not let himself in for Mrs Brook's displeasure, seeing the mouse plague had been a pure piece of invention and he had not the least idea whether the housekeeper was a cat-lover or not. He was considering by what means he could extend the interview when the Mad Bart suddenly said, 'I know you. You're that detective chap. You live across in the new houses.'

'That is correct,' said Faro weakly. 'How did you know?'

'Girl who came to visit my cats, from the convent, told me who you were.'

'Girl?'

'You know, one who was murdered – second one. Teacher. Heard about it. Grocer lad told me. Most unfortunate.'

'So you knew her?'

The Mad Bart looked vague. 'No more than I know you, sir. As I said, saw my cats. Took a notion to buying one. Mice in her room, too. Scared of 'em. Pleasant girl, kind too. Was suffering from one of my attacks of the ague at the time. Told me the nuns made a good concoction of herbs. Brought some. Papist muck, of course, but did the trick. Never saw her again.' His accompanying sigh, a shake of the great shaggy head, more than any words gave a glimpse of the loneliness of his life. 'No. Never saw her again,' he repeated sadly. 'Rotten business. Glad they got the fellow. Deserved to swing for it. *Crime passionnel*, was it?'

'I don't think so,' said Faro vaguely, anxious not to divert the stream of confidence.

'Oh, thought he had led her on, let her down. Damn fool. Had I been younger, I'd have married her myself.'

Suddenly feeling that he was getting valuable information at last, Faro's senses were on the alert. Had the cats been Lily Goldie's excuse for an introduction to the Mad Bart? Had she perhaps had an eye on marrying this mad old man? The idea wasn't as impossible as it first seemed. It was happening every day, girls who married men old enough to be their grandfathers, for the money and, more often, for the title.

'This chap – wasn't the one she hoped to marry then?'

'Not as far as we know. That didn't come out in the evidence, anyway,' said Faro cautiously.

'I naturally presumed . . .'

'Presumed?'

'From what she said, that there was someone . . .'

Faro felt a surge of excitement. So there was a man in existence who had offered Lily Goldie marriage.

'Didn't you tell anyone about this?'

'Why should I? Wasn't any of my business. After all, they got her murderer, didn't they?' He looked at Faro for a moment before continuing. 'Can tell you who it was she hoped to marry, though. If you're interested. That young chap who fell under a train. Turned out that her expectations came to nothing, fellow was penniless, bit of a waster. Sent him packing. Quite right, seeing he had been leading

95

her on. Not the done thing for a gentleman, is it now?'

Faro looked bleak. It had cost this particular young gentleman his life. 'So you didn't consider the police should be told.'

'If anyone had come and asked me, I should have told them. For what it was worth.'

Leaving the kitchen with the kitten miaowing plaintively in its cardboard box, Faro silently cursed McQuinn as the Mad Bart said, 'My felicitations to your young constable. Enjoys a chat over my garden wall when he's on duty. Gather he was brought up by nuns, or some such background. Don't hold that against him even if he is a papist. He's a shrewd young fellow. He'll go far, mark my words. Can all rest easy in our beds, knowing we have such chaps in the police.'

As they shook hands at the door, Faro went away feeling sourly that wherever he went these days McQuinn seemed to have been there first, covering his inefficiency by ingratiating himself with everyone, from nuns to mad baronets. And managing very conveniently to be first on the scene at Cramond Island when the drowned girl was washed ashore.

Faro hoped his feelings were natural ones for having been thwarted by the case of Lily Goldie and not allowed to complete his own thorough investigations. He didn't like McQuinn but he didn't want to fall into a trap he knew of from experience of older detectives, eager to blame young constables for their own failures and mistakes. He also felt a question had been posed to which he must, by tact or guile, find the answer: what did Danny McQuinn know of Lily Goldie's personal life that had failed to find its way into his reports?

'So much for our private investigations,' he told Vince over supper that evening, a delighted Mrs Brook having taken the pretty ginger kitten into custody.

96

Vince looked thoughtful. 'Are you sure that's all the Mad Bart said?'

Faro was hurt. He prided himself on his remarkable memory and the ability to make verbatim reports of conversations where necessary. 'I am sure. Obviously the old gentleman was correct in assuming that Ferris had told Lily he was well off – until he was disinherited, or whatever, after failing his exams.'

Vince sighed. 'On the other hand, she might have been telling our Mad Bart that to keep him at a distance. There's no fool like an old fool in love.' His mocking glance in his stepfather's direction made Faro wince. He refused, however, to fall for that particular piece of bait, and Vince continued, 'Surely if there had been a man involved who loved her honourably and wanted to marry her he would have appeared at Hymes's trial?'

'Only if he was innocent of her murder.'

'You mean, you think that he's the man we're looking for? A Mr X about whom we know nothing but who, for reasons we will never know, might have murdered Lily Goldie? Well, who is he, and, more important, where is he? Tantalising, isn't it?'

'Something to hide doesn't make him guilty of murder. Perhaps his crime was being a philanderer, a bit of a bounder who gained Lily Goldie's favours under false pretences, like Ferris. Or our Mr X might have been married already, in which case he would consider it prudent not to draw undue attention to himself and his extra-marital activities. Or, if he wasn't married, he and Lily could have quarrelled violently. She could have been blackmailing him – anything – there could be some very good reasons why he might not have wanted to appear at a murder trial.'

From his own vast experience of crimes and criminal trials, Faro was fully aware that anyone who so appears, however innocent, is immediately besmirched in the public eye. Respectable Edinburgh society would go far to avoid 'that man who appeared at the notorious murder trial'. Faro also knew that such a notoriety was one that most men would go far to assiduously avoid, even to concealing vital evidence.

'You know, I still incline to our Mad Bart,' said Vince, 'as the most hopeful suspect. Tell me about his hands.'

'His hands?'

'Yes. Did you notice anything about them?'

'Only that they were crippled with rheumatism.'

'That's it,' said Vince triumphantly. 'I thought they would be, because what little I've seen of him walking, his feet are also affected.'

'Small wonder, living in that wretchedly damp tower.'

'Did he have difficulty using his hands?'

'As a matter of fact, yes. Pouring out a dram, lighting his pipe, took him a long time. Obviously, the pressure needed for strangulation would be beyond him.'

'There you are. That's it,' repeated Vince. 'Don't you see, Stepfather? You're missing the whole point. What did I tell you right at the beginning?'

'That Lily was pushed off the Crags . . .'

'And the scarf tied about her neck afterwards, to make it look the same as the Hymes murder.' Seeing Faro's doubtful expression, he sighed. 'Well, if it wasn't the Mad Bart with his rheumaticky hands, who are we left with?'

Faro rubbed his chin thoughtfully. 'Hands incapable of strangling could also apply to a woman.'

'A woman?'

'Yes. I'm giving serious consideration to the missing and mysterious Miss Clara Burnleigh.'

'Are you now? Well, it's a deuced interesting theory.'

'It poses only one question. Why?'

'Jealousy is the most obvious reason. But we can't know for sure until we track her down. And that I'm quite determined on.'

'Dead or alive?'

'Hopefully alive. Because at least we know that Miss Burnleigh isn't the poor unfortunate lying in the mortuary, and the chances are that she is very much alive and not too far away.'

Next morning, when Faro went to the Central Office, Constable McQuinn was waiting to give him a message.

'The drowned girl, sir. Her parents came and identified her late last night. Here are the papers.' The statement said little, but McQuinn was eager to fill in the details. 'Terrible state the mother was in – usual thing. Father showed the girl the door when he knew she was pregnant. Advocate, pillar of the Church, very respectable and all that sort of thing. Suicide it was, just as I thought when I first saw the corpse. Poor girl, with no one to turn to, threw herself in the river.'

A waste of a life, thought Faro. It was the story of so many young girls. But what was left to them? A back-street abortion and a painful death in all probability. Or, if they and the child survived as outcasts from society, the woman bringing up her child alone, with not the least hope that any respectable man would wish to marry her, often resorted to prostitution as the only means of earning a living where her past would not be held against her.

'There is another letter for you, sir. Came by last night's post.'

Faro tore open the envelope. In black capital letters the message read, 'Clara B. is a lying whore. So was her mother. Try asking for them beyond the crossroads at Mrs Wishart's.' It was signed, 'One Who Seeks Justice'.

As he hailed a cab from the stance at Parliament House, where several vehicles were reserved for police use, Faro felt triumphant. His visit to Fairmilehead had seriously upset some person or persons who bore Clara Burnleigh and her mother a grudge. From such disagreeable sources, information was readily forthcoming and eagerly given.

This was the break that all detectives longed for and seldom received. He felt the sure tingle of excitement that within hours the mystery of the missing Clara Burnleigh would be resolved.

He would be one step nearer to discovering the identity of Lily Goldie's slayer, and apprehending the second murderer.

CHAPTER TEN

As the hired gig drove at a smart pace through villages and fields and smoky hamlets towards Fairmilehead, Faro found his thoughts returning to Alison Aird. He wished he had not decided to make this second visit alone. The day was identical in weather to that first excursion with her and it intensified his longing to see her again.

At every stage of the journey, Faro was haunted by Alison's presence: here we laughed at the children playing with a kitten; here she quoted *Hamlet*; here we admired an old water-mill.

The sun disappeared, a chill wind came leaping out of the Pentlands and cut across his shoulders like a cold knife. The walk was sad, as if she was dead and had left him for ever. He could hardly believe that at this moment she was probably sitting happily in her lodgings, sipping tea and going over her script for the next play in the repertoire. He had to steel himself and remember that he had not lost her, that the battle had not yet begun: a battle still to fight is also a battle still to win.

As he opened the gate of Mrs Wishart's residence, which to his relief he found without difficulty, Alison's smiling ghost retreated as the detective swept aside the sentimental would-be lover.

What if there was no one at home and his journey fruitless? The old house stood aloof and shrouded by trees, a short distance from the village. Its windows and front door, its neat garden, spoke of shabby gentility. His second summons brought forth a response and the door was opened by a maid, whose appearance was in keeping with the house. She looked as if she had been serving in the establishment for some considerable time.

'Mrs Wishart?'

'Who wants her?'

'Who is it, what do you want?' An old lady peered over the maid's shoulder. 'We are not at home today.'

'Mrs Wishart?'

'That is my name.' She regarded him, frowning, and he half expected the same reluctance as he had received, a stranger, at the Mad Bart's door. He was soon to discover that her manner was due to deafness rather than hostility.

'I wonder, madam, if you can help me. I'm looking for a young lady. She, er, calls herself Clara Burnleigh.'

'I will deal with this. Go you back to your work.' And dismissing the maid, Mrs Wishart asked him to repeat the question. At the name, she gave a rather violent start.

'I thought that was what you said.' A faint shadow disturbed the serene face, a slight hesitation. 'I know no one of that name.'

'That is a pity. I was advised to make my enquiry to you.'

'Indeed. And who wishes to know?'

Faro decided in his turn to be deaf, and said, 'Burnleigh may not be her real name, but I have good reason to believe she comes from this area. A tall pretty girl with fair straight hair,' he added, remembering the Reverend Mother's description.

The old lady nodded vigorously, as if the description tallied. Then, examining Faro through her lorgnette, she demanded, 'And who might you be?'

'Before I tell you my name, let me say that I only wish to talk to the young lady about one of her friends. An unfortunate colleague who was murdered— '

102

'Murdered – but how horrible. Horrible.'

'A Miss Lily Goldie. Perhaps you knew of her?'

'No. No. As for Clara, I'm not aware . . .' The old woman stopped, confused, her lips suddenly tight closed.

'Aware?' Faro asked.

'What Clara can do to help you with your enquiries. Justice has been done. I read in the newspapers that the murderer was hanged – weeks ago.'

'That is so. But I am here to conduct a private investigation at the behest of a relative,' Faro lied cheerfully. 'This is an absolutely confidential matter and nothing you care to tell me need go any further.'

Mrs Wishart accepted the implication that the relative was one of Lily Goldie's. 'In that case, of course, of course, I will do what I can to help you. Come inside.'

As had been suggested by the exterior, the interior was spick and span and comfortably if plainly furnished.

'Do sit down, Mr . . .?'

'Faro.'

'You will take some tea?' After ringing the bell for the maid, she said, 'What I am about to tell you is in the very strictest confidence, and I rely on your discretion as a gentleman— '

'Before you do so, I ought to tell you that I am a detective inspector – in this case acting in a private capacity.'

'I see no reason why there should not be gentlemen among policemen.' She gave him a shrewd glance. 'I have lived a long time, Inspector Faro, and whatever your profession you have the look of a man I would trust.'

The maid brought in tea, and when it was served Mrs Wishart continued, 'Burnleigh is not Clara's real name. That is her mother's name and was mine before I married. Clara is my grand-niece. Her real name is Clerkwell.' She paused. 'There was a great scandal attached to that name about fifteen years ago. Perhaps you remember it?'

'Of course. A case of embezzlement and— '

'And Clara's mother was deeply involved with the partner in the firm. You know the rest.'

It had been before his time, but was a *cause célèbre* in the records of the Edinburgh City Police. Clerkwell had been cheated by his stepbrother and had committed suicide – a suicide in such suspicious circumstances that it was very probably murder dressed up to look as if Clerkwell had taken his own life. Ethel Clerkwell was tried and acquitted with the verdict: Not Proven.

'The poor child, my grand-niece, lived under the stigma of all that implied in Edinburgh society.'

Faro smiled grimly. Not Proven was a byword with the magistrates. We know you did it, but we can't prove it. Go away and don't do it again.

'Her mother's life was shattered by the scandal. Her health never recovered and Clara had nursed her devotedly. Imagine a child of ten, hardly understanding anything but the terrible cloud that hovered over her mother's reason. By the time the child was eighteen, it looked as if poor Ethel would have to be committed to an insane asylum. But Clara stayed with her until, mercifully, two years ago she died. Clara was heartbroken but free. They had long since reverted to the name of Burnleigh, and it was under that name she sought a situation as a teacher in an Edinburgh convent – I cannot remember the name.'

Faro told her, and asked, 'Did the sisters know her story?'

Mrs Wishart shook her head. 'No. As I told you, she wished to begin a completely new life. She told no one. A year ago, she met a young man of property, well connected in Edinburgh society. They fell in love and he asked her to marry him. She was in something of a dilemma, poor child, for she was afraid that by telling him the truth she would lose him. While she was summoning up her courage, one of the maids was murdered. The police came to investigate and my poor Clara was horrified, guiltily aware that they might well discover the truth about her on the eve of her marriage, which she had kept secret even from the sisters. And so she fled.'

Mrs Wishart paused to refill Faro's teacup. 'I have to tell you that Clara's story has a happy ending. The young man's regard for her was in no way diminished by her revelations. Her story merely strengthened the depth of his love and determination to cherish her as his wife. If you wish, I can ask her if she would be willing to speak to you, privately, of course.'

'If you would be so good. I will give you my address.'

'That will not be necessary, Inspector. She lives not far away – in the next village. Her husband is not at home, alas, a family bereavement has him in Stirling this week. Clara was unable to accompany him for reasons of health.'

'She is ailing?'

Mrs Wishart smiled fondly. 'Shall we say, they have expectations of a happy event and the early stages are somewhat trying?'

'Perhaps I should not intrude upon her at this time?'

'By this hour of the day, the worst will be over. It is only in the mornings when she feels considerably unwell and would be unlikely to feel strong enough to receive a visitor.'

As he pocketed Clara's card and prepared to take his leave, Faro said, 'You have been very helpful, Mrs Wishart. I trust that your grand-niece will receive me as graciously.'

'I think you have my word for that. My poor Clara, having suffered so greatly herself, has learned the lesson early in life, that we should be willing to help others in distress. And this unhappy relative of poor Miss Goldie?' she enquired, inviting further explanation. When this was not forthcoming, she went on, 'My grand-niece has a kind heart. I am sure she will receive you.'

On the doorstep, Faro turned and thanked her once again.

'One moment, Inspector. There is one question you might be good enough to answer – to satisfy my curiosity.'

'And that is?'

'Who gave you my name? I ask because it appears that our secret is not as well hidden as we imagined.'

Faro considered and decided against revealing the scurrilous letter. 'It came without any signature. Do you have an enemy, Mrs Wishart?' he added gently.

The old lady was unperturbed. 'Perhaps everyone has, Inspector. Resentments, old slights, fester through the years in small villages. There were those who were jealous of Clara's good marriage.'

Faro worked on the well-worn principle that there is much to be gained from the element of surprise, namely, the unexpected visit. He knew from long experience that those first minutes are crucial, for it is then more than at any other time that, to the detective's shrewd and observant eye, guilt is revealed or innocence proclaimed without a word being exchanged.

Clara Denbridge, née Burnleigh, lived but two miles away from her great-aunt, and Faro once again left the cab in a convenient lane at a discreet distance from the house. It was a pleasant sunny day and he enjoyed the walk with its prospect of Edinburgh Castle like a great grey ship sailing on the far horizon. Mellowed by distance, it became the castle from a fairy tale. Hard to believe that beyond those great trees and hidden villages lay a thriving bustling city of commerce, a city where every stone was steeped in a bloody history of battles and violence.

Faro sighed. And it seemed to get worse rather than better as the centuries progressed. If there was a lesson to be taken from history, it was that men lived but never learned from the mistakes of the past.

The Denbridge residence was in the modern baronial style, bristling with pepperpot turrets, in blatant imitation of the ruined old castle which frowned down upon it from the hillside. Set in an attractive garden, along an impressive drive with a coach-house, its air of opulence was completed by the trimly uniformed maid who opened the door.

From her slightly flustered, anxious appearance, Faro deduced even before she opened her mouth that she was a local lass, bursting with pride at having a smart new uniform as she twitched at cap and pinafore. Her eagerness to be helpful suggested that she had not been long in her present employment, or, judging by her extreme youth, in any employment at all. It also suggested that the Denbridges had not been long established and had few visitors.

To his question she said, 'The mistress. Oh yes, she's at home – I mean, I'll see, if you'll just wait a wee minute.' Then, turning in her tracks, she remembered the essential, 'Who shall I say is calling?'

Faro took a chance. 'A friend of her great-aunt, Mrs Wishart from Fairmilehead.'

Clara Denbridge appeared with the alacrity of one who had been lurking in the hall. She almost thrust the maid aside in her eagerness to confront Faro.

'Mrs Wishart? Is there something wrong – is she ill?'

Her anxiety indicated the devotion that existed between them, and hastily he put her mind at rest.

'No, Mrs Denbridge. She was in excellent health and spirits when I left her a little while ago.'

Clara sighed. 'Oh, that is good. I was afraid . . .' Calm again, she waited, smiling politely.

'Detective Inspector Faro.'

At the name, her hand flew to her lips. Dread filled her eyes as she whispered, 'The Inspector who came to the convent. What – what is your business with me?'

Indicating the servant, Faro said, 'Your maid holds the letter from Mrs Wishart which explains the reason for my visit.'

107

Hastily tearing open the envelope, Clara read the brief message. 'You had better come in. Annie,' she called in the direction of the kitchen. 'Tea, if you please.'

The parlour into which he was ushered continued the opulence suggested by the exterior. There seemed to be not one possession in that room which was any older than the young bride herself. Everything spoke of proud new ownership. Paintings, ornaments, silver, a rich but not necessarily matching assortment and some half-unwrapped parcels suggested recently acquired wedding presents. From the room itself came the lingering smells of paint, and the upholstery, cushions, sofas and carpets added that indefinable but not unpleasant odour of new wool. Antimacassars and curtains were of fine linen and even the furniture smelt as if the wood from which it was constructed was within living memory of a pine forest.

'Do please sit down, Inspector Faro.'

As he did so, Clara swept aside two of the parcels and apologised for the untidiness. 'We have only been installed in the house since we returned from honeymoon a month ago and, alas, the promised bookcases have failed to put in an appearance. My – my husband,' she continued, a pretty blush declaring that the title was not yet well used by her, 'my husband and I are both great readers.'

Faro smiled. 'Please don't apologise. I have just moved into my new home six months ago, and as both my stepson and I acquire a considerable number of books – he is a newly graduated doctor – we have similar problems. It is good of you to receive me, madam, at such a time, with such short notice.'

'I presume your business is urgent, or else my great-aunt would not have sent you. She is most reliable in such matters. Is there something I can do for you? Is it about poor Lily Goldie?'

Faro explained that this was a routine visit on behalf of a

relative of Lily Goldie. 'After my first visit to Fairmilehead, I feared that there might have been some less agreeable reason for your disappearance.'

'I behaved foolishly,' interrupted Mrs Denbridge, 'and I apologise for putting you to so much trouble and speculation, Inspector. It did not occur to me that I would be inconveniencing anyone by my story. As my great-aunt will have told you, I felt it necessary at the time. Thankfully, that is no longer the case.'

'I can only say that I am delighted for you.'

Clara smiled. 'I fear I can say little that will help you, which is a great shame, you having come all this way. Lily and I had the merest acquaintance. She was a naturally secretive person and I'm afraid she had to do a great deal more listening to my troubles at the time – I was too pre-occupied with my imminent marriage to pay a great deal of attention to her activities.'

'Our enquiries revealed that she had a sweetheart, a possible suitor,' said Faro boldly, taking a chance. 'Is that correct?'

'Why, yes. Such a tragedy. Did you not know?' she added in a hushed voice. 'The poor unfortunate gentleman fell' (the word was heavily emphasised) 'under a train.'

Faro made sympathetic noises and handed her the photograph. 'Do you recognise him?'

'Of course. That is a very good likeness of Mr Ferris.'

'You met him then?'

'A fleeting acquaintance. Hardly that, even, for Lily seemed very anxious to avoid a formal introduction,' she added, with a touch of pique.

'For what reason, Mrs Denbridge?'

Clara shrugged delicately. 'Many young women do not care to introduce their suitors. It is a disagreeable and very impolite trait and it implies that they are afraid of competition. I mean— '

'I see exactly what you mean.'

'Let us be frank, Inspector. For all her bragging of her conquests, Lily was not at all certain of Mr Ferris's intentions. I knew she wished to be married but I gathered there was some impediment to this marriage. I remember her saying that she would have to work on him. "I shall have to use all my woman's wiles if I am to get him to the altar, Clara." I remember, those were her very words. However, one cannot repeat confidences of this nature.' She put her hands together primly. 'I do not in the least wish to talk ill of the dead, of Lily or poor Mr Ferris, but I felt that, er, they had misbehaved.'

'Misbehaved?'

'Yes, Inspector.' Clara blushed. 'As a married woman, I can only suggest that they had been on – er, terms of intimacy.'

'For what reason?' Faro demanded sharply.

Clara shook her head. 'I cannot say more, except that females sharing rooms know certain things about each other rather by instinct than any conversation, which, of course, would be highly improper.'

'I do wish you had told me about this at the time.'

'I was unmarried myself, and somewhat embarrassed. Besides,' she added righteously, 'ladies do not readily cast aspersions upon a colleague's character, especially when she has been murdered, Inspector. And as it seemed that her murderer – the wicked man Hymes – had been apprehended, I guessed that he had been responsible and that was the reason why he had murdered her.'

'Responsible?'

'Yes, indeed, Inspector. You see . . .' She took a deep breath and continued. 'I knew – by certain things – female things, after he died – that she suspected she was – er – in trouble.'

'Do I take your meaning that Miss Goldie had reason to believe she was carrying a child?' said Faro bluntly.

'Yes,' whispered Clara. '"His parents – someone – will have to pay for this little indiscretion." Those were her very words, Inspector. You can imagine how difficult it was for me. Had I announced my suspicions, it would have been a blow to the convent's reputation and I would have been merely blackening her character even further, if my suspicions were not correct. Having suffered deeply from the scurrilous slanders of heartless people – I saw my own mother destroyed by such slanders, remember that, Inspector – I could never have forgiven myself. And it appears I would have been wrong, for there was no mention of what I suspected at the trial. Perhaps you can tell me, Inspector, was I correct?'

'The post-mortem on Lily Goldie revealed no such evidence that could besmirch her character.'

'Then I am greatly relieved.'

'You believe, then, that Hymes was responsible for her murder?'

'I see no reason to doubt it. Perhaps she was desperate.'

'Desperate?'

'Yes. She believed she had to find a father for the child. Anyone who would give it a name and save her reputation.'

'But Hymes was married already.'

'I don't suppose Lily knew that.'

'I'm sorry, Mrs Denbridge, but what you are suggesting simply does not make sense.'

'It makes good sense to me, or to any woman who finds herself in such a situation. You have my assurances on that, Inspector,' she added sharply.

'Surely you would think it strange that such a – lady – as Miss Goldie appeared to be, should have formed an attachment with Hymes in the first place?'

'Not if she was desperate to find a husband in her unhappy circumstances. Besides, perhaps he had some fearful fascination for her, even mesmeric,' she added, eyes gleaming. 'This, I understand, can happen all too often when young ladies emerge from sheltered lives and allow themselves to be preyed upon by creatures from the lower classes.'

Clara's conclusions certainly threw some unusual light on Lily Goldie's activities, and on the ways of womankind in general, thought Faro cynically. As a detective used to dealing in facts, he found it almost impossible to give credence to such an imaginative explanation.

As he was leaving, Faro glanced over the notes he had written. 'When Miss Goldie expressed her fears of being pregnant, did I understand that she said to you: "His parents – or someone – will have to pay dearly for this little indiscretion"?'

'Yes, indeed. Those were her words. I am positive.'

'I merely put it to you that you might have been mistaken, because Ferris was an orphan.'

Clara laughed. 'Now, Inspector, it is you who are mistaken. Tim had a young brother at St Leonard's.'

'You are sure of that?'

'Of course I am. I met him with Lily on two occasions. He's about fourteen or fifteen. Rather slightly built, but a handsome boy, with fine features, from what I could see, as he did not have the courtesy to raise his cap to me. Of course, I understood, it's an awkward age and he was obviously very shy and ill-at-ease.'

'What was his name?'

Clara spread her hands wide. 'Inspector, I have the most appalling memory for names – I even forget those of people to whom I'm introduced, which can be most embarrassing. And in this case, I doubt whether I would have considered Tim's young brother important enough to have it stick in my mind.'

'One more question, Mrs Denbridge, if you will oblige. Did these meetings take place before or after Mr Ferris died?'

Clara bit her lip. 'About the same time. Yes, I remember thinking it very appropriate, and hoping that Lily was a comfort to Tim's brother in his sad loss.'

As he said his farewells, Faro added, 'If the boy's name should come to mind – or any other detail, however trivial it seems to you, I would be most obliged if you would drop me a note. Here is my private address.'

He rejoined the cab, whose driver was enjoying a quiet snooze in the sunshine. On the way back to Edinburgh, Faro decided that the meeting with Clara Burnleigh now presented him with what he most dreaded: a visit to St Leonard's. First of all, he must explain his reasons to the Headmaster, who might not be kindly disposed towards having a detective inspector interview Ferris Minor.

Faro sighed. For a dead man, Timothy Ferris was turning out to be persistently enigmatic. The only remaining hope was that his young brother would shed some light on a particularly baffling case. And one which he now regretted having reopened.

If only he could believe in Clara Burnleigh's reasoning, absurd as it was, and accept that Lily Goldie had given Hymes good reason for murdering her.

If only, to quote Superintendent Mackintosh, he had 'let hanged murderers lie'.

CHAPTER ELEVEN

At the Central Office, there were no new cases for him, merely a routine check on Wormwoodhall to establish the whereabouts of the notorious Black Tam, whose re-entry into society had produced a spate of robberies with violence.

As St Leonard's School lay on the respectable area bordering Causewayside, he might be able to catch Black Tam and interview Ferris Minor in one visit. It was an appealing thought and, closing his door, Faro put up his feet on his desk, sent out for a pint of porter and, for the first time in months, a mutton pie. Then he sat down and, sharpening a pen, drew up a sheet of paper and compiled a complete report from his sketchy notes of his meeting with Clara Burnleigh.

He wondered what Vince would make of his findings as he set off for St Leonard's, a modern building despite its aggressively medieval castellations. The long drive, not yet decently shaded by trees, seemed oddly naked, the house deserted.

'There's no one here,' said a gardener. 'The whole school is away on a founder's day picnic to Peebles.'

Faro thanked him for the information and left. Heading for Causewayside led him past the street where Alison Aird lodged with the other female members of Trelawney's Thespians.

Why not call upon her? His excuse was feeble but

irresistible, an apology for having missed her performance in *Macbeth*.

Mrs Penny, the landlady, eyed him sourly. 'Mrs Aird is not at home.' And without any further question, she added, 'I do not know where she has gone, and I do not know when she will return. And I am unable to take messages of any kind for my boarders. That is my rule. You may leave a note on the hall table, if you so desire.'

Faro regarded the formidable lady with awe. Large, florid, her face painted, and doubtless wearing a discarded theatrical wig of a suspiciously youthful gold. As she spoke, Mrs Penny's appearance suggested the figurehead of a ship come to grotesque life.

And one well able to repel boarders, thought Faro, making his apologies and his way to the gate, under her keen eye. A lady who would take no nonsense from anyone.

He continued on his way into the warrens of Causewayside, with a certain caution and reluctance. He was already known to many of the inhabitants, for he had regularly appeared to run famous criminals to earth in this notorious area.

The cobbled street was quite crowded, but as he walked down, trying to maintain an air of jaunty indifference, most of the inhabitants melted into the shadows of the grimy tenements and dingy hovels. By the time the Quaker Mission came into view, the street was almost deserted and he guessed that word of his coming had already spread like wildfire among the thieves and vagabonds whose presence had sorely tried him in the past.

The mission was situated in a secluded court with a tiny garden. He had never set foot in it before, but Alison Aird's association with the Quakers made him curious, and as he looked inside he thought he saw her sitting under a tree, and reading from a book to an audience of small children.

Could it be? She was against the sun, but yes, it was indeed Alison Aird. He stood in the shadows, for a moment

115

enjoying the contrast between her gentle beauty, her muslin frock and neat hair, and the grimy poverty of the ragged urchins, bare-limbed, filthy, verminous. The sight struck his heart with new tenderness and an overwhelming desire to protect her.

She was unaware of his presence until his shadow came between her and the sun. The children's reaction was immediate – 'Scarper. Peelers.' – and they melted into the distance before she had finished reading the sentence.

'Children? Come back here – what on earth . . .?'

Turning, she saw his tall figure approaching across the grass. She stood up and held out her hand with a welcoming smile – but no more.

'Good day, Inspector.' She frowned. 'This is very unexpected.'

'Not at all, Mrs Aird. This is a neighbourhood which I unfortunately know very well indeed.'

'What brings you here? You have not come to arrest me, I hope?'

Faro laughed at her bewilderment. 'I have come in search of a gentleman known as Black Tam. But I suspect that news of my approach has already reached him.'

'Is he a dangerous character?'

'Very.'

'Then are you wise to come alone?'

Her anxious tone suggested concern. Did she really care? he thought. 'What of yourself, Mrs Aird? I see you have not heeded my advice.'

'Will you be reassured if I tell you that I come armed?'

'Armed?'

'Yes, Inspector, armed.' Despite her solemn tones, he had an uneasy suspicion that she was laughing at him. From her reticule she withdrew a tiny dagger from a jewelled sheath. 'I go nowhere without it.' Handing it to Faro, she continued, 'It was a present from an Indian holy

116

man long ago who said that one day it would protect me from a terrible death.'

Returning it, Faro did not add that it would be useless against a strong assailant. 'A pretty toy, Mrs Aird, but you would be better not to tempt fate and stay away from this area. As I have told you, it is no place for a gentlewoman.'

Mrs Aird laughed. 'As I told *you* before, I am no gentlewoman, merely an actress.' She held up the book of *Tales from Shakespeare*. 'I was asked by the Quakers if I would read to the poor children, in the hope that it might provide the right inspiration for them to make a better life for themselves.'

Faro refrained from commenting that it would take a great deal more than that to wean them away from the sordid existence that was bred in them, from first cry to dying breath.

'You look doubtful, Inspector. There is no danger here. The poor are not all wicked. Sometimes all they have to give is their friendship.'

He made a grimace. 'Not to policemen. And I would advise you, beware the face of innocence. It is most often a mask, and you have chosen to work in the midst of a strong criminal element.'

With a sigh, she closed her book, gathered up her bonnet and basket. 'Since you have scared away my little friends, I might as well return to my lodging. Would you care to accompany me? Mrs Penny will give us tea – her scones are delicious. Where has everyone disappeared to?' she whispered as they walked down the almost deserted street. 'I have never seen the place so empty. What on earth did you do to them, Inspector?'

'Nothing, I assure you. But they know my reputation. I rarely come to Wormwoodhall and leave again empty-handed.'

'Empty-handed? How so?'

117

'Yes. I usually take some member of their fraternity away with the cuffs about his wrists.'

'Good gracious, Inspector. You alarm me. You seemed such a friendly man, calm, full of compassion. I could not imagine you putting the fear of death into anyone. And now I am seeing you in a very different role. I feel quite cheated,' she added, with a mocking smile.

'We all have our obverse side, Mrs Aird.' And he thought of the grieving woman in grey he had first seen in Greyfriars Kirkyard and of his instant infatuation. While he wondered how he might with tact raise the subject of that first meeting, his senses were strangely aroused by her forearms under the parasol she carried. So soft and gently freckled, defenceless and utterly lovely, he longed to seize her in his arms.

Would her reaction be outrage, at being kissed in the public street, he thought, following her along the path to her lodgings where a transformed Mrs Penny greeted their arrival together.

Alison Aird was clearly a favourite and when she went upstairs to her bedroom to attend to her toilette, Mrs Penny, with the undisguised delight of a match-maker, now fawned upon the Inspector.

Full of eye-fluttering apologies for her harshness in sending him away, she whispered, 'So many admirers, and I have my instructions, directly from Mrs Aird: not to admit anyone. Those are her very words. In all the time she has been under my roof, she has never once brought a gentleman back to partake of my tea and scones until this moment.' She gave him an admiring glance. 'But the moment I saw you, I should have realised that you were different. That you were someone special. I do most abjectly apologise for my behaviour towards you, sir, and trust that it will be overlooked.'

Faro, feeling exceedingly flattered, readily agreed, where-upon Mrs Penny was at great pains to inform him that Mrs Aird was A Gem.

'She is the perfect boarder, sir, there are none to match her for gentleness and consideration. It will be a devastation, sir, to me personally, a devastation to lose her.'

'Who are you about to lose, Mrs Penny?' asked Mrs Aird, who had entered the room soft-footed having changed her sturdy outdoor shoes for slippers.

'Well, yourself, Mrs Aird. I was just remarking to the Inspector that I have prayed you would meet some nice gentleman who would persuade you to leave all those actors, and that uncertain life you have on the stage.'

Her bold look in Faro's direction was unmistakable, but Mrs Aird did not blush or look embarrassed, she merely shrugged and said, 'I fear not, Mrs Penny. I have no great wish to marry again and I have passed the age where I am likely to appeal to some eligible man who will sweep me off my feet and wish to have me as his life partner.'

This revelation did not please Faro. It merely emphasised what he already suspected – that his regard for Mrs Aird was by no means mutual. She obviously did not consider him an attractive proposition and had never thought of him in the role of prospective husband.

When they were alone with the tea and scones before them, Mrs Aird said, 'Did you return to Fairmilehead to find the missing lady?'

'I did. The reason for her apparent deception had an innocent explanation.'

'Did I not tell you so? Was I not right?' asked Mrs Aird triumphantly.

'In part, yes.' And Faro was suddenly aware that a successful detective might benefit from a woman in his life, an intelligent woman whose interpretation of the occasional astonishingly irrational behaviour of her sex could be relied upon.

'Your business with the lady is at an end, then?'

'Indeed, I hope so.' Faro decided he was not going to waste precious time with Alison Aird's polite interest in

119

his investigations. 'Am I to understand that you are to be leaving us soon?'

'Yes. Mr Trelawney and the company are booked into Bournemouth for the summer season.'

Faro's heart felt unnaturally heavy as he said, 'I shall miss you.'

She smiled. 'I know.'

Did it follow that she would also miss him? He followed up his advantage. 'It seems sometimes as if I have known you for a very long time,' he said breathlessly, aware that he had said the wrong thing, for she merely inclined her head, smiled and said, 'You are very kind.'

'Will you be sorry to leave Edinburgh?'

She stared out of the window towards the Pentland Hills. 'Not really. I have been here since spring, a whole season. That is a long time for me to spend acting in the same theatre. Normally, it is two weeks and then on the road again.'

Her bleak tones aroused a dismal picture of the drudgery that lies behind those magnificent hours on stage portraying the great Shakespearean roles.

'I know so little about you,' he said helplessly, out of his depth. Where was his customary dignity? Even to his own ears, he heard the desperate note of the love-lorn who expects no mercy.

There was none. 'What is the point, when the chances are that we will never meet again?' As though conscious of her cruelty, she put out her hand and, touching his arm, said softly, 'You know enough about me, Inspector,' and, as a sop for his stricken expression, 'far more than most of the men I meet during my travels. Now, have another of Mrs Penny's scones. Of course you must, they will have been counted and she'll be mortally offended if they are not eaten. Here you are, see, I have buttered it for you.'

He groaned inwardly at this sweet domestic gesture. It struck a chord almost forgotten, for Lizzie always buttered his bread. Never had he felt so alone, so in need of a woman's love and cherishing.

'Are we not even to be friends?'

'Friends? Of course we will be friends, if that will make you happy, for the short time I have left in Edinburgh.' She looked at him, head on one side, smiling, as if she could picture such an association and it pleased her. 'Yes, I would like that very much, Inspector.'

'Then may I beg that you call me by my first name?'

'Of course.' She put a hand to her mouth. 'Oh dear, I think I have forgotten what it is.'

'It's Jeremiah – my mother had a passion for biblical names, but I shortened it long ago to Jeremy.'

'Jeremy,' she repeated softly. 'I like it. It makes you sound like a little boy.'

Faro thought sourly that was not at all the impression he had hoped for, as she added, with a shake of the head, 'No more Mrs Aird – Alison, if you please. And now that we have our friendship well and truly launched, what were we talking about?'

'Your feelings about leaving Edinburgh.'

'Oh yes. Perhaps I have been too harsh in my judgement, since we have been most fortunate with our audiences. Most nights we have played to full houses. Granted the theatre is small and has many drawbacks in the way of scenery and lights, but there is something very satisfying about an enthusiastic audience. And ours, though mostly students, have been so appreciative and kind. Especially the English and Classics students. And we have even entertained classes from the senior schools – a most rewarding experience.'

'You mention students. May I then ask you something personal?'

'Of course.' But her expression was guarded.

'The very first time we met was in Greyfriars Kirkyard. You were wearing a grey cloak and a hat with a heavy grey veil, which got caught in the shrubbery.'

Her expression went completely blank, and for a heart-stopping moment Faro thought she was about to deny it. And if she had, he realised that he would have readily agreed and might even have pretended that he had been mistaken.

But at last she nodded. 'How strange. I wondered – afterwards, when we met again at the theatre – if you could possibly be my rescuer. Remember, I caught only a glimpse of your face in my involvement with my insecure bonnet.'

And the dangerous moment over, they both laughed. 'How extraordinary that we should meet again.'

Faro didn't think it in the least extraordinary, but her good-natured admission led him to ask, rather more sharply than he should, 'You knew Timothy Ferris?'

A sharp intake of breath and her eyes filled with sudden tears. 'Yes, I did. I cannot tell you – he was – he was – like the son I never had. He came to the theatre regularly and it began like so many of my young admirers. Boys who imagine they are in love with me.' She laughed. 'And I as old as their mothers, even if I can play Juliet on stage. Age seems to make no difference to their devotion.'

'"Age cannot wither her, nor custom stale her infinite variety,"' quoted Faro. 'Shakespeare could have written those words with you in mind.'

'You flatter me, but I am no Cleopatra – and I am well aware of the fact.' She sighed. 'Poor Timon. I called him that, after Timon of Athens. I liked it better than Timothy. He was so attentive, so devoted. And in the end I had to send him away.'

She was silent, and Faro saw that she was trembling. 'I little realised that I was destroying him. You know how it ended, that awful, awful death. And I was responsible— '

Sobs racked her and Faro took her in his arms, murmured the same soothing words he used to little Rose and Emily.

'Hush, my dear. Hush, you mustn't carry this guilt. It was not your fault that he died.'

'It was, it was.'

'It wasn't, Alison. Listen to me.' And he tilted her weeping face towards him. Gently, he put his lips to her cheek, with the bitter-sweet salt taste of her tears. As he smoothed back her hair, and she took out her handkerchief and blew her nose, he thought what a relief his next words would be to her. Maybe – maybe she would be so grateful that she might even love him a little.

'You see, Alison, we have it on very good authority that Tim Ferris wanted to marry Lily Goldie . . .'

Her eyes slid away from him. 'You mean – that girl – who died?'

'Exactly. It was because she refused him, discovered that he had been leading her on to believe he had a fortune. Then, when she learned he was penniless, she sent him packing. You see, he apparently had quite a good allowance from some benefactor or other, but when he failed his qualifying exams – so Vince tells me – this was withdrawn. He had always lived beyond his means, gambling, drinking, impressing Miss Goldie. When he knew that was all over, that's why he took his own life.'

Alison stared at him, took a deep breath and then cried out, 'Oh God, dear God. All that pain, all that agony – and no one to comfort him.'

The door opened a sliver and they both turned round.

'I thought I heard you call for more tea, Mrs Aird,' said Mrs Penny, her excuse paper-thin. Obviously she had heard the sobbing, and curiosity as to what was going on in her parlour, where her boarder was at the mercy of a gentleman caller, had overcome her.

Alison managed a bright smile and disentangled herself from Faro's arm. 'No, thank you, Mrs Penny. That was delicious.'

'Delicious,' echoed Faro.

123

Mrs Penny was reluctant to move. She frowned, looking suspiciously from one to the other.

'Mr Faro is just leaving,' said Alison, holding out her hand with a dazzling smile, calculated to convince her landlady that nothing untoward had been happening behind that closed door. 'I will see Mr Faro out, thank you, Mrs Penny.'

At the front door, they were both silent, staring up at Arthur's Seat agleam in the afternoon sunshine.

Faro took both her hands, held them tightly. 'Just one more question, and then this painful subject will never be mentioned between us again, I promise.'

She looked at him squarely. 'If you must.'

'Did you ever meet Tim's young brother?'

'His young brother?' she repeated.

'Yes, we understand he is a boarder at St Leonard's.'

Alison thought for a moment, then shook her head. 'I didn't know that. He never mentioned a brother. But that doesn't surprise me. He took a certain pride in being an orphan.'

Mrs Penny poked her head out, her curiosity further aroused by this prolonged doorstep conversation. 'See and not get cold, Mrs Aird, dear. Remember your voice now.'

Alison gave him an impish smile and hastily released her hands, which he still held.

'May I see you again?' he whispered.

'Are you not coming to *The Merchant*? There are some free seats available and Mr Trelawney's Shylock is very credible,' she said with a mischievous glance. 'The character offers such marvellous possibilities for over-acting.'

'If you are playing Portia . . .'

'I am . . .'

'Then I will come.'

Far below them, the little horse-drawn train arrived at St Leonard's Station.

'I have always promised myself to take a journey along that railway,' said Alison. 'I believe it goes to Musselburgh, and the seaside is so tempting. It is what one misses most without children. It must be years since I built a sandcastle, or dipped my toes in the ocean.'

'Then you need wait no longer. May I take you there on Sunday?'

'Oh, would you do that? Please! I shall get Mrs Penny to provide us with a picnic hamper.' And clasping her hands together like a little child, 'I shall so look forward to Sunday. Thank you – thank you, Jeremy. You have made me so happy.'

Standing on tiptoe, she kissed his cheek. And Faro walked towards Sheridan Place in a daze. Occasionally he touched the place her lips had caressed and considered himself the luckiest fellow in the whole world, from the day Alison Aird had walked into his life and he had decided to re-investigate the murder of Lily Goldie.

Content surged through him, a great wave of bliss, and he looked forward to retiring quietly to his study with its firelight glowing on his rows of books, his familiar chair and his desk. Always untidy, resisting strongly all Mrs Brook's determination to restore order, it was a lonely widower's retreat, heaven or hell, according to his mood. But it was his very own special place, where he could close the shutters against the unhappy world he inhabited by day. There he could seek refuge from his own troubles in some other time or place, in the worlds portrayed in the novels of Sir Walter Scott or Mr Charles Dickens. And there he could now weave his own dreams, more promising than any pages of a novel, about Alison Aird.

125

CHAPTER TWELVE

St Leonard's School was less than twenty years old, but it already smelled of boiled cabbage and wet wood, a familiar odour that Faro associated with boys' schools. It took him back to the Kirkwall of his childhood.

Everything about Headmaster Benjamin Lochhead was larger than life, from his booming voice to his flowing white beard, which instantly transformed him into an Old Testament patriarch. His parents, long dead, had shown a certain lack of insight when they chose his first name, whose initial immediately registered with several glee-ful decades of boys and earned him the nickname 'Old Blockhead'. He received Faro in his lofty panelled study, an awesome place where white busts of Socrates, Homer and other scholastic worthies gazed down sternly from their high pedestals.

'Please be seated, Mr Faro. Perhaps you would like to glance over our prospectus. What age is the young gentle-man?'

'Fourteen or fifteen.'

The Headmaster frowned. 'A difficult age, but one we can readily accommodate,' he added hastily.

'Headmaster, before we go any further, I must tell you that I am not Mr Faro, about to deliver a new pupil into your regime. I am Detective Inspector Faro of the Edinburgh City Police and I am here to make enquiries about a boy already with you.'

The patriarch froze, his hand in mid-air, suddenly an ungenial Santa Claus. His voice was icy. 'And what misdemeanours have my boys committed? Surely it is no serious crime which brings you to my establishment?' he added sardonically.

As Faro tried to give him a brief outline of the Gruesome Convent Murders, he found his placatory speech sounding thinner than ever.

The Headmaster made an impatient gesture. 'Yes, yes, Inspector. I have read the case.' He gave him a long glance. 'A private investigation – at the request of the unfortunate victim's relatives, you say. I do not see what my school can possibly contribute.'

'Miss Goldie was on friendly terms with Mr Timothy Ferris.'

For a moment the Headmaster frowned, and then nodded slowly. 'A former pupil of this school who took his own life. A disgraceful business. Ferris was one of our first boarders. He came to us when he was eight years old.'

This was a stroke of luck. 'And I believe Ferris Minor is a present pupil?'

'Ferris Minor?'

'Yes, his younger brother.'

'You have been misinformed, Inspector. Timothy Ferris was without relatives.'

'Are you quite certain?'

'Indeed I am.' And opening a drawer, the Headmaster handed Faro a bound volume. 'This is our register, a complete alphabetic list of our pupils for each year, back to the year eighteen-fifty when the school was opened. See for yourself if you can find a Ferris Minor.'

When Faro, after glancing through, shook his head, Lochhead continued, 'And may I ask what this Ferris Minor has done to warrant an investigation?'

'He was seen to be on friendly terms with the late Miss Goldie.'

127

'And where, might one ask, were these friendly terms observed?'

'At the Convent of the Sisters of St Anthony.'

Lochhead sprang to his feet, a tower of biblical wrath. 'Intolerable, intolerable. An outrageous suggestion, sir, outrageous and indecent. One of my pupils associating with a member of that establishment. I would have you know that the convent is out of bounds, strictly out of bounds. The punishment for fraternising is severe and none of my boys would risk such a thing.' Recovering from the shock, he sat down heavily and pointed a finger at the Inspector. 'Someone – someone has been leading you up the garden path, deliberately misinforming you in a desire to cast discredit upon my school. The matter, let me assure you, sir, shall not rest here,' he added severely.

Faro was aware of the danger. Should the Headmaster complain to Superintendent Mackintosh, there would be the devil to pay.

'That should not be necessary. You have my assurances, Headmaster. This is purely a private matter which will go no further than this room.'

'I am relieved to hear that.'

Faro rose to his feet. 'Perhaps before I leave, you can tell me something about Timothy Ferris.' The Headmaster made a restless movement, eager to end the interview, as Faro continued, 'May I ask in what manner his fees were paid?'

'Such matters are highly confidential, Inspector. However, in Ferris's case there was a trust fund which dealt with all financial matters.'

Faro was surprised and disappointed, remembering Vince's rumour of a rich benefactor. 'Not an individual?'

'No. It is usual in cases of orphans with well-to-do patrons, who wish to remain anonymous, to set up a trust fund.'

'I don't quite understand.'

128

The Headmaster's lip curled. 'Naturally, Inspector, if you are not a public-school man yourself. It is quite regrettable, but many pupils have, er, unfortunate backgrounds.'

'In what way?'

Lochhead sighed wearily at this lack of comprehension. 'Many are illegitimate sons of noble families, or of prosperous citizens who wish to keep such information secret for the damage it might do to their reputations – or, alas, much worse, to their business or professional life.' At that moment, Faro decided he looked almost human, as if he would have relished the sharing of a piece of gossip. Then, remembering himself in time, 'I won't delay you any further, Inspector.'

'To save embarrassment and litigation, a settlement is made through a trust fund. Yes,' said Vince that evening. 'Of course, I should have realised that. There were several cases in my own school, among the boarders.'

Lizzie had insisted that Vince be 'properly educated'. 'On account of his unfortunate background. We owe it to him, Jeremy,' she had whispered. And nothing would move her. Not even the fact that they could ill-afford fees for a private school.

Faro sighed, realising that as his heart sang with joy at the thought of Alison Aird, he was thinking less and less of Lizzie, who had been up to now the only love of his life, without once proving to be the great love he had once anticipated.

Perhaps his practical mind had been cautioned by his mother's love for his father, love doomed and yet undimmed, impervious to the ravages of time, love about which she continued to speak with such eloquence and emotion after nearly forty years. Their little cottage in Dean Village, living only for each other, the sound of his footsteps, the creaking gate, at the end of each day's labour. Safe home, another day's battle behind him, glorious as a soldier, returning to her arms again.

129

His violent death – his murder, she called it – cut like a knife through her world. After grief, and long before the Queen set the fashion for widows by dedicating her life as a shrine to Prince Albert, Mary Faro had been doing exactly that for her own dear Magnus for nearly forty years. The custom of Indian wives committing suttee and stoically following their husband into the funeral pyre met, not with her horror, but with her full support, as correct and fitting.

In his childhood, Faro remembered that hardly a day ever passed by without some reference to, 'Your dear father – he would have loved to see you do so-and-so, your dear father would have loved to hear you say that' – and so on.

It was his father's ghostly advice during his adulthood that was to spur him on and lead him to the Edinburgh Police Force. Mary Faro was even prepared to accept the departure of her only son to Edinburgh by consoling herself with, 'Your dear father would have been proud to see you this day.' She had refused his offer to accompany him, firmly putting behind her any idea of returning to the place of her greatest happiness and greatest sorrow.

'Besides, you will soon find a wife – and even if I wished to come with you, I have my obligations.' Her obligations were self-induced, to a tide of elderly invalids, mostly remote cousins she had made it her life's work to care for. All her pent-up maternal love had flowed into these bleak little houses on the wild shores near Kirkwall. No one in trouble or sorrow ever came to her door and left empty-handed.

'You are young and handsome, just the image of your dear father. You will soon make a life of your own – with a wife – and with grandchildren for your old mother.'

Ten years were to pass. Constable Jeremy Faro walked his Edinburgh beat, his feet well and truly on the ground, surrounded by the most sordid aspects of crime, while his head remained stubbornly in the clouds, confidently awaiting the great romance his mother had promised. It never happened. He had given up all hope of what the romantic novelettes and the great classics alike describe as falling in love, an emotion he recognised among the great writers and poets: the passions of Romeo for Juliet, of Antony for Cleopatra, both ended in tragedy. Was the reason that such ecstasy, a love one would die for, could not sustain the less rarefied atmosphere of everyday life, the drier down-to-earth elements that constituted marriage? Marriage itself, he thought, must strike the death knell of romance.

He had come to terms with what promised to be lonely bachelordom, with the bleak conclusion that there was no great love set aside for him. Then, one day, a pretty young waitress with a beguiling Highland accent was serving dinner at the hotel where he was making routine enquiries after a robbery.

Lizzie was from Skye, and prepared to be friendly to the young policeman who took her to Jenners for tea on her afternoon off. It was an occasion he found extremely pleasant, as had other occasions when he had taken other young women out to tea, or to hear a brass band. No more and no less.

After the first time, when conversation had been difficult to sustain, for they seemed to have little in common, Faro had almost decided not to see her again, but Lizzie was never good at concealing her feelings, and her look of disappointment was his undoing.

At their second meeting, she was less shy and more expansive about her early life. She and her young brother had been only a short time in Edinburgh and had not made many friends. Faro himself had made few friends since he came from Orkney. He did not consider this a disadvantage, preferring the company of books and solitary walks in the country. Colleagues in the Central Office, of his own age, touching thirty, were mostly married men with young families.

Having thought her less than twenty, he was surprised to learn that she was considerably older than her brother. Her struggles to bring up the lad, whom she was trying to educate so that he might have a better life than had been her lot, created a further bond. Her island story found a sympathetic echo in his own Orkney background.

Conscious of her own inadequacies in the matter of education and the loneliness of city life in Edinburgh, she often sought refuge in the beckoning foothills of the Pentlands. On their third meeting, she brought along her nine-year-old brother. The occasion was not a success; the boy was handsome and extremely like his sister, but he was also sullen and rebellious, ungrateful, ungracious.

Jeremy decided not to repeat the expedition, and in fact thought it as well not to continue seeing Lizzie in case his continued attentions led her to believe that he had serious intentions. The idea of a permanent relationship with the odious brother tagging along filled him with dismay.

For several weeks he returned to his solitary life, then, one day, by accident, he met her walking in Princes Street Gardens with a companion, one of the hotel maids. He found himself genuinely glad to see her again. He had missed her, and told her so. Her suddenly tear-filled eyes, her hand on his arm, beseeching, told its own story of how wounded she had been by his neglect.

Six months of 'walking-out' followed – without a single kiss, a fact which would have astonished his colleagues who from their teasing conversations imagined that the handsome, shy young constable from Orkney was 'a regular dark horse'. The pleasant undemanding relationship might have continued indefinitely had Lizzie not been dismissed by the hotel. Questioned as to why, she reluctantly admitted it was on account of a misdemeanour of her brother.

'He was very naughty and annoyed the manager. Rude to a guest, you know. He is so high-spirited, he didn't mean it.'

Faro doubted that, for although his first impression of the boy had been softened on closer acquaintance, he knew from Lizzie that his behaviour was unpredictable and he could still be a bit of a handful.

'He needs a man – a father – in his life, that's what.'

She and the boy had been asked to leave immediately. Poor Lizzie, in tears, was at her wits' end. She had nowhere to go, and although Faro realised it would hardly be considered proper or respectable to have her living in his digs, perhaps the presence of her young brother would lessen the inevitable eyebrow raising and heavy-handed teasing. His colleagues would inevitably see this step as a prelude to his forthcoming marriage.

One person was less than pleased – his young widowed landlady. Favoured with the largest servings, the best cuts of meat, even Faro guessed what were her hardly concealed designs. Of late, her overtures and hints had increased in boldness, bringing forth delighted guffaws from Faro's colleagues, and a somewhat hunted look into his own eyes.

An unpleasant week followed Lizzie's arrival: of smaller helpings, high dudgeon accompanied by door- and plate-banging from the irate landlady. The boy's behaviour was impeccable. Polite to everyone, to Faro he was friendly and helpful, even charming.

'He is so shy,' said Lizzie, 'but he does like you very much, Jeremy. Perhaps it is the uniform that made him a little nervous when you first met.'

At the end of two weeks, Faro had decided it was very pleasant to have a smiling young woman to welcome him 'home'. He was taken aback when Lizzie announced that she was leaving that weekend for Peebles.

'Why must you go to Peebles?'

'I have a situation there, in a hotel, if I want it.'

133

'Must you go so far away? Is there nothing suitable here in Edinburgh?'

'Nothing that keeps us here. The wage I'm being offered is far better too.' She paused uncomfortably. 'As you can guess, I have very little money left from my savings.'

Suddenly Faro's future looked very bleak. Undemanding Lizzie replaced by the triumphantly predatory landlady. The alternative was a search for new digs, much less than a convenient stone's-throw from the Central Office and most likely with less of the good food and comfort that he had grown accustomed to for the past two years.

'Lizzie,' he said, 'could I persuade you to stay – I mean, if we married?'

She looked at him and her eyes filled with tears. 'Of course I would stay then. Jeremy Faro, are you seriously asking me to marry you?'

'Yes, yes. I'd like that – very much. More than anything.'

Conscious that he was making an idiot of himself with his first ever proposal, he leaned over to kiss her and was surprised by the warmth of her reaction, by her soft and loving arms tight about his neck as she whispered, 'Oh, my dear, I have loved you for such a long time.'

It was then he realised he had said nothing about love, that love in fact had never entered his head. He patted her shoulder, and clearing his throat stammered out, 'There, there – I love you.'

The effect of his declaration was to have Lizzie burst into tears, cast him aside and sit down at the table, beating her arms upon it like one demented. Her attitude of unutterable despair took Faro by surprise. It was not at all what he had been led to believe might be the reaction to his proposal and Lizzie's acceptance.

When he tried to comfort her, she clung to him, rained passionate kisses upon him and then again thrust him aside.

'No. No, dear. It can never be. I was foolish to think you could love me.'

'But I do. Haven't I said so?'

There were more sobs. 'Do not make it more difficult for me, I beg you. I should never have given way, encouraged you to propose. Before you begin to hate me, you must believe that I love you with all my heart. I shall never, never love anyone else. I'll love you and only you until I die. But I can never, never marry you.'

'What are you talking about? You love me and yet you say we can't be married. Why on earth not?' And then the thought struck him. 'Is it the boy? Is that it? Does your brother dislike me so much? Tell me, don't be afraid. Is that it?'

'If only it was that simple,' she whispered.

'It doesn't sound very simple to me. It is the boy, isn't it?'

'It is, Jeremy. But the boy is not what you think.' She clutched his hand so tightly that it hurt. 'You see, he isn't my brother.' And in a whisper, 'He's my son. My bastard son.'

Faro stared at her. 'But he couldn't be – you couldn't . . .'

'Oh yes. He is, and I could – and did. I was fifteen – taken, by force – it was one of the laird's house-guests up for the shooting. You could never want to marry me now. No decent man would want marriage with such a degraded, wicked woman as me,' she sobbed.

'You're wrong, Lizzie, you're wrong about that. I could – and will marry you. And I'll be a father to the boy. The past is gone and we can't change that. It is the future that's our concern – our future together. So now we'll never talk about this again – do you hear? Never.'

Jeremy Faro was good to his word. A good husband to Lizzie and a good father to Vince, who soon became the very apple of his eye. Lizzie was a good wife, although he had to admit that their marriage didn't exalt his senses, nor could he by any feat of the imagination mistake it for the love that he had read about in books. He was not complaining, he was content with Lizzie, shrewdly guessing that in every relationship no two people love to the same measure. There is one who kisses and one who is kissed, one who gives and one who takes.

Lizzie never wavered in her love for him, and his mother, watching them, remembered that it was like seeing her own love for his dear father relived and advised her son, very sternly, 'Never has any woman loved a man as much as that lass loves you, except for the Queen and myself, that is. Treasure it, lad. It's more precious than gold.'

Faro had thought that marriage would last until they were both old people sitting by the fireside together. It had not dawned upon him that his strong healthy Lizzie, who had given birth to two daughters with a minimum of trouble, would give her own life in bearing him a son.

Stricken to the heart, after he laid her in the grave, he decided there would be no more loving for him. He would not ask fate for miracles. He would count himself fortunate to have Rose and Emily, who adored him, and Vince whom he was proud to call his son. He was clever, and the private school had a bursary system, and that, added to Faro's own promotion, saw him through university.

Faro considered that he had been amply repaid for those early sacrifices. In two days' time, Vince would celebrate his twenty-second birthday.

'How shall we celebrate?' he asked.

'Dear Mrs Brook would love to have a tea party,' said Vince. 'She is longing to put on display a full account of her culinary genius.'

'That's a splendid idea.'

'I thought we might ask Rob and Walter, of course, and Hugo.'

'A bachelor tea party?'

Vince grinned. 'You look quite disappointed, Stepfather. Actually I thought you might like to invite Mrs Aird to bring along some young ladies from the theatre. Saturday is a convenient time, before the evening performance, which begins an hour later than normal to allow the cast to recover from the matinée performance. Afterwards, I thought we might go and see Mrs Aird as Cleopatra and then supper at one of our old student haunts.' He laughed. 'No, Stepfather, I don't mean "The Gay Japanee" – somewhere much more in keeping with your respectable image.'

Faro smiled wryly. On two occasions he had been present when the police had searched the notorious Leith Walk howff, a hostelry which was a thinly disguised brothel, beloved of the student population, and especially of those sons of respectable houses who of necessity had to sow their wild oats before settling down to honourable Edinburgh professions in church, state and law.

'I'll write the invitations, if you wish. And now, Stepfather, back to the business of our second murderer.' Drawing up a sheet of paper he began to write.

'I've made a list already, lad.'

'I know, I've seen it. But do bear with me. After all, no two people viewing the same events see them in quite the same fashion. And that is perhaps – that tiny island of discrepancy – where we might indeed find the clue to his identity.'

Faro approved of such thoroughness. 'Very well. Back to the beginning. First of all, we have Hymes.'

'Hymes,' wrote Vince, 'who we have agreed is unlikely to be the murderer of Lily Goldie, on the evidence of the Mother Superior, of Maureen Hymes, and our own conclusions.'

'Which are?'

'That he would have strangled her with his hands, not tied a scarf about her neck afterwards, as I am convinced, from the post-mortem, was what actually happened.'

'If she had been the first victim instead of the second, then Hymes might have murdered her, in mistake for his wife.'

137

'Provided that the early morning light was dim enough and he came upon her from behind.'

'All fairly thin, rather too many suppositions,' said Faro.

'Right. Tim Ferris?' wrote Vince whose reaction had been, 'I told you so, didn't I?' when Faro had reported his conversation with Mrs Aird.

'Highly probable. If he had been alive at the time of Lily Goldie's murder, he would have been the obvious suspect.'

'Indeed he would. He would have had to produce some very good evidence as to his whereabouts at the time.'

'Very difficult when at six o'clock in the morning, when Lily Goldie took her walk up to Salisbury Crags, he and a large proportion of middle-class Edinburgh were still abed.'

'Talking about Ferris, what about the mysterious missing younger brother? Remember it was Lily Goldie who introduced him to Miss Burnleigh as Ferris's brother,' said Vince.

'Yet Ferris never mentioned his existence to Alison Aird, who one imagines he would confide in.'

'Ferris Minor seems to have been a figment of Lily's imagination. I wonder what her reasons were. Why did she lie about it?'

'That is something we will never know, lad. Some woman's wiles.'

Vince nodded. 'And we gather she had plenty of them. Liked teasing and goading other females.' He thought for a moment. 'What about Clara Burnleigh, anyway?'

'Her reasons for disappearing from the convent and giving a false address seem genuine enough. There certainly was this very nasty scandal in her family, and she's very intent upon climbing up the social ladder – and not very bright, I suspect – besides, what was her motive? Lily Goldie wasn't any threat to her. What about your Miss McDermot?'

138

'We know she left before the murder took place.' Vince smiled. 'I would be prepared to vouch for her. If only you had met her . . .' he added with a sigh. So that leaves us with the Mad Bart. By the process of elimination, Stepfather, I can't help thinking he is most likely to be our man. Consider the condition of his hands. That he might have been incapable of exerting the pressure needed for strangulation and therefore, when he pushed her off, he went down to make sure she was dead. Instead, he found her still alive and tied the scarf about her neck.'

'There's one thing you haven't considered. How did the old man get up Salisbury Crags? It's a stiffish climb for an old man with rheumatism in his knees.' Faro shook his head. 'I must confess that is the one improbability in your hypothesis.'

'We've never worked out how the murderer lured her up there in the early morning in the first place, Stepfather. There must have been some irresistible reason, since *rigor mortis* had not set in when she was discovered. When she got to the mortuary she hadn't been dead more than a couple of hours.' Vince threw down his pen.

'Well, it has to be one of them,' said Faro. 'Or else a complete stranger.'

'A passer-by filled with a mad impulse at the sight of an attractive young woman walking in a lonely place is usually a rapist. And we know she wasn't sexually assaulted.'

'Whoever murdered Lily Goldie had a very good reason, lad.'

'And knew about Hymes murdering his wife and took a chance on him being blamed for both.'

Faro shook his head. 'I have a feeling that we've taken a wrong turning somewhere, lad. That the answer is staring us in the face and we're just not seeing it.' He paused before adding, 'There is one other person who could have murdered Lily Goldie and might have had excellent reasons for doing so.'

'You mean – the Reverend Mother?' Vince sounded doubtful.

Faro laughed. 'Seriously?'

'Yes, if she is a religious fanatic, felt that the presence of Sarah Hymes and Lily Goldie had besmirched her reputation.'

'Then she would be insane.'

Vince nodded solemnly and Faro said, 'A mad baronet and a mad Mother Superior?'

'It isn't beyond the bounds of possibility. Or it might have been a fanatical nun who worshipped the Mother Superior and hated Lily Goldie.'

Faro filled his pipe and lit it thoughtfully. 'In my experience, Vince lad, very few murders are planned and executed by madmen or women . . .'

'. . . with the exception of the *crime passionnel*.'

'I grant you that. But the murder we are dealing with has all the indications of having been thought out very carefully by someone of exceptional intelligence.' Watching the smoke spiralling, he said, 'There is one other person.'

As Vince consulted his list again, Faro said, 'McQuinn.'

'Now you can't be serious.'

'Oh yes, I can. Consider him for a moment. He has access to the convent, he is friendly with the teachers, sweet on Lily, according to the maids. Think, lad, there are infinite possibilities.'

'You mean she might have spurned his advances? I thought he had rather a lot of lady-friends and one more or less would have made little difference.'

'But what if Lily was the one he really wanted?'

'There's only one flaw, I can see. If he had wanted it to look like Hymes's work, then being a policeman, he would have made a more convincing job of her murder. He would have strangled her, exactly as Hymes did Sarah, left bruising marks on her throat. He would never have thrown her down and tied that scarf around her neck afterwards.'

When Faro was silent, he added, 'I know you don't like the pompous McQuinn, but you must not let your personal prejudice influence you. After all, this is a murder case.'

Vince succeeded in sounding so like Superintendent Mackintosh that Faro laughed out loud at the apparent absurdity of his hypothesis. But not for long.

CHAPTER THIRTEEN

The next two days at the Central Office were very trying indeed, thanks to McQuinn, whose recent performance seemed to have impressed his superiors so greatly that the Constable had now been allocated as special assistant to Detective Inspector Faro.

Remembering his own early days, Faro knew what that meant. Promotion was on the way. McQuinn had but to prove himself and if he, Faro, didn't watch out, they would be saying he was too old for the job.

McQuinn was clearly bursting with pride and new importance, thought Faro with disgust, watching his over-eager smile charm old ladies, as did his offer of a helping hand. Faro had observed all too often in the Princes Street Gardens evidence of McQuinn's pouter pigeon breadth of chest charming their daughters, especially when accompanied by some outrageous piece of gallantry.

Normally a fair-minded man who scorned prejudices in others, Faro had to admit that the constable showed the makings of a good detective. If only his presence and his patronising manner were less obnoxious, especially when he seized every opportunity of demolishing Faro's long-standing theories with a sneer.

The fact that McQuinn had found a speedy solution to a recent case of embezzlement and a daring jewel theft was even more galling. He could also move with amazing rapidity and, taking off after the thief, vaulted fences and low walls like a race-horse, leaving Faro winded, staring bleakly after him.

Returning triumphant with Black Tam's nephew, railing down curses and promises of his uncle's vengeance, McQuinn found a grim-faced Faro ready with the cuffs. 'Allow me, Inspector, this is my man.' And later, adding insult to his superior officer's injury, 'I'm filling in my report, Inspector, and I'm saying that "we" apprehended him. I hope you approve.' When Faro growled that it wasn't strictly true, McQuinn continued amiably, 'I'm prepared to concede the point. After all, this kind of work, it's really a young man's job. You have to be fit.'

'Damn your impudence,' said Faro, and, snatching the pen, he crossed out 'we' and substituted 'PC McQuinn'. 'I'll have you know I'm not decrepit yet – not by a long way.'

'To be sure you're not, Inspector. Just a wee bit out of condition. Let's face it, this happens, so I'm told, to every man with advancing age.'

Such remarks succeeded in making him feel like a doddering ancient, and it was as well for McQuinn that the Superintendent entered the office at that moment, or the Constable might have received severe chastisement from Faro in the form of a punch on the nose.

On his way home, Faro called in at the Pleasance Theatre to leave the invitations for Vince's party. In the corridor he met a black-clad figure almost unrecognisable as Alison, hurrying into her dressing-room to change out of her Portia costume. Peering round the door at him, she snatched the envelope.

'Forgive me, Jeremy. I cannot talk to you just now. I have an important dinner engagement in the New Town and I'm late already. Do forgive me,' she repeated, and closed the door firmly.

Hugo Rich, however, was disposed to conversation, displaying an almost schoolboyish relish in criminal investigation, the disposal of corpses and other ghoulish matters.

143

Faro finally made his escape, and neither his opinion of McQuinn nor his temper was improved when he discovered the Constable handing Alison into a brougham waiting outside. As the Constable leaned in her direction, with his jaunty confidential manner, that mobile handsome face staring down into hers, peals of laughter reached Faro. Light-hearted as she never is with me, he thought disgustedly. Too much in a hurry to exchange half a dozen words with me, but with all the time in the world for McQuinn.

The sight stirred him to unexpected fury, especially as, at his approach, they both turned, their faces wiped clean of expression, leaving him to wonder suspiciously whether he had been the object of their merriment. And the thought that he had been made to appear ridiculous in Alison's eyes smote him to the heart.

Danny McQuinn and Alison Aird so occupied his thoughts on the way to Sheridan Place that he realised his interest in the case of Lily Goldie was dwindling rapidly. There were too many paths that led nowhere and he realised that if he was to be absolutely honest with himself it was not Hymes, nor his sister, nor even Lily Goldie, that had made him take on this private investigation.

As he opened the front gate, he realised he was never going to solve this mystery, or the identity of the second murderer – if such existed – if he let himself be diverted by destructive emotions of jealousy. Indeed, when he examined his own motives, he saw that personal pride and vindication were both involved. That he might prove to Central Office that they had bungled and that he was indispensable. There was even a small unworthy hope that he might find something to discredit Constable McQuinn and dash that supercilious smile from his face for ever.

Even Vince's original enthusiasm was daunted, and he must give up soon. In a few weeks, he would have served his *locum tenens* with Dr Kellar. Then he would be setting up his own surgery in the house. For his future as a fully fledged medical practitioner, Faro had installed on the front door an elegant brass plate.

Faro waited by the drawing-room window for Vince's return from Dr Kellar's and dashed downstairs in time to witness his surprise and delight at this unexpected present.

'Doctor Vincent Beaumarcher Laurie,' he exclaimed proudly, and, eyeing it critically, 'Do you think the letters are large enough, Stepfather?' He breathed on an imaginary speck of dust, which he polished with his sleeve.

'Big enough, I hope, to bring a small army of Newington and Grange folk trooping up to your door as patients,' said Faro, standing back for a last look before following him inside.

'But only for a while, Stepfather. You know I intend to become Queen's Surgeon, once I have enough money – nothing less will satisfy,' said Vince solemnly.

'Not even being a good doctor and saving lives?'

'There's nothing very distinguished in attending to broken heads and bones, to coughs and sneezes and bringing babies into the world.'

'A lot of doctors spend their whole lives doing it, lad, and consider that reward enough.'

Vince banged his fist on the table. 'Oh no, Stepfather, not for me. These doctors you speak of with their fine surgeries in the New Town, they have mostly come from respectable middle-class homes. They're not like me – I'm different – you're not forgetting that, are you? I'm only the bastard son of a servant girl,' he added bitterly.

Faro winced at the words and Vince smiled. 'Oh, that still hurts, doesn't it? That you weren't the first, that my mother had a child before she married you.'

'I never gave it a thought. I loved you, little devil that you were, from almost the first moment we met . . .'

'And I hated you,' said Vince slowly, 'for stealing my

145

mother, the only person in the world who belonged to me absolutely, the only person I would ever have who was flesh of my flesh, bone of my bone. And now she's gone too.'

This tirade was no new experience for Faro. He knew that Vince thought of Lizzie acutely each time his birthday came round, remembering the pain and shame in which she had brought him into the world. He put his hand on the boy's shoulder.

'You still have me, lad, and you've been more to me than many a son to his father. I've been so proud of you.'

As they waited for the first guests to arrive, Mrs Brook having set a table that was a masterpiece of culinary art, Vince looked out of the window at the afternoon sun gleaming on the Pentland Hills and sighed.

'If only mother could be with us today,' and, turning to Faro, he asked bitterly, 'Why did she have to die, anyway? So unnecessary.'

'That's one of the things you might discover in your life as a family doctor – just why so many women bear children and then both die within days . . .'

They were both silent, in attitudes of grief, as if Lizzie had died just days ago. She seemed to be there in the room with them, with her sweet voice and gentle laughter.

They both started as the door opened to admit the party guests, led by Alison Aird, holding a cake with candles already lit, and followed by Hugo, Rob, Walter and a trio of young gentlemen from medieval Venice.

'Happy birthday to you – happy birthday, dear Vince,' they sang, and everyone applauded. Then, bowing, they swept off their caps, to be revealed as the young actresses still in their *Merchant* costumes.

'Vince, you awful creature, Hugo assured us that it was to be fancy dress.'

146

Vince laughed, rolling his eyes wickedly. 'Fellow couldn't miss the chance to glimpse such fine limbs.'

'You would not have said that if you had seen us wandering along the Pleasance,' said Beth.

'Nonsense,' said Hugo. 'Passers-by were quite unmoved by the sight, as if medieval players were a regular occurrence in Newington.'

'Not even ones with such unmanly curves?' said Vince. 'And why aren't you in fancy dress, Mrs Aird? Having seen your Portia, I'd say you make an admirable Venetian gentleman.'

'We tried to persuade her. She has the perfect figure,' said Marie with an envious sigh. 'Beautiful long slender legs.'

'Ladies, ladies, please,' said Alison, 'spare my blushes.' She looked round, appealing. 'They do exaggerate, you know. Only the very young actresses like themselves can play convincing boys.'

'And the other way round,' said Hugo. 'Boys will be girls, since Shakespeare did not have the original commodity to chose from.'

'No doubt that is why his more mature ladies, like Lady Macbeth and Cleopatra, must have been extremely trying for a youth to play with conviction,' said Vince.

'"Antony shall be brought drunken forth,"' quoted Hugo in profound tones. Everyone cheered as he added in sepulchral aside to an imaginary audience, 'As he is regularly at the end of each performance.' He pointed dramatically at Alison to complete the quotation. When she declined, he continued, '"And I shall see some squeaking Cleopatra boy my greatness, I' the posture of a whore."'

The actresses groaned. 'Do give over, Hugo dear, we're not working now,' said Beth. 'There's a good fellow,' she added with an affectionate peck at his cheek, which received an appreciative embrace and some applause. The two, in Vince's parlance, were 'very smitten'.

147

There were cheers as Mrs Brook brought in the tea tray, and everyone sat down at the table to enjoy her hot buttered scones.

'We were very impressed with your brass plate,' said Marie shyly. 'Beaumarcher – that's an unusual name. Are you related to the famous earls?'

Vince had arrived home a little drunk from a celebratory drink with his medical friends, otherwise he would not have abandoned his normal discretion and waxed eloquent upon his bastardy and upon the identity of the rich man who had fathered him.

'The gratification of a few minutes of lust. A few minutes . . . that's all it takes, to father a child. Did you know that, Mrs Aird?' he asked Alison who sat on his other side.

Across the table, Faro was aware that her happy smile had been replaced by a haunted look.

'Vince, lad – really,' he said. 'Ladies present.'

Alison recovered and gave him a bright smile. Faro realised that if Vince had hoped to shock her, he was in for a disappointment.

She laughed. 'My dear Vince, I have always considered the father's role in procreation somewhat minor, and that it didn't seem quite fair, despite what the Bible says on the subject, that women should bear all the shame but are not supposed to have any of the pleasure.' She added, with surprising frankness, 'And I doubt whether even the cleverest of doctors will be able to change the laws of biology.'

But Vince didn't hear. He had extracted a rosebud from Mrs Brook's arrangement and was endeavouring to attach it to Marie's tunic, an effort requiring considerable assistance from that young lady, who was enjoying every moment.

Alison watched with amusement and swept aside Faro's whispered apologies. 'The young like to feel outrageous on occasions, and what better time than on a birthday, the beginning of a new year?'

'I assure you, he doesn't usually behave so abominably.'

'Perhaps something else upset him,' she said anxiously. 'Whatever it was, I freely forgive him.'

The lad has everything, thought Faro, looks, brains and yet he cannot forget, will never forget, that his birth puts him beyond the pale of polite society. And sometimes Faro took a good hard look at that same Edinburgh society and the seething hypocrisy of its professional and middle classes, that Vince wished to emulate. The respectability that was paper thin and, once scratched, revealed horrors of child abuse, incest, sodomy – a whole world of crawling nastiness that erupted into occasional scandals, quickly suppressed by a handshake containing a large sum of money. Scandals which not even the most forthright editor would allow to be exposed in his newspaper.

'Yes, do let's go there . . .'

'Everyone – listen . . .'

'A picnic tomorrow – over on the Fife coast.'

'We take the ferry, it's only half a mile from the landing stage.'

'What a splendid idea.'

'You must come too, Stepfather.'

Faro looked at Alison, who clapped her hands delightedly. 'Yes, Jeremy, of course you must come with us.'

Faro allowed himself to be persuaded but he was bitterly disappointed. He had been looking forward to taking Alison to Musselburgh on the horse-drawn railway, to having a day alone with her. She had clearly forgotten all about their arrangement and now, apparently, if he was to enjoy her company at all, it must be within the group of Vince's young friends.

The picnic spot had been suggested by Vince. He was to be the leader. Mrs Brook was prevailed upon to pack up the remnants of the birthday feast and wine, which pleased her since the tea table groaned with enough food to feed a regiment.

It was a merry party who dispersed for the theatre in gleeful anticipation that the perfect weather Edinburgh was at present enjoying would hold for a few days longer.

When at last Faro and Vince took their seats in the Pleasance Theatre, the curtain rose on *Antony and Cleopatra*. Faro had only seen Alison thus far in *Othello*, and here was a vastly different portrayal. Unbelievable, he thought, watching the exquisite, irresistible Queen of the Nile, whose beauty turned men to clay in her small hands and 'kiss'd away kingdoms and provinces'. That 'a lass unparallel'd' could on a different night be the simple, innocent, hero-worshipping Desdemona.

Even Topaz Trelawney's Antony was a mercifully subdued performance, although his 'I am dying, Egypt, dying' raised a misguided cheer from a rowdy element in the audience. When Cleopatra died with the asp at her breast, the scene was so heart-stopping, and Faro was so absorbed into believing what he saw, that he felt the curtain should rise on her lifeless form. That was how she should be remembered, not smiling hand-in-hand with a posturing Antony to a tumultuous, ear-splitting ovation.

He felt dazed as they left the theatre, it having been decided that everyone needed to retire early in order to catch the early morning ferry across to Fife, carriages having been arranged to transport them to Queensferry.

Vince declined the invitation to accompany Rob and Walter to Rutherford's and walked rather sharply in the direction of Sheridan Place.

'I've had enough birthday celebrations for one year,' he said in answer to Faro's question. 'And I have an infernal toothache – all those iced cakes. A hot toddy and I think I'll turn in. Of course – I'll be right as rain in the morning.'

When morning came, Vince looked round the door, weary and heavy-eyed. 'Been up all night with this damnable tooth. I think it's abscessed. I feel like death, and a picnic would be the final straw. Be a good soul, Stepfather, give them my apologies. Of course you must go. Everyone is depending on it.' And without further comment, he retreated once more into his darkened bedroom.

Groans of disappointment greeted Vince's non-arrival, and Marie looked particularly sad. An hour later, however, the party had regained their cheerful anticipation and were stepping down from the ferry after a remarkably smooth and pleasant crossing of the River Forth.

A pretty wooded dell was their destination.

'It's the perfect picnic spot for a perfect summer day,' said Faro, who had been appointed their leader, as the little group followed him triumphant through summer sounds of insects busy with their hidden world, to a chorus of seabirds, and larks rising high in the swaying long grass.

As they spread out the cloth on the grass, they found their activities keenly observed by timid rabbits, and even a shy squirrel put in an appearance. Rob had brought his flute along and there was a great deal of merriment, which irritated Faro, as the sun heralded time's passing and he realised that he was to have no time alone with Alison. No time, and so much he wanted to tell her.

At last Hugo intoned in his best Shakespearean imitation of Topaz Trelawney, 'Enough, good Sir Rob. Put aside merriment, forsooth. "Music, moody food, Of us that trade in love." Come, my sweeting,' and taking Beth's hand, they raced towards the wood, their laughter echoing back to the group of friends. Soon other couples had similar ideas, and Marie too found herself a Sunday-afternoon suitor.

To his considerable joy and relief, Faro saw that he and Alison, busily gathering up the remnants of the picnic, were alone. At last she leaned against the mossy bank, hands behind her head, staring up at the sky.

'Isn't it beautiful?' she said. 'So warm, so peaceful. A truly perfect summer's day. Just look at that sky.'

Faro had removed his jacket, rolled back his shirt-sleeves, and lay back beside her, their bare arms touching.

'"Sometimes we see a cloud that dragonish; a vapour sometimes like a bear or lion, a tower'd citadel . . ." What's next?'

'"A pendent rock, A forked mountain, or blue promontory, With trees upon't,"' Alison supplied softly. 'What is it you see, Jeremy?'

Faro looked down at her. 'You. Only you, my dear.' And leaning over, he kissed her gently on the lips.

'Idiot,' but she was smiling and she made no resistance. 'Dear idiot.'

'I grant you that. I think I am idiotically, wildly in love with you. What have you to say to that on your perfect summer's day?' And kneeling, he began to gather her into his arms.

This time there was no gentle response, no acquiescence. She sprang away from him, her eyes searching. 'No, no— '

'Don't concern yourself about our young friends,' he whispered, 'I hardly imagine they have disappeared to gather wildflowers.'

'No, Jeremy. No, I say.' She evaded his hands and sat bolt upright. 'I am not concerned with our young friends, only with you. I absolutely forbid you to fall in love with me.'

'You cannot do that – you are too late.'

'I am not too late to discourage you.' Her eyes, regarding him, were tragic, haunted. 'Be my friend, be anything, but do not seek to be my lover – I implore you.'

'What if I don't wish any of those roles, but something much more permanent in your life?'

For a moment as she looked at him, her eyes filled with tears. 'You dear, dear man. Have you seriously considered what you are suggesting? Not even you, I am sure, can imagine me in the role of a policeman's wife.' Her laugh was harsh. 'Oh my dear, it is too preposterous for words.' And, seeing his expression, she touched his arm gently. 'Jeremy, don't let me hurt you – I don't want that. I am

152

leaving Edinburgh soon and our paths are unlikely ever to cross again.'

'Unless we want them to . . .'

She nodded. 'Oh yes, then the world would not be too wide to hold us apart. But you see, I don't love you . . .'

'You might, given time,' he said desperately, conscious that he had lost her already.

'That is not the way it happens – not for me. I have loved only twice in my whole life and I now know with certainty that it is a process I will never – no, I can never – repeat.' She looked at him. 'But had we two met – in some other circumstances – I think I might have loved you.'

'Hello there – hello?' The echoing calls from the wood announced the return of those other lovers, many with flushed countenances and a certain amount of disarray which announced that they had been more successful in their wooing than Faro.

The ferry's arrival was delayed by engine trouble, difficult to set right on a Sunday, and there was a considerable delay before they restarted. The boatman who made the announcement added, 'I hope ye all have warm clothes,' and pointing up at the sky, 'See those clouds gathering? Weather's changing. See how the water's ruffled? We're in for a bad spell, mark my words. We'll have storms before nightfall.'

The picnic party accepted this setback to their day with good-natured resilience and decided that they might as well consume the rest of the food and indulge in songs and music, accompanied by Rob's flute, until the repairs were carried out.

It was dark and the rain was falling steadily when at last the ferry limped into Queensferry again. Once again the engine failed, half-way across the river, and had to wait for tugs to pull it into the little harbour.

Alison had said little. Like everyone else she seemed tired, irritated by the long delays. Faro offered to see her to Mrs Penny's and was surprised when she accepted.

'I have some magical drops for the toothache, given to me years ago by an old African chief. All the cast swear by them. I'm sorry I cannot let you borrow them. Often at night, a persistently nagging tooth keeps me sleepless. I am too much of a coward to have it removed, so I always have the drops by me. But I'd be happy to come back with you, and administer a dose to poor Vince.'

They arrived in Sheridan Place in a heavy downpour, and all Faro's thoughts about Alison and her obstinate refusal to fall in love with him were completely obliterated by the scene that was awaiting them.

CHAPTER FOURTEEN

Faro let himself in and, directing Alison up to the drawing-room, went in search of Vince. He found him in Mrs Brook's basement kitchen, her normally pristine well-scrubbed table festooned with bloodied linen. His clothes torn, head and hand bandaged, Vince was leaning back in a chair while Mrs Brook attended to his broken face.

Mrs Brook turned to Faro, very near to tears. 'Here's a terrible thing, Inspector. Poor lad here, near murdered. Set upon coming home, he was.'

Faro looked down at him. Where was beauty now? Vince's eyes were swollen, half-closed, his lips bleeding. He looked barely conscious. Faro took his hand, bleeding and bruised, nails broken.

'Vince, lad?'

Vince opened his eyes with difficulty. 'Hello, Stepfather.'

'Who did this to you?'

'Keelies.'

Mrs Brook hovered. 'If you think this is bad, Inspector, you should have seen him when that nice polis, McQuinn, carried him home. I hardly recognised him, covered in blood he was, the poor lamb.'

'McQuinn, you say?'

'Gone now. If it hadn't been for him, I would have been killed. God, I can never thank him enough. Saved my life. That's fine, Mrs Brook. Fine now.' He struggled to his feet. 'Thank you – no more. No bones broken, thank God . . .'

'. . . for small mercies,' added Mrs Brook. 'Such wickedness in a nice respectable neighbourhood. I don't know what this world is coming to, that I don't.'

'Let's go upstairs, Stepfather. All right now. I can manage.'

Faro settled him in the armchair and poured out a large glass from the decanter on the table.

'Thanks, Stepfather. I'll try not to spill your best brandy.' He drank it at a gulp. 'Sorry not to savour it in the proper fashion – that's better.'

'I think we'll consider this medicinal. Here, have another.' Watching him sip slowly and painfully this time, Faro asked, 'Now, what happened?'

'I'm glad to see you again. Did you have a splendid time in Fife?'

'Yes, Mrs Aird's upstairs. With something for your toothache.'

'Toothache – God, I need more than that. What a kindly thought – I'm grateful . . .'

'Vince – for God's sake – I'm waiting to be told what happened to you.'

'My infernal toothache got worse. Went to see Doctor Kellar and, much against his will, it being the Sabbath and so forth, he extracted it. God, that was agony. I felt even worse, groggy, wretched.' He looked at Faro doubtfully, then said, 'I have these friends who open the backdoor of their howff on Sundays – just for a few friends . . .'

'Strictly illegal – I don't think I should know about that.'

'Illegal or not, it saved my sanity. I'll spare you the details, but I left rather late and, feeling much improved, called in at Mrs Penny's to make my excuses to the divine Marie – and found that none of you had returned. I didn't attach a great deal of importance to that, but decided, as the effects of many restorative drams were wearing off, that I'd better make my way home. Took the short cut, down Gibbet Lane.'

156

'Which you should know is notorious for lurking footpads after dark. You were taking a chance – all the scum from the Warrens at Wormwoodhall gather there, hoping for a kill.'

'Which they damned near got!' He sighed. 'I was tired, drunk too, I must admit. Makes one reckless. Anyway – keelies set on me. If it hadn't been for McQuinn appearing when I was still able to yell for help, I'd be dead.'

'I'll get his report at the office. I presume he set off in hot pursuit immediately after bringing you home.'

'I rather think not.'

'He damned well should have done. That's the rule. Quickly attend the victim, then pursue the attacker. He'll have the Superintendent to answer, if he hasn't reported in immediately.'

'Because the victim is your stepson?' Vince smiled through swollen lips. 'All I lost besides my pride was my purse and a shilling – not much in it after a night's illegal drinking.' He paused, and with a shrewd glance at Faro, said, 'You'd like to get McQuinn on this, wouldn't you?'

'That's beside the point. He knows the procedure.'

'In this instance, if he hasn't done his duty, it is because I asked him not to.'

'You – what? After what they did to you?'

'That's right. You see, I'm not the only one they're after. I was just the beginning – it's you next – and maybe Mrs Aird.'

'Mrs Aird?'

'Thought that would bring you up sharp in your tracks. Ouch. God, I shouldn't laugh, hurts like hell.'

'Vince, what's this about Mrs Aird?'

'I'd better tell you the whole story.'

'Yes – and if you can bear it, start at the beginning – and I want all the details.'

'When they jumped me, I didn't stand a cat in hell's chance. Even if I hadn't been a bit unsteady with the drink, I couldn't have fought them off. Anyway, when

157

the beg fellow held me and rifled my pockets, I thought that was all they wanted. The next thing . . .' He stopped and took a quick drink, '. . . the next thing, they had me down on the ground, kicking at me everywhere with their great boots. I thought I was a goner and that their leader – a great brute of a fellow – was going to use his boot to kick my face in, when suddenly he sat me up, took hold of my coat lapels.'

'This big fellow – what was he like?'

'It was pretty dark, but he was built like a barn door. Black hair, beard— '

'Black Tam o' Leith,' said Faro. 'He and his lads have been on our books for a long while. Robbery with violence. We got his nephew behind bars last week.'

'In my case I suspect they were more interested in the violence. This black devil's foul breath was on my face and he said, "I'll let you go this time, Doctor Laurie." '

'Doctor Laurie – so he knew who you were?'

Vince nodded. 'Oh yes, he knew. "If we went any further, it would be murder, ye ken that, laddie. That we could destroy you, finish you off. That would give my lads the greatest pleasure. But what we've done to you is just to show your stepfather a bit of what might happen to someone like himself and that fancy actress of his – her that goes to the Quaker Mission. Tell him to leave me and mine in peace – or else!" '

'The Quaker Mission? I suppose the children told him.' Alison had come in quietly and was leaning against the door, her face pale with shock.

'Or had it beaten out of them, more likely,' said Faro.

'Oh, Vince, my dear.' Alison ran across and, kneeling by his side, took his hands, stroked back his hair, murmured soothing words. It was a scene unexpectedly maternal which smote Faro's heart with love renewed.

Vince was holding out his glass. 'Yes, please, I'd love another drink.'

Alison glanced quickly at Faro before going to the table with its decanters and water carafe.

'I'm used to being threatened,' said Faro. 'Think nothing about it, a hazard of the job. But to use my family . . .'

Alison was again kneeling by Vince's side. 'Drink this.'

'Ugh – what's this? Water?'

'Yes, my dear. And you're going to have a good sleep, which is what you need most. It's only laudanum.'

A sudden growl of thunder shook the room, followed by the angry hiss of rain, like the arrows of an army in search of the three frightened people beleaguered, crouching, behind the room's closed shutters.

Alison shivered. 'I have a request. May I stay here for the night? I am – I am so afraid to go home. I know I shall never sleep, and besides I might be of more use where I can look after him.'

'Mrs Brook can do that – besides we have no spare bedroom prepared . . .'

'You have several comfortable sofas – a rug is all I need.' And looking into Faro's stern face with tragic haunted eyes, she whispered, 'I beg you, let me stay. I had a son once.'

Faro slept little that night. Occasionally he awoke to hear a creaking board or movements in the kitchen below, a tap turned on. Once he went downstairs and found Alison making tea.

'What time is it?'

'Dawn,' she said. 'Listen to the birds. The storm is over, all is well with the world again.'

'Vince?'

'I have kept my vigil. He is sleeping soundly. Now have some tea, it will refresh you. No?' She put a hand on his arm. 'And do not look so worried, Jeremy. Go back to sleep!' And, standing on tiptoe, she kissed him lightly on the cheek.

'I won't sleep . . .'

'Would you like some of my magic drops?'

159

He looked at her, conscious that his heart was in his eyes and that the most magical of all would be to make love to her against that dawn chorus. Afterwards, how he would sleep!

When he came downstairs again at eight o'clock, she had gone and Vince was in the breakfast room. In bright sunlight, his broken face looked even worse than by lamplight.

Faro groaned. 'As Christ is my witness, I'll get Big Tam for this – if it's the last thing I do . . .'

'Careful, Stepfather – it might be just that.'

'Look, lad, this is a situation I'm used to. There are always petty criminals out for my blood, and I wouldn't have thought Black Tam had enough imagination to try to get at me through you – but I've got to do my duty, whatever he threatened. He must be desperate . . .'

'To hell with your duty, Stepfather – hear me out, will you?'

'Of course, lad.'

'You are not the only intended victim. If you don't care about yourself, have a care for her— '

'Her?'

'Mrs Aird. Remember his warning— '

'But why, for God's sake – what's she done?'

'Oh, that's easy – they seem to have eyes and ears, these naughty lads. They seem to know what you're both up to.'

At the glint of amusement in his stepson's eyes, Faro shuffled uncomfortably. Vince made his innocent relationship with Alison sound like an illicit *grande passion*. If only it were true.

Mrs Brook came in and began to set the table, full of apologies. She hadn't expected either of them to appear for breakfast. As she went out she beckoned to Faro from behind Vince's chair, a finger to her lips.

Faro made an excuse and followed her down to the kitchen, where he found her spreading a piece of crumpled paper on the table. 'When I was putting Doctor Vince's clothes to the wash – all muddied and filthy they were, I don't know how I'll get them clean again – I found this. I thought you should maybe see it, before I gave it to the doctor, in his state.'

One glance at the note's ill-formed letters sent Faro up to his study for the anonymous note directing him to seek Clara Burnleigh's whereabouts from Mrs Wishart. Then he showed Mrs Brook's find to Vince, who read, '"Let Lily Goldie rest in peace or Mrs Aird will be next."' He threw it down on the table. 'You see? I'm telling you, take care. This isn't just your usual petty criminal working off his spite, Stepfather. Black Tam means your death.'

'I doubt whether this dire threat was penned by Black Tam's hand. Nor was it written by "One who seeks Justice".'

'I can see that. Different slant to the writing, besides the paper and ink aren't the same.' Vince frowned. 'But if Black Tam didn't put it in my pocket . . .'

'I didn't say he didn't plant it, lad, merely that he didn't write it. I'd be very surprised if he can read or write, or, even if he could, I doubt if he could spell.'

'Then who?'

'That we have still to find out.'

Vince took the note and studied it. 'You think he was paid by someone?'

'Well, there's one thing for sure. If we discover the identity of whoever wrote this, I think he's going to lead us directly to whoever murdered Lily Goldie.'

After he had eaten, Faro took the omnibus to the Central Office. He found Constable Danny McQuinn boldly sitting behind his desk, nonchalantly sorting through papers. One look at Faro's thunderous expression and McQuinn stood up, straightened his tunic, saluted smartly and said, 'I see you've been home, sir. I've been waiting most anxiously

161

to see you. It was a pity that you weren't at home when it happened.'

The implied reproof intensified Faro's own sense of guilt that while his stepson had been in mortal danger he was gallivanting about Fife, bear-leader to a crowd of irresponsible young Thespians.

He controlled his anger with difficulty. 'Perhaps you would be so good as to give me a complete report of all that happened.'

McQuinn pointed to a paper on his desk. 'It is all here, ready for you, sir.'

'I would like to hear it in your own words, McQuinn. Everything that happened.'

'I was on my normal duty-patrol in the area when I heard a man calling for help. I blew my whistle and rushed to the rescue. I used my truncheon to some effect and kept on whistling. That seemed to scare them off. At first I thought the young man on the ground was dead. He was hardly breathing and I could see in the dim light that he was in a bad way. I adopted the usual procedure of going through his pockets for identification. There was none. The light was very poor and it wasn't until I wiped some of the mud and blood from his face, which was swelling by then, that I recognised your stepson, sir.'

'There was no note in his pocket when you searched for identification?'

McQuinn shook his head. 'Nothing, sir. Nothing at all. The contents had been removed by his assailants. May I continue, sir?

'Police Constables McDonald and Scott arrived on the scene and I sent them off in pursuit of the attackers, while I carried the injured man across my shoulders to his home at Number nine Sheridan Place, where I woke up your housekeeper, Mrs Brook, who then proceeded to clean him up and dress his wounds.'

'And what did you do then?'

'I asked her for a pen and paper to make out a statement for Doctor Laurie to sign once he was fully conscious – for use as future evidence when the attackers were apprehended. I had a cup of tea from Mrs Brook while I waited. Doctor Laurie had come round by then and was able to give his account of the attack – signed – here. I left immediately and returned to the Central Office, where I also found Constables McDonald and Scott, who informed me that their pursuit had been unsuccessful and the robbers had vanished in the area of the Sciennes district known as the Warrens, a great place for criminals to go to earth.'

'Have you any clues to their identity?'

'Oh yes, sir. Doctor Laurie's description fitted Black Tam and his lads. As you will remember, sir,' he added proudly, 'it was Caller Jamie, his nephew, that we apprehended and put behind bars last week.'

Faro picked up Vince's statement and read it twice over, with a sense of incompleteness. There was something else about that pathetic document staring him in the face, and he just wasn't seeing it.

Across the desk was McQuinn's blandly handsome face with its suspicion of a supercilious smile. Typical of him to turn in a statement, correct in every detail, just as Vince had told him, omitting any mention of Big Tam's warning.

When he returned to Sheridan Place, Mrs Brook met him in the hall. To his question regarding Vince, she said, 'He is ever so much better now, sir. Been in his room all day, sleeping like a baby, but he managed a bowl of porridge. A wee touch of yon powder works wonders. I hear that even Her Majesty approves of laudanum and has a supply of it when she stays up at Balmoral.' Mrs Brook's awed whisper implied a guarantee of unquestionable respectability.

'Have there been any visitors?'

'Yes, Inspector. Mrs Aird called in before going to the theatre. She left a message that she would return later in the hope of seeing you.' At that moment the sound of the front doorbell jangled through the hall.

'That'll be her now, sir. Shall I send her up?'

'If you please.'

He heard her light step on the stairs and she ran into the room and, rushing over to him, threw her arms about his neck. She was trembling. 'Jeremy, my dear, I am so relieved to see you. What a day I have put in. Something rather awful happened when I got back to Mrs Penny's. This!' From her reticule she took out an envelope addressed 'Mrs Aird'. 'It was waiting for me. Read it.'

In the same ill-formed letters, on identical paper to the note Vince had received, was the warning, 'Let Lily Goldie rest in peace and go back where you belong if you want to stay alive.'

'Jeremy, I'm afraid. I don't know any Lily Goldie. What are they talking about?'

'Lily Goldie is the girl from the convent— '

'You mean – you mean the one who – who was murdered?' He saw now how afraid she was, as her voice rose shrilly. 'Oh my God, how dreadful. But what has that to do with me?'

He put his arm around her trembling shoulders. 'Not a thing, my dear. It just happens that I'm carrying on a private investigation – on behalf of relatives . . .'

'Wait a moment – of course, that was why you were going to Fairmilehead – when you took me with you.'

'Yes.'

She looked at him wild-eyed. 'But that had nothing to do with me. I wasn't helping you – I hardly knew you— '

'My dear, please be calm.'

'Calm!'

'I'll explain everything, but tell me first, when did you receive this?'

'Mrs Penny said it must have been handed in some time when I was out on Sunday. See – there's no postage stamp.'

164

'Doesn't Mrs Penny remember who . . .?'

Alison shook her head. 'The usual thing is for the postman or anyone leaving messages to put them on the table in the lobby. The front door is never locked, so it might have been delivered any time.'

'When did you last receive any mail?'

She frowned. 'I occasionally receive letters from admirers – you know, the kind actresses get – and that is all. We all pick up our letters from the lobby table as we come in. Jeremy, what does it mean? Who would write such a beastly note?'

'Tell me about the other boarders.'

'Only the girls from the theatre, Beth, Marie, Julia – oh yes, and Hugo. He moved in last week, some trouble with his landlady's family arriving, and Mrs Penny agreed to put him in the attic, temporarily.'

She looked at Faro earnestly. 'You can't possibly think – I mean, its unimaginable – the girls are a terrible tease, but they mean no harm. And none of these dear young people are capable of playing such cruel and frightening practical jokes.'

'I'm afraid this is no practical joke.'

'You mean – it is serious, someone is threatening me, just because I happened – quite innocently – to go with you to Fairmilehead? But that is monstrous, monstrous – it's so unfair – oh, dear God . . .' Alison sat down, her face pale. 'What will they do to me?'

'Nothing. I shall look after you. I mean it.' Faro poured out a cup of tea. 'Here you are. Go on, drink it. Do as I tell you.' He drew up a chair opposite, and, scrutinising the letter lying between them on the table, said, 'Vince received a similar threat. By the same hand, I'd say, and in almost the same words.'

'When was this?'

'Mrs Brook discovered it when she was attending to his clothes. It had been thrust into his coat pocket.'

'I still don't understand.'

'I think I'm beginning to – it fits a definite pattern, although I wouldn't have expected it quite so soon.'

'Pattern? What pattern are you talking about?'

'Someone is getting very anxious about our interest in Lily Goldie's murder.'

Alison frowned. 'I don't understand. Wasn't a man hanged – dreadful case, he murdered someone else, didn't he?' She shook her head, trying to remember.

'His wife. However, we have uncovered evidence which leads us to believe that in fact the man who was hanged – Hymes – was innocent of Lily Goldie's murder.'

Alison stared at him. 'Are you saying that there is another murderer still on the loose?'

'I'm afraid so, and he realises – somehow – that we are catching up with him. That is why he is getting desperate, trying to scare us with threats. Have no doubt, my dear, that whoever wrote these two notes is our man. And I mean to get him, and he knows that. Now, I will see you safe back to your lodging and take the opportunity of making a few enquiries.'

'No, please, Jeremy, I don't want Mrs Penny involved and the girls frightened – a murderer on the loose! And Mrs Penny has been so good to me, and now I've brought this terror to her door. I beg you – please don't . . .'

'I'm sorry, I have to do it, my dear. I have to follow up the attack on my stepson and every shred of evidence.'

Hearing them coming downstairs, Vince emerged from his bedroom. Apart from the angry-looking bruises his appearance was considerably better than Faro had expected.

Alison ran to him with a little cry and put her arms around him. Again this display of maternal concern and affection moved Faro deeply. Vince liked her. She would have made a splendid stepmother.

'May I show him the letter?' she said.

Vince read it and whistled. 'You too? That's jolly

166

interesting. Handed in to Mrs Penny's, you say? Well, Stepfather, where do we go from here?'

'"We" don't go anywhere, lad. I think it would be better if I worked alone from now on and didn't involve either you or Mrs Aird.'

Vince sighed. 'If you must, but I do enjoy playing detective – and I have some ideas of my own I would like to put to the test.'

'You take care,' said Faro sternly. 'I don't want any repetitions of last night's misadventure.' And to Alison, 'Let us go now. Rest assured I shall be very tactful with Mrs Penny. You may rely on me not to make it sound like a police investigation.'

Vince waved to them from the window, and Alison blew him a kiss. Closing the gate, she sighed, 'Such a dear boy. Tell me, why doesn't he just call you Father? Or Jeremy, for that matter?'

'Never Jeremy. He wouldn't consider that quite proper.'

'But you are such friends.'

'That has not always been so. When I first knew him, as a little boy, it was Mr Faro. But from the day his mother and I married, he called me Stepfather. And I must confess I rather like the title, seeing that it is perfectly accurate and it makes it somehow special.'

They found Mrs Penny in the garden attending to the roses. She greeted them both effusively and when Mrs Aird went indoors was quite disposed to linger and chat with Inspector Faro, waxing voluble in response to his warnings about a spate of petty thievings from unguarded kitchens in the area, and the necessity of locking the door at night, at least until the criminals were apprehended.

'I've already been warned, Inspector. Constable McQuinn was saying the same things when I found him in my kitchen on Sunday.' She smiled slyly. 'Mind you, I thought it was maybe a wee bit of an excuse – I think Bessie, the pretty little maid I've engaged to help me with the washing, is the reason for his particular interest in these premises.'

'What other callers have you had recently?'

'Apart from Doctor Laurie – he was worried about you all missing the ferry . . .' She hesitated, her smile inviting explanation.

'I mean strangers, Mrs Penny, during the last few days.'

'Oh well, let me see now. On Saturday, there were two wee lads selling firewood, an old beggarman, the minister. And on Sunday, if you please, Inspector, a gypsy woman, selling clothes pegs and telling fortunes. Well, I sent her packing, such wickedness on the Lord's day. I didn't like the look of her.' She frowned. 'She was filthy, Inspector. In fact, I wondered if she could be a woman, she had this long stringy black hair and I thought her hands and feet were rather big and her voice a wee bit on the deep side.'

'You thought she might be a man, eh?' said Faro, thinking here was a stroke of luck.

Mrs Penny nodded vigorously. 'I did indeed. She came just as we were leaving for church, too. What a cheek . . .'

Faro escaped with difficulty and made his way to the Central Office.

'Is there anything on Black Tam yet?' he asked McQuinn, eyeing with disapproval the pipe that the young constable was smoking, since this was a privilege only allowed to senior officers and detectives.

'Nothing yet, Inspector. But do give us time – it's early days, as you know from your own experience.'

Faro shrugged irritably. McQuinn never missed an opportunity of reminding him that once upon a time he too had been a humble policeman doing duty-patrol in the streets of Edinburgh.

'What about routine enquiries in the area?'

McQuinn produced a long list and Faro felt, instead of gratification, annoyance that his efficiency could not be faulted.

'What about Mrs Penny at Marchmont Cottage?'

'Mrs Penny? There was no reason to enquire at her house. The attack wasn't in her vicinity.'

'And yet you went there on Sunday.'

McQuinn blushed. 'Oh, that! Nothing to do with official enquiries, Inspector. I was merely paying court to the pretty little lass in the kitchen. And when Mrs Penny caught us, I felt obliged to make an excuse for my presence,' he added with a smirk that infuriated Faro.

'Indeed, Constable. You might endeavour in future to keep your private life separate from your police duties. It would be a great help. In connection with the attack on my stepson, you might keep a lookout for a tall gypsy woman with uncommon large feet and hands and a be-grimed appearance.'

'You think it might be Black Tam in disguise?'

'Never mind what I think, Constable, and I will be obliged if you will keep your eyes open when you are on duty, less in the region of kitchen-maids and more in the region of possible suspects.'

In the days that followed, there were no more threatening notes or suspicious incidents. With the healthy flesh of youth, Vince's bruises and cuts healed and he had almost forgotten his attack in his excitement about Mrs Penny's mysterious gypsy visitor.

'I'm absolutely certain that she – or more probably he – is responsible for leaving the note for Mrs Aird. Find him, Stepfather, and we have the man we're looking for – Lily Goldie's murderer.'

Faro was inclined to share his enthusiasm, especially as neither McQuinn nor any of the other constables alerted found a trace or a hint of the existence of the gypsy, who had apparently vanished into thin air since the visit to Marchmont Cottage.

There was still the business of Vince's threatening note, which McQuinn swore was not in his pockets when he searched them in Gibbet Lane. That and the fact that McQuinn had also visited Mrs Penny's that Sunday were matters that needed careful and tactful investigation, considering that he had also been 'sweet' on Lily Goldie.

And why should Black Tam be concerned with the murdered girl? None of it made any sense.

Faro now had his own reasons for personal anxiety, which tended to make him less enthusiastic or vigilant about following clues to the identity of the second murderer. In a few days, the Trelawney Thespians – and Alison – would be gone from Edinburgh. At least she would be safe from any vengeful attacks. He had already made up his mind, despite her protests, not to let her go out of his life for ever. No one who had made such an impact on his senses could say goodbye and walk away.

Soon, too, he would be once more involved in domesticity, in his sorely neglected role of father to his two daughters. A letter lay on his desk from Orkney.

Dearest Papa,
    We are looking forward to being all together again, with our dear brother Vince, in your new house in Edinburgh, as you promised. We hope you will like the enclosed which Granny says is a good likeness . . .

He looked at the smiling photograph and it made him acutely aware of time passing. How they had grown – soon they would be young ladies and he would have lost their childhood.

He groaned as he re-read the letter. '. . . as you promised' reproached him. He had forgotten, or rather pushed it to the back of his mind. However, unless the mystery of the threatening letters was solved and Lily Goldie's murderer apprehended and safe behind bars, he felt the presence of any other members of his family would be an added hazard.

170

Already he was wary of providing Vince with any additional information that might lead him recklessly to follow 'clues' on his own with disastrous, and this time perhaps fatal, results.

Faro knew of only one way to resolve his difficulties, and that was to set a police trap. Vince listened gravely to his plan.

'You might as well know, Stepfather, I can't stop you but I'm against it. It's far too dangerous. Take care, you may have gone too far this time and played into the murderer's hands.'

CHAPTER FIFTEEN

That Saturday night was brilliantly moon-lit. As midnight chimed from a vast number of distant Edinburgh churches solemnly proclaiming the Sabbath morn, a white-haired bearded old gentleman wearing a silk-lined cape, top hat and carrying an elegant cane was seen to leave the neighbourhood of the King's Theatre. Merrily, but somewhat unsteadily, he proceeded along Lothian Road and across the Meadows, heading towards the new villas by the short cut at Gibbet Lane.

If any had remarked upon his passing it would have been to the effect that he would have been wiser to hire a cab. Elderly, crippled in the left leg, his progress was further impeded by the condition of one who has imbibed too well. The further he walked, the slower and the more pronounced his limp. Now a shortness of breath, a wheezing cough, added to the picture of decrepitude as he stopped frequently, leaning on his cane.

The onlooker would have further decided that a man, obviously wealthy, was not quite in his right mind to choose such exercise at his time of life when he was so out of condition, as he disappeared from view along the tree-lined lane. But the path was deserted – or so it seemed to the limping man, when suddenly, from behind the trees, three masked men, two of average height and one very large, leaped out at him.

The old man cried out 'Help!' in a voice surprisingly

strong, and even as they descended upon him his bent back straightened and from the cane appeared a fine-bladed sword which flashed in the moonlight as, with limp miraculously cured, he turned upon his assailants.

'Scarper!'

The leader's warning came too late. The old man was using a whistle to ear-piercing effect and from every tree policemen erupted, racing down upon them. In the lead was Constable Danny McQuinn, who, for once, Faro was extremely glad to see.

'A nice piece of work, Inspector. You make a very convincing old man, to the life – as if it was yourself only without the beard.'

Faro wasn't sure what to make of this enigmatic remark but chose, for once, to take it as flattery. 'Put them on a charge and keep them inside. Send someone to get my stepson to identify them.'

Black Tam and his associates were bundled into a cab and escorted to the Central Office. Dr Laurie was at home. Presented with his stepfather's compliments, he was hustled into the second cab.

'What's this all about? Where is Inspector Faro?' he demanded, confronted by the back of the elderly gentleman still in his disguise and whom he failed to recognise in the dim light.

'Why, Stepfather! Your plan worked after all.'

'Come with me, lad.'

A look into the cell and Vince said, 'Oh yes, those are the three who attacked me right enough.'

'Good! You can formally bring charges, then. See the Constable and he'll tell you what's needed. The cab will take you back home.'

'Aren't you coming too?'

'I may be a little while. Goodnight, lad. See you in the morning.'

Faro then confronted Black Tam and his two bullies,

and charged them with assault. 'You know who I am?'

'God perhaps, with that white beard,' said Big Tam sourly.

'It would pay you to be serious.' And Faro removed his disguise, while watching carefully Black Tam's reactions.

'A copper as I live an' breathe,' was the sneering response. 'I might ha' kenned as much.'

'You know me.'

'I do?'

'My name is Inspector Faro.'

'That's a funny name for a copper.'

'It might be a very significant name in your case, my lad. I suspect that you've already heard it.'

'Never. And I don't want to hear it no more, neither.'

'Listen, Tam – I can make it easier for you, if you co-operate. Who paid you to leave a note in Doctor Laurie's pocket when you robbed him the other night?'

Black Tam stared at him blankly. 'Do me a favour, Inspector. Don't know what you're on about. What would I be doing putting things into folks' pockets? Goes against the grain, that does. Opposite is what I'm at – taking things out, as you ken fine well.' He grinned.

'Do you know an old gypsy woman – about your height, with large hands and feet, who sells clothes-pegs and tells fortunes?'

'Never heard of her.'

'You don't know anything of a visit she made to Mrs Penny at Marchmont Cottage, and delivered a note there?'

Big Tam shook his great head from side to side. 'You're talking double-dutch, Inspector.' And, appealing to the silent Constable McQuinn, 'What's he on about the now?'

And Faro felt uneasily that unless Big Tam was an extremely good actor, which he doubted, then he was telling the truth.

'You maintain that you've never seen me before?'

174

'Never. Heard plenty about ye, kenned you was a copper to be avoided, but never been my misfortune to set eyes on ye afore.'

'I also happen to be Doctor Laurie's stepfather.'

With elaborate casualness, the man replied, 'Is that a fact? Well now, wasn't it just ma bad luck to choose a lad who was copper's kin?' He spat on the floor. 'An' all for a miserable two shillings.'

'Read him the charge, Constable, the attack on Doctor Laurie.'

Big Tam listened and shuffled his feet.

'Have you anything you wish to say that might be used in evidence?'

'Don't know my own strength, Inspector. Used to be a wrestler before I fell on hard times.'

'Like robbery with violence. I believe you are also part of a conspiracy— '

'I ain't part of nothing. Work for meself, I do. Only rob the rich to give to the poor.'

'Sit down – here at the desk.'

Black Tam regarded him nervously. 'What for?'

'Because I tell you to. Go on.'

Faro produced the two notes, the one found on Vince and the one to Alison Aird.

'Here is paper. Take up that pen . . .'

Black Tam held the pen, rolling it between his fingers. 'What's it about, Inspector. What's your game?'

'I want you to write something for me. Your name, for instance.'

The pen scratched long and laboriously. 'Thos Macandlish. That's me name.'

'Now let's have your address.'

'Haven't got one.'

'Central Office, Edinburgh. That will find you for some time to come.'

In answer, Tam drew a large and shaky cross under his

signature. Looking over his shoulder, Faro said, 'What's this? I thought you could write?'

Black Tam grinned sheepishly. 'Only me name – learned it by heart lang syne. Was told it would be useful, but I canna write anything else, honest to God, mister.'

'Maybe you can read then?' And Faro thrust the note in front of him. Black Tam looked at it solemnly and shook his head.

'Dunno what it says. Never learned letters, only numbers. I can read numbers,' he said helpfully.

'Take them to the cells,' said Faro in disgust.

There was not the slightest resemblance in Tam's shaky signature to the firm educated hand of the notes, and Faro was more than ever convinced that he was looking at the writing of the man who had murdered Lily Goldie. To his mind there were four classes of murderer. The once-only murderer who, of a violent disposition, often combined with poor mental powers, comes home and finds his woman in bed with another man. He picks up the nearest implement and murders her – and often her lover as well. There is no subtlety involved. He might make a run for it, but most often when his blood-lust has cooled, and he slowly realises the enormity of his action, his run is not away from the scene of the crime but to the nearest police station to give himself up. And even if he tries to escape the law, his getaway is usually easy to follow. He leaves plenty of clues. Almost as if he wanted to be found. Such a murderer was Hymes.

In the second category was the mad murderer, driven to kill for pleasure, or wreaking his revenge on society for some imagined wrong, working out of his system some ancient grievance that had twisted his mind. Prostitutes were their most common prey. Such mass-murderers often evaded the law by the use of cunning and ingenuity. However, they were rarely encountered, thought Faro, thankfully.

176

The third was the poisoner, the man or woman driven beyond all endurance, or by lust, loathing or lucre, to get rid of the impediment to what they imagined was peace, often accompanied by plenty. It rarely worked and, unless they had a considerable run of luck, they were most often caught and hanged.

The first-category murderer was often violent and ignorant, the two latter were considerably more wily and intelligent. So too the fourth and last, the man who employed a bully, a strong man with poor reasoning, 'bought' for the purpose of committing murder or to intimidate the chosen victim. Such as Black Tam, disguised as a gypsy woman, delivering warning notes. No, it was too far-fetched.

So, in which category did Lily Goldie's murderer belong? Once he had reasoned that out, he would be much nearer to his goal. But somewhere, he realised, he had lost the track. There was a great muddle of clues, and none of them made any sense at all.

Again and again he returned to the two notes. Although the writing was doubtless disguised, it was definitely that of an educated hand.

Once again the tide of thefts, assaults, embezzlements and arson took over. As Faro dealt with the routine investigations he hoped fervently that no major crime would erupt on Edinburgh society and cause him to miss the Trelawney Thespians' farewell performance of *Antony and Cleopatra*, and his last evening with Alison before her departure for Bournemouth.

He returned from the Central Office to be met in the hall by Mrs Brook, who handed a note to him.

'Will you please remember to give this to Mrs Aird at the next opportunity?' At his blank look, she said, 'It is a recipe for my pancakes which I promised her. They were greatly enjoyed by those young actresses and it is a recipe they can make themselves. It is quite simple. I would have

177

entrusted it to Doctor Vince, but he is so forgetful— '

Faro cut short the tirade with solemn promises and hurried up to his study and closed the door.

His desk was awash with papers and, carefully laying aside Mrs Brook's recipe, he decided that with the impending visit from Orkney, he must placate the housekeeper by a brisk attempt at tidiness. His study was a constant affront to her sense of order and she insisted that before the family visit the room, from which her activities were normally barred, must be thoroughly cleansed.

The bright sunshine through the window revealed very clearly, even to his undomestic eye, the source of Mrs Brook's anguish. Most of his desk was presently occupied by evidence relating to Lily Goldie's murder. Glad that the case was now finally closed, even if unsolved, he took out a large packet and gathered all the documents together. On top were the two warning notes received by Alison and Vince, which had led to his decision to abandon the investigation.

A sudden shaft of sunlight also took in Mrs Brook's pancake recipe. Faro snatched it up with a surge of excitement. Why on earth had he not noticed that before?

Taking out the two warning notes, he laid the new note alongside.

For a moment he sat back in his chair, dazed with certain knowledge that he had found what he had been looking for. That elusive link, something his acute sense of observation recognised but which lay dormant, nagging him, below the surface of his mind.

He rushed downstairs to the kitchen where Mrs Brook was rolling pastry for an apple pie and, flourishing the recipe, he said, 'Have you any more of this paper, Mrs Brook?'

Somewhat guiltily, he thought, she went to a drawer and withdrew several sheets. 'Here it is, sir. That's all that's left.'

'Where did it come from?' And examining it closely, he said, 'You've cut something off the top, Mrs Brook.'

'Yes, I did, sir. But how did you know?'

'Your scissors need sharpening, their cutting edge is rough.'

'I might as well tell truth, sir, this paper belonged to the late doctor. Seemed a wicked waste to throw it away, with his name printed on it and all. So after he passed on, I decided to use it up for my recipes. Did I do wrong, sir?' she asked anxiously.

'Of course not. Such economies are admirable, Mrs Brook. But, may I ask, where did the ink come from?'

'Oh, the doctor had his ink specially prepared. Very fussy about it clotting when he was writing out his prescriptions.'

'So you've been using up the bottle.'

'Yes, sir. It's rather thick now, not the kind you would want.'

Faro sat down at the table. 'Mrs Brook, can you tell me who had access to this paper – apart from yourself – in recent weeks?'

Mrs Brook thought for a moment. 'Nobody – that is, except Constable McQuinn. That night when Doctor Vince was brought home. He wanted to write out a statement for the poor lad to sign. I was that flustered and upset, sir, I just gave him what came to hand.'

Faro took a gig to the Central Office and extracted McQuinn's handwritten statement regarding Black Tam. Leaving a message for the Constable to meet him at the Pleasance Theatre at seven o'clock, he returned home. As he expected, the two warning notes and Vince's statement had all been written in identical ink, with the same pen on identical paper with a jagged edge.

But not in the same hand. And he knew he had solved Lily Goldie's murder. The thought gave him no satisfaction as even now, reluctant to believe what he knew to be true, he spread the notes out on his study table, pushing aside the smiling photograph of his two small daughters.

For himself, at that moment, he could see no future beyond the next few hours. How long he sat wrestling with his conscience, he did not know, hardly aware in his anguish that Vince had come in and was regarding his slumped shoulders, his downbent head with compassion.

'Stepfather? What is it?'

Faro wearily handed him the three notes, and described the events of the last few hours. 'We've solved the case. Haven't you guessed, Vince lad?'

Vince sat down opposite. 'This lets out the Mad Bart, doesn't it? And McQuinn,' he said, comparing the handwriting. 'We've eliminated everyone else. Except . . .'

'Except?'

'The schoolboy. Yes, it has to be him.'

'A schoolboy who never existed. Except to murder Lily Goldie.'

'Therefore it had to be someone acting the part of a schoolboy.' Vince smiled wanly. 'And as soon as you put the words "acting the part" into context, everything else falls into shape.'

'It was Hugo who gave us the answer, yet neither of us could see it.'

'We didn't want to see it.'

'Dear God, I don't want to see it now, staring me in the face.'

Vince laid a hand on his shoulder. 'What will you do, Stepfather? You can't mean . . .'

Faro stood up, buttoned his coat. 'Lad, I can and do mean just that. And I need you as witness. Will you do this for me?'

And, aware of his stepson's appalled expression, he went out, closed the door behind him and set off for the Pleasance Theatre.

CHAPTER SIXTEEN

He found Alison in her dressing-room. He knew she would be alone as the make-up for Cleopatra took some time.

The mask of beauty took his breath away. How skilfully before his eyes the Queen of the Nile, she whom age could not wither, nor custom stale, was coming to life, as the short, red-gold curls disappeared beneath the heavy Egyptian headdress.

'Don't hover, Jeremy. Take a seat, please. You can talk to me while I put on the finishing touches.'

He sat down heavily, his resolve shattered. Yet there were so many indisputable facts. If his emotional involvement had not blinded him, he would have recognised them immediately. Smiling, she regarded him through the mirror. 'You're looking so solemn, Jeremy. I've promised to be your friend and I will write to you, if that is what you would like. So do cheer up, we want our last evening to be merry.'

Merry, he thought. Would he ever be merry again?

'I have something to tell you.'

'Oh, something nice, I hope.'

'Not nice. Something very serious.'

'Oh?' She swung round to face him. 'And what is that?'

Trying to keep his voice and emotions under control, he said, 'I want you to tell me how you lured Lily Goldie up to Salisbury Crags by pretending to be Tim Ferris's schoolboy brother. We believe you then pushed her over the edge and knotted a scarf about her neck to make it look like the work of Patrick Hymes.'

The make-up was too thick for him to see if she paled at this accusation, but it was a little while before she asked quietly, 'You have proof?'

She did not deny it. Oh dear God, why didn't she deny it, laugh at him?

'You wrote these, didn't you?'

She merely glanced at the notes he held out but made no attempt to examine them. Had she been innocent, she would have snatched them from him with cries of indignation. Had she been innocent . . . but she merely smiled.

'You are clever. You must tell me where I went wrong.'

'First, your reluctance to be seen as a boy, in your Portia costume. You almost slammed the dressing-room door in my face.'

She shrugged. 'I was tired. I had been on stage for hours. Perhaps I do not like being seen by men alone in my dressing-room, "showing off my limbs" as I seem to remember Beth called it.'

'Actresses have no such modesty, as well you know. The girls at Vince's party assured us that you made a splendid boy, and yet you refused to appear with them as one of the young gentlemen from Venice.'

Still she smiled but, watching her, he repeated Hugo's mocking words. '"Some squeaking Cleopatra boy my greatness . . ." '

Her lips moved, but no words came and he remembered that other time, her startled look which he had interpreted as embarrassment, was fear, deadly fear.

'Are you going to arrest me?' she asked lightly and went back to looking in the mirror. How could she sound so casual, uninterested even? Faro realised he had not thought that far ahead. He went to the door.

'Come in, Vince. McQuinn, you take a seat – over there.'

And to Alison, 'Mrs Aird, you are charged with the murder of Lily Goldie – for God's sake, woman, why?' His voice shook and, fighting for control, he added quietly, 'It might make it easier for you if, in your statement, you have good reasons.'

What nonsense, he thought. Nothing would change. They would hang his Desdemona, whatever her excuse. Hang her by that lovely slender neck until she was dead. He wanted to rush from the room, fly from the inevitable, but he was aware of Vince's hand heavy on his shoulder.

'How did you convince her to go with you, Mrs Aird?'

Alison looked at Vince, smiling, and then stared across at McQuinn as if puzzled by his presence, and then with a shrug, she said, 'It was quite simple. Her natural greed. I told her that Tim had left in my keeping, at St Leonard's, a large package for her, just before he – he walked under the train. I indicated that I was certain it contained money and items of valuable family jewellery. That brought her out, faster than summer lightning.' She shrugged. 'The rest was easy. That isolated path, no one around so early. I told her, "I have a nice surprise for you. Close your eyes and hold out your hands." '

Faro shuddered at the suddenly boyish treble. She must have had no trouble deceiving anyone. 'But your reason? I suppose Tim Ferris was your lover, was that it – jealousy?'

'Tim – my lover?' She laughed, and then turned her head away and looked at Vince, a long, tender appraisal. 'Not my lover. Tim was my son.'

'Your son?'

'My son, my only child, and she destroyed him as readily as if her hands had pushed him to his death. She deserved to die. I knew that and I was determined that if I couldn't make her feel the horror of being pushed under a train, at least she would know the full horror of violent death, of being pushed from a great height— '

'Tim was your son?'

'Timon, I called him, after *Timon of Athens*, the play I was in in London when I met his father. Oh, his father was so like him in looks, and, alas, in nature. A handsome plausible rogue who couldn't resist wine, women and a more than occasional flutter on the gaming tables. He married me because it was the only way he could get me into his bed, persuade me to leave the theatre. I was seventeen. Everyone said I was a fool to give up a promising career, but I didn't mind. Marrying him was a triumph and I was blissfully happy – for a little while. Happy as I shall never again be in this life.'

Her face darkened. 'Then, one day when I was pregnant, a woman came to see me with three young children. One glance at them, and she didn't need to tell me that they were his. She handed me a marriage certificate. She was Julian Aird's wife and I was bigamously married. She was determined on vengeance and he was still in prison when Timon was born.'

She clasped her hands. 'Timon was the most beautiful baby. I loved him, he was my whole world, and I could hardly bear to let him out of my sight. I gave up all hope of being an actress until he was older. I was determined that he should have the life he would have had if Julian had really been my husband. I found a rich protector – I'm not ashamed – a dear elderly man who was my lover. He died when Tim was eight years old and left me all his fortune.

'Then, one day, I decided to tell Tim the truth. That the man he regarded as his father was my lover. That I wasn't a widow and that he was illegitimate.'

She stopped, and even through the make-up he saw the tragedy lurking in her eyes. 'He never forgave me. He was a child still but he called me terrible – filthy – names. It was dreadful, but I knew how I had hurt him. He was broken-hearted, so ashamed of the awful stigma I

184

had branded him with. We were living in Yorkshire, in a lovely country mansion, but he had always wanted to go to Scotland. I had told him so much about it. I decided to send him to boarding school in Edinburgh, to St Leonard's. So far away from me, but I hoped that one day when he was older he would understand that everything I had done was for his sake, for his future. Then I set up the trust fund, put every penny into it, so that he could enjoy a good life. I went back to the stage and tried to work with Scottish companies, so that I could be near him.

'I hardly ever saw him. Going back to the stage made matters worse – a mother who was an actress, as well as a kept whore. He did not want to see me in Edinburgh. I thought it would be different when he went to medical school. He would be a man then, he would understand about life. But time made matters worse. He made excuses not to meet me, forbade me to visit his lodgings. When we did meet, he would hardly spend time to speak to me. Then, early this year, I saw a new side of him, besotted with this girl who was out to ruin him. Now all he wanted from me was more and more money, to buy her trinkets, to persuade her that he was a rich man who wanted to marry her. It wasn't until he failed his qualifying exams that I learned – from his own lips – that he had gambled away the entire trust fund that remained on this woman. And when it was all spent, she wanted no more of him.

'Even then I didn't realise how much he loved her. I couldn't believe that anyone could make him suffer so much that he would walk under a railway train. He did so, without a moment's consideration of what I might suffer as his mother,' she added harshly. 'Not one thought as to my agonies, a fine end to all my sacrifices and devotion. I had given up everything for him, a stage career as a Shakespearean actress – I mean a real one – on the London stage, not this absurd company.

'Now it was this woman's turn to suffer and I was determined to destroy her. But how? Then one day, when I was out walking, I found a St Leonard's cap on the railings. Some boy had dropped it. I knew I made a convincing boy – I could convince her, strike up an acquaintance as Tim's heart-broken young brother. She was flattered that a schoolboy should seek her out, pay court to her.

'Soon I saw the perfect opportunity to destroy her. The murder of Sarah Hymes. I could make it look like a double murder.' She laughed. 'You know, I never realised that murder could be so easy. I went back a few times afterwards, hung about the convent gates. That took some courage, just to be seen as a lovesick schoolboy grieving.'

'So that you would never be suspected. And you succeeded.'

She looked at him sadly. 'When I first met you, you seemed determined to fall in love with me, so I felt quite safe, even though I did have occasional qualms. I knew you were clever and I didn't think I could fool you for ever, which was why I was determined to keep you at arm's length. Yet luck was always with me. Even the night you were attacked, Vince.'

She swung round and faced him for the first time. 'I was so fond of him,' she said to Faro. 'He reminded me of my own son, the same age, both studying medicine in the same year.'

Faro exchanged a startled glance with Vince, for the parallels were even closer. Both were illegitimate, both fighting the stigma of bastardy.

'It was because I was so concerned about your toothache, poor suffering darling, that I came to your house and succumbed to the temptation of planting the two notes. It seemed such a perfect chance to plant some evidence that pointed to his attackers. And if I received a warning, who then could possibly suspect me? I'd seen Mrs Brook take out paper and ink in the kitchen to give to the Constable.'

186

'That was your fatal mistake. I might never have guessed, if you hadn't used that special notepaper.'

She shrugged. 'How was I to know? I thought all paper and ink were the same. And now, Inspector – what are you going to do with me? I presume that the Constable is here to arrest me?'

When he didn't reply, she sighed. 'I have one request. In Desdemona's immortal words, "Kill me tomorrow, but let me live tonight." Will you ask him to do that for me, Vince?' And, turning to Faro she said, 'Please, Jeremy, because you loved me once.'

Because I still love you – desperately, were the words he longed to say and could not.

'My last Cleopatra. The Constable may sit outside the dressing-room, quite discreetly.' She gave him a flashing smile. 'I won't run away. You have my word. Besides,' she added, looking wistfully across at Vince, as if seeing in him again the son she had lost, 'there is no place to run to any more. Without love, there isn't very much worth having in a woman's world.'

Or in mine. Oh my dearest . . .

Outside her dressing-room, McQuinn took a seat. 'You go to the front, sir, just in case. I'll stay here, at that rate we'll have both exits covered.'

Vince was waiting for him in the green-room and handed him a large brandy. 'Drink it, Stepfather. You look so ill.'

'I feel ill. If finding out the woman you love is a murderess can count as illness, then I feel like death.'

'What about her? Will you let her carry on with the performance?'

'Yes. I don't see why not. There won't be much theatre where she's going,' he added grimly.

'Has it got to be . . .?' Vince shrugged. 'Tim was so unworthy of her. I never liked him, but what a brute. How could he have treated his mother like that, especially one so sweet and loving.'

'We will never know his reasons now, that's for sure.'

'Quite candidly, one could almost be glad he's dead. He and the Goldie woman. The world's a cleaner place without either of them.' Pausing, he looked at Faro. 'You realise she's not quite sane, don't you, driven mad by his cruelty. If ever there was a *crime passionnel*, this was it.'

'We'd have a hard job convincing the judges.'

'Surely you'll do your best, try for manslaughter?'

'Oh God, Vince lad, don't ask me. Not just now.'

The bell rang for curtain up and they stood at the back, but neither had much concentration left for the play which now enthralled and held its audience captive for the last time.

Between the acts, the green-room was filled with noisy enthusiastic students, and with nothing left to say, Faro and Vince walked outside. They stood gazing up at Arthur's Seat with a pale moon rising, although the sky was still cloudless and blue. A warm, windless, seductively romantic night, but for Faro its beauty merely mocked his agony.

Vince took his arm. 'I think, Stepfather, that we've always known there was something like this. I didn't want to face it.' He looked at the scene before them thoughtfully. 'Remember the night I was attacked, and she stayed, afraid to go home?'

'What happened?'

'I was half asleep, dozing, but I thought – I thought I saw her turn up the lamp and slip something into my coat pocket. Then she picked up paper and ink from the table, as if she had been writing, and carried them out of the door, looking over to where I lay. There was something about her manner, very nervous and furtive. Of course, I'd been so knocked about, I could have been slightly delirious, and next day, when I learned that she too had received a warning note, I decided that I had dreamed the whole thing.'

They heard the bell for the last act. 'It's turning cold, let's go inside, Stepfather.' At the door, he said desperately, 'Look, can't you possibly let her go, pretend none of this ever happened? They're leaving Edinburgh tomorrow.'

'Vince lad, I can't, and you know I can't. My whole faith in myself, in my job – and in justice being done – would be gone for ever if I did. I might as well crawl into a hole, for I'd never live with myself again.'

'And yet the demands of justice have been met. The case is closed.'

Faro felt chilled to the heart. 'Morally, that makes no difference. There is a murderer going free, however you choose to interpret it.'

There were no seats available, but from where they stood near the front they could see the stage plainly, with McQuinn and two uniformed reinforcements hovering discreetly in the wings.

Cleopatra's death scene was played before a hushed audience, that lovely bell-like voice echoing, holding the playgoers spellbound. For them, Edinburgh had vanished, the greasepaint, the over-acting of Antony and the supporting cast was forgotten. This was Egypt and Cleopatra was about to die by her own hand.

'Give me my robe, put on my crown; I have
Immortal longings in me . . .
. . . Husband, I come . . .
I am fire and air; my other elements
I give to baser life . . .
Come then, and take the last warmth of my lips.
Farewell, kind Charmain – Iras, long farewell.'

Beth, as Iras, reeled dramatically and fell with a mighty groan. Cleopatra knelt beside her, regarded her tenderly.

'Have I the aspic in my lips? Dost fall?'

189

Again a mighty groan and writhing on the floor announced that Iras was loathe to lose this dramatic moment, despite Cleopatra's comment,

> 'If thou and nature can so gently part,
> The stroke of death is as a lover's pinch,
> Which hurts and is desir'd . . .'

Faro watched as she took the asp, saw the red jewels that were its eyes glint and flash fire. He stood transfixed, unable to believe that this was Alison Aird, a confessed murderess, and not the Queen of the Nile, Shakespeare's 'lass unparallel'd' as he listened to the dying words, saw the asp's bright jewels plunge.

> 'What, should I stay— '

And then she fell, not back on her funeral couch to lie there regal and dignified. Instead, she jerked once, like a puppet, and slithered to the floor. Her last words were lost as Charmain screamed out loud and the curtain descended abruptly to tumultuous cheering.

Now the audience were on their feet. They began to applaud wildly, stamping feet, unaware apparently that the play was not yet over. Where were the guards and Dolabella and Caesar's entry and triumphant oration?

There was something wrong. Vince took one look at his stepfather and began to struggle through the cheering students. There was movement on stage, a great hush. But it was only Antony. Antony without Cleopatra at his side, who staggered forward and looked somewhat ashen-faced under his make-up.

Trembling, he held up his hand for silence. His plea was ignored; the stamping, cheering began again.

'Cleopatra. We want Cleopatra.'

'We want Mrs Aird, Mrs Aird.'

The stage-hands, unaware of any disaster, set in motion the machinery. Antony's shout – 'Keep the curtain lowered, for God's sake' – came too late.

The curtain rose slowly to reveal Cleopatra lying where she had fallen. It was no ornamental asp at her breast, but the jewelled dagger, embedded to its hilt, and the dark red on her white robe grew to a monstrous rose, as slowly her lifeblood seeped away. It ran, a thin red line, flowing unevenly across the boards to where Faro, with Vince at his side, was already leaping on to the stage.

BLOOD LINE

for
Patricia and Kevin

Chapter One

When the body was found Detective Inspector Jeremy Faro was at home at 9 Sheridan Place, taking afternoon tea with his mother and two small daughters, Rose and Emily. Basking in the rare and somewhat ill-fitting role of father, he hoped that the recent decrease in crime would continue, encouraged perhaps by an August unusually hot for Edinburgh. It would indeed be a pleasant change if he, in common with the City Police and Sheriff Court, might enjoy the small miracle of a respite from vice and law breaking.

He was to be disappointed.

Earlier that month, his mother had written from Orkney advising him to expect her on the 'long-promised' holiday in his new house. After careful deliberation and much heart searching, she had decided to brave the voyage to the mainland.

` 'We must put our trust in the Lord', she wrote, 'that this horrid Prussian war will not spread to our dear land. I tremble at the thought of victorious French troops marching along Princes Street.'

Jeremy Faro had long since decided that his mother's morbid interest in wars and rebellions was worthy of the Queen herself, whose lengthy retreats to her beloved Balmoral much perturbed her Parliament and angered Prime Minister Gladstone.

Personally, Faro was more concerned with the chaos to be expected from this imminent domestic invasion, and, guilt-ridden by his own neglect of the duties of fatherhood, he lay awake composing particularly convincing letters to

7

his determined parent. In the cold light of day the excuse that his house was not yet in order sounded feeble indeed. The truth was less palatable. 1870 had been notable for a tide of personal misfortunes: suspected typhoid, followed by a disastrous love affair, its wounds still too fresh and raw to leave him emotionally capable of dealing with his two exuberant children who, he had sadly to admit, were in danger of becoming strangers to him.

Needless to say, the letters remained unwritten in his head. Every inch the devoted parent, he awaited the Orkney boat at Leith and, with great tenderness, received his two small daughters into his arms.

Mrs Brook, housekeeper at Sheridan Place, regarded the scene with considerable satisfaction. A simple woman, she firmly believed that every man should have his mate. Not for his own amusement had the Almighty ordained that the animals should enter the ark two by two. In her below stairs stronghold, Mrs Brook nodded approvingly as the normally sober household of Inspector Faro and his stepson, Dr Vincent Beaumarcher Laurie, echoed to girlish squeals of delight.

'Come – see this – and this.' Rose and Emily, accustomed to the flat treeless landscapes of their Orkney home, exclaimed wide-eyed as Edinburgh's extinct volcano, Arthur's Seat, filled the horizon from the drawing-room window, while the dining room offered an undulating, sun-shimmering vista of the Pentland Hills. There was even a ginger kitten called Rusty, who had escaped from the kitchen to see what all the fuss was about.

The appearance of their stepbrother, alighting from a gig, brought a fresh wave of excitement. Especially as Vince, who never neglected to bring them gifts, unleashed an armful of picture books and paint-boxes.

Mrs Brook, beaming, delivered her *coup de grâce*. An afternoon tea, calculated to win the hearts of two girls and the secret envy of their grandmother. Pancakes, feather light, with jam made from the garden's strawberries, a Dundee cake stuffed with fruit and enticing small iced cakes.

8

Looking over the scene Faro felt unusually paternal, the bachelor quarters suddenly transformed into the home they might have been had he remarried, as his mother had sincerely hoped he would after Lizzie's death. Wistfully he thought of the difference that female presences brought with them and how this sometimes sterile dining room was now a place warm and glowing, echoing to the affection of these eager young people.

There were undoubted changes since his last meeting with his two daughters. After an absence of some months, he saw in six-year-old Emily for the first time an extra-ordinary resemblance to Vince, Lizzie's illegitimate son.

'Yes, of course I'll take you to Arthur's Seat.'

'And the Castle, please, dear Vince,' said Emily. Wonders were not over. The animated expressions of the two, their fair curls, brought to life his dear dead Lizzie as she had looked long ago.

'I want to go to Holyrood Palace, Vince. I want to see where Queen Mary lived. After all she was a Stuart too – like us,' said Rose, who would soon be nine. Her dark prettiness and delicate features were inherited from his diminutive mother, who had been a Sinclair Stuart before she married Police Constable Magnus Faro.

Vince and Jeremy exchanged wry glances over the girls' heads. Obviously Mary Faro had been at work filling those same small heads with romantic nonsense. All Sinclairs and Stuarts on the islands claimed descent from Queen Mary's half-brother the wicked Lord Robert, Earl of Orkney, who had tyrannised the islands and whose sons, legitimate and bastard, notorious for rape and seduction, were largely responsible for increasing the population with their innu-merable offspring.

'At least Queen Mary couldn't claim a seal woman for a great-grandmother,' murmured Vince.

The girls' grandmother overheard his remark and said acidly, 'It happens to be true, young man, so do not give me your learned doctor's talk on the subject. I know what I'm talking about. I lived with her and she was a very, very odd lady. She even had webbed toes and her long black hair was just like a seal's coat. Why, I remember . . . '

Jeremy Faro finished his tea and retired to the sofa. There he sat back contentedly, happy to remain a spectator in a good-natured argument. Rose and Emily speedily followed his example. With four soft arms around his neck and two soft, sweet faces staring up into his, and a small plump hand occasionally reaching up to stroke his face or kiss his cheek, he was content. There was healing grace as well as pride in the almost forgotten rituals of fatherhood.

At that moment Mrs Brook entered with a constable at her heels.

Taking in the scene, he said, 'May I have a word, sir?'

Trouble, thought Faro. Dammit.

Out of earshot in the corridor, the constable said, 'There's been an accident, man's body found near the foot of Castle Rock.' Hearing the laughter and excited children's voices issuing from behind the closed door, he said, 'Sorry to disturb you like this, Inspector. We were all for moving the corpse straight to the mortuary, but we've been warned by Superintendent Mackintosh that you and Doctor Laurie, as the Police Surgeon's assistant, are to have a look first. Is that right, sir?'

'It is indeed, Constable.'

Returning momentarily to the dining room and consoling his family with a murmured, 'Something we have to look into. We'll be back soon,' he summoned Vince and boarded the waiting police carriage, which bounded across the Meadows and along Johnston Terrace past the King's Stables Road.

Climbing over the railings and up the steep slope to where the two constables stood on guard, Faro and Vince looked down at the twisted broken body under the rough blanket. The sight outraged Faro's senses. Used as he was to sudden death, the contrast between the world of childhood's innocence and family life he had just left, and the cold clay that had once been a dignified elderly man, that dark unholy violence lurking within a summer's day, seemed obscene in its sudden transition.

'Nothing has been touched, Constable?'

'Nothing, sir. Just as we found him after he was spotted from the battlements. One of the Castle guards. Thought it was an old sack.'

Darkness overtook the sun, a clap of thunder followed by a sudden heavy shower. Above them the Castle shimmered through a rain shroud, wrapped in ancient sinister majesty.

Vince followed his stepfather's upward gaze. 'If I am not mistaken, those are the windows of Queen Mary's apartments.'

'Aye, lad. And what a treasure trove for any thief.'

The constable hovered. 'Sure you don't want the corpse taken in, sir? You'd be a lot more comfortable in the mortuary.'

At Faro's sharp refusal, the man's expression as he buttoned up his cape clearly indicated that he thought his superior officer was mad. And it was no secret that Superintendent Mackintosh thought so too: that it was carrying things too far for everything to be left precisely as it was whenever they found a corpse where no corpse should rightly be. If there was a mystery to be investigated and maybe a murder to be solved then they were to wait for Inspector Faro.

Most of the constables agreed that it was very high-handed behaviour, but the Inspector had been adamant. There were too many cases of vital clues being lost for ever, he pointed out, when a body was removed to the mortuary before on-the-spot examination.

Faro knew of one case personally where a policeman had even tidied up a bedroom in the New Town when a woman was brutally murdered, so that her modesty would not be outraged by appearing naked. By the time Faro reached the scene all evidence had disappeared. Evidence, he was certain, that would incriminate her jealous husband as her murderer and not her lover who, protesting his innocence, was found guilty.

11

Helpless to prove his theory, after that incident, as senior detective he reserved the right, unpleasant as it was, to first view all victims at the scene of the crime.

'How did it happen?'

'He must have been trying to break into the royal apartments – there's a window right above us. Up to no good, Inspector, mark my words.'

Vince stood up from his brief examination. 'Rigor has set in a long while past. He must have been here for some time, concealed from the road by this ridge and the hours of darkness.'

'It also rained quite heavily last night, just like this, I suspect,' said Faro, gloomily turning up his greatcoat collar. With a last searching glance at the great bulk of the Castle, which continued to stare down malevolently through the rain sheets, he and Vince turned the body over, trying as they did so to disturb as little as possible, in that first vital search for clues.

'Take particular notice of his garments, Vince. Do they suggest anything to you?'

Vince shook his head and his stepfather continued. 'Here is additional proof of his lying on this very spot for some considerable time. Feel how wet the back of his jacket is, and yet underneath where he lay, face downwards, his shirt and the front of his breeches are quite dry, as is the ground beneath him. Interesting.'

There was no means of identification forthcoming. The man's pockets were empty and leaving the constables in charge of a somewhat cursory routine search, Faro and Vince once more boarded the police carriage, with the corpse on a stretcher in the back.

By the time they had arrived at the Central Office of the Edinburgh City Police, Faro, who remained silent throughout the short journey, had already reached several significant conclusions.

'I doubt whether you will find this unfortunate gentleman in police records as a potential thief and housebreaker,' he told the constable who accompanied them to the mortuary, notebook at the ready. And as the clothes were removed from the body, 'Observe that he is well fed, and tolerably well groomed. Note that his face and lower arms are suntanned or weather beaten, also we may deduce from the fact that this tan continues below the collar line that he does not normally wear a cravat. His hands are calloused, but he is not, I fancy, a railroad worker or a labourer.'

As the shirt was removed, Faro continued, 'Note all the scratches on his lower arms. These swellings, are they insect bites, Vince? What would you deduce from that?'

'That he works out of doors, often with his sleeves rolled up,' said Vince triumphantly.

Faro nodded approvingly. 'I would hazard a guess, judging by the man's respectable appearance, that we have here a factor, a gamekeeper – someone of that class.'

Vince held up the jacket which they had removed from the corpse. 'I'm more interested in this, Stepfather. Feel it, such excellent material, certainly not the kind a labourer would wear.'

'Excellent, Vince lad, and you'll observe that it's of much better quality than his moleskin trousers or his boots. Nor, I suspect, considering our difficulties in taking it off him, was he its original owner.'

The body before them was now almost naked. 'His body linen too. Note that, Vince. Shabby but correct, no doubt influenced by his betters. So many of the poorer classes neglect to wear underdrawers.' Faro indicated the jacket again. 'Have you any ideas why our corpse should be wearing such an unsuitable garment as this?'

'Certainly not to work in. And I'd swear that he never set out with the least intention of climbing –', Vince emphasised the word, '– climbing Castle Rock or doing any violent activity in a jacket with sleeves three inches too short and so tight across chest and upper arms as to restrict all strenuous movement. He would have had extreme difficulty in lifting his arms above his head, let alone climbing . . . '

13

'Without undoing the buttons. See, a central one was torn off, probably in the fall. Well?'

'I know that look, Stepfather. You've already concluded that the poor unfortunate man was pushed off the Rock – or out of a window.' Resuming his examination of the body Vince continued, 'And that bruise to the back of his head was made by some blunt instrument, I suspect, before he fell.'

'Strange that his pockets yielded no information, that he carried not so much as a clay pipe with him. Consider the moustache and the unavoidable tobacco stains.'

Straightening up, Vince said, 'His body is amazingly unmarked. No scars, no evidence of bones broken in the past or operations. Hello, this is interesting. What do you make of this, Stepfather?' And he pointed to a tiny tattoo mark on the inside of the man's wrist. 'I almost missed that. What do you think it is?'

'A shamrock or a clover leaf, but rather imperfectly done. By the look of it, the work of an amateur. Poor devil. It didn't bring him much luck,' said Faro, and picking up the jacket he examined it closely. 'Observe that some of the buttons don't match and have been sewn on rather hastily with different-coloured thread. I rather suspect, lad, that this same jacket of excellent material has all the marks of being handed down – by some prosperous employer or deceased relative.'

'If that is the case, Stepfather, then I know from my boarding school and Medical College days that most Edinburgh tailors leave an identifying mark inside the lining. To assist with ordering of future garments by their rich customers, particularly clients who go to serve overseas, in the Colonial Service and so forth. They often prefer to order their tropical clothes and dress uniforms from a reliable home tailor. Let's see if I'm right.'

At the back of the neck, under the lining, were the marks he was searching for, 'K & J. 154/9'.

'K & J. Kennington and Jenner's,' said Vince. 'I'm a good customer in their gentlemen's outfitting department.

14

A visit to Mr Banks tomorrow should produce the name of the original owner.'

'Good lad. Meanwhile, we'll see what the constables bring back from Castle Rock. I may even go back anyway, and see what I can find.'

'Too dark for that kind of work now.'

'True.' Faro frowned. 'I'm for a walk up to the royal apartments while the trail is still warm. No, you go home, lad. Give them the usual excuses. Nothing scaring, detained at work and not to expect me in for supper. Be so good as to inform Mrs Brook to leave one of her cold collations. That will do me admirably. Well, what is it, lad?'

'Rose and Emily, Stepfather. This is their first night with us. I doubt whether they'll be willing to go to bed before Papa comes home. They'll certainly never go to sleep . . .'

'Then you must deputise for me.'

'Me? How?'

'You're the head of the house when I'm not around. What you do is read them stories, tuck them up in bed. Get in some practice for fatherhood. Might come in very useful some day.'

Vince groaned. 'God grant that "some day" is a million years away.' And consulting his pocket watch, 'As a matter of fact, Stepfather, I'm engaged to meet friends at Rutherford's within the hour. And I don't see how . . .'

Faro sighed impatiently. Domesticity was going to be damnably inconvenient with something in the offing that his every instinct told him was a case of murder.

Chapter Two

Sir Eric Haston-Lennard was an Orcadian who had been a good friend to Jeremy Faro's mother when her policeman husband was killed in Edinburgh. On retiral, with a knighthood, from the diplomatic service in India and Canada, appointed Keeper of Her Majesty's Historical Records in Scotland, he had been delighted to discover that young Jeremy was now Senior Detective Inspector Faro of the Edinburgh City Police.

A bachelor, fast becoming a recluse, Sir Eric had an apartment within the Castle, where Faro was always most cordially welcomed for a gossip, a dram and a hand at cards or chess. As befitted his illustrious role, where historical records existed of the long and turbulent history of Scotland and of Edinburgh in particular, Sir Eric's ability to track down ancient documents was of great assistance to the law.

Faro followed the uniformed guard along the cold stone corridor past the old royal lodging where unhappy, disillusioned Mary Queen of Scots sought refuge for her lying in. There, in a room not much larger than Mrs Brook's pantry, she had given birth to the future King James VI.

There was, however, nothing in the least melancholy about the large room into which Faro was ushered. The high walls were covered from wainscot to ceiling by an imposing gallery of paintings of Scottish monarchs. Neither historic nor contemporary, alas, they were the work of one imaginative artist, commissioned to impress the visiting monarch King George IV in 1822 with an imposing turnout of royal Stuart ancestors.

Announced, Faro thought the drawing room to be empty at first glance. No doubt Sir Eric would shortly appear from the direction of his study. Meanwhile he would enjoy the photographs of modern royalty, splendid examples of that new and magical art now taking Britain by storm. There was Sir Eric with Her Majesty and members of the royal family at Balmoral Castle. Again, Sir Eric in the uniform of the Queen's Royal Company of Archers being graciously received at Holyrood Palace. A silver-framed likeness held the place of honour. It showed Her Majesty in state robes and was signed, 'To Sir Eric, a devoted servant, Victoria R.'

'Inspector Faro?'

He put down the photograph guiltily and swung round to find the occupant of Sir Eric's high-backed chair had stepped into the candlelight. Faro was a little taken aback to find himself face to face not with his grizzled old friend, but with a very pretty girl in her early twenties. Now laying aside the book she held, she came forward, hand outstretched to greet him.

'How do you do? Sir Eric has been detained at Holyrood, I'm afraid, some boring royal business.'

Her handshake was strong and more to the point, it was surprising. Did she not know that etiquette demanded that well-bred young ladies should not touch a man's hand until they were formally introduced? Who the devil was she?

Bowing, he said, 'I'm so sorry to have inconvenienced you. I will return later. Perhaps you will tell Sir Eric when he arrives.'

'Wait. You're surely not going?'

'Well – yes.'

As Faro hesitated, she said eagerly, 'If you are not in a desperate hurry – please be my guest.' The invitation was accompanied by a winning smile.

'He should be here directly. And now, Inspector Faro, tell me all about yourself.' At Faro's startled expression, she said, 'We are not complete strangers you know. I have

17

heard so much about you – you are his clever policeman friend and I've been dying to meet you.'

Faro was surprised to find her on his own eye level. An inch over six foot, he was used to looking down on most of female kind but this girl, studying him so candidly, was almost as tall as himself.

Head on side, she continued, 'You don't look much like a detective, I must say. You look far too young – and jolly.'

Faro's feelings were far from jollity, if truth were to be told, however he was sufficiently vain to be flattered by the definition 'young' from a girl half his age.

'I've never met a detective, of course,' she said apologetically, 'and one gets very fixed ideas about people who are in authority. I've always imagined anyone to do with the Police Force as being quite stern and elderly.' She smiled, head on side. 'Not a bit like you. Sir Eric is always singing your praises and I'm so glad we've met at last.' And leaning forward confidentially, 'I'm terribly interested in crime.'

Faro's eyebrows raised a little at this frank and decidedly unfeminine admission. In respectable drawing rooms such matters were restricted to behind-hand whispers since any interest in improper behaviour was considered not only unwomanly, but wanton.

Here was a very forthright and unusual young female. And although he did not normally like tall women, finding that a certain aggressive manner went with the extra inches, this slender girl before him was most appealing. What Vince and his generation would undoubtedly call 'an absolute stunner'.

A stunner indeed, and enchantingly pretty. Raven-black tresses coiled on top of her head sloped to a widow's peak on her brow, emphasising a heart-shaped face and eyes that in candlelight seemed golden brown. Her figure was exquisite and he was wondering where she fitted into Sir Eric's lonely bachelor life, when she suddenly trilled with laughter at his expression.

'Oh, I am rude. Do pardon me. Of course, I should

18

have introduced myself. I'm Lucille Haston – Sir Eric is my uncle. I've been staying in Orkney with his sister, my Aunt Maud, and I guess I bullied the poor dear to let me come to Edinburgh.'

'You are from America?'

The girl clasped her hands and laughed delightedly. 'Bravo, Inspector – a good try. Actually I'm Canadian backwoods and Orkney isn't much better – a peevish, dull place.'

Faro refrained from comment. 'I hope Edinburgh is to your taste.'

'Not so far, alas.' She sighed. 'All we do is play cards or chess or read books. We never go anywhere. Absolutely no social life, no people of my own age – except the officers of the guard and Uncle says I can't associate with them, since I'm unchaperoned – except for my maid. And who wants to go out to dinner or to a ball accompanied by one's maid? Girls in the backwoods have a little more freedom, thank heaven . . . '

This breathless account was interrupted as the door was flung open by a uniformed maid, eyes discreetly lowered and carrying a tray.

Lucille Haston greeted her appearance with that trilling laugh.

'You see what I mean,' she said, and at the maid's sternly disapproving glance in the direction of this gentleman caller's boots, she sighed, 'No need to look like that, Bet. I am quite safe. Inspector Faro is a friend of Sir Eric's and he is also a policeman, so you needn't apply your eye to the keyhole any longer. I am totally in the hands of law and order and the Inspector is the very soul of propriety.'

Bet, embarrassed by her young mistress's declaration, bobbed a curtsy and, avoiding Faro's amused glance, hurried out.

'Refreshments, how nice. Will you take lemonade, or tea – and these biscuits are very good indeed.' At this hour of the day, Faro would have welcomed something stronger.

He eyed the sideboard with its decanters longingly. Sir Eric was very generous with his drams.

'I suppose you're wondering how my maid appeared with such alacrity.' And Lucille pointed to the large chimney-piece. 'Above that there is a small pantry which used to be the laird's lug in the old days,' she whispered. 'You know, the laird used to go up to his bedroom and listen in to what his guests were saying about him. Hardly the done thing, but very useful where chaperones are concerned.'

Taking a sip of lemonade, Faro asked, 'Are your parents abroad, Miss Haston?'

'Please call me Lucille. My parents? Both dead. In Canada – I was born there – when I was three, I can't even remember them. Uncle Eric is my guardian until I'm of age and meantime I live in Stromness with Aunt Maud, his unmarried sister. You know Stromness? Isn't it the dullest place ever?' she added.

'On the contrary; I'm very attached to Orkney. I lived near St Margaret's Hope and I sometimes miss it – and my family there – very much.'

'Surely not after living in divine Edinburgh all these years?' Lucille obviously regarded such an admission as incredible. 'Tell me about your family. I understand from Uncle that you're a widower. How sad – I am sorry.'

A sound of voices in the corridor and Faro was spared an account of his life story when the door opened to admit Sir Eric. Grey-haired, large and distinguished, he bore the unmistakable air of authority, the stamp of a Court official.

'My dear fellow, how good to see you. I trust my niece has been looking after you. What on earth is that she's given you to drink? For Heaven's sake, why didn't you ask her for a dram?'

'I wasn't sure – '

Lucille laughed. 'My dear fellow,' she said to Faro in a tolerable imitation of her uncle's manner, 'I know all about drams. Why, my dear Aunt Maud owns shares in the local distillery. You should have told me, silly man. You don't have to be polite with me.'

'That's quite enough, young lady. Thank you for entertaining the Inspector in my absence, but now you may retire. Now, Lucille,' he added in a threatening tone. 'Now – meaning immediately.'

Faro suppressed amusement for there was nothing in the least avuncular in this stern aristocrat's manner.

'But, Uncle . . . ' protested a sadly diminished Lucille.

'Now,' Sir Eric repeated firmly. He rose to his feet, a tall, regal, grey-haired disciplinarian. A sight to make strong men quail and more than a match for his spirited niece.

'It's been lovely to meet you,' said Lucille weakly. 'I hope I'll see you again before I leave,' she added with a sigh.

'Seeing that you're to be here until the autumn, I don't see how that can be avoided,' said Sir Eric, his good nature restored. His affectionate glance was followed by a threatening gesture. 'Now, be off with you, young lady. Good night, sleep well.'

'Good night, Uncle. Good night, Inspector.' A pretty curtsy and the door closed.

Handing Faro a dram, Sir Eric relaxed in the chair opposite. 'Hope she wasn't being too tedious. Bit of a rattle, but a sweet child really. Have to watch her with all these soldier lads about in the Castle. Seems to have no idea what men are like – well, you know what soldiers are. Given any encouragement, it could be deuced awkward.'

Drinking deeply, he sighed. 'We inherited her when a Vermont Haston cousin died. Time she had a husband. Her aunt's finding her a bit of a handful. Got this brilliant idea that there might be more chance of a good marriage here in Edinburgh. Perhaps when the Court comes to Holyrood. Anyway, I dare say you aren't here to talk about my niece. What can I do for you?'

'I'm not sure, Sir Eric. There was a body found at the base of Castle Rock . . . '

'So I've heard. Fellow trying to get into Queen Mary's

apartments. Up to no good, I warrant. Expect he was disturbed, panicked and tried to make his getaway. Good Lord, nobody's climbed down Castle Rock and got away with it since the wicked Earl of Bothwell back in the 1560s. Don't make men like that any more.'

'Have you any idea what he could have been looking for? Are there any valuables missing?'

'No, thank God. All safely locked in their glass cases. The rest of it is memorabilia – shoes, gloves, that sort of thing. Then there's a bed with hangings Mary embroidered personally.' He laughed. 'All authentic, dating from the sixteenth century, whether they belonged to the Queen or not.'

'I wonder if I could have a look round.'

'By all means. But you'll be wasting your time, lad. I know every item after all these years. Naturally when I heard about the intruder, first thing I did was to have them checked. Nothing missing, nothing even disturbed, I'm told. In fact, how he hoped to get in and out again is a mystery.'

Faro smiled and Sir Eric continued, 'Which, of course, is why you are here. Who was he, anyway?'

'We have no idea as yet.'

'I see. Well, you're more than welcome to have a search for any clues if you feel my men might have missed something vital. But you'll need to come back in tomorrow. Forster, who keeps the keys, is off duty, away to Haddington, I think. Returns in the morning. Now, time for a game of chess?'

'Not tonight, I'm afraid, sir. My mother has just arrived from Orkney with Rose and Emily – '

'Then I mustn't delay you.' With a sudden tender glance, he added, 'Compliments to your dear mother. It is far too long since we last met. Tell her I shall take the liberty of calling on her very soon.'

'Please do, Sir Eric. She would enjoy that.'

'You really think so?' He sounded eager. 'Such a splendid lady and one I have always held in the highest esteem.'

There was a suppressed sigh. 'We were very close after your father's death, you know.'

Faro did know, but not from Sir Eric. He had gathered from his mother's coy innuendoes that she might have married Sir Eric had she had the notion for a second marriage. But like her adored Queen Victoria she preferred to remain in love with the memory of a dead husband, relishing her widowhood to the full.

'Besides,' she told her son in a moment of confidence, 'it wasn't proper at all. I know my station in life, son, and it was not to be Lady Haston-Lennard. The very idea. What would my Orkney friends think of me, giving myself airs?'

'It's done every day in high society, Mother. Poor-born females are raised up by marriage.'

And now he was left wondering whether Mary Faro could possibly be the reason why Sir Eric had remained a bachelor.

'Do bring the little girls with you next time. I'd like to take them round myself. Tell them a bit of the history.'

'They would love that. They're full of stories about Queen Mary.'

'Good for them. I'll get my niece to go along too. Might stir her interest in the past. Our glorious history leaves her quite cold. All she cares for are pretty clothes and theatres and grand balls. Don't know what this young generation is coming to.'

Faro didn't feel inclined to argue that some of that young generation, like his doctor stepson Vince, were a credit to Scotland's future. At the door the two men shook hands.

'I'll expect you about ten tomorrow,' said Sir Eric.

'Thank you for your help, sir. And I'll bring the family on some later occasion.'

'Of course, of course. Crime and domesticity don't mix, do they?'

Rose and Emily Faro were early risers, so too was Faro's mother – the latter somewhat surprised, on preparing to

23

indulge her son with the special treat of a breakfast tray, to find his bed slept in, but the room empty.

'He left the house half an hour ago, Mrs Faro,' the housekeeper told her. 'Quiet as a mouse he was. 'Spect he's gone for a constitutional. Oh yes, I'm sure he'll be back soon.'

Even as she spoke Faro was perched precariously on the Castle Rock. The point to which he had climbed was some eight feet above the spot where the body had been found. As he conducted his minute search of the area, he kept remembering those empty pockets.

Unless the dead man lived within walking distance, he must have had some money. And a clay pipe and tobacco in his pocket, since evidence had pointed to a smoker.

It was the stem of a clay pipe which led him to the discovery of a large knotted handkerchief, jammed in a crevice and almost hidden by gorse. Inside he found small coins and the pipe's bowl. He had guessed right. Its mode of transport had probably been the trouser pocket, since the hand-me-down jacket was such an uncommon tight fit.

Looking at these anonymous tokens, Faro almost missed the jewel completely. The sun, tardy in putting in an appearance, suddenly blazed forth from behind a bank of cloud. At that moment, Edinburgh's many churches, whatever their denomination, were more or less united in chiming forth the hour.

Eight, nine. Faro sighed. The search had taken longer than he had planned. It was hardly worth returning home for breakfast. He might as well go direct to the Castle, contact Forster and begin his investigations with a thorough search of Queen Mary's apartments.

It promised to be a glorious day, the sunlight swiftly drying the night's dewdrops in a kaleidoscope of delicate colour. Suddenly he strained forward for a closer look. This particular dewdrop was in fact the ruby and diamond glint of a jewel about three feet above his head.

Weighing it in his hand, he thought about the constables' method of investigation. Doubtless they had been conscientious enough but had used little imagination. They had searched below where the man was found, not realising that as a body rolled downwards, through such an uneven terrain of rocks and gorse, items carried in pockets could well be dislodged.

The jewel was a cameo pendant of delicate gold and enamel filigree surrounding a tiny miniature of a man in sixteenth-century apparel. The likelihood of it being 'buried treasure', lying here in this crevice for many years undiscovered, seemed very remote. The gold would have tarnished, in fact it was doubtful if that delicate filigree would have survived the passage of time.

Faro felt certain that the piece was authentic, valuable, and had found its way down the Castle Rock very recently. Looking up at the window of Queen Mary's apartments, he was now sure that the jewel he held had been connected with the man's violent death. When he walked round the glass cases shortly, Forster would confirm that one piece was missing.

There was a thrill of personal triumph in knowing that the mystery was beginning to unravel. In his hands he held the thread to the labyrinth, the very first clue. He was still certain that the scanty clues of the dead man's apparel pointed to his having been murdered, but why? A struggle on the heights with someone else who wanted to gain possession of the jewel? Was it that simple?

He should know part of the answer in ten minutes' time and could almost hear Sir Eric saying, 'Yes, of course. One of our treasures, belonged to Queen Mary. I know it well.'

I know it well. The imagined words repeated themselves over and over. I know it well. True, he knew little about jewellery, but what he now felt was the unmistakable sense of recognition. Just as he was certain that what he held was not a modern reproduction of an antique cameo, he was experiencing a feeling that raised the hairs on the back of his neck.

25

A sensation of times past. Of a happening far off but familiar too. At some other period in his life, he had held this piece in his hands. No, that could not be – one very like it. The remembrance brought with it a rush of guilt and shame. Someone had been very angry with him. His mother? Yes, his mother. No, she wasn't angry. She was upset – crying. And that made him feel terrible.

His fist tightened over the cameo. The possessor of a phenomenal memory, he fought desperately to remember. How, when and, most important, where?

At that moment, his glance took in a shadow moving far above him. Arms gesticulating? A large bird?

No. A black shape – hurtling down towards him.

He flattened himself against the rock and felt the wind of a huge dark object flying past him. A second later and it bounced, cracking, stone upon stone, past the very spot where he had been perched, to crash vibrating the railings far below.

His sudden evasive action dislodged the heath root supporting his weight. The next moment he too was hurtling down – down, the ground coming to meet him, dazzled in morning sunshine.

Chapter Three

Slithering painfully against every rock, Faro's downward progress was arrested with a sickening thud as he hit the ground and his ankle twisted under him.

He tried to stand. The pain was agonising. On hands and knees he crawled the short distance to the railings and stared helplessly through at the road with its bustling morning traffic, walkers and riders, carriages driving towards Princes Street and the West End.

'Help me, help me, please.' But the first passer by, a respectably dressed middle-aged woman walking with a small child, gave him a look of horror and speedily averted her eyes as if from some improper sight. Propelling the child along, ignoring shrill questions and backward glances, she hurried on, deaf and blind to his distress.

Next came three young girls, whispering and giggling as they walked arm-in-arm down the Wynd.

'Ladies, ladies. Please help me.' They slowed down momentarily. 'I'm a police officer,' he added desperately, trying to sound stern and convincing.

Hands on hips the trio regarded him. 'Don't look much like a policeman, does he?'

'Come away, Meg. He'll be one of those dafties, always tormenting decent folk.'

'Please listen,' Faro shouted as they moved away. 'If you won't help me, then tell the next constable you meet . . . '

But the three hurried on with occasional nervous backward glances and furious giggling, leaving Faro clinging miserably to the railings, staring after them. What a ridiculous predicament. Here he was, unable to climb the railings or walk in search of some exit. His hopes of getting anyone to help him steadily diminished – where, in heaven's name, were all Edinburgh's great God-fearing citizens who poured forth from churches each Sunday, eager with their good works?

'Help me please, I'm a police officer,' raised only looks of mocking merriment from a band of workmen.

'Serve you right,' they shouted across at him.

'Aye, hope you rot there.'

Could this nightmare be really happening to him, or would he awake in his bed in Sheridan Place? Now for the first time, he was experiencing a new dimension of crime. How easily attacks, even murders, could be accomplished in broad daylight without exciting more than a flicker of curiosity in passers by. Curiosity that might extend to perverse amusement at the victim's plight without arousing the slightest inclination to rush forward and offer assistance.

At last, the most welcome sight in the world, a police carriage trotting briskly up Johnston Terrace from the direction of the old King's Stables Road. At his frantic waving through the railings, the uniformed passenger jumped down; it was his assistant, and constant thorn in his side, Constable, lately promoted to Sergeant, Danny McQuinn.

The sight of his superior officer seemed to fill him with ill-suppressed merriment. 'Fancy finding you here, sir. Some young ladies said you'd been in the wars and needed help? Well, well – what did you do?'

'I had a slight argument with a falling rock,' Faro snapped and thought bitterly that the girls must have enjoyed relating their story to the handsome young policeman. He could just imagine them with their giggling, their flirtatious glances. Aye, McQuinn doubtless got considerably more of their anxious attention than he had done.

'Falling rock, eh, sir?' McQuinn gazed amused at the scene above them. 'There's a lot of it about, sir. Dangerous place for climbing.'

'I wasn't climbing, dammit. What do you think I was

doing – amusing myself? I was looking for a possible murder weapon.'

McQuinn shook his head sadly. 'You should leave that sort of thing to the young constables, sir.' His accompanying smirk and sidelong glance seemed to indicate that his superior officer had one injured foot in the grave already and the good one sliding dangerously.

'Dammit, man, someone has just tried to kill me.'

Danny McQuinn's eyes widened. 'Is that a fact? I hope you're making a charge, sir.'

'Get me out of here.'

'Can you walk, sir?'

'No, I can't walk. Otherwise I wouldn't be asking for help, would I?'

'I see. Just a moment.' And McQuinn produced from the closed interior of the carriage an extending ladder, part of the routine equipment for rescuing children who locked themselves in upstairs rooms, and for reaching old ladies' cats who got themselves stranded in trees. It was also useful for saving folks who fell into the water – by accident, not intent.

With the help of the driver of the carriage and a considerable amount of painful effort on Faro's part, the two men managed to get him over the railings and hoisted inside the cab.

'Quite comfortable now, are you, sir?'

Faro forbore to reply. His gratitude for the rescue was now exceeded by feelings of humiliation and resentment of his dependence upon the hated McQuinn. At that moment he would have enjoyed nothing more than soundly boxing his ears. Fortunately for McQuinn, he needed that spare hand to support himself in the swaying carriage.

'Anything I can do for you, sir?'

'Yes, you can take me home,' snapped Faro and decided to keep the clues he had discovered to himself. He was furious, in no condition now to search the royal apartments, and if his ankle was broken, as he feared from its throbbing agony, then Vince, in his new role of qualified doctor, would doubtless immobilise him for some time.

Meanwhile a verdict of 'death by misadventure' would be recorded on the dead man whose body, if unclaimed, would go to the medical students. As for his murderer, the law would be cheated again as the trail grew dim and finally disappeared before Faro was fit to resume his investigations.

Sitting back in the carriage, with McQuinn's shrill whistling of an Irish jig adding insult to his injury, Faro realised his accident had made abundantly evident that it was an assassin he was up against. And a desperate one at that, who would attack in broad daylight – he remembered that glimpse of upraised arms against the sky, and the projectile, too well aimed to be an accident.

His search had been observed and noted by his adversary, to whom an encounter with 'falling' rock must have suggested a convenient way of disposing of this inquisitive policeman. Only the presence of what some might call a guardian angel, which was to Jeremy Faro a tangible awareness of lurking danger, had saved his life. He shuddered. But for this uncanny sixth sense, which had paid off many times in his long career, he would now be lying alongside the dead man in the city mortuary.

At last McQuinn delivered him like a large and unwieldy piece of furniture to his own front door. If Faro had thought that his injury was the worst that could happen to him, then he had not bargained for the hysterical behaviour of the four females occupying his home. At that moment he was grateful that three of them were there on a purely temporary basis.

Fuss was a part of Mrs Brook's nature that Faro was teaching her sternly to keep in check. The housekeeper was, however, totally outclassed by his mother, with whom he could do nothing at all.

He only thanked God that he had made light of the incident. He had slipped and fallen, that was all. If Mary Faro had an inkling that the 'accident' had been deliberate then he would have to endure once again the story of 'your poor dear father's' unfortunate death. The long and tortuous account of the events which had widowed his young wife and left their one child fatherless would be retold, complete with tears still remarkably fresh and ready flowing after thirty years.

Rose and Emily were speedily infected by the panic and confusion. Taking their cue from Grandmama, they rushed up and downstairs, 'helping' with basins of hot water which they contrived to spill.

The atmosphere was one of utter chaos when Vince put his key in the front door. Dealing with this chorus of lamentations at amazing speed, he removed Faro into the surgery and closed the door very sweetly but firmly on the hand-wringing female members of his family.

To Vince's enquiry, 'How did this happen?' Faro replied, 'On Castle Rock. Stepped back too smartly. Didn't realise I was so far off the ground.' So disgusted was he by the morning's farcical events, and in general with the whole business, that he grumpily resolved to keep his suspicions of an assassin to himself.

Truth to tell, he couldn't bear one more mocking, disbelieving glance. Especially from Vince, who merely nodded, removing the boot from his stepfather's bruised and rapidly swelling ankle as gently as possible. 'Well, was it worth it? Did you find any clues?'

Mollified, from his pocket Faro brought forth the clay pipe and the handkerchief with its coins.

'That doesn't tell us very much, Stepfather. Hardly worth an injured ankle.'

'But I also found this.' And savouring his triumph, Faro handed him the Queen Mary cameo.

Vince turned it over. 'Looks very old. Are those real rubies and diamonds, do you think?'

'I do. Realise what this means, lad?'

'You think the dead man dropped it. And that he'd stolen it from the royal apartments?'

'I was about to check that with Sir Eric when this

damned thing happened.' And watching Vince minutely examine the jewel, he continued, 'Tell me, do you recognise it?'

Vince shook his head. 'No. Should I?'

'Think hard, lad. You're sure you've never seen one like this before?'

'Quite sure, Stepfather. Why do you ask?'

'Because when I found it I thought that I had. That sometime I'd held a jewel exactly like this in my hands.'

Vince shook his head. 'Then it must have been long before we met.' Producing bandages from the cupboard, he said. 'By the way, I went to Kennington & Jenner's. At the crack of nine, I presented myself to Mr Banks. He was very disappointed when he learned that I wasn't wanting a tropical outfit . . . '

'The jacket – what did he say?' Faro interrupted impatiently, biting his lip at the pain as Vince gently manipulated his ankle.

'Some little success, Stepfather. The admirable Mr Banks checked the reference number in his little book and found that it was made specially for a very good customer, Sir James Piperlee – his place is near Glencorse.'

'Well done, lad. When do we go? Ouch!'

'Sorry, Stepfather, I'm being as gentle as I can.'

'Broken, is it?'

Vince laughed. 'Of course not. Bad sprain, that's all. You'll be right as rain in a couple of weeks. But you're to keep off it until then. Rest's the only cure.'

'Rest? And what about Sir James Piperlee?'

'Oh, I dare say he'll still be around.'

'We're wasting valuable time, lad.'

Vince went on with his bandaging. 'Nature has laid down through the ages her own rules regarding healing flesh – and that includes broken bones and sprained ankles. She has her own timetable for everything. There are no exceptions and she can't be hurried. So, like other mortals, Stepfather, you must learn to bear it all patiently as possible . . . '

'Look, you've said it was just a sprain,' Faro interrupted irritably. 'A sprain's nothing serious, but this is bloody painful. Are you sure you've got it right?'

Vince sat back on his heels and regarded his stepfather candidly. A moment later he went again to the cupboard and returned with the brandy bottle.

'Just exactly what I need,' said Faro with a sigh.

'Yes, and in this instance purely medicinal, so don't enjoy it too much. You're fairly shaken, aren't you?' And as Faro handed him back the empty glass, 'I suspect that you're not telling me everything. You're not usually careless, or prone to step off rocks without first looking right and left very cautiously. So how about telling me exactly what happened, and how you came by this? The truth now – did you fall – or were you pushed?'

'A rock was hurled down at me. I stepped aside – and fell. Someone tried to kill me, lad.'

While Faro filled in the details, Vince completed his bandaging in silence.

'That's it, then. As far as I can go, Stepfather. The rest is up to you.'

Thanking him, Faro tried to stand up. When he swore, Vince grinned.

'Don't take it out on me, Stepfather.'

'It's damnably sore.'

'Give it time.'

'Time! And don't you go round blabbing what I've told you to them,' said Faro with a fierce nod towards the closed door.

'You must think I'm a fool. Two ladies with the vapours and two hysterical little girls. Life, for us mere men, would hardly be worth living. Anyway, you should be jolly thankful that it wasn't your neck. I expect that was the intention – a more fatal area, I assure you, that doesn't respond to healing with time.'

'Hold on, this bandage – it is too bloody tight.'

'Tight is what it has to be, if it's to get better, so do stop complaining, there's a good fellow.'

33

Faro seized his boot, and watched by Vince finally gave up the unequal struggle to get it fastened.

'How am I expected to do anything if I can't get a boot on and I can't walk?'

Vince grinned. 'The answer is simple. You don't even try.'

'God dammit.'

'Precisely – and all criminals too. You'll have to let them rest for a while.'

'Damnation – are you certain about this ankle?'

'Oh indeed I am, Stepfather. Allow me to know a badly sprained limb when I see one. And if you want a second opinion I can get Dr Kellar to look at it. As Police Surgeon, he's more used to handling the dead than the living, of course, so don't expect him to be as gentle as I am.'

Seeing Vince's offended expression, Faro patted his arm. 'Sorry, lad, but it is a cursed nuisance, you must admit.'

'I dare say you'll get quite adept at hopping up and downstairs,' said Vince with a cheerful grin. 'A sprightly man like you.'

Faro gave him a sharp glance. 'Thank you for not reminding me I'll soon be forty – at the moment, McQuinn's favourite taunt.'

'Really, Stepfather. You're getting as sensitive as a dowager about your age. Forget it. Probably McQuinn envies you that abundant head of hair – as I do. I reckon I'll get half an inch more face to wash with every passing year,' said Vince with a rueful glance in the mirror. 'Besides, you've got good bones, a fine strong Viking face, a splendid figure and an excellent constitution – barring regrettable accidents like typhoid and sprained ankles, which can happen to anyone. You're really wearing very well,' he added sternly. 'And you don't need my assurances that you don't look your age.'

'As a matter of fact, you're the second person to tell me so in the past twenty-four hours,' said Faro smugly.

'Good.'

To continue was irresistible. 'Yes, indeed. The first was a very pretty young lady – not much more than "sweet and twenty".'

His stepson's weakness for any female young and pretty was immediately kindled and at the end of Faro's story of his meeting with Lucille Haston, Vince stressed how anxious he was to help. His fervent offer of assistance, by taking his injured stepfather's place on a personally conducted tour of the royal apartments, was too eager not to be also quite transparent.

'Sounds like a splendid idea, lad, if you can manage my mother, Rose and Emily too,' said Faro carelessly. Seeing Vince's doubtful look, he added, 'I'd really be grateful. As you know, they're longing to visit the Castle and I honestly haven't the least idea about entertaining little lasses.'

This admission put Vince on his mettle. 'Really, Stepfather, where the family is concerned, you certainly don't appear to exercise that famous logic of yours.'

'And what do you mean by that?' asked Faro indignantly.

'Why, they leave clues everywhere about what they like. All very easy to follow. Even I, who am no detective, can interpret the desires of little girls to perfection. Mind you,' he added with a rueful grin, 'I'm not always quite so astute where their older sisters are concerned.'

In the days that followed, Faro discovered the advantages of being a temporary invalid. With injured ankle resting on a stool, he was the centre of attention. The entire household pivoted around him, making him once again conscious of all that he had lost of the joys of parenthood. He also recognised that this unexpected and enforced inactivity was a small blessing in disguise. Miraculously, it had drawn him closer to his little daughters than he had been since their mother died.

And even when Lizzie was alive, how uncomplaining she had been of his constant neglect, his shortcomings as husband and father. How humbly she accepted his dedication to the Edinburgh City Police and all that being a detective entailed. His duty was never to be questioned, and must come always ahead of wife and family.

It was not until he heard his mother in his study upstairs, a shrill note of protest in her voice as she talked to Mrs Brook, that the spell of domestic harmony was broken at last.

Chapter Four

Stirred into action and spurred on by indignation, Faro found that he was now able to hop upstairs quite rapidly.

His study, that holy of holies, was in mortal danger. Hadn't Mrs Brook warned his mother that it was sacrosanct? That no woman was ever permitted, without his consent and supervision, to cross its threshold armed with broom, duster and intention to make clean and tidy the desk with its heaps of papers and documents, the piled up volumes on the floor. To the casual eye the sight was chaotic, but Faro knew the precise location of everything, and exactly where to lay hands on that vital information he was seeking.

Breathlessly reaching the landing, he was met by the indignant and reproachful face of his diminutive mother. With her rosy cheeks, her sharp black eyes and hair untouched by grey, she looked for all the world like an angry robin prepared to defend her territory.

Before he could open his voice to protest, she shook her fist at him defiantly.

'Jeremy Faro, you should be ashamed of yourself.' And pointing to the open study door, 'To think that a son of mine should live like this. Such a rat's nest in there as I never saw in my whole life.' And turning to Mrs Brook, who looked extremely uncomfortable and embarrassed at having to witness her illustrious employer's chastisement, Mrs Faro added sternly, 'It wasn't the way he was brought up by me. Oh dear no. I just don't know where to begin . . . '

'I don't expect you to begin – anywhere, Mother,' Faro interrupted coldly. When she looked as if the ready tears were about to overflow, he added hastily, 'You're here on holiday, remember.'

'Holiday or not, rooms have to be kept clean and tidy. Do you think I can rest easily downstairs now that I've actually seen spiders cavorting – over there – in the corners? And I shouldn't be surprised if there's worse than spiders,' she said with a shudder.

'And what's wrong with spiders, I should like to know? Remember Robert the Bruce.'

'Now don't you give me your clever talk, son. Mrs Brook will bring up her feather duster and we will set to work immediately.'

As the housekeeper gratefully disappeared downstairs, Mrs Faro marched into the study and tried in vain to reach the high shelf. 'And now if you'll just push across that footstool, I'll get down your poor dear Papa's hamper.'

'I'll do that, Mother.'

'Very well.' And dusting her fingers she added accusingly, 'From the grime on it, I don't suppose you've even looked inside since I sent it down from Orkney.'

'I haven't had time, Mother. I've been rather busy this summer.'

'Then you should have made time. First things first, that's what we've always said in our family. And your poor dear father, he would have wanted you to show a little interest in his work, and respect for his memory. Especially when you took after him so greatly and went to be a policeman.'

Once again, Faro was torn between guilt and irritation at his mother's reproaches on the subject of his 'poor dear father'. Constable Magnus Faro had been thus immortalised by his devoted widow, ever since the day he met his death making his way homeward at the end of a night's duty with the Edinburgh City Police.

Being run over and fatally injured at night on Edinburgh's

steep, cobbled High Street made treacherous by rain and fog was not unknown in the annals of the city. But according to Mary Faro, her husband's death was no accident. She insisted that it was deliberate murder, although no one would listen or give credence to her wild accusations, and her indignation burned undimmed by the passing of more than thirty years for that death unavenged.

Jeremy had been nearly five. And looking back, he realised that his mother's hero worship of her dead husband, those epic tales of his marvellous exploits, had filled their son's earliest days with only a burning desire to leave Orkney. For as long as he could remember Jeremy Faro's one unswerving ambition had been to go to the mainland and follow in the footsteps of his illustrious father.

When at eighteen he left, Mary saw glumly that her enthusiasm for her late husband had badly misfired and life in the Edinburgh City Police was not what she had ever imagined or intended for her only son. More than anything else, she had wanted to keep him near her, to see him settled down on a croft like his forebears. They had been farmers since the sixteenth century, when a Royal Stuart bastard had given a piece of land to the female Sinclair he had already bestowed twins upon.

'Have you never even been curious to read all those notebooks your dear father kept?' asked Mary Faro. 'Every one of his cases, he would sit up writing half the night. "Getting the facts straight", he called it,' she added proudly.

Jeremy didn't answer as he considered how best to transfer the hamper into some prominent position that would placate her. He had no wish to stress his neglect by confessing that he wasn't much of a reader of police reports. He'd seen and participated in too many in his twenty years as a policeman and, as far as he was concerned, they made very dry reading for an off-duty hour.

Inspector Faro preferred his crime to be of the fictional variety, in the swashbuckling adventures of Sir Walter

Scott's novels, the marvellous mysteries of Charles Dickens. Especially the latter, based on fact and a criminal element in London which had its counterpart in Edinburgh too. The intimate knowledge Mr Dickens displayed showed how well he understood crime and the courts of justice. How Jeremy admired and envied his talent to write such highly readable and entertaining novels where – unlike real crime or anything resembling life itself – virtue was always triumphant, with all the mysteries solved and all the loose ends tied together in a most satisfying way on the very last page.

Jeremy's deepest regret was that he was still a child in Orkney when Mr Dickens was given the freedom of Edinburgh in 1841. How wonderful to have heard the great writer reading from his own works and how infinitely sad, like losing a friend, to read of his recent death.

As he eased the hamper from its lofty perch, his mother hovered anxiously. 'Are you sure you can manage? It can wait until Vince gets home,' she added helpfully.

Vince might not arrive until evening and the thought of being gently nagged on the subject of spiders and general untidiness set Jeremy's teeth on edge. Better to keep her quiet with her feather dusters.

'Of course I can manage. It isn't all that heavy. Just a lot of papers,' he said cheerfully. However, he had reckoned without the footstool that lurked behind him. Stepping backwards, he staggered against it, lost his balance and both he and the hamper landed heavily in a painful collision with the nearby sofa.

'Oh your poor leg,' said his mother. 'I hope you haven't made it worse.'

Faro, wincing with renewed pain, made light of the subject, grateful that her first thoughts had been for him, since the hamper had been even less fortunate in its encounter with the sofa's wooden back.

'Oh dear, oh dear, just look at that now,' said Mrs Faro, transferring her attention to its broken lid. Hanging forlornly by one hinge, it had burst open, spewing papers everywhere over the well-polished floor. 'No, son, you stay where you are, I'll get them.'

Jeremy sank down thankfully on to the sofa as the noise brought Rose and Emily on to the scene. They added their lamentations, their offers to bring Papa a glass of water, while Jeremy rubbed the sore skin of his injured ankle. Weakly he suggested that they would be better employed assisting their Grandmama, down on her hands and knees, retrieving the hamper's contents and considerably hindered by the playful Rusty, who regarded anyone on the floor as fair game.

Soon all three were reverently gathering together the yellowing notes that had burst out of covers, and papers tied with tape. A new sound was added, his mother's barely suppressed sniffs, as if it had been only yesterday that she had laid her dearest Magnus in his grave.

As she retied the bundles and kissed each one, Jeremy watched in amazement, and some envy, that any love could be sustained so long or so deeply.

Rose and Emily, kneeling beside her, exchanged helpless glances with their father over her head. At a nod from him, rightly interpreted, they saw immediately what was needed. They hugged and kissed and petted their grandmother, while she dabbed at her eyes and called them her 'wee darlings' and apologised for being so weak.

At last all the documents were tidily restored to the hamper, the girls bringing additional contributions which had slithered over the polished floor and had vanished, with Rusty in hot pursuit, under the less accessible pieces of furniture.

Before closing the damaged lid, Mrs Faro withdrew one packet. 'If you ever feel inclined to read any of your dear father's cases, I urge you to look at this one. His very last, the one he was working on when he was murdered.' And touching the faded ribbon tenderly, 'I tied these papers together myself on the day he was

41

buried,' she said sadly, 'with the bow from my wedding bouquet.'

Jeremy glanced at his father's neat handwriting.

'"The Mysterious Corpse of a Baby Discovered in the Wall of Edinburgh Castle. 1837",' he read. 'Sounds intriguing.'

Mrs Faro nodded. 'Yes, it does and I curse the day he ever became involved in it. Mark my words, son, I would not have been a widow all these lonely years, had he left well alone.' With a sigh she added, 'I still remember as if it were yesterday, just a few weeks after our dear Queen came to the throne it was, he came home so excited about some secret he thought he'd discovered. What it was we'll never know now.'

Two hours later it was a vastly improved study that Faro entered, cleaned and tidied with a gratifying lack of any disturbance to his papers and books. His mother, on whom he had lavished abundant praise, was now taking a well-earned afternoon rest and the house was silent but for the poignant song of a blackbird in the garden mingled with his daughters' faint laughter downstairs.

Faro sighed. He was rarely at home at this hour of the day and there was undoubtedly a most agreeable sense of repose and wellbeing in the domestic sounds of a summer afternoon. His investigations into the death of an unknown man lying in the city mortuary seemed remote and unimportant, along with his own monstrous suspicions that only days ago he had been the victim of a murderous attack.

Afternoons like this, tranquil with sunshine, resplendent with birdsong, convinced a man of his own immortality. Small wonder the general populace of a respectable Edinburgh preferred to believe that crime and sudden death were none of their business, and he could find it in his heart to forgive their indifference to his plight on Castle Rock.

He wondered how Vince had fared in his mission to

the Castle. He had promised, if Dr Kellar released him in time, to take the cameo to Sir Eric and have its theft from the glass cases in the royal apartments confirmed. For once, Faro was quite happy to leave the routine investigation in his stepson's capable hands and decided that he might well profit from this unexpected break in his busy life by reading up his father's last case.

The connection with Edinburgh Castle intrigued him and a casual skimming of the notes, left incomplete at Constable Magnus Faro's death, revealed that a tiny coffin containing the remains of a child had been found by workmen, entombed in the wall of the royal apartments.

How had it got there and why? Here was a mystery worthy of Sir Walter Scott himself, thought Jeremy, but hardly the reason for foul play outside the imaginative realms of fiction. Even if his father's accident had been deliberate, and he had always been rather doubtful about that, it was hard enough solving crimes that happened last week or last month. There was no possible way of solving a thirty-three-year-old mystery.

Faro came back to the present to the sound of voices upraised. Of shrill screams – issuing forth from the same region where only a short time ago had drifted his daughters' delighted laughter.

His peace broken, resentfully he opened the study door.

'Girls – Emily, Rose –' his mother's voice was added to the noise. 'Stop it at once. Stop. Jeremy – Jeremy, come and do something about your children.'

Reluctantly emerging, he saw his mother's angry and flustered countenance.

Clutching the banister, he limped downstairs. 'What's all this about, Mother? Can't you deal with it?'

'No. They need a father's discipline.'

Pushing open the door, he saw Rose and Emily rolling on the floor, fighting, clawing, screaming. Faro groaned inwardly. His little girls, happy and laughing, were angelic. Quarrelling had made them into ugly little monsters, charging his serene and comfortable bachelor existence, his retreat from the world of sordid crime and violence, with exactly the sort of unpleasant domestic situation he most dreaded.

'Rose – Emily – please . . . ' His command went quite unheeded. Even to his own ears, it sounded most ineffectual.

'I'm the princess and you're my wicked stepmother.'

'I'm not. I'm not.'

'You are.'

'I'm older than you – and I get to wear it.'

'Oh no you don't. I want it. I found it.'

'You promised turns.'

'You've had your turn, now I want it back. It's mine.'

'It is not.'

'It is.'

'You wicked liar. I found it on the floor.'

'I hate you. You're cruel and horrid.'

'I would cut off your head if I had half a chance.'

'You little beast – beast . . . '

As the two fell upon each other with renewed frenzy, Jeremy entered the fray and separated them with difficulty, trying desperately to keep his injured leg away from flailing arms and legs as they tried to kick each other.

'Girls – girls! Stop this at once. Are they often like this?' he asked his mother desperately. 'You told me they never quarrelled.'

'They don't. I can't understand it. Something must have upset them,' she said, clutching Emily while Jeremy seized the opportunity to hold Rose in a firm grip.

Red faced, tear stained, the two girls stared mutinously at each other.

'Now, behave and say you're sorry to your sister, Rose.'

'Shan't!'

'Oh yes you will, if you want any supper tonight.'

'Don't want any.'

'Very well. You will stay in your room – no Arthur's Seat with Vince tomorrow.'

44

'And no Edinburgh Castle either,' Mrs Faro added for good effect.

The two girls looked thoughtful and distinctly mollified at this punishment.

Then Rose shook her head defiantly. 'All right, I'll behave, if that's what you want, Papa.'

'I do indeed. And you can begin by saying you're sorry to your sister. Ouch – what was that? What have you got in your hand?'

Rose immediately put her hand behind her back.

'Let me see. Come now . . . '

'It's a brooch. I found it.'

'No, she didn't, Papa. I found it,' yelled Emily.

'Never mind who found it. Give it to me – at once.'

And Rose placed in her father's hand a familiar cameo, the Queen Mary jewel which should, at that very moment, have been with Vince on its way to Edinburgh Castle.

'You stole this from your stepbrother, didn't you?' Rose trembled at her father's angry expression. 'Didn't you, you wicked child?'

'I did not,' was her brave reply.

'Oh yes, you did. Rose – and Emily – I am ashamed of you.'

'So that's what you were quarrelling about,' said Mrs Faro. 'You naughty, naughty children. Your Papa has you here for a holiday and you repay him by stealing things.'

'We didn't steal anything, Papa. We – or rather I – found it on the floor, under the table in your study. Rusty was playing with it . . . '

'What a dreadful lie. Really, Emily.'

'It isn't a lie.'

'It's true, Papa,' said Emily, now staunchly coming to her sister's defence. 'It was after we helped gather up the papers . . . '

'And there's no use protecting one another now. It's too late for that,' said Mrs Faro. 'I'd never have believed the two of you were capable of such wickedness.'

'But we didn't do anything wrong . . . '

'Honestly, Grandma . . . '

'Let me see that, will you, Jeremy? Oh dear, oh dear.' Mary held it in her hand, and then with a shudder, she handed it back.

'You've seen it before, Mother?' Jeremy looked again. At first glance identical to the cameo he had found on Castle Rock, there was a difference. The tiny miniature in its centre was not of a man, but of a woman in sixteenth-century dress.

'Aye, I've seen it before, lad,' said his mother. 'Your poor dear father came across it during his last case. When he was killed. It might even be the reason why he was killed. I never wanted to see it again. That's why I put it in the hamper with that letter.'

'What letter, Mother?'

'From some antique dealer he knew – an old man in the High Street.'

'What did it say?' asked Faro eagerly.

'Oh, I don't know. I can't remember. All I know is it was too late to save my poor love,' she added with a sniff. 'There was a curse on it – and there still is. Look how it turned our two darlings into wee devils, tearing at each other's throats,' she ended dramatically.

'This is the envelope that it fell out of, Papa,' said Rose, taking a crumpled packet out of her pinafore pocket. 'You see, Papa, we weren't lying,' she added triumphantly, taking Emily's hand.

'And we didn't steal anything from anyone, did we, Rose?'

'Rusty found it under the desk.'

'It was so pretty we only wanted to play with it while Grandma was resting and you were busy in your study.'

From the envelope Jeremy withdrew the antique dealer's letter.

Dear Magnus: This is undoubtedly an interchange-able piece of jewellery particularly popular in the

46

sixteenth century in the Court circles, when the monarch would give one part to a particular favourite as a love token, bearing his or her likeness. Also among wealth noble families, for sentimental reasons, parts were exchanged between lovers and parents/children. There are usually two or more pieces which can be worn separaͺͺly or together as a pendant. In my opinion, this work dates from the mid-1500s and as the miniature is undoubtedly of Queen Mary may indeed have originated from her collection of jewels.

Incidentally, the rubies and diamonds are authentic, making this a very valuable piece. I am intrigued to know more of its history. When next we meet you must tell me how you came by it – I am, Your obedient servant, Chas. Pilter.

There had been no next meeting. The letter was dated 3 August 1837, the day after Magnus Faro died. The address, 'Fayre's Wynd, High Street', and presumably Mr Pilter had both vanished a generation ago.

'That lady in the little painting, Papa. I've been thinking,' said Rose, looking over his shoulder, 'isn't she like the drawing we have at home of Queen Mary?'

Jeremy looked at his daughter approvingly. Rose might be only a child, but he was pleased to note that already she showed signs of having inherited his keen powers of observation.

Queen Mary. And the matching cameo, he was certain, would prove to be a portrait of her consort, Lord Darnley, to be worn together or separately as the antique dealer had said.

'Well done, Rose,' he murmured approvingly.

'Am I right, Papa?' she beamed at him.

Hugging her to his side, he asked his mother, 'Didn't you know this might be valuable?'

Mrs Faro shuddered. 'All I knew was that it brought bad luck. It had taken your poor dear father. I never wanted to see it again.'

47

And listening to her, Jeremy Faro heard another echo from the past and knew why the jewel he had found on Castle Rock had been so tantalisingly familiar. Memory clicked into place and presented a small boy whose curiosity had led him to the mysterious hamper so revered by his mother. Caught with the forbidden cameo in his hand, he was scolded severely. He remembered her anger clearly, her tears and his desolation, his fears of God's wrath for naughty children.

What did it all mean? Where was the vital link? For the facts remained. The two pieces had indeed brought a trail of destruction. His own father, Constable Magnus Faro, had died. More than thirty years later a mystery man had also died. And, but for the grace of God, Jeremy Faro himself would have been the third victim.

His mother called it cursed. That label was too easy for Faro, who was not a superstitious man. His logical mind refused to accept the existence of curses. If they existed, then he believed they were brought about by man alone, by his folly and greed, which had a habit of rebounding upon him.

He could hardly wait for Vince's return, but with his daughters forgiven, kissed and cuddled and rewarded with goodies from Mrs Brook's inexhaustible supply, Faro decided to read carefully his father's notes.

Somewhat cynically, remembering how he had found clues and the cameo overlooked by the police searchers on Castle Rock, he decided that tomorrow, with Vince's aid and a walking stick, he was now fit enough to go out to the Piperlees estate. To interview the laird, Sir James, on the subject of the dead man's jacket.

And then he would go up to the Castle and take a careful look around the royal apartments. Trust no one, not even your own first observations. Check and double check, was a motto that had served him well in the past.

But as he climbed the stairs to his study, although

the sun shone brilliantly, he shivered as if a cloak of ice had been thrown around him. He knew the feeling well. It was his demon, his own personal premonition of disaster.

Chapter Five

In his study, his door closed with the warning that he was not to be disturbed, Faro began to read his father's notes.

'The Mysterious Corpse of a Baby Discovered in the Wall of Edinburgh Castle. 1837.'

Constable Magnus Faro had been thorough. In his neat, precise handwriting, 'Copied from the *Scotsman*, 11 August 1830,' Jeremy read:

Sensational Historic Discovery

Two workmen, engaged on renovating the royal apartments at Edinburgh Castle after a fire, have made the gruesome discovery of a tiny coffin. Nearly in line with the Crown Room and about six feet from the pavement to the quadrangle, the wall was observed to return a hollow sound when struck.

On removing a block of stone, a recess was discovered measuring about 2 feet 6 by 1 foot, containing the remains of a child enclosed in an oak coffin, evidently of great antiquity and very much decayed. Wrapped in a shroud, a cloth believed to be woollen, very thick and somewhat resembling leather, and within this the remains of a shroud of a richly embroidered silk and cloth of gold which suggested some portion of a priest's vestment, most likely used in the Masses secretly held in Queen Mary's oratory.

Such a sanctified garment would be approved as suitable for the interment of one of royal blood, a little prince, born and baptised in the Popish faith, rather than for the hasty disposal of some Court lady's indiscretion. Further evidence being two initials wrought upon the shroud, one alas, was indecipherable, but the other, the letter 'J', was distinctly visible.

From the coffin's concealment in the wall, secrecy of the closest character was evidently the object, and being wainscoted thereafter, no trace remained.

By order of the Castle officials the remains were restored to the coffin and the aperture closed up.

Attached was a further newspaper cutting, dated 12 July 1837.

Egyptian-Style Curse in Edinburgh Castle.
Two workmen, Matthew O'Hara and John Femister, died tragically when the high scaffolding on the battlements of Edinburgh Castle collapsed under them. A third man, Peter Dowie, suffered serious injuries. All three had been engaged for renovation work on the inside of the royal apartments and when the old panelling was removed in line with the Court room and near the quadrangle, the workmen's attention was drawn to a loose stone just above their heads. Further investigation revealed the presence of a child's coffin which had been interred behind the wainscoting a short distance from the bedchamber where, on 19 June 1566, Queen Mary gave birth to the future King James VI (and I of England), the only issue of her marriage to Lord Darnley.

Following upon the recent suicide of Colonel Theodore Lazenby, the officer in charge of Castle renovations, the accidental deaths of the two workmen irresistibly raise the question in the minds of gullible and superstitious persons, as to whether these unfortunate happenings were mere coincidence, or the fulfilment of an Egyptian-style curse for disturbing the dead?

It is now almost seven years (August 1830) since

the original discovery was made. Then as now misfortune and death struck the unhappy individuals who disturbed the oak coffin containing an infant's mummified remains. Reverently reinterred, this gruesome mystery from Queen Mary's tragic reign has lain undisturbed until last week when repairs and renovations were ordered to make all in good order and readiness for Her Majesty Queen Victoria's first visit to her Scottish kingdom since she ascended to the throne last month.

Concerning the deceased. A full obituary of Colonel Lazenby, a distinguished officer and gentleman who was recently married, is to be found on page 2. Of the two workmen who died, Mr John Femister, aged 35, from Leith, is a widower with one daughter. O'Hara, aged about 23, an itinerant labourer, is believed to hail from Ireland, as is Dowie who sustained serious head and back injuries and has been admitted to the Infirmary.

Attached to the newspaper account was Colonel Lazenby's obituary, a glowing tribute to his service at home and abroad in India and Canada. Magnus Faro had underlined heavily that he was the only son of Lord and Lady Phineas Lazenby, Aberdale, East Lothian.

Magnus Faro's report followed. Of how he had been on duty in the High Street when the scaffolding collapsed. He had raced to the scene, where he had found two men already dead and one so critically injured as to be near death. His account continued:

My attempts to investigate the accident further were impeded by Colonel Lazenby and other army officials who refused to allow me to proceed, in the interests of my own safety, and insisted that I inform the Central Office immediately and return with other constables to assist me. By the time I returned, half an hour later, the debris was in the final stages of being carted away and the dead men were on their way to the mortuary. I realised, of course, that any evidence, of negligence or of unsafe timber and ropes, if such existed, had also been lost.

The report went on:

Later:

I am very sceptical about Egyptian-style curses. The two men who died in 1830 were drowned, washed ashore at Granton. It was thought they had purloined a boat which capsized. Their names were Connor and Doyle, 'believed to be from Ireland' (like most itinerant labourers, poor starving wretches who arrive in droves from Ireland and the Highlands). Christian names would have been a help for further investigation, but employers of casual labour are frequently careless about such details.

Notes:

Tomorrow I intend to see Dowie (if he is still alive and capable of speech) then proceed to Leith and talk to Femister's relatives.

On another sheet of paper, hastily scrawled:

Tried to see Dowie, but he is far gone.
    Was the cameo buried in the child's coffin?

Jeremy felt the surge of excitement. He had been right. The jewelled cameos were connected with the royal apartments –

If so, is it one of a hoard [Magnus Faro's account continued], hidden for safe keeping? Could buried treasure be the reason for the earlier 'accidents', and is this a case of murder? Was the drowning of Connor and Doyle also murder? There is something

53

very suspicious about that 'purloined' boat.

Have talked to Dowie. Have learned enough to be warned that I must go carefully now.

Went to see Dowie again, but was turned away. Perhaps he is already dead. These devils will have no mercy and I must protect my dear Mary and the boy.

There could be danger.

The last words were heavily underscored. Faro turned the page, but there were no more entries. Again he read that last entry. It was dated 1 August 1837.

Two days after his interview with Dowie, Constable Faro had met his death. Returning from duty in the early hours of the morning, crossing the High Street, a runaway cab had hurtled towards him, and trying to seize the horses he had been trampled to death.

The cab was never traced and the inquest recorded 'death by misadventure', with Mary Faro protesting that the verdict should be 'murder by person or persons unknown' and that her husband had been killed by someone with a grudge against him. What better reason, thought Jeremy sadly, re-reading his father's last heavily underscored words, '*There could be danger.*' What had Dowie warned him of in his dying breath that threatened Constable Faro and his entire family? As he put the notes together, he heard the clock in the hall chime four. The Police Surgeon might not release Vince for several hours.

Faro sighed. He did not count patience among his few remaining virtues and sending Mrs Brook out to summon a gig, armed with walking stick and supported on a wave of enthusiasm and excitement, he decided to begin his investigations with a visit to the royal apartments of Edinburgh Castle.

The effect of reading his father's casebook as well as the attempt on his own life on Castle Road made Faro more than usually watchful. His sixth sense warned that

54

his home was being watched and as he awaited the arrival of the gig at the dining-room window, was it coincidence that a strange man, his face well concealed by a high collar, was apparently searching for a house number? On the rare occasions when Faro rode out with Vince, he felt uneasily that they were being followed at a discreet distance by a small carriage with blinds drawn.

He patted his greatcoat pocket containing Queen Mary's jewel. If this formed part of a treasure hoard long concealed in the walls of Edinburgh Castle, he might be dealing with desperate men anxious to get their hands on it. The presence in 9 Sheridan Place of his mother and daughters gave him added cause for anxiety. How to warn them without causing unnecessary distress? He shook his head. A tricky situation which would need urgent but careful handling.

There was only one method, a method which although hazardous had paid off in the past. Lay the bait, draw the enemy fire. As a carriage swung into the street and he limped towards the front gate, it was no shadowy watcher who erupted before his startled gaze, but the substantial shape of Constable Gregg, who, saluting smartly, indicated the vehicle.

'Superintendent Mackintosh's compliments, Inspector, and will you be so good as to present yourself at his office immediately? The Superintendent knows about you being lame at the moment, but I am to assure you that you would not be troubled unless it was a matter of the utmost urgency.'

At the Central Office, he found Superintendent Mackintosh in a less than understanding mood and dismissive of his Senior Detective Inspector's injury. His scornful manner declared more than any words that this had been caused by incompetence combined with a reckless disregard for personal safety.

'Clambering about rocks, Faro. You should leave that sort of thing to the constables. That's what we employ them for.'

Useless to murmur that they didn't always use their imagination when looking for clues.

'Imagination? What has that to do with it? We don't keep them to use their imaginations. Evidence based on solid fact and logic, that's all we pay for, all we get and indeed, all we have a right to expect,' he added self-righteously.

'Is that what you wanted to tell me, Superintendent?' asked Faro heavily.

Mackintosh made an impatient gesture. 'Of course not. Jock Clavers has been seen, in the neighbourhood of Glencorse. We have information that he has gone to earth, winged by one of the gamekeepers during the last robbery. Anyway, our informer tells us he is hiding in the folly on Lord Wylie's estate.'

'When did you hear this?'

'Just before we sent for you.'

Faro wondered who had clyped and why. If it had been one of his regulars then the Superintendent would have told him.

'It won't be dark until ten o'clock,' he continued, 'so this is an opportunity not to be missed. Clavers's daughter worked there as servant lass. Bearing in mind that his lairdship is a sheriff, I thought he might appreciate having the arrest made by someone in authority, rather than a bevy of police constables descending on him. Just in case the report is false. Don't you agree?'

At any other time, Faro would have been delighted to know that the elusive Clavers had been run to earth. Safely behind bars, the baffling six months of unsolved robberies would be at an end. All were from stately homes and bore the Clavers gang's unmistakable imprint. Jewellery, ornaments, plate, pictures and other valuable items worth several thousand pounds had been taken, and the irate owners were increasingly annoyed by the Police Force's singular lack of success in tracing the thieves and restoring their property.

'I don't need to tell you that this would be a feather in your cap, Faro, if you could nab Clavers. He's damned clever, but he's bound to make a mistake sooner or later.'

'Who is your informer?'

Mackintosh shook his head. 'The fewer who know this person's identity the better, Faro. That was part of the bargain. We've been trying to get Clavers for a long time now and all you need to know is that our informant is very much in our debt and anxious to prove reliable. Take some lads in readiness. I don't need to tell you to spread them around discreetly in case he makes a bolt for it.'

'Any word on the Edinburgh Castle break-in yet?'

'No. And I rather fancy there won't be any either. Clear as daylight that this is a case of death by misadventure. Man was climbing where he had no business to be in the first place.'

'Is there anything in the missing persons file that would identify him?'

The Superintendent sighed. 'That's the first place we looked, Faro. We've made the routine enquiries, had a couple with missing fathers, half a dozen absconding husbands, but none of them identified the corpse.' He chuckled grimly. 'Most of the wives we saw were very put out and distressed, I might tell you, that the dead man wasn't the absconded husband. Bitterly disappointed they were. You should have heard the reproaches from a couple of them, as if we had lured them to the Office on false pretences, with a guarantee of widow's weeds and the chance they had been waiting for, to enjoy the insurance.'

Picking up some papers on his desk in an attitude of dismissal, Mackintosh said, 'We'll give the corpse another week to enjoy the mortuary's cold hospitality and then we'll have him tidied away and the case closed.'

'Tidied away' was the Superintendent's delicate way of saying that the unclaimed body would be given to the Medical College for dissection.

'And if someone claims him?'

'I would imagine they'd want him underground as soon as possible. They don't keep well in this weather. Nor do

I imagine they'll want to be involved in any scandal about what he might have been doing on Castle Rock. Elderly relatives can be embarrassing, they get odd ideas.'

And as Faro rose from the chair with some effort, Mackintosh added, 'McQuinn was just going off duty. I asked him to stay. You won't be much use if it comes to a chase and he's a good man to have along with you if Clavers turns nasty or makes a bolt for it.'

Remembering that Glencorse bordered Piperlees, Faro collected the dead man's jacket and ordered a police carriage. While waiting, Faro stood at the window of his room and considered the Queen Mary cameo now reposing in his pocket in a new light.

Could it have any connection with Clavers's robberies? Had they been planning a grand *coup* on the royal apartments, and was the unknown man a member of the gang?

No. Much as the tidiness of the theory appealed to him, Faro decided that this was a case of imagination and wishful thinking gaining precedence over common sense. Years of experience had lent him an ability to recognise instantly the habitual criminal and house-breaker. Whatever had led to that clumsy attempt on the Castle Rock, the dead man's age and air of genteel poverty did not fit the pattern of Clavers's highly organised and successful gang, most of whom were under thirty-five and extremely agile.

There was only one way to make certain. Make a drawing of the jewel he had found and have the police show it at each of the houses where the robberies had taken place.

No mean draughtsman, Faro was quite pleased with his effort when a short time afterwards he emerged from his office to find McQuinn waiting impatiently.

Half an hour later, the carriage turned into the leafy drive of Lord Wylie's estate, admirably situated for concealment of the police reinforcements.

With McQuinn unhampered by a walking stick in the lead, Faro cautiously approached the folly, using the natural screen of vegetation to give as much cover as possible.

McQuinn leaped up the steps and at his touch the door flew open without the least effort. Even before he could issue his stern warning, Faro knew that they were too late.

Clavers had eluded the net once again.

With a raging, frustrated McQuinn cursing at his side, he limped back along the drive. The sustained effort of walking quickly was still painful and he was glad to take a seat in the waiting carriage.

'Seeing we have come this far,' he told McQuinn, 'we might as well continue to Piperlees and try to find out something about the jacket here while there's still light.'

A look of annoyance crossed McQuinn's face. He knew he could not refuse this extra duty much as it irked and inconvenienced him. 'I was wondering about that. Could it possibly be one of yours, I thought. A bit shabby for a Detective Inspector.' He laughed. 'But men who are getting on seem to prefer old clothes, more comfortable, they tell me . . . '

Another splendid chance of indicating that his superior was old and decrepit, thought Faro, biting back his anger and resolving to cheat McQuinn of the satisfaction of seeing him rise to the bait.

Truth to be told, Faro would have vastly preferred to have Vince with him at Piperlees, but when they were so near it seemed an opportunity not to be missed. Especially with a police carriage at their disposal, for it would be a dismal and wearying journey on his own from Edinburgh and back again in his present crippled condition.

Turning into the drive of Piperlees, Faro decided that his mission would appear more casual if he visited Sir James alone. The presence of the police could be intimidating. An almost unfailing reaction which Faro had witnessed with carefully suppressed amusement through the years. How even the most respectable and innocent of citizens were prone to display feelings of resentment, reticence and, at the pricking of uneasy conscience, even unaccountable guilt at the presence in their house of a uniformed sergeant or constable.

As the drive swept round towards the handsome mansion, lights blazed from the windows and the presence of several carriages with waiting coachmen indicated that Sir James had guests.

'Looks like a party,' said McQuinn.

Faro ignored the obvious. 'One more carriage won't matter then.'

With instructions to McQuinn to wait, he limped up to the front door, which was opened with alacrity by a manservant.

'Is Sir James at home? Detective Inspector Faro.'

The servant was unimpressed. 'What is your business?'

Faro thought hard. He could hardly present Sir James with one of his discarded jackets in the middle of dinner.

'It won't take long, just a routine enquiry.'

'Then you had better enquire again tomorrow and perhaps Sir James will see you then.'

The servant stood firm, ready to close the door. Turning to leave, cursing this lost opportunity when time was such an important factor, Faro thought quickly. If not Sir James, then there was one other person who might have the information he sought.

'Sir James's valet – I don't suppose he would be available for a word?'

The servant smirked. 'You suppose right. Mr Peters is out for the evening and I don't know when he'll return. Besides, if you have questions to ask any of the staff, you will have to seek Sir James's permission first.'

Retreating to the carriage, he was met with, 'Wouldn't see you, sir? Too bad.' McQuinn enjoyed seeing the Inspector discomfited.

'I'll see him tomorrow. And I'll be obliged if you do not mention this visit. Keep it unofficial,' Faro added, disliking intensely asking this favour and thereby putting himself under an obligation to the Sergeant.

McQuinn merely nodded, his thoughts plainly elsewhere. And so with the feelings of frustration so familiar to him in his role as detective, Faro sat back to gloomily endure the rest of the journey. If there was any satisfaction to be gained it was in bequeathing to the odious McQuinn the unenviable task of imparting to Superintendent Mackintosh that Clavers had escaped them once again.

As he left the carriage outside his home, the sun had already set in scarlet glory behind the Pentland Hills. Another day ended. Faro's conscience smote him anew. Soon his family would be returning to Orkney, leaving him full of guilt at having spent so little time with Rose and Emily. Each time they met, he was surprised to find yet another stranger child. Taller, subtly changed, escaping into girlhood, and leaving him still yearning for the wee bairns he had unaccountably lost. One day, if he wasn't very careful, he knew that he might find to his eternal regret two young women, complete strangers, asking his permission to marry and the family life he had hardly known would be ended before it had properly begun.

Stepping through his own front door, he was full of splendid resolutions. It felt good to be home, especially to have his little daughters waiting in their nightgowns to embrace him. Their well-scrubbed faces, their shining hair, their squeals of delight, indicated how much they had missed him. Here was dear Papa, the long-absent traveller returned at last. Such a welcome would have melted the hardest of hearts and Faro, who rarely shed tears, was choked with emotion as he gathered them to his heart.

Mrs Brook was there with anxious enquiries about his supper. His mother fussed as usual. He smiled wryly. For her he would never be Detective Inspector Jeremy Faro, a man of responsibility and decision, approaching middle age. For her he was just one other child.

'Now you've seen Papa home again. They were allowed to wait up for you,' said Mrs Faro. 'Do let Papa have some peace, girls. He has been working hard all day. So say good night and off to bed with you.'

'Just a little longer . . .' whispered Emily.

'Please, Papa,' sighed Rose.

'We would love a story – please, Papa.'

'Oh yes, yes, indeed we would.'

'Then you shall have one.'

Climbing the stairs between them, holding two tiny hands in his large fists, while they accommodated their nimble steps to his awkward gait, solicitous for his poor injured ankle, Faro felt uncommonly cosseted and well blessed. The picture of doting fatherhood, he proudly settled them in the big spare-room bed.

'Now, what sort of story would you like?'

Emily pointed towards the window. 'Tell us about King Arthur.'

'Yes,' said Rose reproachfully. 'You promised you would.'

He told them how Arthur's Seat had got its name. How King Arthur and his knights fought the dog-faced warriors of the Hybee tribe on that very spot they could see where the last rays of the day's sunlight glowed red and faded into the dark. How bravely they fought for a day and a night and the sound of the battle reverberated like a thunderstorm over the surrounding countryside.

Hopelessly outnumbered, bleeding from many wounds, defeat and death seemed inevitable. But the faery kingdom was on Arthur's side. When all seemed lost, a great door appeared in the hillside and the King with his loyal knights were whisked inside. There it was promised they would live for ever. Unless a day came when their country was in dire peril from other invaders and the horn which had slipped from King Arthur's saddle was found again. Should someone blow that faery horn, then the great door would again open and the King and his knights would ride out to victory.

'Is the horn still hidden, Papa?'

'I hope no one blows it by accident,' whispered Emily, who was inclined to be nervous.

'I wonder if there are any clues as to where it might be hidden,' was the practical Rose's response. 'I shall certainly keep my eyes open, Papa. You may rely on that and I shall look for anything unusual the next time Vince takes us . . . ' Her words were lost in a sleepy yawn.

62

Having kissed them good night, Faro went downstairs somewhat cynically concluding that there was as much hope of Rose finding King Arthur's horn as he had of unravelling a thirty-three-year-old mystery. If it hadn't been for the coincidence of the two identical jewels he would have been almost inclined to let it stay unsolved.

The dead man's identity was vital. Dowie, if he were still alive, would be the right age. However, he had been present at Vince's examination of the body which had revealed no injury or scars to account for the 1837 report of 'serious injury' and Magnus Faro's remark 'He is far gone' surely indicated approaching death.

In a few days it would be too late, anyhow. Corpses couldn't be kept indefinitely and once the body was disposed of to the Medical School, Faro could not imagine Superintendent Mackintosh allowing him to waste his time on an investigation based on purely nebulous speculation. The Superintendent was a tidy man and he would be keen to have the case closed and the unknown Castle Rock victim would become just one more mysterious death in Edinburgh's turbulent history.

Lost, unsolved, for ever.

Chapter Six

At ten o'clock next morning, Faro limped across the Castle quadrangle only to be told that his journey had been in vain.

'Sir Eric has been summoned to Balmoral Castle – by HM,' said the young officer, adding 'Her Majesty', apologetically, in case the jargon of officialdom was unknown to a Detective Inspector.

'Mr Forster, Sir Eric's personal assistant, is unable to be here. I have been left in charge: Lieutenant Arthur Mace,' he said by way of introduction. Then solemnly consulting a list: 'Yes, Inspector, you are expected. Sir Eric states that you are to examine the royal apartments in connection with the recent attempted break in.'

Over the short distance to their destination, Faro observed his companion carefully. The smart new uniform somewhat self-consciously worn suggested that he was new to responsibility and to the regiment of Scots Greys. Faro would have hazarded a guess that the lad was little past twenty, and his upper-class English accent indicated that after leaving public school his family had bought him a commission.

Unlocking the door, Mace turned. 'Sir Eric said I was to assure you that since your last meeting he had instructed Mr Forster to make a most careful search and Mr Forster was satisfied that nothing had been disturbed in the attempted burglary.'

Walking round the glass cases, Faro merely nodded. There was no evidence of locks being forced and a brief examination of the windows was enough to confirm the assistant keeper's report.

Faro cursed silently. The trail, if any had existed, was already cold.

'I have always been absolutely fascinated by Mary Queen of Scots,' said Mace with a sigh. 'Look at that dear little shoe of hers and the glove. Such tiny feet and hands and I'm told that she was six foot tall. Tall, indeed, for a man in those days.'

'Or for anyone, if the height of doorways is to be believed.'

Mace opened the door into the Queen's bedchamber and sighed again. 'I wish I had lived then.'

Faro looked at Mace's high forehead, his long pale face and long slender hands. Quite remarkable. Mace might have stepped down from a portrait of that period and he smiled in sympathy.

'A savage, cruel time, it was.'

'But there was beauty, such chivalry, don't you think, dying for a young and beautiful Queen.'

Faro said nothing. The lad was half in love with a ghost, as he himself had once been. Let him keep his illusions. Romantic young fools like this one had gone to bloody death in their dozens, by way of the torture chamber and the block, their lofty ideals and sufferings vanished into the dust of passing centuries. Of that tragic long-ago only a few pathetic faded artefacts remained, objects which might, or might not, have once belonged to the Queen. He touched the bed curtains reputed to have been embroidered during her long years of imprisonment. What secrets, what thoughts of agony and grief had she woven into those delicate patterns which had alone remained impervious to time?

'Isn't our present Queen the one you would gladly die for,' Faro asked, 'seeing that you have taken her shilling?'

Mace looked confused and embarrassed. 'Yes, I suppose so. Of course,' he added, but without any true conviction.

Faro smiled. The poor lad's heart wasn't in it, to die for the royal widow, whose preoccupation with mourning Prince Albert, unpopular and misunderstood by the masses, suggested neglect of important matters of government, as well as the rumoured neglect of her subjects. A Queen who, stout after much child bearing, could only command her generation of romantic young fools to die on the battle-field of yet another outpost of her ever-growing Empire, hard won and even harder to hold.

Mace pushed open the door of the tiny room high above the Castle Rock. In area it was not much larger than a linen closet in Sheridan Place, yet here Queen Mary had given birth to the future King James VI of Scotland and I of England.

Here, as in no other room in the Castle associated with the Queen, Faro was conscious of a lingering sense of disaster and doom well beyond a monarch's personal tragedy. Here, from these very stones, emanated the events that had reverberated through Scotland's subsequent history, when a once-powerful nation took the wrong turning to wither and die from the effects of Jacobitism and the Clearances.

Standing by the window, he was engulfed by a miasma of foreboding. Distorted whispers, faint cries echoed around him, as if only a thin veil divided the long-ago from now. He closed his eyes, seeking desperately to renew his own link with that time, half remembered, hovering on the brink of what his mother called 'long memory': their Stuart blood, via the Orkney Sinclairs and the Wicked Earl, an explana-tion too fanciful for her son's fierce logic to accept.

Again Faro considered the steep slope of Castle Rock. Inaccessible from inside or outside the barred window, he concluded that no man in his right senses would have the folly or initiative to attempt its scaling. He would have given much to have known how the dead man had spent his last hour.

Mace locked the doors behind them. 'Is there anything else I can do for you, Inspector, any information I can help you with?'

66

It was a forlorn hope, but Faro produced the two cameos. 'Have you ever seen these before?'

Mace studied the jewels carefully. 'No, I haven't, I regret to say. But I am almost certain these miniatures are of Queen Mary and Darnley, possibly at the time of their marriage.' His voice increased in excitement as he continued, 'May I ask how you came by them, Inspector?'

'They came into my possession recently.' Faro was not prepared to say more that that.

'Are they from a collection?' Mace asked eagerly.

'Perhaps so. I know little of their history. I was hoping they might have come from the royal apartments.'

'Stolen, you mean?' Mace sounded profoundly shocked.

'Yes, that is why I am here, to discover if any items are missing.'

Mace smiled sadly. 'I wish they were mine. You see, my family has a great many trinkets of this period, and I would be willing to swear that these pieces are authentic.' He nodded enthusiastically. 'Yes, indeed, you can take my word for it. These are more likely to have been the personal possessions of Queen Mary than most of the artefacts in the Castle.' He paused. 'If you have a moment, Inspector, I should like to check the inventory of the Queen's jewels.'

Mace walked quickly across the quadrangle and unlocked a room containing narrow stacks of dusty files. He pointed across to dismembered suits of armour, swords and pistols, heaped together with a rusty 'iron maiden' off its supports.

'These are awaiting reconstruction, for exhibition in the new museum. I am something of an expert in this kind of work. A labour of love, one might say,' continued Mace happily.

Faro declined the invitation for a closer inspection and took the opportunity to rest his ankle. A much frayed and dilapidated velvet chair, upon whose interior he suspected rats had freely feasted, did not deter him. He sat down and a few moments later Mace emerged from the labyrinth triumphantly clutching a roll of yellowed documents.

'This inventory of the Queen's jewels is absolutely fascinating and quite unique. Much of it dates from the time of her reign, written by her Lord Chamberlain. Later we have documents from the time of her first imprisonment at Lochleven and later in England when her possessions were being listed by her jailers at the request of Queen Elizabeth. The miniatures should date these two pieces fairly accurately. Most likely painted and exchanged at the time of their betrothal early in 1565 and certainly not later than Darnley's murder at Kirk o'Field in 1567.'

'So short a time,' said Faro. 'Presumably they were disposed of immediately after she married the Earl of Bothwell.'

Mace nodded, rifling through the parchments. 'Indeed, in the circumstances, it's highly unlikely that the Queen would wish to keep any mementoes of her second husband.' Mace paused and looked across at Faro. 'How very strange. The inventory of the jewels. It isn't here in its usual place. Quite extraordinary.' He shrugged. 'Perhaps it is away being catalogued. Yes, that would be the answer. I'm sorry to disappoint you, Inspector. Mr Forster will know. I'll find out from him and let you know.'

'If you would be so kind, a note to the Central Office will find me.'

'Very well. And now, how else can I help you?'

'I'm not sure. You are very knowledgeable about Queen Mary.'

Mace beamed. 'History is my speciality. My own family dates from the sixteenth century. Such a time to live, so rich in romance.'

'And in mayhem and murder,' said Faro, a suggestion which Mace chose to ignore. 'Do you happen to know anything of a child's remains allegedly discovered hidden in the wall of the royal apartments?'

'Oh, that fairy tale.' Mace laughed. 'We know now that it was a practical joke.'

'Surely someone with a rather macabre sense of humour?'

'It was the idea of the officers of the guard apparently, to frighten the workmen repairing the wall.'

'I dare say they succeeded,' Faro remarked drily. 'To be frank with you, a child's body doesn't sound like a practical joke in the best of good taste.'

'But to the uneducated labouring class, Inspector? Take the bones of some small animal, most likely a monkey, wrap them in an old vestment. Tell them these are the mummified remains of a child interred long ago and such information, from their superiors, would be accepted without the least question. Surely you can imagine, Inspector, how irresistible such a prank would seem to young, high-spirited army officers. One knows how gullible Irish workmen are,' Mace giggled, with a touch of malice.

Faro eyed him with sudden distaste. 'A highly reputable newspaper – the *Scotsman* – also accepted the discovery as fact and, indeed, reported it in considerable detail.'

'Come now, Inspector, we are all aware that news reports are prone to exaggeration,' said Mace with a pitying smile. 'Sensational stories are what they rely upon to sell their newspapers. And I don't imagine, for one moment, that the writer was encouraged to examine the contents of the coffin in case he realised that these were not, in fact, the bones of a child at all.'

'Not any child, Lieutenant. The remains were rumoured to be those of a royal prince, the son Queen Mary bore to Darnley.'

Again Mace laughed. 'No scholar would take such a preposterous supposition seriously, Inspector. You are surely not suggesting that King James VI of Scotland and Queen Elizabeth's legitimate successor was an impostor?'

Faro smiled. 'You know, I really hadn't got that far. But now that you mention it, yes, perhaps we have a point worthy of consideration.'

Mace looked nonplussed. 'If this were true, Inspector, then a lot of history would have to be rewritten. And I can assure you that no loyal servant of HM would ever harbour such treasonable and sinister thoughts,' he added severely.

Faro nodded. 'The Castle officials made absolutely certain that no one else would have any opportunity to investigate. The remains were immediately re-interred and the aperture sealed.' He took advantage of the Lieutenant's sudden bewildered expression to add sharply, 'Have you any idea why Colonel Lazenby committed suicide in 1837, at the time of the second discovery?'

'I gather he was involved in some scandal.' Mace's tone expressed contempt and disapproval. 'Why do you ask?'

'As he was in charge of the Castle restorations, I just wondered if there might be some possible connection.'

Mace laughed out loud. 'Good heavens, Inspector, it was nothing to do with a practical joke on some ignorant workmen that drove Lazenby to such dire straits.'

'You think falling off a scaffolding was a practical joke?'

'Of course not, Inspector.' Mace's countenance flushed red with indignation as he added stiffly, 'You are deliberately misunderstanding me. I was referring to our earlier discussion.'

'What about Lazenby then?'

'I understand it was a sordid matter, hushed up by the regiment. Lazenby was involved with a married woman, the wife of a fellow officer. Disgrace to his colours . . . '

'Oh indeed,' Faro interrupted. 'I understood from his obituary that he had been recently married.'

Mace had recovered. He raised one eyebrow mockingly. 'Since when, Inspector, did such peccadillos influence a man's reasons for making a suitable marriage? When he was challenged by the woman's husband, suicide was the only decent thing left to him to avoid a scandal.' He stood up. 'And now, is there anything else I can do for you?'

Faro sensed by the way he gathered his papers together that Mace's co-operation had been replaced by a somewhat chilly impatience.

'There is one more thing, Lieutenant. My history book contains only one chapter on Queen Mary's reign. I wonder if you have a more comprehensive volume in your library.'

Mace seemed relieved by the request, his good humour restored. 'Of course, Inspector. Over here.' He went to the shelves. 'An excellent account based on contemporary records. The only copy in existence. It's very valuable and I'm afraid it cannot be removed from the building. However, you may consult it here at your leisure.'

Seeing the Inspector settled at a table by the window, Mace shook hands, wished him good day, saying what a pleasure it had been, and promising to be in communication as soon as Mr Forster revealed the present whereabouts of the missing inventory.

Through a regular study of lengthy documents, Faro had acquired of necessity an ability to read fast. He also possessed a remarkable visual memory and, although the prose of the book was stiff and awesome to a modern reader, he knew exactly what he was looking for.

Two hours later, he heard the one o'clock gun fired from the battlements. Armed with copious notes copied from the volume, he was leaving the building when he caught a glimpse of Lucille Haston alighting from a carriage in the quadrangle outside Sir Eric's apartments. As he drew nearer, he saw that she was in the process of upbraiding her maid.

'And stop being so sullen – remember you're getting all my old clothes, so do try to look happy and grateful for once.' Catching sight of the Inspector, Lucille giggled apologetically. 'I am quite exhausted. So much shopping.'

'So I see.' And Faro limped forward gallantly to offer the dour Bet a sympathetic hand as she staggered out of the carriage buried in an assortment of boxes bearing the names of Edinburgh's mantle and millinery shops.

'For heaven's sake, she can manage,' said Lucille, watching him indignantly. 'Men look so ridiculous carrying hat boxes.'

'It seems that you find our shops to your taste,' he said.

'I do indeed. Such rapturous clothes. Quite on a par with London and Paris fashions, I understand. Uncle Eric is away to Balmoral Castle, if you please. At the command of Her Majesty, who didn't see fit to invite his poor niece.'

Bet opened the door for her mistress and as Faro deposited the two large boxes in her charge, Lucille removed her bonnet, fluffed out her hair and sighed. 'Really, Inspector, it is too bad. Here I am positively dying of boredom. If only one had friends of one's own age, it would be bearable.'

And, he thought, regarding him very intently, she added, 'I'm starved. Have you had luncheon? No? Good. Then Bet will find us something.'

'Thank you, but I'm afraid you must excuse me. I am expected home to Sheridan Place. My daughters . . . ' he ended somewhat lamely.

'Oh, I had forgotten. The two little girls.' And wistfully, 'Tell me their names again.'

'Rose and Emily.'

'Rose and Emily,' she repeated slowly. 'I would so love to meet them. I wonder – I wonder, if I might take them to the Botanic Gardens this afternoon. I have the carriage at my disposal.' And laying a hand on his arm, she said, 'Please say yes, I really am quite desperate for company and I have no idea how long Uncle Eric will be absent.'

There was, Faro knew, only one answer. 'Then permit me to invite you to luncheon with us. I am sure Rose and Emily – and my mother – will be delighted to receive you.'

Lucille clasped her hands, jumping up and down with excitement and truth to tell, he thought, looked so ingenuous and charming that she seemed little older than his own daughters at that moment.

'Oh, do you mean it? Really? Oh, I would so love that. Such paradise. I can't tell you how this dreary old Castle gets on my nerves. It isn't a bit as I imagined it. Artists always make it look so romantic – and I suppose it is on the outside. But inside, its exactly like living in a barracks. I so long for female society.' And indicating the carriage. 'Shall we go?'

'Hadn't you better tell your maid?'

She frowned. 'Oh yes, I suppose so. But you had better come with me. Tell her that you are an old and trusted friend of Uncle Eric, and so on.'

Confronted by the stony-faced Bet, Faro was astonished at his young companion's elaborations. Not only was he a family friend of Sir Eric, and a policeman, but Uncle Eric had especially entrusted her into his keeping while he was visiting the Queen.

At the end of this glowing testimony, with only the vaguest indication of when to expect her return, Lucille hurried him out of the door, down the stone steps and into Sir Eric's private carriage, which he soon discovered was a vast improvement on the police vehicle in the matter of interior furnishings. As they trotted briskly down the High Street he was amazed to find that the well-upholstered red plush seats with their buttoned padded backs left passengers quite impervious to the normal jolts and discomfort of travelling over the cobbles.

All the way to Sheridan Place, hardly stopping to draw breath, Lucille prattled happily on a vast assortment of topics, with such speed and diversity that Faro soon lost the thread.

He felt his concentration glazing over, but soon discovered that his silence went unnoticed. A pleasant smile, a nod of approval and an interested expression were enough. When Lucille asked a question she never waited for nor, he suspected, did she even expect an answer.

Handing her down from the carriage and opening his front door, he tried not to observe that his mother's jaw had dropped open at the sight of the pretty young girl at her son's side. A look that was swiftly replaced, he noted with some amusement, by one he knew well. His mother was already hearing the distant chime of wedding bells.

Nor was his mother alone. The same thoughts were obviously running through Mrs Brook's mind.

'No, Inspector sir, of course I can lay another place for luncheon. No, it isn't in the least inconvenient,' she added to his whispered aside. 'Delighted, I'm sure.' The latter was accompanied by an approving though markedly sly look in Lucille's direction.

By the time luncheon was at an end. Mary Faro had summed up Lucille Haston. She had all her case history and was clearly weighing the evidence. Was this a just case for a verdict of marriage? What an admirable detective his mother would have made, thought Faro.

On the other side of the table, Rose and Emily, with Lucille between them, chatted happily.

'Just look at that, son,' said Mary Faro. 'How they've taken to Miss Haston. Why, anyone would think they had known her all their lives,' she added in a tone laden with significance, as the two little girls were sent upstairs to wash hands and faces before the promised outing to the Botanic Gardens.

'You must come too, Miss Haston,' said Emily.

'Yes, Papa has an inside closet, you must use it,' said Rose, always practical.

'Girls – really,' said Mrs Faro in a shocked voice. 'We don't boast about such things.'

Lucille beamed upon her. 'I'm delighted by the information, Mrs Faro. We haven't anything so modern in the backwoods where I come from.'

Faro was waiting when they came downstairs. 'May I beg a lift in your splendid carriage as far as the High Street?'

'Delighted, I'm sure.'

He sat between Rose and Emily, who held his hands with a distinct air of possession and occasionally leaned over to kiss his cheek while Miss Haston, seated opposite, gave him her undivided attention. The glances in his direction were so unmistakably admiring that Faro felt idiotically happy, out of all proportion to the occasion.

'Why do you smile, Papa?' asked the observant Rose.

'I was just thinking that this is a perfect day for a visit to the Botanic Gardens. I do envy you.'

'Come with us, Papa.'

'Yes, please, Papa.'

'Such a waste to remain indoors on a beautiful day,' was Lucille's reproachful comment.

Faro shook his head. Criminals did not cease from crime because of fine summer weather.

'How lovely the hills look, all shimmering and mysterious,' Lucille continued, opening the window so that a pleasant breeze wafted into the carriage. 'They remind me so of home – I must go there and walk one day before I leave.'

Faro was tempted to make the offer which he felt that this remark with its accompanying glance blatantly invited. However, he remembered that other occasion not so very long ago when he had taken pity on a lonely lady, a stranger to Edinburgh, and how their first excursion together had been to the Pentlands. To think how that had ended . . .

No. He must not remember. He had trained himself in forgetfulness and he would not allow Miss Haston to open that storehouse of bitter memories.

As he left them in the High Street, his daughters bestowed their ritual of smacking kisses while Miss Haston watched wistfully, as if she would have liked to be included.

Faro felt quite confused as he walked towards the Central Office. Perhaps he had hurt her feelings, perhaps he should have kissed her gently and innocently on the cheek, indicating that he regarded her in the same light as Rose and Emily. To kiss or not to kiss. Oh dear, what was a man to do?

Once inside his office, all such domestic problems were instantly forgotten. His presence was being eagerly sought by the Superintendent, who had just been alerted to yet another hiding place of the elusive Clavers, recently sighted at Leith.

The police carriage with its reinforcement of constables set out at a brisk pace for the harbour. They were too late. There was no evidence of Clavers and his gang in the now deserted shipping warehouse where they had allegedly gone to earth.

At this stage, Faro began to have serious doubts as to the integrity of the Superintendent's informant. He had a strong suspicion that his superior officer was being extremely gullible, deliberately misled by one of the gang or even one of Clavers's doxies (of which he was reported to have a considerable number, along with a remarkable capacity for keeping them all happy).

Retracing his steps to the police carriage waiting in the shade offered by the nearby church for the hot dusty ride back into Edinburgh, he read, 'St Patrick's Roman Catholic Church. Reverend Father James O'Rourke.'

Faro remembered his father's casebook. The John Femister who had died in 1837 had been from Leith. His fellow labourers were believed to be from Ireland in which case they were most likely Catholics. So there was always the remote possibility that they might have been interred in the one burial ground of that denomination in Leith.

Instructing the driver to wait, he wandered round the kirkyard inspecting the graves. As the church bore the date '1820' carved in stone, most of them were relatively modern.

There was no Matthew O'Hara or Peter Dowie and he was ready to give up when he came upon a headstone half-hidden by weeds, 'Jean Femister, died 1832, aged 29 years, beloved wife of John Femister, died 1837 aged 35 years. R.I.P.'

Returning once more to the grave of the sadly young couple, he suddenly realised the significance of its neglect. The Femisters had left no close and caring relatives. Yet, according to the newspaper, Femister had left a daughter. Was she the reason for her mother's early death? He did a rapid calculation. She would be about his own age, and with luck, she might have survived.

There was one way to find out. He set off along the gravel path leading to the church, where his further investigations were thwarted by a locked door. Disconsolately, he walked around the building and was about to leave when a priest hurried across the grass, his eager expression suggesting that Faro's attention to the gravestones had not gone unnoticed.

'Is there someone in particular you are seeking, sir?'

As Faro explained, his hopes of success faded. This rosy-faced cherubic priest was considerably less than forty.

'Alas, I cannot help you. I am new to this area. Father Bruce would have known. He was here for fifty years.'

'Perhaps I could talk to him?'

The priest shook his head and pointed solemnly to a new grave with a shining monument of a hovering angel. 'There he lies, sir. Buried three months past. Your best hope now is the parish records. If you'll come with me.'

Inside five minutes Faro had all the information he needed: John Femister's marriage in 1831 and a year later, the birth of a daughter, Griselda, and the death of his wife, Jean.

He found Father O'Rourke in the dim, cool interior with its odours of incense and the smell of old Bibles peculiar to stone-walled churches.

'Griselda Femister? No, I am certain there is no one of that name in our congregation. If she was only five when her father died then it is most likely that relatives took care of her – if she had any.'

And perhaps took her many miles from Leith. Without knowing their names it would be a hopeless task to trace her. Besides a child of five might have only the vaguest memories of her father and remember even less about the circumstances surrounding his death.

'If she had no relatives,' the priest continued, 'then she would have been placed in one of our orphanages, either in Edinburgh or in the Lothians. However, if she remained in the district and eventually married, then of course, she would most likely have been married at our church.' And when Faro looked hopeful, 'Perhaps you would like to consult the marriage register?'

Back in the vestry, Faro ignored all entries before 1848 as it was unlikely that Griselda Femister would have married before she was sixteen. It was not until March 1853 that he found the entry he sought, 'Griselda Femister, daughter of the late John and Jean Femister of this parish, and Malcolm Penfold, baron, of Heriot Row, Edinburgh.' Neither of the witnesses, alas, were Femisters.

Lord Penfold was well known to every member of the Edinburgh City Police. A High Court judge, a respected member of Edinburgh society, he was also a pillar of the Church of Scotland. What of his wife? Had she changed her religion?

Thanking the young priest, Faro made his way back to the police carriage, eminently satisfied with his afternoon's work and delighted by the discovery of a lead, however tenuous, to those events of 1837.

There was always the chance that Lady Penfold might produce foster parents, relatives or friends with long memories. And it was by painstakingly following such minor clues that a detective whose character was strong in patience and persistence might discover a path through the labyrinth. At the end of it, such a man might be rewarded by the revelation of many long forgotten – and often dangerous – secrets.

Chapter Seven

Faro returned home to find Vince alone in the drawing room studying Magnus Faro's notes.

'Fascinating stuff, Stepfather.'

'Where's the family?'

'Long past their bedtime. Haven't you noticed the time?'

'Did they enjoy the Botanic Gardens?'

'Positively wild with delight. By the way, I had a tantalisingly brief meeting with the delectable Miss Haston as she was leaving.'

'Did she stay to supper?'

'She did indeed. After putting the girls to bed and reading them a story. Even then she was disposed to linger. Anxiously enquiring for your welfare. Did they always keep such late hours at the Central Office?'

With a teasing glance, Vince added, 'You know, I had the distinct feeling she was most reluctant to take her departure before you returned. Wished to thank you for – I quote – introducing her to two such delightful little girls. Tell him I have had a marvellous time and that, with Mrs Faro's permission, I shall call on them tomorrow.'

And clearing his throat gently, Vince said, 'I think, seeing this is my day off, that I shall make myself quite indispensable.'

'You will enjoy riding in Sir Eric's splendid carriage.'

'That is not all I hope to enjoy, Stepfather.'

'Then I wish you joy of the lady, but do bear in mind that she is Sir Eric's niece.'

'And what do you mean by that?'

'You know what I mean, Vince lad. She is not to be regarded as one of your easy young women.'

'Easy young women? Somehow I didn't get the impression that she would be difficult or inexperienced in the ways of the world.'

'Come now, Vince, if you are intending to make a conquest . . . '

'A conquest, Stepfather? Seduce that delightful creature? Nothing is further from my mind.'

'So be it. If any harm comes to her while she is under my roof, you'll have me – and Sir Eric, who is even more formidable – to answer to.'

'You are losing your sense of humour, Stepfather. Or could it be that you have a fancy for the lady yourself?'

'You talk nonsense.' And irritably shrugging off the hand Vince had placed on his arm, he added, 'If I had, then I should certainly not have missed an opportunity of spending a pleasant summer afternoon in the Botanic Gardens.'

Seeing Vince's puzzlement at his rather violent response, he sighed apologetically. 'I've seen them many a time, lad, that you know, in peace and in the pursuit of criminals . . . '

'But not, I imagine, with anyone as adorable as Miss Haston.'

'Who is young enough to be my daughter.'

'When did that deter any lusty male? God created men to love for ever.'

'Then let me put it another way. Do you think I'll ever fall in love, after what I have been through – or have you forgotten?'

And seeing his expression, Vince patted his shoulder. 'No. And never will,' he added gently. 'Forgive me, Stepfather, I am being crass and more tactless than usual. I realise it's early days for you – after . . . '

'Yes, yes,' Faro interrupted. He could not bear to go into the agonising details of his recent loss. 'And now, let's get down to these notes you've been reading.'

As he ate Mrs Brook's standard 'cold collation' left for either the doctor or the Inspector if they were unfortunate enough to miss supper, Faro filled in the details of his visit to Edinburgh Castle and his meeting with Lieutenant Arthur Mace. As he spoke, he spread the two Queen Mary jewels side by side on the small table before them.

'What do you make of it all, lad?'

Vince sat back in his chair. 'I should say, Stepfather, that, regardless of Mace's theory, whatever that tomb in the wall contained – and I'm inclined towards a treasure hoard personally – we can certainly dismiss any notion that the small coffin was a hoax and contained the remains of some small animal.'

'They couldn't have made a mistake?'

Vince shook his head. 'You don't have to be a medical man to know about such things. You couldn't mistake a mummified monkey for a child, could you?'

Faro shook his head. 'I don't think so.'

'Nor, I assure you, could the most ignorant of workmen, unless they were also half blind, which I doubt. And having read your father's notes, I am convinced that this discovery was no practical joke, but one to be taken very seriously indeed.' Pausing, he put the tips of his fingers together and regarded his stepfather thoughtfully. 'Has it not occurred to you that the existence of this small coffin hidden for nearly three hundred years might well pose one of history's most intriguing questions? Was the man who succeeded Mary as King of Scotland and England really her son or was he an impostor?'

'Yes, and in the words of Lieutenant Mace, if that were so, a great deal of our history would have to be rewritten, especially in regard to the royal succession,' Faro added slowly.

'If the baby was James, then what have we in support of our theory? Where does the secret of that tiny coffin begin?'

'Has your history improved, lad?'

Vince grinned. 'Not much. It was always my weakest

81

subject. Too dry and dusty when there were so many urgent matters in the present to engage one's interest. However, no one living in Edinburgh could be immune to Scotland's tragic Queen.'

'You recall David Rizzio's murder?'

'I do indeed. Every schoolboy worth his salt has gloated over the bloodstained boards in the Queen's supper room at Holyrood. Do you think it still gets another dose of ox's blood from time to time to keep it fresh?'

Faro sighed. Keeping his stepson's mind on historical facts had always been difficult. 'Doesn't it intrigue you as a medical man to wonder why the Queen, who was six months pregnant when she witnessed Rizzio murdered before her eyes, with Ruthven's sword point at her stomach, did not miscarry?'

Vince nodded. 'Wasn't her husband Darnley in the plot too?'

'He was indeed. Listen to this. It's a contemporary account from a volume in the Records Office – very forthright in its language. The Queen's Secretary, Maitland of Lethington, is reported as saying of Darnley, "He misuses himself so far towards her that it is an heartbreak for her to think that he should be her husband." Yet when he had smallpox in Glasgow she went to nurse him personally.'

'Poor Mary. Reading between the lines that smallpox was a polite name for another pox – syphilis, in fact,' said Vince.

'What an appalling discovery for any young bride – especially the Queen of Scots,' said Faro.

Vince smiled grimly. 'A discovery, alas, none too rare even in our own respectable society here in Edinburgh, if truth be told. Too much sowing of the wild oats down Leith Walk can leave a very nasty souvenir.'

'Aye, and there's a suspicion that ladies of easy virtue were not Darnley's only debaucheries.'

'A penchant for page boys?'

'Indeed. Mary must have been horrified and disgusted when so soon after marriage she discovered that her golden lad was perverted. Perhaps even worse was to know that his love for her – if it ever existed outside her imagination – came a very poor second to his lust for the throne of Scotland.'

'Let's go back to Rizzio's murder,' said Vince. 'I seem to remember the hint was that Mary and Rizzio were lovers. Do you think there was any truth in it?'

Faro snorted indignantly. 'I most certainly do not. An old grizzled hunchback. His intellect and talent as a musician must have excited and entertained her, but certainly would not be calculated to arouse her carnal appetite. From all accounts, we know that Mary was a very fastidious woman.'

'So Darnley used Rizzio as an excuse?'

'An excuse indeed. It was the throne of Scotland that Darnley was after and Mary carried the unborn heir who could displace him. He and the other conspirators were hoping that the Queen would not only miscarry but might also die and they would be rewarded for their efforts by the new King of Scots.'

'They must have planned it very carefully, especially as her health was always problematic,' said Vince. 'Sixteenth-century medicine was based on a few simple premises. Doctors believed that the human body was governed by four cardinal humours – blood, phlegm, choler and melancholy, also known as black melancholy, and it was their abundance or absence which determined a person's temperament.'

In his best textbook manner, Vince continued, 'We now know that Mary had all the symptoms of porphyria, attacks of severe abdominal pain, vomiting and diarrhoea, sometimes accompanied by a complete mental breakdown. These attacks are very severe but not long lasting and there are many women who have chronic illnesses but lose all such symptoms during pregnancy and are remarkably fit and well. And Mary must have been one such case to have survived.'

'She not only survived, lad, she used her woman's wiles.

83

Still wearing her gown soaked with Rizzio's blood, she persuaded Darnley she still loved him and, insisting that the conspirators meant to kill him too, she got him to help her escape from the royal apartments and flee to Dunbar, riding pillion behind one of her servants. Once she begged Darnley to slacken pace for the child's sake. "Ride on," he told her. "We can always make another bairn." God, how that thought must have revolted her.'

'What happened at Dunbar?' asked Vince.

'She was rescued by the loyal Provost of Edinburgh and the citizens and returned to the fortress of Edinburgh Castle, safer although a lot less comfortable than Holyrood, to await the birth of her child.'

'In those days, Stepfather, it was the usual custom for noble ladies to ceremoniously take to their lying-in chamber a few weeks before the birth was due and to remain there like Indian ladies in purdah.'

'What rumours there must have been down below the Castle in Edinburgh as the folk looked up wondering what on earth was taking place within its grim walls.'

'And with good reason,' said Vince. 'A husband riddled with syphilis when the child was conceived. An expectant mother who had witnessed Rizzio stabbed forty times, and her own life threatened by the murderers. Then forced to endure a twenty-five mile gallop to Dunbar – about five hours, riding pillion. Well, Stepfather, even in these civilised days, I wouldn't give much for the chances of delivering a normal child with such a prenatal background.'

'Aye, and in a less enlightened age, everyone expected her to give birth to a monster. Certainly no one expected her to leave her bed alive,' Faro added grimly.

'How did they pass the time in all those weeks of waiting?'

'The usual womanly pursuits, I imagine. Baby clothes, reading and playing the lute – and playing cards.'

'With plenty of time to make plans.'

Faro smiled. 'You are absolutely right, of course. Can't you just see them whispering together, while the Queen slept. If there was ever an opportunity, then this was when the Queen's ladies must have decided that whatever happened, on no account should Darnley rule over Scotland.'

'And if the Queen died, or the child was still-born, then a substitute royal Prince should be found. Were the four Marys still with her?'

'Only Mary Beaton, married to Ogilvie of Boyne, and niece to Margaret Forbes, Lady Reres, also in attendance. And Mary Fleming's sister was there, too – the Countess of Atholl, reputed to be a witch.'

'A loyal but strange collection of ladies, don't you think?'

'And two of them related to the original four Marys,' said Faro. 'Her oldest, dearest childhood friends. Any one of them would have died for her.'

'The perfect material for a conspiracy.'

'Let's look at Lady Reres, who was somewhat significantly, in the light of later events, also pregnant. The story of those days before the Queen was delivered . . . '

'The details of that historic royal *accouchement*, which every Scottish medical student hears about at some time,' Vince interrupted. 'It is one of the few sixteenth-century examples to be documented. A long and difficult labour . . . '

'"With the Queen so handled that she began to wish that she had never been married",' read Faro from his notes, '"and those who attended her feared for her life and the Countess of Atholl cast the childbirth pains on Lady Reres, who lay suffering with her mistress."'

'Now that is an extremely interesting coincidence. Both the Queen and Lady Reres, not only pregnant, but in childbed at the same time.'

'Was it a coincidence, or had this been carefully taken into account in the conspiracy? Remember the blood royal. Lady Reres's niece, Lady Jean Stuart, was the natural daughter of James V.'

'Mary's half-sister.'

'"When at last the Queen's sufferings were at an end, the child was born with a thin membrane over its face."'

'No mention of its sex – a Prince or Princess?'

'Nothing. On 19 June, it was announced that a royal Prince had been born whom Mary proclaimed her heir. But the child was not shown immediately to the waiting populace as was the custom. Even the doctors who one imagines would be in attendance maintained what might be called a stout silence. Not one word or comment on its condition.'

Vince whistled. 'In fact the doctors behaved like very loyal and cautious men.'

'Or very frightened ones. And the first time young James appears is some hours after his birth, when he is shown to Darnley. Here's the scene in the Queen's bedchamber as described by Lord Herries. "About two o'clock in the afternoon, the King came to visit the Queen and was desirous to see the child. "My Lord," says the Queen, "God has given you and me a son begotten by none but you." Then she took the child in her arms, and discovering his face said . . . "

'"Discovering his face?"' interrupted Vince. 'Did Herries mean "un-covering"?'

'I agree it is an odd expression. Does it give you the feeling that Darnley came reluctantly and wasn't offered a close look?'

'All newborn babies look alike. I should think, however, that they would want him to keep at a safe distance in his diseased condition.'

'Very convenient for our conspirators. I imagine they laid great stress upon Darnley's unwholesome presence at his wife's childbed.'

'Exactly. Proceed . . . '

'Here are Mary's words. "My Lord, here I protest to God, as I shall answer for him at the great day of Judgement, this is your own son, and no other man's son, and, as I am desirous that all here, both ladies and others, bear witness, for he is so much your own son that I fear it may be the worse for him hereafter."'

Faro laid aside the notes and waited for Vince's comments.

'Rather unusual, wouldn't you say, Stepfather?'

'"Methinks the lady doth protest too much", as the Bard would have it,' said Faro grimly.

'And there's more than a hint of warning in such an extraordinary public statement, "begotten by none but you". Suggests that Lord Darnley had been casting doubts upon the child's paternity.'

Faro consulted his notes. 'The next visitor, eight days later, was Killigrew, Ambassador of Queen Elizabeth, who reported, "I was brought to the Queen's bedside where her Highness received thankfully her Majesty's letters and commendation . . . "'

Laying aside the papers, Faro smiled grimly. 'Rumour had it that Elizabeth received the glad tidings of her cousin's safe delivery by screaming, "Alack, the Queen of Scots is lighter of a bonny son, and I am but of barren stock." But to continue. Killigrew remarked upon the Queen's "delicate condition and she spoke with a hollow cough. I took leave and was brought to the young Prince sucking of his nurse."'

'Lady Reres?'

'The same.'

'How very convenient. Do go on.'

'Killigrew continued, "Afterwards I saw him as good as naked, well proportioned and like to prove a goodly prince."'

'A moment, Stepfather. Let's consider that very convenient spell of the Countess of Atholl. Since Lady Reres was wet nurse, she must have given birth recently, either immediately before or after the Queen was delivered. And if we are considering a changeling, then Lady Reres appears to be the likeliest person to provide a substitute Prince.'

'Especially as it was announced that she was to be *governante*, a kind of foster mother to the boy while the Queen was absent from Edinburgh.' Faro paused before addding, 'There is one other contender, however – the Countess of Mar. Young James was brought up in her household and I'm told that his portrait bears an uncanny resemblance to his foster brother the Second Earl of Mar, who was six years older. It is quite possible that the Countess also had another son at the same time as the Queen, and because she was related to the Lennox Stuarts she might have been persuaded to substitute her own child.'

'Which would account for that mysterious rumour which has persisted through the centuries of an infant being lowered in a basket from Edinburgh Castle. In this case, it would be the other way round,' said Vince.

'These were desperate times, lad. Loyalty was a gamble and it was all too easy to choose the wrong side. What if Mary died childless and Scotland fell into the hands of Lord Darnley and the power-crazed Lennox family? I dare say there were many frightened nobles who had a lot to lose, including ancient lands and titles, aye, and their heads, too. The only hope of peace was for Mary to leave a legitimate heir.'

'To have told Mary the truth that her agony was all in vain and that the royal Prince was still-born or so delicate that he was unlikely to survive, in her exhausted postnatal condition might well have been the fatal blow,' said Vince. 'So why not solve all her problems by substituting the lusty newborn baby of the willing Lady Reres or the Countess of Mar?'

'One thing seems certain, lad, that closed and devoted circle in the lying-in chamber had ample opportunity.'

'Do you think Mary knew?'

Faro shook his head. 'I think that the Queen was innocent of any deception and never believed otherwise than that the child placed in her arms on 19 June was the one she had just brought into the world. Listen to this letter she wrote many years later, from imprisonment at Tutbury in 1585, two years before her execution, "Without him I am and shall be of right as long as I live, his Queen and Sovereign, but he independently of me, can only be Lord Darnley or Earl of Lennox, that being all he can be through his father." '

'Sad and pathetic, isn't it, that her love and longing remained constant for the son she had not seen since infancy. He was ten months old when she abdicated in his favour and lost him for ever after Darnley's murder at Kirk o'Fields and her disastrous marriage to the Earl of Bothwell.'

'But didn't he plead his mother's cause with Queen Elizabeth,' said Vince, 'try to get her released from that long and terrible imprisonment?'

'No. Not once did he voice even the mildest protest. In fact, he made it so abundantly plain that he was hell-bent on securing the Crown for himself that even Queen Elizabeth was shocked by his eagerness to sell his own mother. "That false Scotch urchin!" she called him. "What can be expected from the double dealing of such an urchin as this?"'

'Since Elizabeth wasn't noted for her kind and gentle nature, then James must have been a monster, if not in outward shape then certainly in mind and heart.'

'Yes, Vince. But all the evidence points out that only substitution could decently explain his complete indifference to his mother's fate.'

'I agree. That picture of heartless betrayal is only less terrible if in fact James knew that there was no blood tie between them.'

'There is evidence, albeit too superficial to convince judge and jury, in his appearance too. Even in youth he had a wizened old man's face. His tongue was over large for his mouth; his personal habits were disgusting and obscene even when he wasn't slobbering and fondling his effeminate favourites. He was untidy, dirty, and as he seldom if ever washed more than the tips of his fingers he smelled abominably.'

'There certainly isn't much likeness in the portraits to either of his tall and strikingly handsome "parents",' said Vince.

'His mother was one of the bravest women who have ever lived, right through her life to her death at Fotheringhay. But James's craven cowardice was a byword and the legendary charm of the Stuart monarchs was replaced in him by political cunning.'

'"The wisest fool in Christendom", wasn't that what he was called?'

'Aye, and with good reason.'

'I wonder when he learned the truth?' asked Vince.

'It might have proved to be a secret very hard to keep. And in large families skeletons have an unhappy way of falling out of the cupboard when least expected. At a guess I would say he learned the truth from his tutor George Buchanan, who was Mary's enemy.'

'And thereafter lived forever in mortal terror of denouncement,' said Vince. 'No wonder drawn swords and any violent movement terrified him.'

'Aye, knowing what he knew. But not knowing how many other people were privy to the secret – and Scotland's nobles had a long and notorious record of getting rid of their unwanted kings. Very, very few ever died in their beds.'

'And if James VI of Scotland and I of England was an impostor, then he had good reason to be on the alert for assassins lurking behind every dovecot and in every closet.'

'And if the coffin in the wall contained Mary's real son, then the discovery of that long lost secret has more significance than any other episode in Scottish history.'

'I can see that, Stepfather. The curtain-raiser to the long-drawn-out tragedy of two succeeding centuries, culminating in the tragedy of Culloden, the downfall of the Clans and the doomed Jacobite cause.'

'And more up to date, Vince, we could also add the present clearances of the Highlands.'

'If Mary had died childless, then the whole course of Scottish history might have been very different. No Stuarts, no Charles I and no Charles II ... '

'Whose illegitimate offspring conveniently founded many of the most noble families in the land.'

'A very different "Kingdom of Scotland".'

'Or just Scotia, the northernmost county of England.'

'No Hanoverians, and no Queen Victoria,' said Faro.

'Our dear Queen isn't the most popular monarch Scotland ever had, if truth be told. You hear a lot of discontent voiced in the howffs of Leith Walk.'

'Aye, and we have it on good authority at the Central Office that there's a lot of dissatisfaction in Parliament at the amount of time she spends at Balmoral.'

'Behind the respectable closed shutters of the New Town, there are a lot of old men whose fathers were "out" in the '45 Jacobite rebellion. Even in England the early years of her reign, long before you were born lad, were fraught with problems. As well as the far corners of Empire, there were rebellions much nearer home – in Ireland and Wales.' With a laugh, Faro added, 'Get your Grandmother Faro on to the subject, wars are her speciality. If women had been allowed in Parliament, she would have made a superb politician.'

'God forbid,' groaned Vince. 'One woman ruling over us is enough yet the newspapers give the impression that her subjects are all devoted and loyal to a man.'

'Aye, and those same loyal subjects once demanded that her beloved Prince Albert be put in the Tower of London as a spy. There have always been assassination attempts on her life.'

'And, as you well know, not even Balmoral is safe.'

Faro nodded. 'When she's travelling in Scotland, the police are constantly on the alert. Never made public, of course.'

'Fenians?'

'Aye, but not only Irishmen.'

'So I gather. There had always been troubles in Ireland, but it appears that her loyal dominions, like Canada, are having problems.'

'I heard it being discussed in Central Office. Some trouble with French-speaking people who don't want to be Canadians?'

'More than trouble, Stepfather, it's a full-scale rebellion.' Vince gave him a hard look and said slowly, 'Only last week, Colonel Wolseley set out with a brigade of staunch men and Iroquois Indians to quell a threatened uprising.'

91

'How very interesting. I must read it up sometime.'

'Stepfather, why do you never read the newspapers?' asked Vince gently.

'I rely on you – and my mother when she's here – to keep me in touch with any interesting items of news. I'm too busy everyday with my own crime reports, lad, to consider wars and rebellions as a source of pleasurable reading. Especially in summer when our police are responsible for the safety of members of the Government – and the Royal Family – passing through on their way to Balmoral.'

Vince smiled. 'I'd have thought the first requirement of a detective was to be knowledgeable about current affairs.'

Chided but unrepentant, Faro indicated a file of papers on his desk. 'That's tonight's work. At any given moment I have to be able to reel off for Superintendent Mackintosh the whereabouts of every suspected lawbreaker and revolutionary in Edinburgh and the Lothians – aye, and a few north and south too, who might decide to extend their activities. In the circumstances, I shall continue to devote my leisure hours – the few I have – to the world of crimes I don't have to solve . . . '

Vince looked at the line of leather-bound volumes on the shelf. 'Such as Mr Dickens'?'

Faro nodded enthusiastically. 'Exactly. And times past – Scott, Shakespeare – how the spirit soars – I assure you a very necessary escape when a man has done wrestling with today's dark and sordid deeds.'

'You are incorrigible,' said Vince, with a shake of his head.

'That's as may be, lad, but let's not digress. Let's get back to Queen Mary and the question mark poised over the discovery of that tiny coffin.'

'And why so many might have died to keep its secret,' said Vince.

'And where do these', said Faro, indicating the cameos on the table beside them, 'fit into the puzzle? Let's hope

Lieutenant Mace has found the answer by now. He promised to track down a missing page of the inventory of the Queen's jewels.'

'And you think these might be on it?'

'I'm almost certain they will be.'

'You suspect they are part of a cache of buried treasure, don't you?'

Faro shook his head. 'I'm not sure what I suspect until we can learn a bit more about the man who died on Castle Rock. I must talk to Sir James's valet, find out what he knows about the jacket. Then I must try to track down Femister's daughter.'

'If she's still alive.'

'True. At thirty-eight, we hope so, if she hasn't succumbed to cholera or childbirth. We know who she married and where Lord Penfold still lives, in a handsome town house in Heriot Row. That is where I go next. But what became of Dowie, I wonder?'

'It seems very unlikely that he's still alive considering his serious injuries thirty-odd years ago. It's even less likely that he could be our dead man, seeing that broken bones heal but also thicken and the body was remarkably unblemished, apart from that tattoo on his wrist.'

'A clover leaf – for good luck, I suppose.'

'Didn't bring him much, did it?' Faro was silent. A second later he shook his head and said excitedly, 'No, lad, not a four-leafed clover – a shamrock. That's what it was. An Irish shamrock.'

'Of course. Poor devil.' Vince paused and then asked, 'Where next, Stepfather?'

'Tomorrow I'm off to Piperlees, but first of all I have to look into the Central Office and see what reports the constables have collected, if any, on my drawing of the cameo. See if it fits any of the stolen property taken during the Clavers gang's robberies. And if it does, then we may have a clue to the one with my father's papers.'

'After more than thirty years, do you think . . . ?'

'No, I don't, lad. That would be the easy solution.' Faro

shook his head. 'I think it would also be a miracle, but we must make sure.'

'And then?'

'Off to the Castle to see Mace.'

'Dr Kellar has promised me a day off. Rose and Emily are longing to see the Castle. We'll meet you there, of course,' he added hastily. 'That will leave you free to make your own arrangements.'

'And you, of course, free to entertain the enchanting Miss Haston.'

'Why, Stepfather,' said Vince in mocking tones, 'what an absolutely splendid idea. It's so sad to think of that lovely creature bored and unhappy in her gloomy Castle when she could be enjoying the benefits of fresh air and gentle exercise.'

'And where are you hoping to find that in the centre of Edinburgh, might I ask?'

'Oh, there are lots of places,' said Vince vaguely. 'We might go down the coast to East Lothian. The girls would love the seaside. And sea air is so beneficial, brings a glow to their cheeks.'

'Your conniving, Vince lad, brings a glow to mine. You are certainly in the right profession to make a fortune out of gullible patients.'

Chapter Eight

A hired gig took Faro out to Piperlees, where a long wait at the front door and the shuttered windows confirmed his worst suspicions. At length a horseman appeared on the drive, with the unmistakable look of a stable-boy.

'Heard you as I was going by. What do you want?'

'Is Sir James at home?'

'No he isn't. There's no one at home at this time of year.' And with an air of amusement and condescension at such ignorance of the gentry's habits, he continued, 'Now, where else would Sir James be but away up to Deeside for the shooting?'

'They were here in the midst of a party only two days ago,' Faro said sharply, furious at this further setback.

The stable-lad shrugged. 'Well, they've gone now. No, I don't know when they'll be back exactly, 'cos I'm not in their confidence. It depends a lot on the weather. Could be next week, or next month.'

'Are the servants with him?'

'Aye, some of them. Sir James is a good employer,' and, indicating the shutters, 'has the house closed up so that the other servants can get away to their own homes for a wee holiday too. What was it you were wanting, anyway?' he added, his curiosity aroused by this questioning and the brown paper parcel under Faro's arm.

Faro decided against declaring himself. The presence of a detective inspector on the premises might be calculated to spread alarm and despondency, put the innocent and guilty alike on their guard. By the time the family returned, tales of the 'polis's visit' would have gathered momentum

among the tenantry. Rumour and speculation would be rife
and Sir James, a personal friend of the High Constable of
Edinburgh, would not be pleased at hints that his public
record and private life were less than impeccable.

'I was wondering what Sir James does with his discarded
clothes?'

'So that's what you're after, guv'nor, from one of them
charity organisations are you?' Amusement was now replaced
by contempt as he scanned Faro from head to foot, no
doubt assessing the origins of the caller's wardrobe. With
a shrug, he added: 'We don't get none of them down the
yard. Her Ladyship packs them off to the poor house in
Edinburgh, I suppose.'

Faro cursed silently at the prospect of continuing his
quest for the jacket's new owner, faced by such daunting
odds.

'What if there was something special – some garment
too good to give away?'

The stable-lad shook his head. 'Might give it to his valet.
But I wouldn't be knowing for sure. I'm only concerned
with the horses and their welfare.'

'Is the valet around at present?'

The lad guffawed. 'Come on, guv'nor, where would Sir
James's valet be but on holiday with the master? Doesn't
move a foot – or a boot, come to think of it, without Mr
Peters.'

Thanking him for his help, Faro limped back to the
gig. Further investigation was pointless. The only person
who could help him, if not Sir James himself, would be the
valet, Peters. And next week or next month would be too
late. By then all that remained of the dead man on Castle
Rock would have been distributed among the eager young
medical students from Surgeons' Hall.

On the outskirts of Edinburgh, Faro decided to call on
Lady Penfold before going to the Castle. Heriot Row was
bathed in milky afternoon sunshine. The day was oppres-
sively warm, the heavily burdened trees silent of bird-song.

As he climbed the steps he felt certain that again his luck would be out. This was the time of day when ladies in Edinburgh society took a nap before calling for afternoon tea. The door was opened by a uniformed maid.

'Is Lady Penfold at home? Detective Inspector Faro.'

The maid glanced at the card. 'I will see if her ladyship is receiving visitors.' A moment later she returned and, opening the door wider, ushered him into the morning room. 'If you will wait here, please.'

Faro took stock of his surroundings. The perfect proportions of the Georgian room, the furnishings, the velvet and satin, the silver and crystal. He looked at the roaring coal fire in the grate and thought of this further extravagance for a late August afternoon. How sparse and even poverty stricken was his home at Sheridan Place. A waft of violet perfume announced the approach of Lady Penfold.

His first thought was that he had been mistaken, that the woman before him was far too young to be the Griselda Femister in the parish register. His experience of the *grande toilette* was limited, but she appeared to be attired in the manner of one going to a ball. With her flounces of satin and lace, and rich jewels, she was almost as over adorned as the room itself.

'Do please sit down.' As he did so, conscious of her ladyship's searching glance and, remembering Sir James's stable-boy's contempt, he was acutely aware of his own rather shabby dress.

Lady Penfold smiled. 'I'm afraid his lordship is away from home. We have just newly returned from abroad, a short summer holiday for a family wedding. His lordship's niece married an Italian count.'

As she warmed her hands before the blaze, her smile became coquettish. 'Weddings are such fun and all the noble houses of Rome and Tuscany were present. I revelled in every moment.' And with a faint shudder, 'I am finding Edinburgh a trifle chilly by comparison. Everyone who matters, all one's friends and acquaintances are away to

Balmoral or to shoot with some Duke or Earl of something on his estate in the Highlands.'

Another sidelong glance. 'Edinburgh is very dull and boring in summer. Do you not find it so?'

Faro shook his head. 'I'm afraid, your ladyship, that criminals, robbers and villains are quite indifferent to the conditions of weather. They even find certain advantages in remaining in Edinburgh when wealthy houses are deserted by their owners. The work of the police increases rather than otherwise.'

'The police? You are a policeman?' She sounded shocked.

'A detective. I gave your maid my card.'

'I'm afraid I did not look at it carefully. The silly girl is new here and all she said was that there was a gentleman downstairs. I presumed you to be some acquaintance and I have been trying in vain to place you. We meet so many persons in our social round, you understand.'

'I do indeed, your ladyship.'

'And you are a policeman?' She repeated the words carefully, as if giving this information time to sink in.

'Detective Inspector Jeremy Faro, your ladyship.'

She beamed on him. 'I thought you couldn't be just a policeman.' Again the sidelong glance. 'You look much too distinguished. However, you are surely rather young to have such a responsible position. You must be very clever,' she sighed. And Faro, managing to keep his face expressionless, received a look that even the most unobservant of men could not mistake as anything but an overture to flirtation.

The door opened to admit the maid. 'You will stay and take tea with me?'

Faro thanked her and the ritual of tea pouring and plate passing began, accompanied in the maid's presence by some trivial conversation from Faro concerning the splendid view of Queen's Street Gardens from the windows and a particularly fine collection of volumes of Sir Walter Scott, which he was invited to examine.

'They are all signed, Sir Walter was a close friend of

98

my father-in-law.' And in answer to his eager question, 'No, I have not read any of them, I'm afraid, I find there are too many pages and too closely printed to hold my interest for long. Candidly, I prefer real people and real-life adventures. So much more exciting than can be dreamed up in novelettes.'

And before he could think of a reply, 'Almost every day, life offers us some unique opportunity of experiencing a new sensation, a thrilling adventure, if we keep our eyes open.'

She looked across at him and her eyes, he observed, were very open indeed. 'Don't you agree, Inspector?'

Faro replaced the delicate china cup on its saucer. 'I'm afraid I haven't given the matter a great deal of thought.'

She lowered her gaze thoughtfully. 'You should, you know, you really should. Opportunities must often come your way, more than to most men. Such a very exciting and interesting life.'

'It can also be very dull. All routine enquiries are not as pleasant as this one.' That cheered her up considerably and he continued, 'Perhaps I may be permitted to explain the purpose of my visit.'

'Of course, Inspector. But I have enjoyed meeting you and I hope we will meet again. His lordship . . . '

'You mistake me. It is your ladyship I wished to see.'

'You wanted to see me?' The eyelashes fluttered. 'How absolutely splendid.' And leaning forward, eyes narrowed so that the pupils grew large and black, her lips slightly parted, she whispered, 'But really, Inspector, my conscience is quite clear.' And then stretching out diamond braceleted wrists for his inspection, she laid her soft cool hands on his. 'I suppose all criminals tell you that. Am I to have handcuffs now – or shall we say, a little later?'

Managing to remove his hands with a gentle smile, he said, 'Nothing so dramatic, I assure you. I only wish to recreate a piece of old history.'

'How very boring, Inspector.' And with a sigh: 'But if you must, I am yours to command.'

'I understand that both your parents died when you were a child.'

'That is so. I never knew my mother. She died bringing me into the world. That is why I am childless.' She paused and then asked, 'Are you a married man?'

'I was. I am a widower.'

'A widower. How sad.' But her look, hopeful again, belied such sentiments. 'Recently?' When Faro nodded, she asked, 'May I ask what happened?'

'My late wife died in childbirth.'

'So you are childless too.'

'No. We had two daughters.'

'How fortunate. I, alas, have always been so afraid, indeed so repelled at the prospect of all that agony that I have been grateful, nay, fortunate even, that his lordship had a son and heir by his first marriage. The first Lady Penfold died of a fever while they were travelling in Italy. Tell me about your poor wife.'

Faro shook his head. 'There is little to tell.' He could not bear to uncover his grief and agony over losing poor Lizzie and their longed-for son. The girls had been too young to understand, but Vince had been inconsolable. Part of his dedication to the study of medicine came from his determination to specialise in this branch of medicine with all its superstitions and prejudices. Dr James Young Simpson's discovery of chloroform in 1840 had been frowned upon by those who believed that ever since Eve it was woman's duty to bring forth children in suffering. For her ninth child, Prince Leopold, Queen Victoria had eagerly seized upon the use of chloroform thereby bestowing respectability upon painless childbirth.

Determined to change the subject, Faro said, 'Tell me about your father. How well do you remember him?'

'Not a great deal, I'm afraid. Except that he used to carry me on his shoulders down to the harbour at Leith to watch the big ships sailing away.'

'So you don't remember his accident?'

'Accident?'

'Yes. When he was killed working on the masonry at Edinburgh Castle.'

'Working on what masonry, Inspector? I don't understand you.'

'A wall in the royal apartments. He and another labourer named Dowie were repairing it, in 1837, in preparation for the Queen's coronation visit in 1838. The scaffolding . . .'

Lady Penfold held up her hand. 'A moment, Inspector. I am quite bewildered by your remarks. You have been grossly misinformed, I'm afraid. My father – a common labourer – a workman?' Her laughter had a strangled sound and before he could reply, she continued gently, 'You have got your facts wrong, this workman person cannot possibly be my father. John Femister was an officer and a gentleman and he died in the Canton rebellion in 1843. On the wall behind you is a painting of him in full dress uniform, the year before his death.'

Faro regarded the painting solemnly. There was little or no resemblance to the dead man on Castle Rock. She was watching him closely and there was nothing to be gained by refuting her claim. He apologised.

'Who brought you up after your father died?'

'A great-aunt in Fife. My only relative, alas, and now dead – the year I was married.'

'Was she also a Femister – from Ireland, were they not?'

Lady Penfold laughed. 'Ireland? Whatever gave you that idea, Inspector? These Femisters were Scots through and through. Great-aunt was on my maternal side, of course.'

'Of course. One more question. Did your father by any chance have a brother, possibly older than himself?'

'My father was an orphan, Inspector.' Her easy, flirtatious manner had been replaced by a certain watchfulness and carefully-thought-out statements. Faro had interviewed too many criminals in his twenty years not to know when someone was lying. He was certain that Lady Penfold was most anxious to conceal the truth.

Could there be any other reason than the very obvious

101

one: that she was a fearful snob, determined to impress with her good connections? Had she built this fantasy about her father, complete with portrait, in order to establish herself as Lord Penfold's wife and when she married deliberately turned her back on her humble parentage? A heartless verdict, but, Faro knew from experience, not altogether rare in those who wished to rise in society from a poor working-class background.

There was nothing to be gained by prolonging the interview, but as he apologised for wasting her time and bade her goodday, she made a rapid return to coquetry. With a great fluttering of eyelashes, she begged him to stay and tell her all about his fascinating work in capturing criminals.

He shook his head, murmuring thin excuses. At length, sighing, realising she had lost a conquest, she rang the bell for the maid to show him out.

'It is my turn to be curious, Inspector. What is your reason for all these questions?'

'Oh, have I not told you?' Faro faced her squarely. 'A man was found dead on Castle Rock recently and we had reason to suspect that he might in fact be related to your late father, John Femister, and that his fall was no accident.'

'You mean this – Femister person – might have been deliberately murdered.'

'That is what we suspect.'

There was a moment's pause as she sought to recover, then with a deep breath, she drew herself up and said sternly, 'I can assure you, Inspector, there is absolutely no connection with this house.'

Faro had observed her reactions carefully. Her horrified whisper, her sudden change of colour, her hands clasped tightly together, all were the confirmation he needed that this was indeed John Femister's daughter. Even more to the point he suspected that she had some knowledge of the dead man. What that connection was remained to be revealed and he was fairly certain that Lady Penfold would give him no help whatever.

As they walked towards the door, she said, 'It is only idle

curiosity, Inspector, but where do the police bury murder victims who are unclaimed by relatives?'

'They become the property of the Medical College. For dissection by the students.'

Her voice as she said goodbye was curiously unsteady, all coquetry long since forgotten. As the door closed behind him Faro had the satisfaction of interpreting her look of terror and guilt. The fact that her dreams that night might be haunted by remorse, and the thought of her discomfort, afforded him considerable pleasure.

At the Central Office there were six very short reports awaiting him, collected from the properties robbed by Clavers and his gang. In each case, according to the constable who made the investigation, Faro's drawing of the Queen Mary cameo had been carefully scrutinised and, in every case, the robbed gentleman denied ever having seen it before.

Superintendent Mackintosh came in as Faro put down the last report.

'If that piece is genuine,' he said indicating the drawings sternly, 'and no one has claimed it, then the proper place for it is in the collection at Edinburgh Castle. See to it, will you, Faro. Oh, and before you go, you had better sign this certificate for the Fiscal.'

The document related to disposal of the remains of an unknown man found on the Castle Rock. All the usual procedures of investigation had been carried out, but no claimant had come forward.

'He definitely wasn't one of Clavers' gang either, Faro. I had my informant take a look at him.'

Faro reluctantly put his name under the presumed cause of death – 'By misadventure' – and handed the document back to the Superintendent.

There was little point in protesting. A jacket that might have been distributed to the dead man by any of Lady Piperlee's charitable organisations, and not necessarily first hand. It could have had several owners.

Lady Penfold had been his last hope, a woman too

103

proud to admit a common labourer as her father, who had invented a grandiose background suitable to her present position in society.

He handed the certificate back and the Superintendent gave an approving nod. 'Good. That's settled then. Case is now closed and we can get him tidied away. Thank God. No one will be sorry about that, I can tell you. Complaints already about keeping bodies around in this weather, a very unpleasant business. Very nasty indeed, Faro.' And his reproachful glance seemed to indicate that his Detective Inspector had been personally responsible for the inconvenience caused.

He was leaving the building when a constable hailed him. 'Message for you, Inspector.'

Marked 'Urgent' the note read, 'Have stumbled on something which you ought to know. Come at once. Highly confidential.' The last words were heavily underlined and the signature was 'Arthur Mace'.

'When did this arrive?'

'An hour ago, maybe more. I didn't realise you were in the building.'

But Faro was already at the door stepping into a waiting carriage. As it climbed the steep High Street towards the Castle, he felt the stirrings of excitement.

With or without the corpse of the mystery man, with or without his superior's approval, the case for him could not yet be closed.

As long as he had a shred of evidence.

And his sixth sense told him that whatever Lady Penfold's denials, however unsatisfactory the interview had been, her manner had betrayed evidence that the dead man was either a relative of John Femister or somehow connected with him.

It was by following such frail uncertain threads that mysteries were solved and Detective Inspector Faro brought criminals to justice.

Chapter Nine

At the entrance to the royal apartments, a gentleman, swarthy of countenance with the proportions of a wrestler and a decidedly foreign appearance which belied his very English name, announced himself as Forster, Sir Eric's personal assistant.

'Mace? Not here. On duty.' And without offering another word, Mr Forster retreated into his small office and closing the door firmly indicated that all further communication was superfluous.

Faro shrugged. No doubt Sir Eric would be able to contact Mace. As he walked across the corridor he thought about Forster's clipped English. His appearance and carefully enunciated words, few as they were, suggested that this was not his native language. The other explanation was more feasible, that Mr Forster was a Highland gentleman and that his native tongue was the Gaelic.

Entering Sir Eric's apartments, he found himself in the midst of a party which, by the evidence of the table set with the remnants of a considerable feast, had been enjoyed by an entire turnout of his family.

Rose and Emily were fully absorbed by a set of toy soldiers and a fort. This activity, he guessed by their rapt attentions, held more interest than playing with dolls long neglected in their nursery. Rose was bookish and Emily good with her hands.

By one window, Sir Eric and his mother sat in deep conversation. The closeness of their heads and the faint flush on his mother's cheek, her downcast eyes and shy smile, her hair untouched by grey, created an illusion of youth regained and suggested to her son that Sir Eric might indeed be renewing his past overtures.

Faro was happy to remain in silent observation to enjoy this delicious spectacle. How extraordinary that he had never until this moment seen his mother as other men might, as a still desirable woman. And he was also aware, for the first time, that Sir Eric's exceptional good looks and distinguished presence might commend him to ladies of all ages.

He had certainly failed to use his much-vaunted sharp eyes, his powers of logic and deduction where his own family were concerned. Wouldn't it be extraordinary if Sir Eric, that faithful family friend of forty years, whom Faro had long regarded in the affectionate guise of a foster-uncle, should become his stepfather? What would young Vince think about that?

From the other window embrasure, not clearly visible from where he stood, a woman's soft but sensual laugh reached his ears. The guffaw that followed was one he recognised and, taking a step forward still unobserved, there was Vince with Lucille, she looking down into the quadrangle and he watching her, narrowly, intensely, with his heart in his eyes.

Romance was most decidedly in the air; the two couples, a vignette out of a light operetta, were much too involved with each other to notice his arrival. To come suddenly upon the scene would be to everyone's embarrassment.

There was only one thing to do. He stepped back outside, knocked loudly and threw open the door.

His daughters noticed him first and, laughing, greeted his arrival with shrieks of welcome. He had given the two couples time to compose themselves and noted with some amusement that they greeted this interruption with perceptibly less enthusiasm than did Rose and Emily. He fancied that upon the faces of both men he detected fleeting shadows of annoyance.

His mother, however, managed to resume her mantle of caring motherhood with commendable speed. Had her boy eaten? Was he hungry? He was looking tired. Was his ankle painful?

Such concern made him feel irritable and quite a bit older than Sir Eric, whose overtures had obviously been receiving some encouragement. The magic of romantic dalliance had brought a youthful sparkle to his eyes and a new lightness to his step as he walked across to welcome the newcomer.

Lucille had meanwhile made a rapid transformation into the role of her uncle's hostess. In a very short time she had Faro seated in the most comfortable armchair with a stool on which to rest his ankle. Her personal ministrations further included a cup of China tea and a scone, heavily buttered and overflowing with raspberry jam, which she proudly presented to him.

Made suddenly at home by such thoughtful gestures and enjoying this charming young woman's undivided attention, out of the corner of his eye Faro was amused to observe his stepson's reactions. Vince was watching them with the same mutinous expression that in boyhood had followed the forcible removal from his grasp of some desirable but forbidden object.

Regardless of the potential hazards of raspberry jam, Rose and Emily both attempted to sit close by and hug him, at the same time regaling him with stories of their day.

'Dear Miss Haston has been so kind –'

'And dear Vince.'

'We have been everywhere in the Castle.'

'And met some real soldiers, Papa.'

Listening to his two daughters, Faro saw across the room Sir Eric relating some amusing anecdote to Vince, who appeared to have regained his good humour. Near the window the two ladies had their heads close together consulting a magazine devoted to the latest Paris fashions.

Faro smiled to himself. In a short space of time, the two couples had reverted to being four very practical people, all suggestions of romance carefully swept away as if he

107

had imagined that golden glow when he first entered the room.

Putting down his cup and plate as soon as possible without offending Lucille, who seemed infected with his mother's determination to fill him full of scones and cups of tea, he left his chair with some difficulty and approached Sir Eric, wondering how he could politely extract Vince to tell him of the visit to Lady Penfold and the surprising developments.

'So glad you came, lad,' said Sir Eric.

'I'm here to see Mace, sir. He sent a note to the Central Office, saying it was urgent.'

Sir Eric nodded absently. 'I was just saying to Vince how I bless you for being so good to my niece while I was away. An old man like me isn't much joy for her. Needs taking out of herself. Had a rough old time of it at home . . . '

As he spoke Faro tried to direct Vince's attention to Mace's note, but his facial contortions were ignored and Vince, with a murmured 'Excuse me', seized the opportunity to withdraw once more to Lucille's side. Faro watched him helplessly before turning again to Sir Eric, only to find he had lost the gist of the conversation. Sir Eric frowned in his niece's direction in the manner of one who would like to say more and then, with a shake of his head, lapsed into silence.

'How was Balmoral, sir?' asked Faro tactfully.

'Oh, excellent. Some quite excellent fishing,' and then with a rapid change of subject, 'Mace, was it, you were wanting? Excellent fellow, Mace. Damned efficient too, not like some of these young officers. Splendid background in history. More use to you than Forster. Did he have any useful information on Queen Mary?'

'He did indeed. He was looking for a missing part of an inventory and I gather he found something . . . '

'Capital, capital. Then that's all settled.'

'Not quite, sir. I haven't seen him yet.' And Faro explained that the enigmatic Forster had told him Mace was on duty.

'But he should be off by six o'clock,' said Sir Eric. 'It isn't long to wait and you must make yourself at home with us meantime. In fact, why not join Lucille and me for dinner in the Mess this evening?'

Hearing her name, Lucille drifted over with Vince at her heels. 'Please come. We would love to have you, wouldn't we, Uncle?'

'I have already invited him, niece.' Sir Eric's sharp rejoinder sounded to Faro's ears unnecessarily irritable. Was this charming, high-spirited visitor beginning to pall on the elderly bachelor with his set way of life? 'We're taking your dear mother, and Vince, of course.'

Again addressing Faro, he smiled. 'No ceremony, just the regular chaps and I expect young Mace will be there. Chance for you to find out what this message was all about.'

Mary Faro, that normally shy and retiring widow, was all excitement as she turned to her son. 'Miss Haston's maid is taking the girls back home to Mrs Brook and – and Sir Eric assures me that I don't need to dress for this occasion.'

'You look quite lovely as you are, my dear, doesn't she?' Sir Eric beamed on the company in general to give their assurance.

'Your costume is quite perfect, so elegant,' said Lucille. Her wholehearted agreement and smiling glance in her uncle's direction suggested that this was a romance that would meet with her approval.

As Rose and Emily were put into their cloaks for the exciting drive back to Sheridan Place in Sir Eric's handsome carriage, Lucille whispered, 'Don't look so anxious, Inspector,' completely misinterpreting Faro's brooding glance. 'Bet is most reliable. And she dotes on children.'

Faro smiled. Fondness of children was the last thing he would have suspected of the dour-faced, enigmatic maid.

The room seemed strangely empty after the girls had left. Faro sighed. He missed them and found himself

109

wishing that they had either stayed at the Castle or that he had accompanied them home. He felt suddenly that a fifth person was an unnecessary and not altogether welcome addition to the foursome he had come upon. Absorbed in each other's company, they were now forced politely to include him in more general and less personal topics of conversation, while he tried in vain to angle his bemused stepson aside to discuss more urgent matters.

As they took their places at the table in the Mess, Faro was unable to see Mace from where he was sitting. If the information implied by the note had been urgent enough to require his immediate presence, he felt a little put out that Mace had not made any effort to contact him before dinner.

Again he was conscious of urgency, of passing time. In a few days Rose and Emily and his mother would have returned to Orkney. Did that account for this feeling of unease, of living on a stage set with something monstrous lurking in the wings, and waiting for a cue that never came?

Lucille sat next to Vince, but it was to himself that she gave her undivided attention and catching his stepson's eye he received many a sad, cold and reproachful glance.

His mother was in deep conversation with one of their table companions. The subject was her favourite: politics. He listened to her candid observations on what was wrong with the French, as characterised by Napoleon III and the Prussians and, in particular, the shocking behaviour of French Canadians, unwilling to accept the benefits offered by British imperialism.

Looking up he saw Sir Eric watching her with a curious expression, a mixture of pride and apprehension. Conscious of Faro's gaze, he turned, smiled and proffered his cigar case.

'Your mother is a most remarkable lady. Shall we adjourn for a smoke?' he whispered. 'I doubt whether we'll be missed, this discussion could go on all evening,' he added

110

with a groan. 'I know old Boyd once he gets an interested audience, particularly a pretty woman.'

And as they took a dram together, Faro studied his companion with new interest. Could it be that his mother's 'remarkable' qualities were the secret of her attraction for Sir Eric? And for the first time he realised that such a marriage would have made good sense, since his host was much too intelligent to wish for a merely decorative adornment to his drawing room.

Misinterpreting his thoughtful look, Sir Eric asked, 'I've noticed you looking rather ill at ease, lad. Anything troubling you?'

Faro shook his head. 'Not really. Except that I was hoping to see Mace.'

'Mace? Of course. I'd forgotten. The reason for this very welcome visit.' He frowned. 'Come to think of it, I didn't notice him at dinner, did you?'

'No.'

'To tell the truth, it completely slipped my mind.' Sir Eric thought for a moment. 'His fellow officers are usually seated at the far end of the Mess and in such a crowd it's difficult to pick anyone out. But he should be back in the main barracks now if you care to go and search for him.'

'If you'll excuse me, sir.'

'Of course. You know the way.'

Faro walked across the now dark quadrangle, where a rather lopsided moon seemed to mock at mortals. Its jaunty angle annoyed him, like a picture hanging askew on a high wall that he longed to set straight. When it suddenly vanished behind a cloud he shook his fist at it. 'All right, old moon. You're safe enough now but don't let it happen again.'

Suddenly he laughed out loud at his own absurdity, chiding an untidy moon. How many glasses of claret had he drunk? After the first two his glass had been constantly replenished by attentive servants, and he must have consumed at least the better part of a bottle.

111

At the barracks he was told that Lieutenant Mace had come off duty before dinner.

'You've just missed him,' said the young officer, giving directions. 'Room 223. Down the corridor, turn right. No, he wasn't at dinner. Bit under the weather, I imagine,' he added with a grin. 'We had a birthday celebration for one of the lads last night.'

Following directions, Faro tapped on the door, waited and receiving no reply looked inside. The room had an air of general untidiness with a dress uniform spread out on the bed, as if waiting for its owner who was going to need it in a hurry when he came off duty.

His way back to the Mess led him past the royal apartments. He stopped outside. Perhaps that was where Mace expected to meet him. But the doors were locked, the corridor empty.

'Where on earth can Mace have got to?' he said, returning to Sir Eric.

Sir Eric shook his head. 'The most likely thing is that having missed you and not knowing that you were dining here he has gone down to Sheridan Place.'

'You are probably right.'

'In that case, he'll be back directly.' Seeing Faro's look of preoccupation, he said, 'All right, lad, if you're worried, take the carriage. Roberts came back while we were at dinner.'

'That's very good of you sir. Will you tell my mother and Vince, please? They'll understand, they're used to my sudden arrivals and departures.'

Mary Faro, who had been watching them, came over. 'What's wrong, son?' When Faro explained about missing the Lieutenant, she nodded. 'Then we'll come with you. It's getting late.'

Sir Eric looked over her shoulder to where Vince and Lucille had their heads together deep in conversation. 'Shame to break up the party, Mary my dear. It's early yet. Besides we see so little of you,' he added, his hand coming to rest tenderly on her shoulder.

112

She smiled up at him and seemed to have no objection to his air of possession. 'But you're coming to tea tomorrow, Eric, aren't you?'

So it was Eric and Mary now, thought Faro. Well, well.

'And it really is late for me. I go to bed with the birds in Orkney and rise with them in the mornings.' Suppressing a yawn in evidence, she added, 'There you are, see – maybe that was the wine. You must forgive me, Eric, I'm very sleepy, all of a sudden.'

She paused to glance approvingly in the direction of the young couple. 'I'll just go with Jeremy, leave Vince to make his own way home.'

Sir Eric sighed. 'If you must go, then I'll see you down to the carriage.'

But there was no concealing their departure. Vince drew himself reluctantly out of the circle of Lucille's magic web.

'How boring that you must go, Inspector,' she said, pouting prettily. 'We were having such a lovely party.' At the door her whisper and the warm glance that accompanied it were for Faro alone. 'We have had so little chance to talk together. I do hope we are going to meet again very soon.'

Handing Mary Faro into the carriage, Sir Eric bent down and kissed her cheek. 'Good night, my dear. Sleep well.'

'Good night, Eric.'

Far from giving continued evidence of weariness, Mary Faro prattled happily all the way back to Sheridan Place with quite as much energy as Miss Haston had shown on a previous occasion. At last, asked a question, her son failed to respond.

'I'm sorry, Mother – what was that?'

She sighed. 'Nothing important, dear. You're very silent tonight.'

'I thought you were very tired, Mother.'

'You're a silly boy sometimes, son, but you're my very own.' She kissed his cheek, and he put his arm around her and with her head resting against his shoulder, they arrived at the locked gates of Sheridan Place. Dismissing Roberts and the carriage, Faro took out his key while Mary Faro looked up at the drawing-room windows. 'I wonder why Mrs Brook hasn't closed the shutters. And the girls' bed-room too, the early sun wakes Rose. She's always been a light sleeper.'

A sickness erupted in the pit of Faro's stomach as he unlocked the door. He knew only too well the unmistak-able aura of an empty house.

'Mrs Brook! Hello – we're back,' called Mrs Faro, slip-ping out of her cloak. 'Shall we ask her to make us a pot of tea?' she whispered.

'She's probably gone to bed,' said Faro carefully. And trying not to alarm his mother unnecessarily, he added, 'You go on upstairs. I'll be with you in a moment.'

'No. I'll come downstairs with you. I must make a cup of tea. I'm so thirsty, I'll never sleep.'

Mrs Brook's basement kitchen was empty of all but the ghostly shapes of furniture, the phantom smells of cooking. He tapped on her sitting-room door.

'Mrs Brook?'

'Where can she be?' asked Mrs Faro anxiously.

But Faro was already across the room, tapping on the door of Mrs Brook's bedroom. As he expected, there was no answer. Looking inside, the bed was neatly made, still with its crocheted daycover undisturbed.

In a curious way, he realised that the deserted room struck a familiar chord of approaching disaster, a feeling of dread that he had been unable to shake off since he had opened the door of Mace's empty room in the Castle barracks.

Mary Faro looked over his shoulder. 'She'd never go out and leave the girls in the house alone, surely. Would she?' And before he could utter any reassuring words, she cried out, 'The girls, oh, the girls, Jeremy!'

Leaning weakly against the table, Faro heard her swift footsteps echoing up the staircase.

A second later, her shrill scream rang through the house.

'Jeremy, Jeremy, come quickly.'

And even as he tried ineffectively to leap up the stairs, she screamed again.

'Rose, Emily. They're not here. They've gone!'

Chapter Ten

The girls' bed was empty. The sight made Faro sweat. Pristine, neat as it should never have been at this hour, it conjured up the same sinister vision as Mace's bed with its sprawled dress uniform. If he hadn't been so damned desperate to see the Lieutenant none of this would ever have happened.

Even as his horrified realisation checked up the dreaded facts – that his daughters, who had left the Castle three hours ago, had never returned home – his mother was crying.

'Oh, my precious bairns. Where are they? I knew it, I knew it in my bones – that maid.' And with the certainty of hindsight, 'I never liked the looks of her, sly, sleekit, she was. I knew we shouldn't have trusted them to her. Oh dear God, Jeremy. Something must have happened to them. An accident, like your poor dear father – that's what . . . ' she whispered and, a hand over her mouth, she leaned against the bedpost, moaning and looking ready to faint.

Faro caught her as she swayed and held her to his side. 'Calm yourself, dear, do be reasonable now. If there had been an accident, Sir Eric's coachman – or the maid – would have reported it when he came back to the Castle – while we were still there. Mother, please, listen to me. He brought us home here in the very same carriage, remember?'

Mrs Faro dabbed at her eyes, tried to regain her composure. 'Of course, son, of course, you must be right. And he would have seen them safely into the house here first, surely?'

Faro hoped so. Sheridan Place was a public thoroughfare

for vehicular traffic during the day. After ten thirty the gates were locked by the lodge keepers and each resident had to use his own key.

'Then why aren't they in their bed?' she demanded tearfully.

'I don't know, Mother, but I'm sure there must be a very simple explanation. Since Mrs Brook isn't here either, we can conclude that they are with her, safe and sound.'

'Safe and sound. Two little girls who've never in their whole lives been out at this time of night? They should have been in bed asleep two hours ago, Jeremy Faro.' Eyes flashing angrily, she added, 'Don't be so stupid. I'm not an idiot, you don't fool me with your simple explanations. I can see it in your face, too, you're sick with fear as I am.'

Then sobbing she threw her arms around him. 'Oh dear God, how I wish I'd come home with them. I knew I should never have let them out of my sight.'

'You mustn't blame yourself. Nothing could possibly have happened to them between the carriage and the house . . . '

'I know what's happened. One of your criminals has kidnapped them,' she said accusingly. 'That's what. Or one of those white slavers . . . '

'Mother, please don't be ridiculous. White slavers wouldn't be interested in girls quite as young as those two.' It wasn't true and he knew it. He only wished that his mother hadn't put into words the terrible suspicion that had already crossed his mind.

By way of consolation, he smiled wanly. 'You surely can't imagine slavers giving that dour, sour-faced maid a second glance?'

'She's a woman, isn't she?' was the caustic reply. 'And that's enough for some men. Anyway, maybe she's in the plot too. In with the kidnappers . . . '

'Listen . . . '

At that moment, they heard the most welcome sound in

117

the world. A key in the front door, and the next moment Mrs Brook let herself in.

Mrs Brook. Alone.

She looked up at them, their horrified faces staring down over the banisters. 'Good evening, Mrs Faro – Inspector sir . . .'

'Where are the children?' shouted Faro.

'With you, of course – aren't they?'

'Come upstairs, Mrs Brook.'

'What's the matter? Has something happened to them?'

'Where have you been, Mrs Brook?'

'Me, Inspector sir? To the Women's Guild concert.'

'Until eleven o'clock?'

Mrs Brook drew herself up stiffly. 'I went to visit friends afterwards for a bite of supper. This is Saturday, Inspector sir, my evening off,' she added reproachfully. 'Or had you forgotten?'

Faro had forgotten. At his side, clutching his arm, his mother began to whimper. 'The girls – they weren't with you?'

'No, Mrs Faro. How could they be? They were with you.' And in a voice touched with panic, she whispered, 'Tell me – has something happened?'

'We don't know. Please sit down, Mrs Brook. We have been at the Castle and we stayed to dinner, sent the girls home to be put to bed by Miss Haston's maid. They aren't in their bed. Or anywhere in the house.'

It was Mrs Brook's turn to stifle a cry of horror as she looked from one to the other. 'But Inspector sir, they wouldn't be able to get in unless you gave them your key. Oh dear, if only you had remembered that it was my evening off.'

'You're not to blame, Mrs Brook. I expect they have gone back to the Castle. That must be it – and we've missed them.'

Faro tried to sound calm, watching them helplessly, the tears welling in Mrs Brook's eyes, his mother quietly moaning, and knowing he was only minutes away from having to deal with two distraught and hysterical women.

He thought rapidly. If only he knew for sure whether the maid Bet was back at the Castle. She had not been in evidence when they returned to Sir Eric's apartment after dinner. But that was quite normal. A lady's maid would stay in her room unless – and until – summoned by her young mistress.

If she had not returned, he could only conclude that she had let Sir Eric's carriage leave them at the entrance to Sheridan Place, presuming Mrs Brook to be at home. When they couldn't get in, she would have tried to find an omnibus to take them to Lothian Road. A stranger in the district, could Rose and Emily have helped her, have known about such things? And what if the maid had no money with her?

With a sick feeling of disaster, he realised that if they had taken any kind of transport, then she and the girls would have been back at the Castle long before he and his mother left.

Even if they had had to walk all the way.

So where were they? Where were his two precious bairns, his little daughters that he had always sadly neglected, who played such minor roles in a life where his duties as a detective inspector came always first and foremost. So relentless at tracking down criminals, he was suddenly made vulnerable by the presence of two small girls; had crime come to roost on his own doorstep?

Would he ever see them again? His mother hadn't been too far out with her speculations about white slavers. Every day small girls vanished from the poor streets of Edinburgh and Leith. Not for anything as exotic as white slaving, but for the thriving business of child prostitution.

Although arrests were few and the guilty were ready to pay a great deal of money to keep such scandals from being made public, Faro was grimly aware of this particular method of child abuse. The prettier small girls were first stripped of their rags, bathed and fed, before being led naked to the bed of some elderly debauchee for 'initiation'. Those who were not virgins bypassed the handsome private houses in the New Town, and were sent direct to discreet gentlemen's clubs patronised by Edinburgh's wealthy decadents.

Oh dear God.

The two women before him, both in tears, were speculating on what might have happened, neither of them, thank God, with an inkling of what he knew of that other society where no corruption that money could buy was inaccessible.

Numbly he stood, put out consoling hands, heard himself uttering platitudes, wildly untrue, as the doors of nightmare closed around them, while the ginger kitten Rusty the girls so loved demanded affection and a warm lap and was surprised and indignant at being denied them.

'Listen . . . '

'Someone at the door . . . '

Two raced down the hall. Faro hobbled after them.

This time the newcomer was Vince.

Vince. Alone.

Even as Mrs Faro threw herself sobbing into his arms, Faro looked at Vince's stricken face.

'The girls?'

'They aren't here?' whispered Vince. 'I had hoped . . . ' He followed them into the drawing room. 'Ladies, would you please make a pot of tea – very strong.'

'Tell me what has happened . . .'

'They are alive and well, so stop worrying.'

'But . . . '

'Tea. Strong tea, first.'

As the door closed, Faro seized his arm, noticing how pale he was. 'Is it true – they're alive and unharmed – you've seen them?'

Vince took his arm, attempted to lead him to a chair. 'Calm yourself, don't you go to pieces like those two. Stepfather, for God's sake . . . '

'Then for God's sake – tell me . . . '

Vince shook his head. 'All I know is that Lucille's maid

120

– Betty or whoever she is – came back to the Castle just before I left. She was in a terrible state. They couldn't get into the house, Mrs Brook was out . . . '

'Yes, yes – I know all that.'

'Then listen, for God's sake. The maid was in a state, wringing her hands. Rose was the only one to show presence of mind. She thought she knew the road where the omnibuses were. She had never been on one herself, but she was game to try it . . . '

'My dear, enterprising Rose,' whispered Faro.

'They boarded the omnibus all right but one stop further on and the driver put them off. The woman had no money to pay the fares. And now they were lost, but Rose thought they were near the Meadows and a short cut might bring them out near the Castle. They began walking and a gentleman's carriage stopped and when they explained their predicament, the coachman offered to take them to the Castle. They thought this was a tremendous piece of luck . . . '

'Luck, God Almighty!' said Faro. 'You know what all this implies, don't you, Vince, picking up children at night . . . '

Vince held up his hand. 'I'm trying not to think of that, Stepfather. And I advise you not to either. The facts are bad enough without us being over imaginative. We need time . . . '

Faro sank down on to a chair, buried his face in his hands. 'Time. We might already be too late, Vince. Even now your two stepsisters, my wee bairns, may have been violated by some rich pervert whose sexual impulses require . . . '

'Stop it, Stepfather. Stop this, at once!' Vince banged his fist on the table. 'For God's sake, let's concentrate on what we know happened, not what we think might have happened.'

There was a pause before the detective's alert mind gained possession over the distraught father. 'What else did this woman say?' he asked heavily. 'And how did she know it was a gentleman's carriage?'

'Because although it was empty, it smelt of cigars and pomade. She was quite definite about that.'

'Was she now? By God, I could kill her. And I swear I will if anything has happened . . . '

'She was guiltless, Stepfather. Gibbering with terror, I can tell you. She said that if it hadn't been for the presence of mind of one of the girls looking out of the window and noticing in the moonlight that Arthur's Seat was on the wrong side if they were travelling towards the Castle . . . '

'That would almost certainly be Rose, my bright, observant lass,' said Faro, his voice broken, near to tears.

'The woman said she then tried to get the coachman to stop, but he pretended not to hear and whipped the horses on faster. She guessed that they were being taken somewhere against their will. She then showed great presence of mind. The carriage had to stop momentarily at the crossroads, to let another vehicle pass, and she pushed the girls out. She intended jumping down after them, when the carriage took off again at high speed and took her with it. It stopped at some big gates – no, she had no idea where. She tried to get out and when the coachman saw that the girls had gone, he struck her down and when she came to, she – where are you going?'

'I'm going to the Central Office, to have every constable alerted.'

'I've already done that, Stepfather. On my way here. I reported two small girls abducted, and a constable left immediately for the Castle to interview the maid.'

'You stay here – tell the womenfolk any story you like. I'll be back as soon as I have news.'

Cursing the limp that hampered him when he most needed speed, Faro hurried towards Newington Road, where he found a hackney carriage setting down passengers. Grumbling about the late hour, the driver was persuaded to take the Inspector to the Central Office.

And there, walking towards a waiting police carriage was the most welcome sight in his whole world. Two small girls in the custody of Sergeant Danny McQuinn.

Faro called out. A moment later, he had them gathered to his breast. And for those prayers answered, a peace passing all understanding reigned in his heart.

'Papa, Papa.' Speechless, tearful with joy, he held them in his arms. 'We've had such an adventure, Papa.'

Over their heads, he looked at McQuinn, grinning with delight. For once, if there had been room he would have included his old enemy in that grateful embrace.

'Thanks, Sergeant.'

McQuinn grinned. 'I was just about to escort these two young ladies back home. Constable McDonald found them wandering along the High Street. That elder lass of yours – Rose is it? – shows great enterprise. Told me some amazing story, mind you, about escaping from a carriage on the Meadows.'

In the police carriage on the way back to Sheridan Place, hugging them to his side as if he could never let them out of his sight again, he listened to the rest of Rose's story.

'It's true, Papa. It was a horrid carriage, all dark and enclosed and smelly – with the blinds down.'

'I didn't like it one bit and that horrid maid of Miss Haston's pushed us out and left us to find our own way back,' was Emily's indignant contribution. 'We were lost, Papa, and anyway we knew there was no one at home.'

'You couldn't have seen anything anyway, you were so busy crying, Em. Luckily the moon helped and I managed to guess from Arthur's Seat and the Castle where the High Street might be.'

'She made us keep walking, for hours and hours, Papa,' wailed Emily. 'And I was so tired. Look at my best shoes. They're ruined, Papa. And they were so pretty. Grandmama will be so cross,' she added with a tearful sniff.

'Never mind, my precious. You shall have a new pair, I promise.'

'As I was saying,' interrupted Rose sternly, 'when I recognised we were near the High Street, after that it

123

was easy. We saw a constable and told him we were lost.'

'I told him that you were our Papa,' said Emily.

'He took us to that nice Sergeant who was just going to take us home in the police carriage. But oh Papa, we were so glad to see you,' whispered Rose, snuggling a little closer so that she could kiss his cheek.

'We were very frightened, Papa,' whispered Emily.

'No, we weren't, Em,' said her sister indignantly.

'What a fib. I saw you crying once.'

'Just when we were very lost, and just a little bit, Em. But it was an adventure, wasn't it, Papa?'

One, thought Faro, that he fervently hoped he – and they – would never experience again.

'Do you think the nasty coachman was going to hold us to ransom?'

'Not really, Rose. I think it was all a bit of a mistake.'

'Mistake, Papa? How?'

He didn't want them to have nightmares. 'He might have been a little deaf and just didn't realise that you wanted to get out.'

'Then why was he going the wrong way?'

'Maybe he got the maid's directions wrong.'

Rose regarded him severely. Her small face registered disappointment. 'You don't really think that, do you, Papa?'

He didn't. But at that moment, the carriage stopped outside Sheridan Place, and leaving them to the rapturous reception from the three eager anxious people awaiting their arrival, Faro told the driver to take him to the Castle.

'It's very late, Inspector.' It was indeed.

The Castle gates closed at eleven and midnight was striking. He must content himself with a scribbled note, 'All's well. Girls safe and sound at home.' Leaving this with the gatekeeper to be delivered to Sir Eric immediately, he ordered the police carriage to return him to Sheridan Place.

As he looked out of the window, the moon was bright

as day and he felt a strong desire to propitiate the pagan moon goddess. What would have been the answer to tonight's sinister happenings if there had been no moon by which his enterprising Rose could recognise Arthur's Seat and discover that they were prisoners in a sinister carriage taking them in the wrong direction, away from Sheridan Place?

He shivered, longing to reach home where the girls were now safely asleep and there was laughter, smiling faces and a certain feeling of celebration in the air. Celebration – or was it deliverance from evil?

Suddenly he realised that the disappearance of Rose and Emily had put out of his mind all thoughts about Lieutenant Mace's failure to appear regarding the urgent message. A message which had brought Faro to the Castle in the first place and thereby set in motion the nightmare events of the last few hours.

He slept late next morning and awoke to the sound of church bells ringing. Downstairs Mrs Brook told him that his mother had taken the girls to morning service, leaving strict instructions that he was not to be disturbed.

Inspector Faro and Dr Laurie were lapsed Presbyterians, their kirk-going limited to somewhat perfunctory family occasions. Normally Vince took the opportunity of discreetly sleeping off Saturday night's hangover and did not appear until Sunday luncheon.

Hopeful that he might be awake, Faro looked into his bedroom. There was no response to his whispered 'Vince?', so ignoring Mrs Brook's lavish breakfast for his digestion's sake, Faro made his way up to the Castle.

He was anxious to speak to Bet and be in time to talk to Arthur Mace as he came off church parade. From the maid he learned that Sir Eric and her mistress had gone to morning service at St Giles's Cathedral, but her first question was for Rose and Emily.

'If any harm had befallen them, I would never have forgiven myself, Inspector. Never.' Her distress was obvious and the passion of her words genuine, making Faro realise once again that one should not make hasty judgements based on appearances only. Faces had their own reasons for presenting a dour expression to the world, but that did not mean that the hearts they hid were cold and uncaring.

'I'd like you to tell me what happened last night. First of all, why did you send Sir Eric's carriage away when you reached Sheridan Place?'

'Because the gates at the entrance weren't open, sir.'

That was true. After dusk they were locked and residents had to produce their own keys to gain admittance. As he listened to the maid's story, he realised it was almost word for word what Vince had related to him. At the end, she regarded his stern face apprehensively.

'You do believe me, do you not, sir?'

Some odd turns of phrase and her swarthy appearance had decided him even more than her faint accent that she was probably French.

When he said so, she smiled. 'From French-speaking Canada, sir. But I have been with Miss Haston's family since she was a little girl.'

And that fact put an end to any further doubts he might have had about the truth of her story. 'What about those big gates, where you managed to leave the carriage? Do you know how long it took you to reach them?'

'Ten minutes, maybe more. Half an hour? I have no means of being certain of the time.'

'You say that the coachman threw you out with some violence.'

'He struck me and, yes, I fell to the ground.'

'I trust you were not injured in any way.'

Again she shrugged. 'Not even bruised, sir. I fell on grass and I fainted only with fear, you understand.'

'Would you recognise those big gates again?'

She hesitated and then shook her head. 'It was moonlight, a road with a long wall. But I was so frightened and, as you know, Inspector, I've never been in Edinburgh before. I only know this area round the Castle here and, of course, Princes Street, where I go shopping with Miss Haston.'

126

'Have you any idea what was intended by this abduction?'

'Ab–duction – what is that, sir?'

'The attempt to kidnap the girls and yourself.'

She thought for a moment. 'It was not I they wanted, for sure. It must have been the little girls.' She looked at him steadily. 'Perhaps they hoped to hold them to ransom. Is that not the way with such kidnappers?'

'Only if they knew who they were, and I am by no means a rich man.'

At his words, Bet opened her mouth as if some thought had occurred to her, then she shook her head.

'Well?' said Faro.

She shrugged. 'It is nothing.'

'Allow me to be the judge of that, mademoiselle.'

'It is too silly, but – but it occurs to me that perhaps you were not the, er – target, is it? And that your little girls were never really in danger. That they were – somehow – only there by accident.'

Her slow speech as she sought for the right words made Faro unnecessarily impatient. 'What are you trying to tell me, mademoiselle?'

'Sir Eric – he is a rich man, yes?'

'Yes.'

'And he has influence with people in high places, yes?'

'He has.'

'And Miss Lucille is his niece – that is so?'

Faro agreed.

'I am only thinking that perhaps it was not myself and your little girls that the kidnappers wanted. You see, Inspector, Miss Lucille gave me her hooded cloak the day after we went to the shops on Princes Street.' She looked up at him. 'This was the first time I am wearing it.' She shrugged. 'Perhaps it is of no significance, but maybe this coachman made a mistake and took the maid for the mistress.'

A remote possibility but one worth bearing in mind. Faro asked, 'Tell me about this coachman. Would you recognise him again?'

127

The maid drew herself up stiffly. 'I do not look at such men, Inspector,' she said, a touch indignantly. 'All I can tell you is that he had a tall hat and was muffled up to the eyes, even though it was a warm night. As he never got down from his box, I do not know if he was short or tall, thin or fat.' She shivered at the memory. 'I was very frightened. Coming from the backwoods with wild beasts and wild men is one thing, but a respectable woman does not expect such behaviour in a civilised big city like Edinburgh and living in a titled gentleman's establishment.'

Faro hid a smile at her innocence, and thanked her for her presence of mind in engineering his daughters' escape from the carriage. Trusting she was none the worse for her adventure, he gratefully thrust a couple of guineas into her hand and went in search of Lieutenant Mace.

The corridor to Room 223 was deserted. He tapped on the door and, receiving no reply, opened it. He was not really surprised to find it empty again.

For some reason Mace was being very elusive, but what really disturbed Faro was that everything looked exactly as it had been last night, even to the dress uniform spread out awaiting the young officer's return. As neither it nor the bed had been disturbed, the obvious conclusion was that Mace had not slept in his room, nor had he returned there after dinner in the Mess.

Faro sat down on the only chair. He had to think this out. If Mace was missing, the connection with last night's events and the attempted kidnapping of his daughters on their way home from the Castle took on a very sinister aspect indeed.

The decision for the girls to go home with Bet in Sir Eric's carriage had been quite spontaneous. To believe otherwise was to take into account what appeared to be an elaborate string of coincidences, whereby the kidnappers had some connection with the Castle and that Miss Haston's maid and Sir Eric's coachman, Roberts, were in league with them.

And Faro found himself remembering how often of late he had felt sure that his house was being watched. He went quite cold at the thought of what such vigilance might imply.

And what of the missing Lieutenant?

Should he give credence to the maid's theory about her mistaken identity and, if the plot was to kidnap Lucille Haston, had Mace received some warning of what was to happen? In fact, had his information nothing to do with the Queen Mary jewel or the missing page of a sixteenth-century inventory? Dangerous information which threatened repercussions on Faro and all his family.

Chapter Eleven

As he entered Sir Eric's apartments, Lucille was removing her apple green satin bonnet, a perfect match for her gown. Her uncle, distinguished and resplendent in full Highland dress, handed Faro a glass. As he savioured the excellent Madeira, their first concern was for Rose and Emily.

Assured that the girls were well and quite unharmed by their ordeal, Sir Eric said. 'I took Roberts to task. He won't forget in a hurry that in future he waits with the carriage until his passengers are safely indoors. When I think of what could have happened to those dear children . . . '

'At least Bet didn't lose her head,' said Lucille proudly. 'I know you've never cared greatly for her, Uncle . . . '

Sir Eric shrugged. 'I was wrong. Worth her weight in gold,' and turning to Faro, 'good of you to come so promptly, lad. We were all desperately anxious, even after we received your message.'

'I really came to see Mace.'

'Mace?' Sir Eric frowned. 'I had quite forgotten. What was that about again?'

'I had a message from him. I believe it had something to do with this,' he said, taking the Queen Mary cameo out of his pocket.

Sir Eric and Lucille studied it carefully.

'Quite genuine, is it? Remarkably fine piece.'

Lucille took it and held it against her neck. 'To think that it is so old, and that the Queen of Scots probably wore it,' and closing her eyes ecstatically, she whispered, 'just like this, touching her bare flesh as it does mine, three hundred years ago.'

Sir Eric watched her with a tolerant smile as, suddenly shivering, she handed the jewel back to Faro. 'I'm not really sure that I would care to wear it, not after all that sad history.'

'You aren't likely to get the chance, m'dear,' laughed Sir Eric. 'I can't imagine the owner wanting to part with it. Must be worth a small fortune.' And to Faro, 'Who owns it, anyway?'

'We don't know.' He explained that it had been found on Castle Rock after the attempted break in and that, as it was unclaimed, Superintendent Mackintosh had decided it belonged with Queen Mary's jewels in the museum.

'Quite right, of course, once we have checked its authenticity. I'll get Forster to look into it. He should know – or Mace, even better. He's a very knowledgeable young man. I presume he's seen it.'

'He has.'

'I dare say he has found out something.'

'Do let us know. It's all very exciting,' said Lucille.

'What's wrong, Jeremy lad? You're looking very solemn.'

'I can't understand why he hasn't contacted me, sir.'

'Oh, I dare say he will.'

'But I went to his room and it didn't look as if his bed had been slept in.'

Sir Eric chortled. 'Come now. You obviously don't know army life, young lad, or what these chaps get up to. He would be off duty until tomorrow morning. Probably got a lady friend tucked away somewhere in Edinburgh and courting will have banished all other unimportant details from his mind.'

A clock struck and Sir Eric said. 'Good heavens, I had almost forgotten. You must excuse me, Jeremy lad, I have an engagement – a rather dreary Council meeting.'

As Jeremy prepared to depart also, Lucille sighed. 'I haven't any engagement for this afternoon, alas.'

'You may have the carriage, m'dear. Get Roberts to take you out somewhere and take your maid with you.'

Lucille smiled slyly. 'Perhaps Inspector Faro would escort me.'

'Good idea, if he's not too busy.'

'I am rather anxious to get back to the family. However . . .'

'Take the girl with you. Have the carriage. Your dear mother and the girls would enjoy a drive on an afternoon like this.'

'That's very kind of you, sir.'

'Not at all. Anything to keep this young lady entertained for a while.' At the door Sir Eric looked back. 'I will leave the pair of you to arrange things. Don't let her be a nuisance, Jeremy,' he warned.

'Beast,' shouted Lucille at the closed door.

On the way to Sheridan Place, he encouraged Lucille to talk of her life in Canada. Losing her parents when she was very young, he gathered that living with an elderly spinster Haston cousin and in a remote backwoods area had great disadvantages and severe restrictions. Little wonder that a young lady of spirit and restless ambition had been eager to escape.

'We only came across in May, you know. Uncle thought it advisable that we leave for a while as we lived in the Red River area, where all the trouble is brewing with the Metis.'

When Faro looked blank, she explained. 'Metis are half-breed Indians. They have a strong French and Roman Catholic culture and they resent being taken over by English-speaking, Protestant Canadians. Their leader is a very brave man called Louis Riel.'

She was silent for a moment and then continued. 'I didn't realise that I was going to be sent away to another backwoods. Orkney wasn't much better than Canada,' she said in disgust. 'And you can imagine, having heard so much of Edinburgh, I was so looking forward to coming to Uncle Eric for a while.' She sighed. 'Maybe things are always better looked forward to than when they actually happen.'

Faro smiled. 'That is one of the first valuable lessons in life, Miss Haston. Never expect too much, in fact, expect little and then one can never be disappointed, only pleasantly surprised.'

Lucille sighed.'You are so wise and I am such an idiot.'

Faro shook his head. 'No, not an idiot, just young.'

'Young.'

'Yes, young. And that is the one trouble time will cure.'

'You make it sound like an unpleasant illness.'

'And so it can seem sometimes. Growing up is not a condition of my own life that I would care to repeat.'

Lucille laughed. 'Oh Jeremy, you are so solemn. Why, I have been grown up for years and years.'

'Hardly.'

'It's true. I can scarcely remember what it was to be a child. Anyone living where I did, and with Cousin Haston, would not long be allowed the luxury of childhood, I can assure you.'

The carriage turned into the gates of Sheridan Place and Mrs Brook came to the door.

'I saw you from the upstairs window.' Seeing his startled expression, Mrs Brook beamed. 'No, nothing's wrong, Inspector sir. All is right as rain. When you didn't arrive back, we thought you had been delayed and seeing it's such a nice day and this is their last Sunday. Doctor Vince hired a gig and has taken them all to – where was it, now – Cramond, I think he talked about.'

A sublime day, Arthur's Seat shimmered, already crowded with small figures on its summit. Poor Vince would be furious when he learned that he has missed the opportunity of another visit from the delectable Miss Haston.

'You could probably catch up with them.'

'What a good idea.'

'Will you wait a moment, Inspector sir?' said Mrs Brook, darting back into the house.

Feeling benign, Faro turned to Lucille, 'Shall we got to Cramond? Would you like that?'

'I should like to go anywhere with you.'

Faro smiled, pretending not to notice the amorous glance, the gentle sigh that accompanied her whisper. He was giving directions to the driver, when Mrs Brook re-appeared breathlessly with a covered basket and a cloak over her arm.

'Those girls forgot the extra food I made for their picnic and Doctor Vince's bottle of wine. Oh, and here is Mrs Faro's cloak in case the sun goes in. If you don't mind . . . '

As the carriage trotted briskly towards Cramond, Faro told Lucille that this was their favourite place, how he had spent a considerable time canoeing with Vince during his student days. The tide was out and the island glittered across the causeway.

Lucille shaded her eyes. 'I wonder where they are?'

'Probably on the shelterd side. Shall we walk across?'

Leaving Lucille to give instructions to the driver to wait along the promenade among the other carriages lined up while their owners took the popular Sunday afternoon stroll across to the island, he took up his stick and led the way. Lucille insisting on carrying the picnic basket and wearing Mrs Faro's light cape thrown over her shoulders.

When they reached the other side, she exclaimed with delight at the sight of the canoes on the smooth water. 'What a divine place. But I don't see Vince and the others.'

'They are probably in the Dell. It's a rather secret place Lizzie and I discovered with Vince long ago. Sheltered and quiet, superb for a picnic. Yes, that's no doubt where they are.'

The Dell was empty. 'We must have missed them,' said Faro.

'Never mind,' said Lucille. 'We have the picnic, we might as well enjoy it. I'm hungry and I suspect you missed luncheon.'

That was true and Faro realised that he was indeed hungry. There were three boulders which he pointed out made a natural table and chairs. Spreading the contents of the basket, she said, 'What a divine spot. I can understand how you must have loved it here. And Vince must have been a great comfort to you after your wife died.'

'He adored his mother,' Faro replied, opening the wine.

'Tell me about her. I realised that you couldn't be his real father, you were too young. Does he always call you Stepfather?'

'Yes.'

'I would have thought Jeremy more appropriate.'

Faro shook his head. 'No, I like being Stepfather. It's like Father, I am the only one to be called that name by Vince.'

'Tell be about his mother.'

'There isn't much to tell.'

'Isn't there? She must have been considerably older than you.'

'Not really. She had Vince when she was sixteen. They were so close – more like brother and sister really.'

'You must miss her very much.'

When Faro didn't reply, she continued, 'Did she love you very much?'

'I expect she did.' He looked at her sombre face. 'What an odd question.'

'Why odd?'

'Because most people take it for granted that husbands and wives love each other.'

'I don't think it's always true, do you? And you are a strange man. You give so little away of your emotions.'

'That is because in my job emotions are best kept hidden.'

'Have you ever loved anyone since your wife died?'

Faro looked at her. To be honest or diplomatic. 'Well, yes, I have.'

'Then you would marry again?'

'I have no strong feelings on the subject.'

'Didn't you want to marry this other woman . . . '

135

'Do you mind if we don't talk about it, Lucille? It was all very recent and very painful.'

'She didn't want you? She didn't love you? How could she fail to love you?'

Faro shook his head violently, as if to shake away those terrible bitter memories of agony and guilt. Bad enough that they should still haunt his dreams and would, he suspected, for the rest of his life. He was certainly not prepared for – he did not even think he was capable of – a solemn discussion with this extraordinarily frank young woman about his past loves.

'Please – I've told you – I'm not going to discuss it.'

Seeing his expression, she put her hand on his arm. 'Forgive me, I've hurt you. I didn't mean to. Only I think things are best talked over.'

'Not for me. Not for me. And I don't think it's a very good idea for us to be on such personal terms.'

'Why not – what on earth is wrong in that . . . '

'Nothing's wrong, Lucille. Now let's talk about something else. There's a good girl,' he added, managing to sound to his own ears amazingly like Sir Eric. As the conversation slid, at his instigation, on to more impersonal topics, he began to relax. Although he kept a token lookout for his family, he was secretly pleased to have this unconventional and quite delightful companion all to himself for the afternoon.

Mrs Brook's box of candies was soon demolished, mostly by Lucille since Faro lacked a taste for 'sweeties'. However, the wine was heady on an empty stomach and he realised that he was suddenly tired, suffering from the effects of last night's terrifying ordeal.

As Lucille prattled on, back to her usual form, full of engaging trivialities and speculations, he found his attention wandering, hypnotised by the bright glare of the River Forth with its occasional canoes passing by, its white-sailed ships.

He blinked furiously, trying to stop his heavy eyelids closing. It was that delicious wine. He must have had several glasses more than Lucille and he was not a wine drinker, a good, solid, ale man. He thought yearningly of sleep. He might just close his eyes, Lucille would never notice.

Just for a few moments.

He dreamed that he was being kissed. The feeling was so real. Then he opened his eyes to find Lucille's face inches from his own.

He put his hand to his mouth and she smiled. 'I'm so glad you are clean shaven, I hate the fashion for beards. You have such nice lips, a firm strong mouth.'

Faro sat upright. This wasn't in the plan at all. He had no intention of making a fool of himself over Lucille Haston or encouraging her ardent but dangerous flirtation. 'What time is it?'

'It's early yet.'

'Is it?' And taking out his pocket watch, he struggled to his feet.

'What's the matter? We aren't going yet, surely?'

'Time and tide wait for no man, Lucille. And in this case, if we don't move sharpish the tide will be in and we'll have to stay here until tomorrow morning.'

'How wonderful – oh how romantic,' sighed Lucille, fluttering her eyelids.

Faro seized the basket, the glasses. 'Come along,' he said, offering his hand.

'No.' Reclining against the rock, Lucille shook her head obstinately and stared out across the Forth, a rebellious child again.

'What do you mean, no, Lucille?'

'I want to stay here.'

'We can't stay here. Don't you understand, once the causeway is covered the tide will cut us off until tomorrow morning.'

'Of course I understand. And I want to stay here – until tomorrow morning – with you, Jeremy. Just the two of us,' was the whispered reply.

Trying to misunderstand the implications of her remark,

he said lightly, 'Surely you don't want to stay here all night? I warn you, it gets very cold and uncomfortable.'

She looked at him directly. 'We have each other. Besides I noticed that there are cottages – someone will give us a room for the night.'

Faro looked at her. 'My dear girl, what are you suggesting?'

'Isn't it obvious? That we stay the night here.' And before Faro could do anything but continue to stare, she threw her arms around him, clinging, kissing his face. 'Uncle is sending me back to Orkney next week,' she sobbed. 'This is our last chance.'

'Our last chance for what?'

'Oh Jeremy darling, I love you. I love you so.'

'Nonsense, Lucille, you hardly know me at all. We have only met a couple of times.'

'What has that to do with it? I've loved you from when I first saw you. I know you love me and nothing else matters.'

'Lucille, dear child – even if I did love you as you imagine, lots of other things matter.'

'They don't, they don't – I love you and I will make you happy, I promise. And if we stay out all night . . . ' she stopped, looked at him.

'And if we stay out all night,' he finished slowly, 'what then, Lucille?'

'Then you will have to marry me, I suppose,' she said.

It sounded so absurd, so pathetically absurd and Faro knew that, even compromised, he would take the consequences. He could never share his exacting, dangerous life with this wordly-wise butterfly.

'Lucille, I don't love you.'

'I'll make you love me.'

'I'm far too old for you. You want a young man, full of hope in life, not a middle-aged widower with a growing family.'

'I love Rose and Emily – and Vince too. I'd make a good stepmother.'

Faro chuckled in spite of himself. He could just see

138

the kind of complications that might arise for Vince with a stepmother as attractive as this, and only a couple of years between them.

'What is so amusing about that? Besides many of my friends have married men a lot older than you. And I don't care for boys. Besides, I know about love.'

'I hope we all know about love, Lucille.'

'I don't mean in theory. I mean – I mean, well, I am not inexperienced where men are concerned. I have had a lover – one of the rebel leaders. That was why they made me come across to Orkney.' Seeing Faro's solemn expression, she laid her head against his shoulder. 'Oh, I shouldn't have told you that. It was very indiscreet of me.'

'And very honest too.'

'But it's made a difference. It's made you hate me now.'

'My dear girl. It hasn't made the slightest difference to my feelings for you. If I loved you and wanted to marry you, I assure you the fact that you've had a lover wouldn't matter a damn to me – or to any other decent man, I hope, who loved you.'

'Then why . . . '

'Look, Lucille, Sir Eric is one of my dearest friends. How would he feel if I stayed out all night with his niece, the girl he trusts me to look after?'

'We could make up a story. He would believe it. No one but us need ever know that we slept together. He likes you.'

'He would cease to like or respect me if I compromised you. He is a very honest, honourable man. And his greatest hope is that you will make a good marriage.'

'I don't want a good marriage. I only want you.'

'I doubt whether Sir Eric would be all that delighted to have a policeman in his family.'

'Even though he loves the policeman's mother?' Lucille giggled. 'I thought that would surprise you. And he has loved her for years and years. Oh Jeremy, we would be such a happy family.'

'No, Lucille. We wouldn't. I wouldn't be happy and

neither would you after the honeymoon was over. Detectives make very bad husbands. If you doubt that, ask Mrs Brook how often she makes meals and I don't appear, ask Vince how often arrangements are cancelled.'

As they left the Dell and began to walk towards the causeway, Faro heard the magic words, 'Papa, Papa.'

Rose and Emily were racing across the sands towards him, led by Vince and followed by his mother, a little breathless.

Explanations, exclamations of mutual surprise and delight followed. Vince had noticed Sir Eric's carriage and had come in search of them.

Faro hoped that Lucille's disappointment would not be obvious. But she rose to the occasion. As they hurried across the causeway, with the water creeping ever closer to their feet, Mrs Faro taking her son's arm with Vince and Lucille and the two girls racing ahead, Lucille's trilling laughter floated back to them.

'I'm so glad we found you in time, Jeremy. I don't know what would have happened if you'd missed the tide.'

'Nor do I, Mother dear.'

'That was a narrow escape you had.'

'It was indeed. The narrowest. And I was never so glad to see anyone,' he said, pecking her cheek gratefully.

Before boarding Sir Eric's carriage, Faro drew Vince aside. 'I must speak to you, then I will see Lucille home.'

Vince gave him a disagreeable look. 'Indeed. I rather hoped you were going to offer me that privilege.'

Faro felt compassion for the sullen, disappointed boy's face before him, conscious that he was helpless to avert the misery in store. Vince must go on with his hopeless infatuation for Lucille.

He must never know the truth. The truth that could only blight their happy bachelor existence. That it was the father Lucille Haston wanted, not the stepson.

With a sigh, Faro produced Mace's note. 'I would most willingly let you escort Miss Haston, but it so happens that I have to see Mace.'

140

As Vince read the note, Faro explained that Mace had failed to contact him. 'Incidentally, I have made some progress with the identity of our dead man – at last.'

Vince had dined with the Penfolds. He was immediately interested in Faro's abbreviated version of his visit, although Faro left out the flirtation.

'Come along, you two. Do stop gossiping.'

'What a dreadful woman. You must tell me more,' said Vince as the two parties made their farewells.

Faro, with a silent and subdued Lucille at his side, was driven back to the Castle, where Sir Eric was waiting for him, sitting at his desk, pen in hand. 'Been a bit of an accident, lad. Young Mace. Body's just been found. Cleaning an antique pistol, didn't realise it was loaded. Tragic business. I'm just writing to his parents.'

Faro realised that he was not surprised, that he had been expecting something like this. 'Have the police been notified? May I see the body.'

'If you wish, lad.' And looking round to see that Lucille was not in earshot, 'Half his face blown away. We had him moved to the barrack infirmary. And had the room cleaned up a bit.'

Faro groaned. And all the clues cleaned up too.

'Hell of a mess. You would wonder where all the blood came from.'

'You are quite sure that it was an accident?'

'Of course, lad. Forster heard the shot and rushed in, but it was too late. Called out medical man right away, but of course nothing could be done but sign the death certificate.'

'May I talk to Forster?'

'Of course.'

Faro could hardly reproach Sir Eric, but he did not enjoy the next half hour. This was the sickening side of detective work that he could well do without. He often thought his stomach was too delicate for viewing bodies that had died by violence, their own or someone else's. He found himself looking at the mutilated face, remembering

141

that interview with Mace and wondering again why the young officer had failed to meet him at the Castle.

He found the silent, swarthy Forster waiting for him in the infirmary corridor.

'Sir Eric told me you were here.'

'I wish to see the museum room.' Forster led the way and opened the door.

Faro looked round quickly. Bloodstains had been washed away, a chair straightened. But there was nothing left in the way of evidence. And there was no place anyone could have hidden. 'Tell me exactly what happened.'

'Sitting in my study. Heard a shot from in here.'

'How did you know it was a shot?'

A faint smile touched Forster's face. 'People who live in military establishments do not make mistakes about guns and explosions.'

'You went immediately?'

'Yes. At first I thought the room empty. Then saw Mace's feet sticking out.' He shrugged. 'Quite dead.'

'There was no one else here. You are quite sure of that.'

Only one door. They would have had to meet me on the way out.'

'Could anyone have hidden anywhere?'

Forster gave him a penetrating glance. 'Before I went for the doctor and to tell Sir Eric, I locked the door behind me. I thought that was the proper thing to do.'

'It was indeed.'

'Thank you, Inspector.'

Faro looked at him quickly. Was he being sarcastic? There was no sign of anything but patience on the man's face.

'Will that be all you are wanting?'

'For the moment. Yes. You will need to sign a statement.'

'I have already done so. For Sir Eric and the police.'

As the man turned to leave, Faro said: 'One thing more, if you please. Are you quite satisfied that Mace's death was an accident?'

142

Forster thought for a moment before replying. 'Lieutenant Mace was an agreeable man. He did not make friends easily, or enemies either.'

'Can you think of anyone who might bear him a grudge?'

'No one.' There was no hesitation in his reply.

'He sent me a note. That he had found something important. I think it might have been concerning the inventory of Queen Mary's jewels. Do you know anything about that?'

'Only that he asked me for a missing page. I did not have it and told him it had disappeared when the items were being catalogued. It had been mislaid at the printers.'

'When was this and who were the printers?'

'A local firm who I am told were burnt down two years ago. All this happened before I came to work at the Castle.'

Dismissing Forster, Faro could not rid himself of the uneasy feeling that Mace's accident had been stage managed. For reason or reasons unknown someone had found his presence inconvenient.

If his suppositions were correct, then the exploding pistol was the work of the same hands that had pushed the dead man to his death on Castle Rock. He saw again that vision of a huge spread of wings above him and heard the rock crashing past him.

And all these dire events, he was certain, bore the mark of the same assassin.

Chapter Twelve

Vince looked at the note Mace had sent. 'Now we'll never know what it was.'

'If only I could have examined the body,' said Faro, 'that would have given some clues. But what can I do? I can hardly insist to Sir Eric that we have a full police investigation.'

'Death by misadventure is becoming somewhat commonplace, associated with these unfortunate jewels.'

'I have still some avenues left unexplored,' said Faro, taking out his father's notes. 'Tomorrow I shall try to interview Colonel Lazenby's widow. We've made enquiries and she still lives in the same house at Aberdale.'

The day was bleak, grey and the sunless peninsula echoed to the despairing cries of sea birds. Through the dismally unwashed windows of the hired gig, which had seen better days, Faro stared out along the twisting road, through a plantation of sea buckthorn, twisted and deformed into grotesque shapes by the harsh winds blowing across the Forth from the North Sea. Even on a sunny day, he suspected that the atmosphere of direst melancholy hinted at by those unhappy trees would persist.

The house, set well back from the road in comparative isolation, had a look of neglect, of continuing sorrow. The door was opened by an aged servant, whose suspicious expression suggested that there were few visitors.

'She doesn't receive callers.' And the door was about to be closed again. To say 'Detective Inspector' would further confuse and would be even less likely to gain him admission.

'Tell her, please, that I wish to talk to her about her late husband, the Colonel. My father knew him,' he said, with a complete disregard for the exact truth.

This statement did not have the softening effect he had hoped for. The servant leaned out of the door. 'Get away from here. Get away – at once.' Suddenly alert and looking over her shoulder into the dark shuttered interior, she said, 'And tell whoever sent you that Mrs Lazenby is not to be drawn on that subject. That subject was closed long ago.'

Faro was immediately alert. The maid's attitude was promising. It hinted at a mystery, and clues might be forthcoming.

'For God's sake, leave her alone,' the old servant now pleaded, almost tearfully. 'Let her stay in her daft world – she's safe from everybody there.'

'What is it, Wilson?' The voice was followed by a shadowy figure emerging from the gloom.

'Just a caller, madam. A traveller. Nothing important. Go you inside where it's warm.'

'A traveller did you say?'

'Aye. But he's away now.' As Wilson made to close the door, Faro caught sight of a pale face, long untidy white hair and a bedraggled gown. Wilson's attempt to close the door finally was impeded by Faro's walking stick.

'Good morning, madam. Have I the pleasure of addressing Mrs Lazenby?'

'You have, young man. And who are you?' And pushing the maid aside, she said sharply, 'Oh for goodness sake, Wilson, let me see him. Who are you? Who sent you?'

'I'm Detective Inspector Faro, Madam. My father, Constable Magnus Faro knew your late husband, the Colonel.'

'Theodore, Theodore,' she whispered and all suspicion vanished. 'Is there news of my darling at last?' An angry expletive from Wilson and Mrs Lazenby turned sharply. 'You may go, Wilson, I will take care of the gentleman. Come inside. I will be with you in a moment. Meanwhile, Wilson will prepare tea for us.'

Wilson bobbed a curtsy and ushered him into the dark hallway with a look of ferocious anger. 'Now you've done it, Mister Clever Detective,' she whispered. 'This was one of her rare times of being in her right mind. And now she'll be back again in that terrible darkness. All thanks to you. Damn you and damn all men.'

'What's that you're gossiping about, Wilson?' Mrs Lazenby had returned with a shawl covering her bedraggled bodice, in her hand some yellowed papers and a key.

'Just telling him I hope his feet are clean,' murmured Wilson.

'Quite correct. Quite correct.' And handing the key to the maid: 'Unlock the drawing-room door, if you please.'

'But madam – you can't . . . '

'Do as I say. We have a guest who knew the master.'

As he stood beside the frail old woman in the dark hall the smell of old flesh, long unwashed, filled him with faint disgust. From the opened door there floated out the disused air of many years, mixing with this miasma of human misery and tragedy. In this inappropriate setting he was even more conscious of bad odours than in the foul-smelling, rat and human infested warrens of Edinburgh's slums.

'And now the shutters, if you please.'

The room was flooded with light, revealing an expanse of ghostly sheeted furniture and ornaments, their outlines lost in the dust and tight cobwebbing of many years.

As if aware of the appalling picture of neglect before them, Mrs Lazenby gave a cry and tottered quickly towards what at first glance looked like a table, but seizing the sheet she revealed a grand piano. Coughing at the dust disturbed, she raised the lid.

'Theo's darling wedding gift to me. My beautiful piano. Listen to its lovely tone, sir. I play very well, he tells me.' She pressed out a few chords and hummed a tune which she tried in vain to find. With a sigh she put down the lid again.

'I seem to have forgotten it. I do play it very well.'

146

Suddenly she leaned against the piano and looked round, as if seeing the room for the first time. 'I was about to offer you a chair, Inspector. But I think we will be more comfortable upstairs.' With a shake of her head, she said, 'This used to be such a pretty, elegant room, Theo's favourite. It is a little large, of course, but so many parties, filled with people.'

And now it's filled with sad ghosts, thought Faro with a shiver, as he followed her up the handsome oak staircase. She opened a door.

'I trust you will not think it indelicate to be received in a bedroom. In my young day, ladies always received morning guests in the boudoir. But things have changed very much these days, not altogether for the better, I'm afraid.'

Faro looked round. If anything this room was more appalling than the ghostly drawing-room. Here was a temple of mourning and one that their dear Queen would have approved. What was worse, the room stank. And the next moment, he knew the reason why.

'This is the bed my beloved Theodore slept in. These are his sheets and his pillow. See the dent where his dear head rested. Nothing has been changed since the day he died, his nightgown and nightcap are there waiting for him. See. Over there his razors.' Pausing she opened a large wardrobe. 'And all his clothes as they were the morning he went out, went out never to return.' The sentence finished on a sob. Dabbing at her eyes, she continued, 'Do sit down, Inspector.'

He took the only chair, at her insistence, while she sat on the dressing table stool. What did she see in the mirror, he wondered? Not an old woman in a gown that had once been satin ruffled and now hung in filthy shreds and tatters, for, aware of his eyes and mistaking his expression, she smoothed one sleeve in a coquettish gesture.

'This was his favourite dress of mine. A little out of fashion, I fear, but I wear it for him, so that when he returns, he will know nothing has changed. Nothing.' She looked at Faro through the mirror. 'He is coming back soon? Is that what you have come to tell me, that his tour of duty has finished? Please tell me what I long to hear. I have waited so long.'

Faro was struck dumb. How could he remind this mad old woman that her Theodore had taken his own life, that her life with him had been a lie. That he had chosen death rather than return to her after his sordid involvement with the wife of a fellow officer had caused a regimental scandal.

As if interpreting his thoughts, she said, 'You must not believe what they tell you. There is no other woman, there never was anyone but me in Theodore's life. We live only for each other, live only for the days and nights we can be together. Soon he will have his dream – and mine – his son, our lovely baby son.' At that she began to weep. So sudden a change of mood caught Faro unprepared and he was helpless before this storm of grief.

The noise alerted the maid Wilson, who burst into the room. 'What have you done? I told you so, I told you so. Now I hope you're satisfied. Don't say I didn't warn you. Come on – out.'

'Wait a moment,' said Faro. 'I want to talk to your mistress. I'm sure she'll calm down.'

'Calm down.' The maid burst out laughing. 'Calm down. Her? You'd better go while you're safe, before she gets violent. When she remembers that this isn't nearly forty years ago and that her beloved Theo is dead and gone . . .' she sighed. 'A few more minutes, that's all it takes, then she'll be a raving madwoman.'

Faro looked at the sobbing prostrate figure now lying on the bed, as the maid continued, 'You wouldn't think she was very strong but she is. And violent too.' She rolled up her sleeves, showing deep scars, long healed. 'That was a knife she turned on me. I have other marks too, on my scalp. Everywhere. Come along, sir.'

At the front door, Faro asked, 'Why do you stay with her?' The maid shrugged. 'Been with her since we were both youngsters. She was only seventeen when she met the master. It was love right away and they got married before he returned to his regiment. They were married only two years when he died and she lost the wee lad. She was never sane after that, but I've stuck by her. I'll not let them put her away. She gave me a new life when I was going to be transported. I owe her that life and I'll stay with her till the day she dies.'

'Then why does she attack you?'

'She looks for the master. And when she can't find him, she thinks that I have done him in, in her poor confused mind.' The noise of sobbing had changed in intensity. The old woman was screaming now, beating her fists and her heels on the bed. 'Come quickly, Inspector, don't linger. If she doesn't see you before she opens her eyes, she'll have no idea that you were here. I'll tell her that it was another of her nightmares, soothe her with a drop of laudanum. With a bit of luck, she'll be right as rain in the morning, back again in her lost world, the poor love.'

'She has no idea what really happened to the Colonel?'

Wilson shook her head. 'Not now, not any more. She would never believe that he took his own life.' She looked at Faro. 'And it wouldn't surprise me if she was right at that. For I can tell you one thing, sure as God's in His heaven and Jesus Christ is His son, my master never committed suicide over a woman. That I'll never believe, no more than she does. He worshipped his young wife. After it happened, way back, she appealed, you know, tried to clear his name, but no one would listen.'

'This appeal – on what grounds?'

'Oh, she believed he was murdered and it was made to look like suicide. You see, he was left-handed, but the gun was in his right hand.'

'And did the police investigate this?'

'They didn't get a chance. It was a regimental matter, not a civilian thing, quickly hushed up. The police didn't bother themselves.'

'One of them did.'

149

'Oh, and who was that?'

'My father. He also died soon after the Colonel. In an accident.'

'My God. Is that true?'

Her words were lost in screams from the room above.

'I'll have to go to her. She may do herself a mischief. Listen to that.' The screams had turned into a tuneless chant.

'What's that? Singing?'

'Is that what you call it? This is where it all begins – the violence. I'll have to look sharp.'

Faro listened. 'That tune. That's the one she picked out on the piano.'

'That was the master's favourite. Can't remember its title, something about a red river. They used to sing it together.'

Those few chords mingled with the screams of Mrs Lazenby continued to echo dismally in Faro's head long after he thankfully boarded the waiting gig and headed for Edinburgh. An hour later with McQuinn and a police carriage, he set off for Piperlees.

The door was opened by the housekeeper. Sir James was not at home. At the sight of a uniformed policeman, and mention of a jacket that might have been stolen from Sir James, her attitude changed to one of cautious politeness.

'Sir James's valet, Mr Peters, might be able to help you.'

The house, built to look medieval, Faro recognised as being of fairly recent date. The lofty hall was not an unpleasant place to take a seat, surrounded by splendid portraits of Piperlees past and present, as well as their favourite racehorses and dogs.

Peters the valet was elderly. He descended the vast and heavily ornamented staircase cautiously, but to Faro's delight he recognised the jacket immediately.

'Yes, of course. I remember this garment very well. Sir James wore it about two years ago. A favourite of his, when it was the height of fashion. You will notice that the lapels

are narrower now, seats are broader, and – those buttons.'
Shaking his head, he added, 'How well I remember those
buttons and the trouble they caused, Inspector. You see,
Sir James lost one and we could never get a perfect match.
Well, the master being a stickler for perfection as you might
say, he refused to wear it ever again.'

'What happened to it after that?'

Peters frowned. 'I seem to remember that it hung in the
wardrobe for some considerable time, until he decided to
get rid of it.'

'Have you any idea who he might have given it to?'

Peters scratched his cheek thoughtfully. 'Now that's
a poser, Inspector.'

'Someone on the Castle staff, perhaps,' suggested Faro
helpfully.

Peters shook his head. 'Hardly, Inspector, more likely
one of the tenantry or some benevolent institution. We are
of a size, the master and myself,' he added ruefully, 'but I
am never allowed to inherit any of his grand clothes. He's
very strict about such things, bit of a hoarder. He would
get positively enraged if he happened to meet any of the
Castle staff wearing his discarded clothes.' He smiled
grimly, 'Especially his own valet, if you see what I mean.'

Faro sighed deeply. After this promising start, it looked
as if he had now reached yet another road that led to
nowhere.

'May I ask you how you came by it, Inspector?' asked
Peters with a nervous glance at the jacket.

'Of course. It was worn by a man who was killed in
an accident – and who had no other means of identification.'

'Dear, dear. Nothing to identify him. That was awkward.'

And Faro, on impulse, withdrew the cameo. 'Only this.
It was found beside him. Fell out of his pocket.'

'May I, sir? Very old, isn't it? Am I right in thinking
it's very valuable?'

'You don't happen to recognise it?'

'No. It isn't one of our treasures.' And as Peters handed

151

it back, Faro studied his face carefully. Unless the old valet was also a superb actor, he was speaking the truth. Noting the Inspector's doubtful expression, Peters added, 'You might ask Sir James when he gets back on Friday, Inspector – if you wish. However, you could take my word for it. I've served Sir James and his father before him for forty years. I think I can say I know every family trinket quite intimately.' And pointing to the cameo he said, 'That one I have never seen in this house before. I'm certain of it.'

Ushering Faro towards the door, and the waiting sergeant, he added, 'If you doubt my word, Inspector, you might have a word with Mrs Wheeler, the housekeeper. She's been at Piperlees for as long as I can remember and there isn't much that goes on in this family that she doesn't know about. She's a kindly soul.'

Peters rang the handbell and, as they awaited the housekeeper's arrival, Faro asked, 'Has Piperlees been troubled at all with this recent spate of burglaries in the neighbourhood?'

'No, thank goodness, we have not. We've been very lucky, or rather Sir James is a great stickler for bolts and bars on everything.' Looking at Faro, he smiled, 'Curious that you should mention those burglaries, Inspector, because it did just occur to me, that that piece, old and obviously valuable, might have come from one of the big houses.'

As the baize door opened, Peters introduced Mrs Wheeler and bid them goodday. 'Please let me know if I can be of further service to you, if you wish me to arrange a meeting for you with Sir James.'

Mrs Wheeler shook her head and confirmed Peters' statement that the brooch, as she called it, didn't belong to the Piperlee family. She showed even less knowledge on the subject than the valet. 'A pretty bauble, Inspector, and of course those jewels will be paste. They do these imitations very well these days, don't they? A body can hardly tell the genuine article any more.'

'What about this jacket, Mrs Wheeler? Have you seen

152

it before?' asked Faro, holding up the garment for her inspection.

'I should just think I have, Inspector.' And looking round to make sure that they were alone, she dropped her voice to a whisper, 'I know that the master dislikes meeting any of the staff wearing his discards, as you might say – and what an eagle eye he has for that sort of thing. However, when Mr Peters said it was to go to some charitable organisation I thought, well, charity begins at home. So I gave it to Jess at the bakery, for her old uncle.' She touched her head. 'He's not all there, poor man, but he's harmless, a good worker, too . . . '

'Works on the estate – out of doors?'

'Why yes. How did you know that, Inspector? When he was young he was a lumberjack and a gold miner, oh the tall stories he'd tell if he had the notion . . . '

But Faro was no longer listening, preoccupied with the vivid picture of a dead man, elderly with tanned arms and neck, and scratches on his arms.

Mrs Wheeler was shaking her head sadly. 'Such a lot of misfortunes, he'd had . . . '

'What was his name?' Faro interrupted.

'Name?' Mrs Wheeler seemed surprised by the question. 'Harry.'

'Harry what?'

'I don't know. We don't go in much for surnames among the estate folk, unless they're tenants.'

'What is his niece's name then?'

'Porter. Jess Porter.'

'And where does Mrs Porter live?'

'She isn't married – and she lives at the west lodge. Just go down the main drive, turn right then left, about five minutes away.'

Thanking her, Faro turned at the door and asked, 'One more question, Mrs Wheeler. Do you happen to know if Harry had a brother?'

'I think he had, older than him, but dead long ago.'

153

'Does he ever talk about him? About how he died, for instance?'

'He was killed – in an accident.'

'Do you happen to know where this accident took place?'

Mrs Wheeler's expression indicated that the conversation had taken a curious turn. 'In Edinburgh – I think it was up at the Castle.'

Again Faro thanked her, shaking her warmly by the hand. It all fitted perfectly and he had no further doubt that the dead man's name was Harry Femister, who would have been a young man in 1837 when his brother John died. He was so certain of his deductions that he sent McQuinn back to the police carriage with a message that they might have to take an extra passenger back to Edinburgh.

As he walked along the twisting, tree-lined path towards the west lodge he had a sense of jubilation. Here was the stroke of luck, the link he had hoped for. Found, he thought, with considerably less effort and legwork than he had bargained for. For once, fortune had smiled on him and soon he would have the mystery unravelled as well as the secret of the two Queen Mary cameos: whether they were part of a treasure hoard and worth another Queen's ransom.

A delicious aroma of baking bread, borne on the summer breeze, warned Faro that he had almost reached his destination.

'You can't miss the cottage, Inspector, it's one of the originals, a lot older than this house. Been here for two hundred years or more, thatched roof and all. Jess is the local baker,' Mrs Wheeler had explained, 'makes her bread in the same oven as her father and grandfathers before her. The Porters didn't go in much for progress.'

Chapter Thirteen

The bakery door was open.

'Miss Jess Porter?'

A plump and comely woman of about forty whose rounded arms showed evidence of recent contact with flour came to the old wooden bench that served as a counter.

Faro's early training led him to realise how very important were those first thirty seconds of meeting and how many details, relatively unimportant at the time, were to prove of great significance afterwards. Even as he took in her pleasing appearance, he had observed that her eager greeting died on her lips. He was not the one she had expected. She was disappointed.

Once he had introduced himself, without further question she invited him into the large kitchen which served as bakehouse. Taking a cloth she wiped the table clear of flour.

'Take a seat, won't you. Would you like some refreshment? It's a warm day.'

As she bustled about the kitchen, Faro was aware that her eyes wandered constantly towards the window. He had only half her attention as she watched over his shoulder for that other caller so anxiously and imminently expected. Then, with a final despairing look, she took the seat opposite and spoke, as if suddenly aware of him for the first time.

'Inspector – did you say?'

'Yes, Miss Porter. We are making a few enquiries.'

'Enquiries?' And with a puzzled expression that betrayed nothing of fear or guilt, she set the jug of home-made

155

lemonade beside him. 'Then I dare say it's thirsty work in this weather. Help yourself.'

Thanking her, Faro refilled his glass. 'I will, it's delicious.'

He was heartily glad of the cooling drink. Despite cooking smells calculated to stir even the most flagging appetite, the kitchen with its huge baking ovens was intolerably hot for a summer's day.

'What was it you wanted?' Jess asked.

'Mrs Wheeler told me that you have an uncle lives here with you.'

'He isn't at home just now. I can't tell you when he'll be back, either. Took himself off to Edinburgh a few days ago on a wee errand.' Her smile was cordial, unperturbed. Obviously if Uncle Harry had been contemplating a break in at the Castle, then she was in complete ignorance of such nefarious activities.

She paused and Faro prompted, 'What kind of an errand would that be?'

Jess laughed. 'Oh, don't ask me – I wouldn't be knowing that. Uncle Harry is a law to himself and he often takes himself off on little jaunts. Being a bachelor and so forth.' Then, conscious of Faro's unflinching gaze, she coloured slightly and said, 'Well, I might as well tell the truth, Inspector. You see, he's a wee bit – well, fey – simple, some folk hereabouts call it. Oh goodness, please don't mistake me, Inspector, he wouldn't harm a fly – not wicked with it, not that sort at all. It's just that he likes solitude, to commune with nature, he says, writes a wee bit of poetry and so forth.'

'But he tells you where he's going?'

'Sometimes, if he feels talkative.'

'And this time . . . '

'Oh yes, he had to see someone – at the Castle.'

Faro's sense of triumph was now suffused with the dismay and indignation he always felt in having to break the shocking and totally unexpected news to an anxious relative that the loved one they expected home was never to return. This part of police duty even after twenty years

156

had never ceased to offend his natural humanity. He felt the sickness growing at the pit of his stomach and asked, 'Did he tell you why?'

She bit her lip, looked uncertain and then said, 'Well, I'm sure there was no harm in it. All rather silly, really – and romantic, but then Uncle is romantic. A long time ago – before I was born – his brother came across from Ireland because they were terribly poor and he expected to find the streets of Edinburgh lined with gold. He was disappointed, like a lot of other folk. Anyway, Uncle John . . . '

'John Femister, was that his name?'

'That's right. Well, he was strong and went into building work, got married to a nice Leith lass, my aunt Jean, and they had a bairn, a lass.'

A shadow darkened Jess Porter's face and Faro gave a silent hurrah at this confirmation of his deductions so far. It all fitted so perfectly.

'Then one day when they were doing repairs at Edinburgh Castle Uncle Harry's brother was killed in an accident. But Uncle Harry refused to believe it was an accident, some strange warning dream he'd had – I know you'll laugh, Inspector, but I told you he's fey. Anyway, he was sure it was part of some dark plot. Though why should anyone want to kill a poor Irishman working as a labourer? What could they possibly get from him? I can't think, can you?'

Faro shook his head obligingly and Jess added slowly, 'Unless there really was buried treasure. That's why Uncle Harry believes his brother was killed.'

A note of excitement crept into her voice. 'Their father was a school teacher and he taught them their sums and their letters. They wrote to each other, John trying to persuade Harry to leave home, but he felt honour bound to stay and help his father, dying of consumption he was. Two little sisters and no mother either. Then just before the accident, Uncle John wrote telling him that he must come without delay as he had found something that would make their fortune.'

'That's what he said – a fortune?'

'Oh yes. A fortune. The exact words. My goodness, I couldn't mistake that,' she laughed. 'I've had that letter read often enough to me through the years.' Hesitating, with an anxious glance, she continued, 'I'm sure it's all right telling you, being a policeman and so forth and I've no doubt he'll tell you all about it himself if you come when he's at home. He's always on about the buried treasure at Edinburgh Castle. Tells everyone and that's really how he's got the name of being a bit simple with folk around here. They don't believe a word of it – how there's a fortune hidden away in a hollow wall in the Castle for anyone that finds it.'

From his pocket Faro withdrew the Queen Mary cameo. 'Do you recognise this, by any chance?'

Jess laughed delightedly. 'I do indeed. That's part – the only part, I might add – of the treasure he's always going on about. Shows it to everyone who'll listen, "My only brother died for this and one day I'm going to find the rest of it." He's devoted his whole life to this quest, Inspector, he even went to the United States and Canada, worked as a lumberjack and a gold miner, to try to raise money . . . '

This was the second time he heard of Femister's work abroad and although he had only half-listened to Mrs Wheeler's account, he felt there was something else he should remember, some vital fact here that was in danger of being overlooked.

'What did you say?' He was aware of Jess Porter's anxiety as she pointed to the cameo.

'I said, Inspector, that my uncle never lets that out of his sight – or his possession. So how did you come by it?'

Solemnly he opened the parcel containing the jacket. At the sight of it, realisation slowly dawned, and she raised her hands to her mouth with a small scream. 'Oh – oh – something's happened to him . . . '

'I'm afraid so, miss.'

'Oh, how dreadful, poor Uncle. Is he – is he . . . '

'Yes, I'm afraid so.'

The tears welled from her eyes unchecked and suddenly helpless in the face of her grief, Faro took her hand. 'Oh poor dear Uncle. What was it?' she sobbed.

'He met with an accident in Edinburgh.'

'An accident? Him too? And he's dead? Dead,' she repeated. 'I can't believe it – I just can't believe it. Is he in the hospital?'

'No, miss. In the city mortuary. And I wonder, could you come back with me, just to identify him?' A convulsive shudder shook her and Faro stretched out a comforting arm. 'I know, miss, I know. It's not a nice thing to ask a young lady, but you seem to be his nearest relative.'

'I am that,' she sighed. 'His wife Jean was my mother's sister. I'm all he has since his other niece went up in the world. Her that married a title. I'll never forgive her, she could have done so much to help him. He wasn't asking for charity, just wanted a little money to help with his enquiries and he was willing to work for her, to earn something. Bitch that she was, she had him put from her door. "Don't let that mad old man come near my house again, or I'll get my husband to have him put away in the asylum."'

She began to sob again and Faro put his arm around her plump shoulders. 'Come, we have a carriage waiting down the drive, it'll take you into Edinburgh and bring you back home, of course. It won't take long,' he ended lamely.

'That's kind of you, Inspector, but I can't come this instant,' she said, with a glance towards the ovens. 'I have my batch of loaves to take out. That'll be another half-hour – and oh dear, there's my morning rolls to get in and by the time I get back . . . ' She made a helpless gesture. 'I'll never manage. And then . . . ' Again that glance towards the window.

'Are you expecting a visitor?' asked Faro gently.

'Well, not for me really. A man wanting to see Uncle urgently about some enquiry he had made.'

159

'Does that happen often?'

'Sometimes. He's always asking about history. I don't think he'll be coming now, but I'll leave a note on the door for him. If you'll wait till my baking's ready, please . . .'

In desperate need of breathing fresh cool air, Faro decided that sitting in this over-heated kitchen any longer was a frightful penance which even delicious home-made lemonade could not comfort. 'I'll wait for you down the drive.'

With his hand on the door, he turned: 'Those letters you mentioned – did your uncle keep them, by any chance?'

'Yes, he did, and they'll be in a big tin box he has hidden away in his bedroom.' She smiled sadly. 'I never let on that I knew about it, and I've never looked inside.' Her eyes filled with tears, and she took a handkerchief out of her pinafore. 'I don't suppose it will make any difference to him if I read them now, will it?'

'There might be something to help us with our enquiries. We'd be very grateful, especially as your uncle seemed certain that his brother's death wasn't an accident and if there is some evidence in those letters, then the police should know.'

'You're quite right, Inspector. He would have wanted that – oh poor Uncle,' she sobbed again. 'I'm sorry, Inspector, I just can't believe that all this is happening. He went out so bright and cheerful, just the way he always does – and now – this.' Drying her tears, she went to the table and with an air of determination floured the board and took up the huge baking bowl.

Faro watched her and asked, 'Did he have any friends in Edinburgh that you knew of?'

'A few drinking cronies and he used to visit an old friend who was in the hospital.'

'One thing more. Did your uncle ever mention a fellow he used to know – Dowie by name, dead long since, I imagine.'

'Peter Dowie, you mean.'

'The same.'

160

Jess Porter smiled sadly. 'He didn't die, Inspector. He's still alive – the one in the hospital.' She coloured and added, 'The East House.'

'The asylum, you mean.'

'Yes. Uncle just told folks it was the hospital. He didn't like to say asylum because folks round here thought he was a bit of a daftie, himself. And he knew it.'

'What about Dowie?'

'He's been there for years, he was a lot older than Uncle and he'd been crippled and gone the way old folks do sometimes, so they said, because of the accident long ago. Same one as killed poor Uncle John.'

So Femister was fey and simple and Dowie was senile. They must have made a pretty odd pair, thought Faro, as Jess continued, 'Uncle hasn't visited him for a while now. They told him at the hosp – asylum that he wasn't well enough to have visitors any more. That he'd turned violent. For a while Uncle went faithfully each week, but he gave up when they kept on turning him away.'

'Did you know him at all?'

She shook her head. 'When I was a wee lass, I went to the hospital with Uncle, but it frightened me, you know the way bairns are.' She smiled. 'But he seemed a gentle, quiet soul. It was a great shame, they were great mates, loved talking all about the past.'

Faro decided on an immediate visit to Dowie. Even in madness, there could be lucid flashes of the past which might yield useful information.

As he was leaving, with a reminder about the letters, she nodded. 'I'll just have a quick scan through.'

'The whole box would be a great help, miss, if you would.'

She smiled wanly. 'I don't suppose the dead have secrets any more, do they?'

He bit back the rejoinder, 'You would be surprised, miss, how many of them do. A look at our files in the Central Office would convince you.'

This was better, far better than he hoped. If it hadn't

seemed like an intrusion on her grief he would have offered to read the letters on the spot. Poor lass, she was very upset and taking it very well, trying hard to be normal.

As he limped back in the direction of the main drive, he discovered that his feelings of triumph and jubilation on having solved the dead man's identity had been overtaken by that strange sense of foreboding.

The closed-in path was overgrown and dim, the uneven ground made rapid progress difficult and when the bushes rustled at his side, he felt his scalp tingle with apprehension. This was so strong that several times he stopped and looked over his shoulder with his walking stick clutched as a ready weapon.

After the third time, he shook his head: I'm being fanciful, this won't do at all. But the shadowy arm of nightmare poised above the Castle Rock persisted, the moving shadow at the corner of his eye which swiftly melted into invisibility. The feeling of being followed by someone who was no fool, no newcomer to the business of tracking his quarry.

He was greatly relieved to emerge in the drive, where he found that McQuinn, at the housekeeper's invitation, had established himself in the kitchen and the handsome young Sergeant was surrounded by the usual bevy of twittering, admiring females.

As always, the sight annoyed Faro out of all proportion. McQuinn, who had so little to offer in the way of entertainment as a companion to his superior officer, beyond a taste for tuneless Irish jigs whistled uncomfortably shrilly at close quarters, was once again showing that he had hidden depths when it came to amusing the ladies.

'We're ready to move now, McQuinn,' he said with a brusqueness that quelled the maids and sent them scuttling away on their kitchen activities, with reproachful sniggers in his direction.

'Right, sir. Back to Edinburgh.' McQuinn, who could move very fast, could also on occasion act with such deliberate slowness that amounted almost to insolence. Heavy footed, reluctant to withdraw from his circle of admirers, he followed Faro on to the drive.

'Where are we off to now, sir? Carriage is down the drive.'

'I know that, McQuinn. I've found out who the dead man is – his niece is coming back with us to identify the body. We'll take the short cut – this way.'

'That was a piece of luck, sir,' said McQuinn prepared to be agreeable for once. He adjusted his long stride to his superior officer's stumbling gait, while Faro briefly supplied the details regarding Jess having recognised the jacket.

'The cottage is over there, where you see the smoke.'

'Looks like the lum's gone up,' said McQuinn.

'It's a bakery,' said Faro impatiently.

'Smells like burning thatch to me.'

Faro sniffed the air. McQuinn was right. 'Come on, hurry, man.'

Faro, using his stick to propel himself along, left the clearing just as McQuinn reached the cottage door. From every aperture smoke billowed out and flames shot from the chimney and the burning roof thatch. As he hobbled across with a growing sense of disaster, he saw McQuinn trying to open the door, his efforts encouraged by a small band of estate workers who had also raced towards the blaze.

When the door refused to move, McQuinn put his shoulder against it. Smoke billowed out and Faro limped after him.

'Don't come in here, sir. You stay clear, I'll bring the woman.'

Jess lay just behind the door and before McQuinn picked her up and carried her outside, Faro heard the crack of breaking wood.

'Keep away, sir,' yelled McQuinn.

Ominous sounds from above indicated that the roof was about to cave in. Through the smoke, Faro saw on the floor, near where Jess had fallen, a tin box. He seized it, winced with pain and threw the jacket over it. The roof collapsed with a thunderous roar as McQuinn laid Jess on the ground, her body hidden by the curious watchers. Faro pushed them aside.

'She's dead, sir,' said McQuinn, 'hit by a falling beam, by the look of it.'

Faro gazed helplessly down at her, the tin box in the jacket under his arm. Before them the cottage was already subsiding in a volley of small explosions and smoke, while Jess Porter's eyes were wide open, staring in disbelief as death had overtaken her.

One of the men pushed forward. 'We've warned her, haven't we?'

A woman took up the chant. 'Those ovens – far too hot, such heat she had for her baking.'

'With a thatched roof, we thought something like this would happen.'

'Mark my words, haven't I always said it . . . '

'Aye, a spark, that's all it would take.'

But was a spark all that had caused the inferno and why had it happened in such a short time? Turning his back on the curious watchers, Faro unwrapped the tin box. The lid was open and the papers in it, those letters dating from 1830 that he was hoping would shed so much light on Queen Mary's jewels, were charred, blackened.

Summoned by McQuinn's whistle, alerted by the smoke, the police who were waiting in their discreetly concealed carriage on the drive now raced across the clearing. Someone, smelling smoke and anticipating trouble, had had the foresight to bring a canvas stretcher and a blanket.

'Accident, would you say, sir?' said McQuinn.

Faro shook his head. 'It was no accident. The fire was deliberate.'

'The door was locked, sir.'

'Did she usually lock her door?' Faro asked a woman nearby.

'Never.'

'No, never.' The chorus was taken up. 'You could come by at any time of the night or day and Jess Porter's bakehouse door was always open.'

Faro walked carefully round the tiny garden. The glint of metal, in the sun beside a rose bush, was a key. The cottage had been set on fire, and Jess locked inside. When she died clutching her precious box she had been struggling to escape.

'I can't understand it at all, ye ken,' said one old man. 'Heavy thunder shower we had last night, thatch was wet through.'

'I ken that fine, Archie, I have a cottage just like this at east lodge.'

'I can't understand it. That thatch should never have gone on fire today.'

But it had and it had burned like a tinderbox, thought Faro, following the sad cortège across the clearing.

But the murderer wasn't to know that.

Faro cursed silently. This tragedy need never have happened. It was his own fault, he should have stayed, read the contents of the tin box while he waited for her.

He had no doubt that the mysterious visitor she had been expecting, who had wanted to see Harry Femister so urgently, had murdered them both. And the clue to the mystery would never now be solved for it lay in the contents of the tin box, the letters Henry and John Femister had written to each other, the charred and useless evidence that he now clutched beneath his arm.

Chapter Fourteen

Faro reached Sheridan Place anxious to accompany Vince on a visit to Peter Dowie, who, he was certain, was the last link in the chain of that day's extraordinary and tragic events. The authorities at East House Lunatic Asylum might react uneasily to Inspector Faro, but Doctor Laurie could produce impeccable reasons, not to mention powers of persuasion, for seeing a patient outside visiting hours.

Instead of finding his stepson alone, as he had hoped, he found the whole family assembled for yet another interminable mealtime. His own arrival had been eagerly awaited as the central figure in the ritual of suppertime.

'Do sit down, Jeremy. Didn't I tell you, girls, that Papa would be here in time?' said his mother.

As he hesitated, the door opened and Mrs Brook came in with the soup. He sat down reluctantly and around him, heads were obediently downcast, hands placed together in prayerful attitudes.

'Come along, Jeremy,' whispered his mother. They were waiting for him to say grace. Never had he felt less thankful, although he was hungry enough with only Jess's lemonade to sustain him. He seemed to have missed several meals that day.

'Amen. Amen.'

As soup spoons were wielded, Vince, seated opposite, obligingly passed the condiments.

'I hope you haven't an engagement this evening, lad,' Faro whispered.

'I was planning to take Lucille to a concert.'

'Can it not wait?'

'Indeed it cannot,' said Vince, outraged at such a suggestion. 'Why?' Then, glancing at his stepfather's solemn face, 'Trouble?'

Faro nodded. 'I'll tell you when we've finished.'

Catching his mother's reproachful glance, he gave his full attention to the soup.

'And what are you two whispering about?' she demanded.

Faro pretended deafness, while his more diplomatic stepson smiled and said winningly, 'Just passing the time of day, Grandmother.'

'Oh, is that the way of it?' demanded Mary Faro suspiciously. 'Well, whatever the pair of you are concocting, there's no need to eat your supper as if you haven't a minute left to live. You set a fine example to the children, I must say.'

Jeremy smiled wryly. His mother had the happy gift of arousing in a widower and a father approaching forty, the exact sense of wrong-doing he had suffered as a small boy. It was quite remarkable.

'Girls – Rose – Emily. There's no need to imitate your Papa, you don't want to have heartburn for the rest of your lives. Your complexions will be ruined and no nice young man will give you a second look.'

At this awful warning, the two girls ate with exaggerated slowness, gazing at dear Papa for approval. He gave them instead an embarrassed smile. Supper finally ended, they were loth to let him go. It seemed they didn't want to go back to Orkney next week.

'We want to stay here – with you – in lovely Edinburgh . . . '

'For ever and ever.'

If only their holiday had not coincided with his involvement in a new case. He was guiltily aware that he had spent precious little time with them, and that grudgingly and impatiently, his mind on more pressing matters. By next week he and Vince would be on their own again, the house's emptiness echoing to his remorse.

'Ready, Stepfather?'

'Yes, of course.'

Vince was already making their apologies, kissing and hugging the girls and their grandmother and promising that Papa would be back in time to tell them a story, with an impish glance in his stepfather's direction.

Faro gave him a cynical look. Oh, the stories that could be, and never would be, told.

Leaving the house, he asked, 'Can you get us into East House Lunatic Asylum?'

Vince chortled. 'Do you really think we're quite worthy of admission yet – we'll have to prove insanity . . . '

'We're going to visit Peter Dowie,' Faro interrupted sternly.

'Peter Dowie – the man who was so seriously injured in 1837? He's still alive?'

'He is – just, I fancy.'

'That's incredible, Stepfather. How did you come by this information?'

As they turned in the direction of Morningside, Faro told him of his discovery at Piperlees that the dead man's name was Harry Femister. Cutting short Vince's jubilant congratulations, he ended with Jess Porter's tragic death in the bakery fire.

'Dreadful – dreadful,' said Vince. 'Can you prove it was deliberate?'

'No. But I'm certain that it was.'

They walked in silence through the leafy suburbs. They were very near to the asylum when Vince said, 'When you consider our main list of characters, the discovery of that child's coffin has an alarming number of sudden deaths to its credit.' And enumerating on his fingers, 'Two deaths by drowning in 1830, two by falling scaffoldings in 1837 . . . '

'Let's not forget my father, lad.'

'My apologies. Plus one street accident and one suicide.'

'I'm not at all sure that Lazenby committed suicide.' And Faro gave a rapid account of his visit to the mad widow at Aberdale.

Vince whistled. 'How very odd – and she really believes that her husband was murdered?'

'Aye, and so does her maid. And what is more, I'm inclined to agree with them.'

'Which means that Lazenby's suicide might well have been a very useful method of dealing with an awkward situation?'

'Exactly. And the same goes for Mace.'

'Ah, so you think his death was murder?'

'Let's say I'm not happy with the label of firearms accident,' said Faro. 'It's all a mite too convenient, the body tidied away, the room cleaned up and no police investigation, if you please. This is a matter for the regiment.'

Vince thought for a moment. 'So today we have one death by climbing the inaccessible Castle Rock, one by a mysterious fire, one by exploding pistol. And if we add 'em all up including Lazenby's violent end . . . '

'Then we have nine potential murders.'

'You could well be right, Stepfather,' said Vince in awed tones. 'But why in God's name did these unfortunate people all have to die?'

'Because they were on to something so important that they couldn't be allowed to survive. Do you remember my father's last note?'

'The Egyptian-style curse, you mean?'

'No, lad, I don't. I'm as sceptical as he was about such things. "These devils will show no mercy" – human devils, Vince lad, definitely human.'

'About that fire, Stepfather, pity that the evidence was lost. You realise we have just about run out of clues.'

'Aye, a boxful of charred letters . . . '

'You brought them.'

'I did indeed. We have a man in the Central Office who's an expert in the particularly painstaking matter of deciphering charred letters.'

'What about this chap Dowie? You surely don't think a poor old mindless chap . . . '

'There might be some vital fact that he remembers.

169

And I'm rather relying on the cameos jolting his poor disordered mind with the clue we need.'

'You may well be right. It's exceedingly strange that the senile can be remarkably lucid about the past and decidedly vague about what happened yesterday. All their yesterdays become as one.' A moment later, Vince asked, 'One poser is – why didn't the mysterious "they" get rid of him too? They must have had ample opportunity.'

Faro sighed. 'Perhaps because he was hopelessly crippled, virtually a prisoner who could be cut off from the outside world. I imagine his visitors were very carefully scrutinised. Like Harry Femister, another harmless lunatic.'

'You're right, of course. Who would give credence to the fantasies of two daft old men about a buried treasure in Edinburgh Castle?'

'Aye, they were safe enough – until Harry Femister tried to prove it with his last desperate bid to storm Castle Rock.'

Vince shook his head. 'But why? That still doesn't make sense, Stepfather.'

Faro didn't answer. He was conscious that his pace had quickened as he remembered all the hours that had elapsed since his return from Piperlees. He had an overpowering sense of foreboding, that their visit to East House Asylum was already too late.

'I see that ankle is healing remarkably well,' said Vince as the gates came in sight.

Faro slowed down, suddenly aware that Vince's observation and the extra spurt of activity had not brought its usual painful reminder. He stared up at the grey stone building, which exuded a certain grim-faced respectability. There was an air of withdrawal and enforced seclusion about its narrow close-curtained windows with their iron bars.

As the bell pealed, Faro said, 'Say any prayers you might find appropriate, Vince, for mark my words, herein lies our last chance of success.'

The maid who opened the door had visage, colouring and a stern but remote expression in perfect keeping with her background, as if she had been specially chosen to blend with the institutional surroundings.

'Visiting's over for today, hours since. You're too late.'

Faro was wondering how any person could speak with so little facial movement when Vince stepped forward.

'I am Dr Beaumarcher Laurie, here to see a patient,' he handed her a card. As she read it somewhat reluctantly, he added, 'I am personal assistant to Dr Kellar who is no doubt known to you and I am to interview the patient . . .' He flipped open a pocketbook, frowned over a name, 'ah yes, Peter Dowie – in connection with Dr Kellar's research on mental problems. Dowie, we are given to understand, has been here for many years and has an interesting – a very interesting – case history.'

Faro listened to this pack of lies with extreme admiration as the maid, still doubtful, stared over her shoulder helplessly. Seeing none of the nursing staff, whom Faro hoped were off duty, and in mortal terror of offending someone in medical authority, she admitted them to the bleak and sterile hall.

Pausing only to consult a list and take a key from the appropriate numbered hook, she said, 'Night staff won't be here for an hour yet, but I expect it will be all right, you being a doctor.'

Vince nodded importantly and as they followed her along the deserted corridor the air of sterility was now overlaid with carbolic, in a losing battle to keep at bay less agreeable odours.

'Where are all the patients?' asked Vince.

'Locked up in their rooms, of course. Where else would they be? That's the rule, doors locked from eight at night till six in the morning.'

Their footsteps alerted the hearts of the imprisoned with new hopes of release, and their progress was followed by a tirade of screams and curses, sobs and pleas, animal howls, and furious banging on the locked doors as if a pack of wild animals was trying to escape.

As they climbed the stairs, the large window gave glimpses

of an Edinburgh suburb: its villas far below, with back gardens facing the asylum, were peaceful and domestic on this gentle summer evening. Children played on swings, a dog chased a cat up a tree barking fiercely, a couple sat at a table with glasses in their hands. Such scenes, such glimpses of normality played out against the screaming madness all around them, were an affront to the senses.

As the maid paused to unbolt yet another door, Vince pointed down to the scene below. 'Incredible, isn't it, that two such variations of humankind should inhabit so small an area.'

'I was thinking the very same thing.' It was appalling, the thought of those wild, tormented, mindless creatures, hopeless, locked away, unlikely ever to walk in a summer garden, feel the warmth of the sun or enjoy family life again.

'Is it quite necessary that they all have to be locked away?' Vince asked the maid.

'You know the rules. If we opened those doors, some of them would tear your throats out. They all believe that we are their enemies. Here it is. Room 49.' Pausing with the key in the lock, she turned to Vince. 'I presume you gentlemen are armed.' His non-committal nod was taken as agreement and she opened the door.

'You're lucky with this one. He's a cripple, out of his mind of course, but non-violent. He's had a fever recently, too. Weakened him considerably. You needn't expect much trouble.' She pointed to the candle. 'Light it, if you need. But be sure to blow it out before you leave. We don't want him setting fire to the room.'

Dowie's eyes were closed and he leaned back against the pillows. An old man with a mop head of tangled grey hair, a face pale and worn as the walls around him. At their entrance his eyes flickered open.

Vince leaned over him. 'I am Doctor Laurie.'

Dowie stared for a moment, trying to recognise them and then made the effort to sit up. 'Ah, a new doctor, eh? A new face and glory be to God a young one just for a change. Have you come like the good angels to set the prisoner free?'

'I've come to help you, if I can. And this gentleman too wants to help you. He is my stepfather.'

'Honoured to make your acquaintance, sirs.'

'We are friends of Harry Femister.'

Dowie smiled. 'My old mate, Harry – to be sure. And how is he – well, I trust? He has not been to see me for – for . . . ' He frowned. 'I cannot remember exactly. Time, hours, days, they are all the same to me – all the same – in this place.'

'You have known Harry for a long time.'

'Harry?'

'Yes, Harry Femister.'

Dowie shook his head. 'Long, long time. I forget when. But we were young lads. And I had two good strong legs on me then.'

Vince mouthed the words, 'John Femister, he's confused.'

Seizing the opportunity, Faro asked, 'The accident, what caused it?'

Dowie's mouth clamped shut and he shook his head violently, looking imploringly at Vince.

'What's the matter?'

'I'm not supposed to talk about it,' Dowie's voice sank to a whisper. 'I suppose you being a doctor . . . ' He leaned forward. 'If I don't forget, they told me, then they'll shut my mouth for good. They'll be after me again.' His eyes, bright now and suspicious, roamed past them searching the dusk-filled corners of the room. Suddenly he clutched Faro's arm, 'Don't let them get at me – for God's sake, keep them away from me.' Then aware of the strange faces, he cried out, 'Holy Mother of God, you're not the doctor. You're one of them – one of them.'

Vince came forward. 'Calm yourself, Mr Dowie. We mean only to help you. And you can trust my stepfather here, tell him all about it. He's a policeman, he'll see that no harm comes to you.'

'A policeman.' The old eyes regarded him with new respect. 'I've never had a visit from the polis before. Can you get me out of here – into the sunshine, for God's love – for pity's sake?'

'I'll do my best, if you can tell me everything you remember about the accident. Maybe then I can help.'

Dowie looked doubtful, turning his head from side to side, gnawing at his lower lip. 'I'm on your side, Mr Dowie, I've been fighting injustice all my life. As did my father, Constable Faro.'

The name obviously meant nothing to Dowie. He remained stubbornly silent. What pictures from the past were filtering through that poor demented mind, Faro wondered. He made a helpless gesture to Vince, who mouthed, 'Be patient.' At last Dowie seemed to come to a decision, nodded a few times and then said, 'We were working at Edinburgh Castle. Or at least that's what we had them believe. We were looking for King James, trying to find where they had hidden him away.'

'King James?'

'Aye, him that was Queen Mary's son and died – or was smothered – and holed up in the wall. An impostor it was took his place on the throne of Scotland – and England. An impostor who this new Queen is descended from, an impostor Queen who reigns over us now.'

'You have proof?'

'Aye, we could produce all the proof that was needed, if we found the body, it was all there.'

'All – you mean – a treasure trove,' said Vince.

The old man looked at him blankly. 'I don't get your meaning, sir.'

'The hidden jewels – where the cameo came from.'

'Oh, that.' Suddenly Dowie laughed and shook his head. 'There were two, a lad and a lass. John and I found them in the wee Prince's coffin. I gave mine to the constable who befriended me, for safe keeping. John's went to his young brother, as he would have wished.'

'What happened to the other jewels?' Vince persisted.

'There were no others, just those two cameos, lying on the Prince's crossed hands, one of his mammy, Queen Mary, the other of his daddy, Lord Darnley, proof positive that he was their bairn.'

'And that was all?' said Faro.

'It was enough, enough to bring the truth to light, the truth that has been hidden away all these hundreds of years. The body of Queen Mary's rightful successor, not only to Scotland but to England too, was all the treasure there was. If we made it public, got the people to believe us, we'd have them on our side, get the English out of our native land – usurpers, liars and cheats – they'd be the laughing stock of the whole world.' Abruptly he stopped, looking past them again, staring anxiously round the room.

'Your native land,' said Faro gently. 'Ireland?'

'Oh aye, Ireland too. But it's Canada is my home. I was taken there when I was ten, before all the troubles started.'

'Canada?' Vince and Faro exchanged glances. This was not what they expected to find. The predomination of Irish workmen who had met their deaths and what they now learned suggested a Fenian plot to discredit the monarchy. Dowie was whistling under his breath now, looking round frantically, a man who is conscious suddenly that he has said too much already.

'You were telling us about the accident.'

'The accident. Aye, they got two of the lads the first time. Before the Victorian Guelp as we called her, the bloody Queen of England came to the throne, there was a chance of revolution, of a republic. But in 1837 we knew it was now or never. The time was ripe. Prove that she and her whole line were impostors. Produce the corpse of the ancestor from whom she claimed her descent.' He chuckled. 'The succession was so shaky that the people would have seized any excuse with open arms. The scandal would have toppled the throne with a bang loud enough to be heard all over the world.'

'You almost succeeded,' said Faro. 'What went wrong?'

175

'Someone was on to us. They rigged up the scaffolding, made us walk on to it. John Femister and another Irishman, O'Hara, were killed. Both my legs were broken, my spine damaged. I've never walked again, but I'm strong, strong enough to survive. They thought I was useless and I suffered so much they expected me to die, otherwise they would have put paid to me on the spot. There was a policeman who knew what they were up to and he used some threat to expose them. Saved my life he did.'

He paused and looked across at Faro. 'He looked a lot like you, young man.'

Faro smiled. 'He was my father.'

Dowie nodded sadly. 'And a lot of good it did him trying to help us. They got him too, poor lad. Made it look like an accident . . . '

The door behind them flew open and a furious, red-faced matron filled the doorway. 'What is going on here. Visitors? Patients having their rest disturbed by intruders . . . '

Vince stood up and began to explain.

'I know Dr Kellar,' she said, 'but you will have to produce written proof from him before you disrupt my patients again. Now go – both of you – leave these premises at once.'

Vince's face was furious. He began to protest. 'This patient . . . '

'No,' whispered Faro, seizing his arm and nodding towards Dowie, 'don't make it worse for him.' And bending over Dowie, he inspected his wrists as he shook him by the hand. 'Good to meet you, sir.'

Dowie smiled sadly. 'And you, lad, remember me to your father.' And suddenly afraid at the approach of authority, he nodded towards the formidable matron breathing heavily at the door, outraged and impatient to have his visitors gone, and he grasped Faro's arm, 'Remember the Red River Valley men,' he said. 'Remember the Red River Valley.'

'At once, gentlemen.'

176

As the matron locked the door behind them, they heard Dowie whistling. Faro hesitated, for it was a tune he remembered, the one that mad Mrs Lazenby had played on the piano.

And he knew that he had solved two of the mysteries.

'Saw you looking at the shamrock on his wrist, same as Femister's,' said Vince as they walked down the drive. 'The good luck charm. So there was a connection.'

'There was indeed. But it isn't a shamrock.'

'No?'

'No, lad, and it's much more than a good luck charm, lad. I should have recognised that it wasn't an inexpertly tattooed shamrock at all. It was a maple leaf.'

'The symbol of Canada.'

'And I think that we'll find that this particular tattoo is also the badge of a dedicated band of French and Irish Canadians, dedicated to throwing off the yoke of British imperialism.'

'Of course, Lucille was telling me about troubles with the Metis, the half-breed Indians – the reason why she came to Scotland.' Vince whistled. 'So that's the reason for the murders, but who were the executioners?'

'Not were, lad, who *are* they? This is larger than individuals bearing grudges, we must set our sights on a relentless, well-disciplined political organisation.'

They had reached the main road where a horse-drawn omnibus bore the welcome sign, 'Newington'. As they took their seats and waited for other passengers, Vince said, 'I must confess that I'm a little disappointed. I was hoping for treasure trove and a reward for finding it.' When Faro laughed, he continued, 'We can only presume that the placing of the two cameos was a mark of respect for the Prince's unroyal burial. I wonder what became of those shadowy figures who placed the coffin in the hollow wall so long ago.'

'I imagine that everyone who knew was speedily eliminated, especially if they survived until King James was old enough to know and fear the truth. His years in Scotland

177

were full of monstrous happenings, like the quite brutal murder of the Gowries . . . '

'You mean the Gowrie Conspiracy, when the Master of Gowrie and his young brother were assassinated by James's order, while he was a guest in their house?'

'That's just one incident – there are plenty more.'

'I wonder what kind of people they were, how they thought, Stepfather.'

'We can only judge their seeming barbarity by our own standards and I think we've had ample proof in this case that it hasn't gone out of fashion and we aren't any more civilised than our remote ancestors.'

Sheridan Place was a hive of activity, or so it seemed to one tired man who came home, envying his stepson's boundless energy. Too late decently to call upon Lucille that evening, Vince immediately rushed off to Rutherford's bar in earnest hopes of meeting up with his young friends Rob and Walter.

In the drawing room, Rose and Emily were seated at the writing desk, penning 'thank you' letters to Sir Eric and Lucille.

Mary Faro was reading the *Scotsman*. 'Have you heard what has happened to dear Colonel Wolseley?' she asked dramatically.

Bewildered for a moment, and preoccupied with his own forebodings, Faro stared at her, wondering for a moment whether this was yet another disaster at Edinburgh Castle for him to investigate.

'You really must read this, Jeremy dear, it's all about how Colonel Wolseley and his Iroquois Indians quelled a quite nasty rebellion.' Adjusting her spectacles, she observed her son's blank expression and laughed. 'To think that I was afraid to come to the mainland because of that silly man Napoleon. And there on the other side of the globe, these gallant soldiers were making that fearful journey into the wilderness, travelling by canoe, packed with ammunition and food, in unknown territory, down the rapids.'

With a sigh, she added, 'News takes such a long time

to get here. I have been following his Red River campaign most anxiously.'

'Remember the Red River people.'

Now Peter Dowie's parting words took on new significance.

'Think of it,' continued Mrs Faro, 'they arrived safely at Fort Garry, not a man lost, thank God, on the very day we landed in Leith and we haven't heard until we are about to leave . . . '

'You arrived here on 24 August,' interrupted Faro.

'Yes, son. Two days after your poor dear father's birthday . . . '

And the same day that Harry Femister's body was discovered at the base of Castle Rock. Faro stretched out his hand for the newspaper.

'May I, please, Mother?' He read rapidly of Wolseley's advance through heavy rain and deep mud on the fort, on the left bank of the Red River:

> When all were in position, our gallant troops stormed the fort. But to no avail. Their attack went unchallenged and a cautious investigation by brave scouts revealed that the place was deserted. The Metis leader, the traitor Louis Riel, had been forewarned and had fled, it is believed, to the United States of America.

The report ended with a glowing account:

> This was the first independent command of Colonel Wolseley, already being described as the best and ablest of soldiers. His campaign was most successful. It had accomplished its objective and not a life had been lost. The troops had benefited physically by their gruelling journey and had also gained invaluable experience in quelling future uprisings against the Queen's Empire.

Faro handed the newspaper back. Kissing his mother's cheek, he said, 'What would I do without you, dear?'

179

'The same as I do without you, my darling,' she said sadly. 'Miss you dreadfully.'

'Then I promise to come home to Orkney, very, very soon.'

'For Christmas, Papa,' said Emily.

'Please, dear Papa,' said Rose.

'Time you were both in bed.'

'We haven't finished our letters yet. Granny promised . . . '

Faro leaned over and regarded his daughters' efforts. Rose already wrote a neat copperplate while Emily battled with shaky capitals.

'I am ready to write the envelope. Will you do it for me, Papa?' she asked wistfully. 'Names and addresses are so hard to spell properly.'

'I'll help you with the spelling. No, you must write it yourself, or you'll never learn. Right? "Major General Sir Eric Haston-Lennard, Edinburgh Castle", that should find him.'

As the girls went upstairs with Mrs Brook, their father promising to read a very short story to them, Mary Faro picked up the envelopes and sighed. 'I shall miss Eric very much. He's such a dear, good friend.'

'Then invite him for Christmas too.'

Mrs Faro gave a little shriek. 'What? In my tiny house – what would the neighbours think?'

'I imagine they would think you were very lucky to have such a beau.'

Mary Faro blushed very prettily. 'Get along with you, Jeremy Faro, he isn't my beau.'

'But he would like to be? You know that perfectly well, Mother dear, and you're flattered by his attentions. I can see that.'

She sighed again. 'What it is to have a detective for a son – one hasn't a bit of privacy for one's emotions.'

He put his arm round her, hugging her. 'All these wasted years, the two of you. Why on earth didn't you marry him years ago?'

She looked up at him solemnly. 'I don't know, Jeremy.

I think I've always loved him, but something has always said, "No."'

'It's your silly snobbery — thinking yourself not good enough for him, that's all. It isn't too late to change your mind, you know.'

She shook her head obstinately. 'No. I had a bad dream just after your dear father died. Sir Eric was so good to us but I never, ever forgot it.'

'But Mother, dreams are nonsense. You can't throw away happiness for a dream.'

'I could for this dream. No — I'm not going to tell you any more, so don't ask me. Listen, that's Mrs Brook. Your daughters are ready for their story now, son.'

Next morning at the Central Office, Faro was in time to sign the papers identifying the dead man but not to halt the process of his being, as Superintendent Mackintosh delicately referred to it, 'tidied away'. And although Faro now knew the reason why Harry Femister had been on the Castle Rock that day, he could not change the clause 'Death by misadventure'. That must stand until such time as a murder charge could be brought, and first he had to catch his murderer.

'Well, Faro?' said the Superintendent. 'Get on with it. We're in for a busy day. Her Majesty left Balmoral yesterday. One of her whims to stay the night in Perth and proceed on another private visit to Peebles. She has expressly commanded that none of this is to be made public but we'll have to post extra constables as usual.'

'Are we expecting trouble?'

'No, but we'd better be prepared — just in case. There's a lot of isolated country *en route* where a Fenian could lurk. Don't suppose your services will be needed though,' he added sarcastically and turned his attention again to the papers on his desk in a gesture of dismissal.

In a room down the hall the charred contents of Harry Femister's tin box had been examined by the expert Sergeant Adams. Warned that they needed very careful

181

handling, since they would readily disintegrate, Faro soon discovered that what had survived were merely personal and not particularly literate or interesting letters exchanged between the two brothers.

He had almost completed his reading when Adams came in and set before him a crumpled piece of paper, which he smoothed out carefully.

'This came from the mortuary, Inspector. The dead woman had it clutched in her hand. I don't suppose it'll make much sense, but we have orders not to destroy anything till you have had a look at it.'

Faro picked up the paper. It was charred at the edge and it contained only the scrawled letters 'rich as'.

'Rich as – who?' Was this the last remaining clue to the Queen Mary jewels? Faro sat and looked at it for a long time, then he sharpened a pen and began idly to copy the letters in the hope that they might provide a clue. As he did so a picture sprang to mind. Of the last moments of a woman trying to fight her way out of a locked bakehouse, desperately trying to write a message. Another picture took its place. Of two small children laboriously writing at a table.

His hand trembled so much he could hardly pen the short note. At last he threw down the pen, engulfed by an icy sense of disaster which even the knowledge that he had solved the Edinburgh Castle mystery could not diminish.

'Found something interesting, Inspector?'

'Take this to Superintendent Mackintosh. Tell him where I've gone and that he's to come at once.'

Chapter Fifteen

At the Castle, Sir Eric was sitting at his desk, writing. He looked up, smiling. 'Jeremy, come in, lad. I've been expecting you. Do sit down.'

Faro remained standing. 'You know why I'm here.'

'Of course I do. From the moment I heard you'd found Dowie, I knew the rest was just a matter of course.' He gave him a shrewd glance. 'You're a clever chap, Jeremy, no doubt about that. Your dear mother must be proud of you.'

'Let's leave my dear mother out of this conversation, if you please.'

Sir Eric spread wide his hands. 'As you wish, dear boy. Anything you wish.' His manner was gentle, benign.

'Then first of all, tell me, who murdered Harry Femister? You know who Harry Femister is, I imagine.'

'I do indeed. A foolish old chap whose sympathies with the French Canadian rebels were well known. He climbed Castle Rock presumably with some idea of breaking into the royal apartments and finding that allegedly hollow wall on the very day Wolseley stormed Fort Garry.' He shook his head sadly. 'Only a madman would have tackled such a hazardous – and impossible – venture.'

'Who did you get to kill him – Forster?'

'Good Lord no. There was no need for anyone to kill him. The moment he set foot on the Rock, he was doomed. He had sealed his own death warrant.'

'Helped by one of your loyal servants, of course.'

Sir Eric shook his head. 'No, Jeremy, without any external help, you must believe me. His death was an accident,

183

self-induced. He slipped and fell, a misadventure that could easily have happened to a young strong man half his age.' He sighed. 'However, it was just as well it happened that way. His attentions were becoming a bit of a nuisance, too persistent to dismiss as harmless eccentricity.'

'Was Mace's death also a fortunate accident?'

'I'd rather not go into that, if you don't mind, Jeremy,' said Sir Eric with a delicately expressive shudder. 'I'd have chosen a cleaner end then relying on his taste for antique pistols. He had come upon some evidence that we were not very keen to share with the world in general. And being a very moral chap, that was the only – rather messy – way to silence him.'

'You're admitting conniving at his death?'

'It was necessary. A soldier's duty to his Queen and country is to protect her at all times and Mace's information could have been disastrous to the safety of the realm.'

'What about all these other murders? All the people who died because they wanted to tell the truth – that the child's body in the wall here was that of Queen Mary's son, James, and that every monarch since has been descended from an impostor?'

'How romantic,' said Sir Eric mockingly.

'There's nothing romantic about eight murders.'

'Eight murders!' Sir Eric threw down his pen violently, an impatient gesture betraying the first emotion he had shown so far. 'Haven't you the least idea how many men – thousands, tens of thousands – I have ordered to certain death in the field in my years of army command – and you expect me to have feelings of guilt about a mere eight?'

'In the battlefield you were fighting against an enemy,' Faro reminded him.

'Is that so? Are not all men, eight or eighty thousand, composed of the same flesh and blood, capable of the same emotions, of feeling the same joy and pain? Besides,' he went on hurriedly, 'what do you think these men were but enemies of the Queen?'

'One of them happened to be my father.'

Sir Eric sighed. 'Magnus Faro was a fine fellow, one of the best who ever lived. I was sadder about Magnus than almost anyone I have ever known. Truly sorry, Jeremy.'

'Then I'm afraid you'll be a great deal sorrier when I do my duty to my Queen and country and arrest you as an accessory to murder.'

'You won't do that, Jeremy.'

'It is my intention, and who will stop me?'

'I will, lad,' said Sir Eric sadly. 'It is my intention that you are to be put under immediate restraint.'

Faro looked over his shoulder. Forster had entered with three other civilians. Of equal stature, they bore unmistakable signs of having served an apprenticeship in the wrestling ring. He braced himself. He was hopelessly outnumbered but he wouldn't go down without a fight. In a tight corner, he could give a good account of himself, for there were some very devious tricks he had learned in his time with the Edinburgh City Police calculated to throw even strong men off guard.

'Take him,' said Sir Eric tonelessly.

As they pinioned his arms to his sides, Faro said, 'Have you another accident in mind for me? I hope it's a convincing one this time.'

'You may rest assured on that score, Jeremy. We are very efficient in that department.'

'So I've observed. Tell me one thing, Sir Eric.'

'With pleasure, my boy.'

'You have been like a father to me, you supported my mother and I believe you have a certain fondness for her. You knew that I was in danger. How did you reconcile your conscience with giving orders that I was also to be disposed of, by an "accidental" fall of rock?'

Sir Eric regarded him steadily. 'You will keep forgetting that I am a soldier first and foremost, lad. Many times in my life I have had to obey orders, as you are doing now, because they were given by the highest in the land, Her Majesty the Queen herself. As you must have experienced

185

many times yourself, doing one's duty can be unpleasant, sometimes it can even wring a man's heart.'

He stood up. 'We are ready to leave now.'

'Where is Lucille?'

'Lucille should now be at sea on her way back to Orkney. When I suspected that you were on the right track and might arrive at any hour, full of accusations, I thought it best to terminate my niece's visit. Especially as the foolish girl seems to imagine she's in love with you.'

'Does she know anything of all this?'

'Of course not. She's a silly romantic girl.' He looked at Faro and that moment's compassion, more than any threats, chilled him to the heart. 'I'm sorry, I hope you don't reciprocate her feelings because I'm afraid you are unlikely ever to meet again.'

'Tell me, where did the plot to kidnap my two daughters fit into the plan? Was that just to scare me off too?'

Sir Eric shrugged. 'There never was any plot to kidnap your little girls, Jeremy. Their abduction that night was, I suspect, just what it appeared to be. Another attempted child abduction, common enough in the sordid annals of Edinburgh's underworld.'

He signalled to the four silent men. 'You know what to do.'

Faro was led by his captors, arms held firmly but unobtrusively, downstairs to a carriage waiting at the open door leading to the empty quadrangle. There was no point in crying out – nor any opportunity to do so – as he was bundled inside.

The window blinds had been drawn and one of the men tied his hands together behind his back while another blindfolded him. He cursed them roundly, realising that he was to be executed like a trussed fowl instead of being despatched, as he had always imagined, in a straight fight to the death.

The carriage moved off. They were travelling down the steep High Street. It was a road he had travelled often enough in his twenty years, strange that this was to be the very last time. Time, he thought, had almost ceased to exist for him. He had been denied even the condemned man's last requests, that he might say farewell to his mother, to Rose and Emily and to Vince. Especially Vince, dearer to him than any man alive, and very nearly his own son.

At last the carriage stopped. He was helped out and felt the warmth of summer sunshine on his face. Savouring that moment of finality, he took a deep breath before being led forward, warned of a step and propelled through a succession of stone corridors.

Were they going to put him in some miserable dungeon and leave him there to die? At least he was glad there was no resemblance to the creaking wooden floors of East House Asylum. They meant that he should have a less lingering end than poor Peter Dowie.

He realised that stone had given way to polished marble, for once his injured ankle, unused to such speed, slipped and only his jailers' support kept him from falling. Around him the echoes signified space, indoor space for there was no longer summer warmth or birdsong. He had the impression of a large room, the creaking of doors opening and closing, sounds of breathing, the clank of arms, as if the doors were guarded. Where in God's name had they taken him?

'Stand there.'

He did as he was told, wishing he could identify his place of execution. A moment later, the blindfold was removed. The large room was familiar. He was in the Palace of Holyroodhouse. He had been here before with the Edinburgh City Police during an attempted break in.

A tall man, grey haired, stood with his back to the window in the manner of one who does not wish to be recognised. A moment later, Sir Eric entered a little breathlessly, glanced at the document handed to him by the silent man and walked over to Faro.

'Got you here safely, eh, Jeremy.' He smiled. 'Sorry to keep you waiting.'

Sir Eric motioned towards the handsome desk across the

room, its only adornment an inkwell, sand and somewhat ironically a service revolver.

'Sit down, dear boy.' And walking across the room he put a paper in front of him. 'I'm afraid we will have to ask you to sign the Official Secrets Act, saying that you will not divulge anything that has been said between these walls or anything remotely connected with the recent disturbances in Red River . . . '

'And emphatically nothing regarding the possibility of a child's coffin being hidden in the walls of Edinburgh Castle,' boomed the other voice across the floor.

Faro began to read the document. 'You can believe us, it's all there as stated. Nothing else, nothing more.'

Faro looked up at Sir Eric. 'And what if I refuse?'

'I don't think you should, dear lad. Your freedom is in peril.'

'And what about my immortal soul, Sir Eric? Or maybe such matters are unimportant to you.'

Faro turned and addressed himself to the tall man, who seemed anxious to remain in the background despite his air of authority. 'I have done no wrong, sir. My only interest is and will continue to be to do my duty by my profession, by detecting crime and bringing criminals to justice. In such matters, I refuse to be compromised. And I'm not interested in being bought by anyone, not even the Queen herself.'

'Your attitude is commendable, but in the present circumstances inadvisable, very inadvisable,' said Sir Eric.

'You said there would be no difficulties, that he would sign. Get him to do so, dammit. We've wasted enough time,' said the other man.

Ignoring the interruption, Faro asked again, 'And if I refuse?'

Smiling beyond him, Sir Eric nodded, 'You had better ask Superintendent Mackintosh about that.'

Hampered by his bound hands, Faro swung round and came face to face with his superior officer, who had entered unobserved. Faro marvelled that the Superintendent, his one hope of survival, had come to his rescue without question and with remarkable speed. Did he have some plan for his escape?

'If you refuse, Faro, then I can tell you exactly what will happen,' said Mackintosh heavily. 'You will be dismissed from the Edinburgh City Police.'

There was a moment's silence, of disbelief, on Faro's part before he replied, 'So you are in this too. I might have guessed,' he added bitterly.

Mackintosh merely shook his head, looked at the other two men and made a helpless gesture.

'You convince him, Mackintosh,' said Sir Eric.

'Listen to me, Faro. Your loyalty to the Force does you proud. But if you don't do as they wish, I'm afraid, official sources will make it quite difficult for anyone to employ you – or your stepson, Dr Laurie, of whom Kellar is giving us such excellent reports. He has the makings of a brilliant career but your refusal to co-operate will destroy him too, especially as he has been concerned in your investigations.'

Faro saw all too plainly what his refusal meant. That the only place he could live in future would be in the ranks of the criminals themselves. What sort of life was that for him? But worse, much worse for Vince, at the beginning of his professional life, whose dream was to be Queen's Physician one day.

'If you are still in any doubt, take a look out of the window,' said Sir Eric. 'Oh, for heaven's sake, do untie him. Inspector Faro is a man of honour. He won't do anything desperate. You have my assurance on that.'

Untied, Faro left his chair, with one fleeting look at the service revolver, and the ardent wish he could prove Sir Eric wrong in the matter of chivalry. Moving stiffly to the window, he found that the room overlooked the private grounds of the Palace of Holyroodhouse.

And there was the last sight he expected on this earth: his mother, Vince, Rose and Emily walking together across the grass.

Brought no doubt just to make sure that I'd sign, he was about to remark bitterly, when he suddenly observed that all four of his family were wearing their very best clothes. They were all looking very happy and excited, especially Rose and Emily, who turned constantly towards a door directly below the window.

A moment later, he knew the reason why. A small plump woman, plain and middle-aged, in a purple satin gown, had emerged. A sudden breeze caught at the streamers on her widow's cap and as she half turned against it, the sunlight flashed on diamonds and emeralds, and touched the Gartar ribbon across her breast.

He watched his mother and the girls curtsy, Vince bow elegantly.

'If you need any further convincing, dear lad,' said Sir Eric at his side, 'HM is in it too.' And dipping the pen into the inkwell, 'Now, are you ready?'

The presence of his family outside removed any further hopes of escape and retaliation. Reluctantly he took up the document, added his signature, and as Sir Eric sanded it Faro indicated the revolver.

'Was that the alternative?'

'Think no more about it, dear lad. That is all behind us now.'

'And what if I had still refused to sign, after all these pressures put upon me and upon my family. What then?'

'A mere precaution – I've told you.'

'But if it had to be used,' Faro insisted.

Sir Eric shook his head. 'Then that would have lain very heavily upon my conscience. Disposing of you, and the sorrow it would have caused to one who is also dear to me.'

'But you would have done it.'

'Oh yes indeed. For I am as fiercely loyal to my duty to the Queen and all I hold dear as you are to dispensing justice.' He looked at him steadily and said quietly, 'If necessary I would have pulled the trigger myself. Come now, Superintendent, you will accompany us.'

190

And together, they marched with Faro across the room to the tall man who had listened with an expressionless face.

'You know Mr Gladstone, of course.' And handing the rolled document to the elder statesman, he said, 'And now, Prime Minister, shall we join the ladies?' And to Faro, 'You too, lad. Her Majesty has commanded that you and your family be presented.'

Deadly Beloved

In memory of Elizabeth Byrd

Chapter One

Two weeks after the police surgeon's wife vanished on a train journey from Edinburgh to North Berwick, when all enquiries discreet but exhaustive had failed, the first grim evidence appeared. A bloodstained fur cloak and kitchen carving knife, discovered in the melting snow near the railway line at Longniddry Station, were ominous indications that the case could no longer be regarded as a 'missing persons' enquiry.

Who could have imagined a furore over the burnt roast at a dinner party as prelude to another sordid domestic crime?

Such were Detective Inspector Jeremy Faro's thoughts as he painstakingly sifted through memory's tedious details of the evening's events.

Aware from long experience that the first place one searched for a motive to murder was within the victim's family circle, he concluded that it had been a very dull party indeed. Until Mrs Eveline Shaw went to the piano and played the Beethoven Appassionata. Up to that moment boredom, rather than the very modest amount of indifferent wine served at the police surgeon's table, was responsible for the blunting of Faro's normally keen powers of observation.

Once upon a time he had believed that mayhem and murder, his daily round and common task with the Edinburgh City Police, were confined to the criminal world. Now he knew that the miasma of molten corruption, seething from grim wynds and tall 'lands' under the

Castle's ancient shadow, could no longer be confined to those wretches who stole and stabbed and procured and perverted.

In recent times crime stalked the respectable New Town, like some ghastly retribution by the ghosts of all those he had hunted down and brought to justice. Now it seemed that their evil shades threatened to roost in the circle of his own family and friends. He would have hesitated to include Dr Melville Kellar in the category of personal friend, but here was a crime brushing uneasily close to 9 Sheridan Place and his own hearth. His stepson Dr Vincent Beaumarcher Laurie was the police surgeon's assistant and the confidant of the missing woman.

Without having the least pretentions to medical diagnosis, Faro had recognised for several weeks before the event that his stepson was suffering from a malady of the heart. Secretive, vague and preoccupied, Vince was displaying all the symptoms of romantic involvement. Faro wondered if the sudden decision to take a short holiday with his doctor friend Walter in the Austrian asylum for consumptives was a sensible retreat, a prudent flight into neutral territory that would give him time to get his emotions into the right perspective.

It was not, however, until after Vince's return from Vienna and Faro's disclosures concerning the missing woman, that he learned with surprise and misgiving that the object of his stepson's affection was Mabel Kellar.

Vince's face had paled as he listened. 'I can't believe this, Stepfather. You must be mistaken. Couldn't she have had an accident? Lost her memory?'

'That was our first thought, lad.'

'You've tried the hospitals?'

'Aye, and the workhouses too.'

'I visited her the morning after the dinner party, to say goodbye before I went on holiday,' Vince whispered in awed tones. 'She was preparing to leave, to visit her sister in North Berwick. It's dreadful, dreadful. Unbelievable.'

8

Faro poured a large whisky and handed it to his step-son. 'Drink this and when you're feeling calmer, we'll talk about it.'

'Calmer? Oh dear God! Who would want to harm her? She was one of the sweetest, kindest creatures on this earth. I loved her, yes, loved her, Stepfather,' he added defiantly. 'I would have died for her.'

Faro said nothing, inclined to dismiss his stepson's infatuation for what it was: the inevitable attraction to a mother figure. Mabel Kellar was older than his own mother, Lizzie Faro, would have been and Vince, determined to avoid matrimony at all costs, had chosen yet another love where no lasting commitment was possible.

'She had no enemies. Everyone who knew her loved her,' said Vince.

The evidence, thought Faro grimly, suggested that someone had hated her. Hated her enough to destroy her.

Later Vince gave Faro an account of that last visit.

'Thinking about it now, I realise that she was considerably agitated. Very upset. There had been yet another unholy row with Kellar after the guests departed. Serious enough for her to be seeking refuge with her sister. Actually leaving her husband, as he rightly deserves. She should have done so long ago, if she hadn't slavishly adored him.'

'What was this row about? Did she tell you?'

'She spared me the exact details, hinted at a very unpleasant post-mortem on the culinary disasters of the dinner. Kellar blamed her entirely for her unfortunate choice of housekeeper. I offered to escort her to the railway station as I was catching a train there myself, but she refused. She wasn't quite ready to leave. Packing to complete, instructions to leave and so forth. Oh dear God – I can't . . . ' And Vince, covering his face, began to sob.

Faro put a compassionate hand on his shoulder. 'There, there, lad.' He felt the words were inadequate to deal with his stepson's unrequited passion, since Mabel Kellar had adored only her husband.

Melville Kellar occupied a position of authority with the Edinburgh City Police. He was highly respected and esteemed, although Vince's daily grumblings painted a picture of a harsh disciplinarian, bigoted and intolerant of human error and inefficiency. Pompous and overbearing, Dr Kellar emerged as utterly callous in his dealings with medical students. Perhaps in order to sleep well at nights, the police surgeon had of necessity retreated into a remote unfeeling shell, a refuge denied Faro, aware that even if he was spared to serve with the City Police for another twenty years, he would never become accustomed to scenes of bloody murder, or be unmoved at a life hideously snuffed out by sudden violent death.

'Kellar could give his dissecting knives lessons in sharpness,' the students who endured his sarcasm were wont to say. And not only students, thought Faro. The honest peeler walking the beat and the hard-working underpaid domestic within the Kellar kitchen existed on a separate plane. They belonged to a sub-species he never cared to let his eyes dwell upon or acknowledge as fellow human beings with the same capacity for joy and suffering as himself. There was a rumour that, in common with Royalty, Dr Kellar expected domestics to stay out of sight unless summoned to appear.

'If he comes face-to-face with a servant going about her duties, he'll dismiss her on the spot. What do you think of that, Stepfather?'

'If it's true, it's incredible.'

Prior to the dinner party, Faro's encounters with Kellar had been limited to the police mortuary, where his first impression had been of a man slightly below middle height with piercing blue eyes, who made up for his lack of stature with a biting tongue and a high opinion of his own lofty intellectual stature.

In Kellar's eyes, even senior detectives were mindless fools.

Faro still recalled uncomfortably the occasion when

he had ventured an opinion about the cause of a victim's death at a post-mortem.

Kellar had rounded upon him, eyes flashing, brows lowered like a charging bull.

'Are you questioning my findings, sir? Are you insinuating from your somewhat meagre education in forensic matters that you are more capable of an effective diagnosis in this case . . . '

Faro had wilted beneath that volley of invective. As it turned out, his theory was proved correct and Kellar was quick to bask in all the praise without the slightest qualm of conscience. Apology never occurred to him or acknowledgement of the Detective Inspector's shrewd observations which had led to the capture and subsequent sentencing of the murderer.

Faro shrugged such incidents aside, realising how they could influence his own judgement. In his profession, prejudice could be fatal to the fair-mindedness that was the very essence of justice.

To be entirely fair, the gruesome daily round at the mortuary presented the surgeon in a very different guise to the host in full evening dress, presiding over the dinner table.

Faro was at once struck by Kellar's commanding appearance which might well have awed his medical students, who would not necessarily have noticed that their tormentor was good-looking in a silver-haired distinguished way, allying the chilly classical features of a marble Greek god with a smile that was charm itself.

His smiles that evening, however, were as rare as his replenishment of the guests' wine glasses, too long empty for politeness and indicating that rumour was true. Kellar was tight-fisted and his wife down-trodden and pathetic.

'A somewhat ill-assorted pair, didn't you think?' he asked Vince.

'I know what you're thinking,' was the defensive reply.

11

'Mabel was an heiress and he had married her for her money.'

Faro shrugged. Handsome men often married plain wives. And Mabel Kellar's exterior did indeed hide a heart of gold, if appearances were anything to go by. He had been touched by her devotion to her protegée, Mrs Shaw, that young and beautiful woman scarce past girlhood.

After lighting a pipe, Faro poured himself a dram and when Mrs Brook had cleared the supper table, he found his concentration wandering from the police report on a fraud case he had recently successfully brought to justice.

One thought persisted, refusing to be ignored. He had the gift, not always a happy one, of being able to put himself squarely in other men's shoes. In Dr Kellar's case, had his wife gone missing then surely the first places he would have searched, after hammering anxiously on the doors of close friends and relations, were the hospitals.

There was always the possibility in view of the damning evidence that she had been attacked on the train and flung out of the carriage. There were also several other alarming possibilities which suggested that if she was still alive she might be very seriously injured. As police surgeon, Kellar enjoyed a unique advantage in having easy access to discreet perusal of hospital admissions and a look into their wards if necessary.

And yet he had failed to do so. Why? And Faro's thoughts returned again to the events of the Kellars' last dinner party. In a pattern that was familiar after twenty years of fighting crime, he found himself meticulously examining every detail of that evening, searching for the first clue into the labyrinth, imagining his host in the role of potential wife-murderer.

Only two weeks ago . . .

Chapter Two

Dr Kellar and his wife lived in a handsome mansion in the Grange, in the recently developed south side of Edinburgh. Built at the beginning of Victoria's reign, strenuous efforts had been made to make it look considerably older. Nothing had been spared in mediaeval turrets, Gothic flourishes of gargoyles and even hints at a drawbridge and studded door.

As an architectural purist, a stickler for the clean lines and uncomplicated plans of the Georgian era, Faro dismissed the result as yet another nightmare in domestic architecture.

'Have you ever noticed,' he asked Vince, as the hired carriage bounded down the drive, its myriad twists and turns designed to establish in the minds of arriving guests an illusion of parkland and a rich man's estate. 'Have you ever noticed,' he repeated, 'how often houses resemble their owners?'

Vince laughed. 'Never. Aren't you confusing your similes? I thought that particular one referred to dogs and pets only. Come, Stepfather, not so glum. You'll enjoy meeting Mabel Kellar. And I'm sure there'll be excellent food and wine, and grand company too.'

The first snowflakes were falling as they pressed the bell a second time. Faro, dragging up his greatcoat collar, tapped his foot impatiently. 'What on earth can be keeping them? One would imagine an army of servants lurking about such an establishment.'

He was to discover that servants were almost non-existent at the best of times, Dr Kellar's excuse being

13

that he couldn't abide such creatures and more than an absolute minimum posed a dire threat to his privacy.

At last the door was opened by the housekeeper, her flour-covered hands explaining the delay. A lady of ample proportions in starched apron and large white cap over untidy wisps of grey hair, her chin was swathed in a large muffler.

'Come in. Missus will be with you in a wee minute,' she whispered hoarsely and indicated the staircase. 'You'll find master up there, drawing-room, first door left.'

At that moment, Dr Kellar appeared on the landing. 'Is that Flynn down there?'

The housekeeper with a nervous hand adjusted her spectacles and bobbed a curtsey. 'Yes, sir.'

'Your place is below stairs, Flynn. Where is your mistress?'

'In the kitchen, sir.'

'I want her here – at once. Does she not know the guests have arrived?' And for the two visitors staring up at him with some embarrassment, he summoned a wintry smile. 'Come away, gentlemen. Come away.'

After they climbed the stairs, he greeted them with an apology. 'My wife employs local domestics and allows them home at the weekend.'

This indulgence was not, as it appeared, out of kindness, Vince told Faro later, but because Kellar's chronic meanness made him suspect servants of stealing food and so forth. Most men in his position would keep a resident coachman, too, but the luxury of board and meagre lodgings was the sole perquisite of the housekeeper.

As for the excellent company, Vince had been sadly mistaken and Faro was dismayed to discover their fellow guests were Superintendent McIntosh of the Edinburgh City Police and his waspish wife, known irreverently in the Central Office as The Tartar.

Faro suppressed a sigh. He had few off-duty hours,

14

especially as criminals took full advantage of the possibilities offered by long dark winter nights. He had no desire to spend one of his precious free evenings in the company of his superior, a man he found opinionated and tiresome at the best of times. McIntosh's acknowledgement, briefer than courtesy prescribed, spoke volumes on his own astonishment and displeasure at seeing Inspector Faro.

As Kellar ushered them into the drawing-room, Faro observed, sitting at the grand piano, an extremely pretty young woman in deep mourning. Since Kellar did not deign to introduce her, Faro presumed that this was a poor relative, recently widowed, and doubtless regarded by the doctor as just one more mouth to feed.

The atmosphere was less than cordial and Faro was heartily glad when the distant doorbell announced another arrival. A few moments later Mrs Kellar ushered in Sir Hedley Marsh.

Known in the Newington district as the Mad Bart, he was the last person Faro and Vince expected to encounter at the lofty police surgeon's dining-table. Their exchange of puzzled glances was a wordless comment on this odd company of dinner guests. How had the hermit of Solomon's Tower been lured away from his army of cats?

Faro looked sharply at his hostess. Since it was well known that Sir Hedley despised and avoided all human contact, perhaps Mrs Kellar did have extraordinary powers of attraction, not evident at first glance. Despite Vince's commendations, he was to remember no lasting impression when it was vital to do so. He recalled a plain woman, tall and thin with dark hair pulled tightly back from indeterminate features. What colour were her eyes, was her nose short or long, her face round or oval?

Faro shook his head. Even details of the elaborate velvet gown had vanished. Was it blue or green? The colour was unimportant for it served only to emphasise her lack of style, while her fingernails testified to her agitation, bearing

15

traces of her recent domestic activity in the kitchen.

Another surprise was still to come, for the Mad Bart had been introduced as: 'My dear Uncle Hedley.'

As they shook hands Faro decided that although Sir Hedley's dress was correct for the occasion, albeit a little out of date, he had not escaped completely from his cats after all. He had, at close quarters, brought their ripe odours with him.

'I believe you two know each other already,' said Mrs Kellar.

'We do. Inspector and I are near neighbours. How d'ye·do?'

Mrs Kellar smiled. 'And I might add, Inspector, you are the chief reason for Uncle Hedley accepting our invitation.'

Sir Hedley grinned sheepishly. 'Like good conversation. See you often passing by. Haven't chatted since you took one of my kits. Big fella now?'

'Yes, indeed.'

Sir Hedley nodded vigorously. 'Gave him a name, I hope.'

'Rusty.'

'Rusty, eh. Like it. Like it. Good mouser?'

'Very.' And aware of the old man's frowning glances in Vince's direction: 'Let me introduce you to my stepson, Dr Vincent Laurie.'

Faro suppressed a smile. He detected a certain distaste as the fastidious young doctor took the extended and none–too–clean hand.

'From these parts, are you, young fella?'

'I've lived in Edinburgh for most of my life, sir.'

Sir Hedley frowned. 'We've met before, of course. What kind of a doctor are you?'

Vince was saved a reply as Mabel Kellar ushered the young widow towards them. 'Now, Uncle, you can talk as much as you like at dinner. I want dear Vince to talk to my dearest friend and companion, Mrs Eveline Shaw.'

Not a poor relative after all, thought Faro, observing

16

Mrs Kellar watching benignly as Vince and Mrs Shaw shook hands.

'The Superintendent is waiting to meet you, Uncle Hedley,' said Kellar and led the old man, glowering ferociously, in the direction of the waiting McIntoshes. Turning, he addressed Mrs Kellar: 'I take it that dinner is ready? Will you lead the way?'

Formal etiquette demanded that Dr Kellar lead in Mrs McIntosh; the Superintendent took in Mrs Shaw and as Sir Hedley was intent on questioning Vince rather loudly, Faro brought up the rear, offering Mrs Kellar his arm.

'You will be nice to Uncle Hedley, won't you?' she whispered.

'I will, indeed. You are to be congratulated on getting him out of Solomon's Tower. Quite extraordinary.'

Mrs Kellar laughed. 'Don't I know it! But as I said, I have you to thank – and the Superintendent.'

'Indeed?'

'Yes, he is absolutely fascinated by crime. He's a great admirer of yours. And so am I, Inspector. I have heard so much about you from dear Vince. You have such kind eyes. You don't look at all like a policeman.'

Faro intercepted the long glance over a fluttering fan, a look that in any other woman he would have considered highly coquettish. Embarrassed, he chuckled: 'Indeed? I don't know quite how to answer that one, ma'am. What, pray, do policeman look like? "If you prick us, do we not bleed? if you tickle us, do we not laugh? if you poison us, do we not die? and if you wrong us, shall we not revenge?"'

Mrs Kellar did not acknowledge his smiling glance. She was staring straight ahead, white-faced, her expression one of sudden terror.

'Ma'am?' said Faro gently.

The fan had closed and was clutched tightly between white-knuckled fists.

'Ma'am?' he repeated gently, ushering her towards the table.

Suddenly aware of him, the fan fluttered free again and she laughed. 'Dear Vince told me of your passion for Shakespeare. Did you see Sir Henry Irving in *The Merchant*?'

'I did indeed.'

'Are we not very privileged to have his annual visit to Edinburgh? We never miss a performance.'

Acutely aware as he was of changes in atmosphere, Faro had sensed a dangerous moment, and wondered upon whom that dark glance had fallen. Now as he seated her at the table, she tapped him on the wrist.

'Not ma'am, Inspector. You must please call me Mabel – as your dear Vince does. For I hope we are also to be friends.'

On the other side of the table Vince suppressed a smile, conscious of the admiring glances of both Mabel Kellar and Eveline Shaw in his stepfather's direction.

Faro, so shrewd and observant, could never see himself as he appeared to others, thought Vince, especially to the ladies – certainly not as a sober widower approaching forty and therefore to be dismissed as thoroughly ineligible. True, his interest in dress was negligible, but despite his declaration that the only function of clothes was a decent covering for nakedness, he managed by instinct to choose the right thing to wear.

Examining his stepfather feature by feature, Vince noted the heavy silver-gilt hair and the wide-set dark blue eyes of the psychic. They didn't look *at* you, but right *into* you as if they read a fellow's very soul, a fact which many a criminal had found disconcerting. True, his nose was rather long and his lips were thinner than made for beauty but that was out of the habit of pressing them together in contemplation rather than their natural shape.

He had inherited good looks and a splendid physique from his Orkney ancestors, but there the resemblance to those fierce warriors ended. Vince, from the threshold of youth, had long guessed the secret of the Inspector's attraction to the opposite sex: an irresistible combination of those qualities which appealed to women, strength and reliability with that most disarming of manly features, a gentle smile and a compassionate heart. Here was a strong man who could also cry and was not ashamed of his tears.

Vince's attention was distracted from his stepfather as Dr Kellar poured the wine and Mrs Kellar excused herself.

'Mabel,' bellowed her husband from the other end of the table. 'Mabel, where are you going now?'

'Just to the kitchen, my love. To look at the oven.'

'Can't Flynn take care of that?'

'I've told you, dearest, she's most unwell.' And to the guests she fluttered nervous hands. 'The poor creature. She has such a cruel toothache. You saw her, didn't you? Her face all swollen?'

The guests murmured sympathetically and Mrs Kellar continued: 'I couldn't possibly ask her to prepare dinner, swooning with agony.'

'Go on then, woman, but hurry up,' was Kellar's ungracious dismissal. And as the door closed, 'I must apologise. My wife is too indulgent. She thrives on waifs and strays.'

Sir Hedley squeezed Faro's arm and whispered hoarsely, 'He means me. Doesn't like me much. Came for Mabel's sake.'

But Faro observed that the barb had also been intended for another guest, as he caught Dr Kellar's hooded glance in the direction of Mrs Shaw, who studied her plate intently.

The food served failed to come up to Vince's hints of excellence; it was uninspired, insipid and disappointing to both men used as they were to their housekeeper Mrs Brook's abundant and excellent cooking.

Faro could, however, sympathise more than most with Mrs Flynn's problem. He knew all about the agonies of toothache since he frequently cornered desperate and violent criminals and disarmed them of deadly weapons with considerably more aplomb than he ever faced a dental surgeon's chair.

19

Considering the housekeeper's malady which necessitated their hostess's frequent excursion below stairs to give 'a hand', Faro, a kind and sympathetic employer himself, would have readily overlooked tepid soup and the long delays between courses, had the wine – even Dr Kellar's somewhat substandard table wine – continued to flow in agreeable abundance.

After a longer wait than usual, during which the guests, and Sir Hedley in particular, with much clearing of the throat stared meaningfully into empty glasses, Mrs Kellar reappeared looking warm and flustered, bearing before her a serving dish from which blue smoke issued forth.

Dr Kellar sniffed the air and, it seemed in retrospect to Faro, looked up quite murderously from the task of sharpening his carving knives, an action which he had carried out with the pride and expertise to be expected of a brilliant surgeon. Later Faro was to wish he had paid a little more attention to those knives, one of which went a-missing and whose reappearance in sinister and dramatic circumstances was to play a vital part in the murder evidence.

Overcome with rage, Dr Kellar had shouted, 'This is an outrage – and I hold you directly responsible, Mabel. We seldom have guests to dinner these days and when we do, I expect perfection. Perfection, do you hear, madam? Intolerable food and intolerable serving, a housekeeper who cannot even cook a decent meal! This is an unforgivable insult to our guests—'

'Her references were quite excellent, my dear, you read them yourself and approved,' Mrs Kellar interrupted defensively. 'Please be patient, she has such dreadful toothache, in awful agonies.'

'Then she must see a dental surgeon and have it extracted.'

A delicate shudder passed round the table. Faro was not alone in his cowardice.

'Yes, have it ripped out,' Kellar continued, 'But not on my time,' he roared, thumping the table. 'I have had quite

20

enough of her. Enough. I do not pay domestics to indulge themselves with petty indispositions. You are to give her a week's notice immediately. Do you hear, woman, one week's notice.'

'But what are we to do?' wailed Mrs Kellar. 'We cannot be left without help in the house.'

'Then set about finding a replacement.'

'Please be reasonable, my love. I cannot possibly find anyone in a week.'

'One week,' thundered Kellar. 'You have one week. And that is my last word on the subject, madam.'

'As you wish, my love.'

In the heavy silence that followed, Mrs Kellar's sniffs indicated barely suppressed tears while the guests did their best to avoid each other's eyes. They concentrated in a half-hearted way on staring ahead at nothing in particular, resisting at all costs a curious or speculative glance in the direction of the ruined roast, still smouldering like a burnt offering on the centre of the table.

'And where is our maid this evening?' demanded Dr Kellar.

'You allowed Ina home for the weekend. Don't you remember, my dear – that is our usual procedure.' Mrs Kellar looked round the table, her helpless gesture begging affirmation and approval.

'Hrmmph,' growled Dr Kellar, his indignant shake of the head indicating that this generous impulse had been ungratefully reciprocated.

Emboldened, Mrs Kellar went on: 'And might I remind you, my dear, that the necessity for acquiring a new housekeeper need never have arisen, had you not given Mrs Freeman notice.' Again she appealed to the guests: 'Mrs Freeman's services gave no cause for complaint, an admirable housekeeper in every way.'

'A self-opinionated fool,' sneered Kellar. 'And rude. Damnably rude.'

'You forget, my love, that she had looked after this

21

house for nearly thirty years and regarded it as her own.'

'Hrmmph. Small disagreement, that was all. Ungrateful wretch left in a huff without working her notice. No character need she expect from me, nor this new one either. You may tell her that, as a parting gift.' Kellar's sneer as he continued to flourish the carving knife now assumed sinister and monstrous significance.

Faro shrugged aside such imaginings. A ruined meal, problems with the servants, were hardly just cause and impediment for murdering one's spouse. If that were the case, then the daily press would have no news of anything else but domestic crimes.

The dessert, an apple tart also somewhat charred about the edges, was served plus a Scotch trifle sadly lacking in sherry as its main flavouring.

There was a momentary revival of cheerful spirits around the table as the guests noted the appearance of the port decanter.

Faro declined the cheese and concentrated on trying to attract Vince's attention, wondering how soon they could decently and discreetly excuse themselves. His hopes sank when Mabel announced: 'Our dear friend Mrs Shaw has been prevailed upon to play for us very shortly. She is an excellent performer,' she added reassuringly.

As there was no possibility of bringing the evening to a close, Faro considered his host dispassionately. Dr Kellar was a snob and worse, a pompous parsimonious bore whose choice of conversation seemed limited to promoting his own importance to the Edinburgh City Police with the addition of graphic descriptions relating to his dissections of interesting cadavers of criminals past and present. The mere flicker of an eyelid from Vince indicated to Faro that they were in agreement about the suitability of this topic for light dinner-table conversation.

Despite Vince's high commendation of their hostess, none of her sterling qualities was evident and Mabel Kellar was soon to retreat into a blurred memory, a well-meaning bungling nonentity, her sole virtues being to suffer incompetent servants gladly and acquiring waifs and strays.

When she wasn't scuttling back and forth to the kitchen, Faro observed that her attentions were devoted almost exclusively to Vince and Eveline Shaw. Her colour grew more hectic as she beamed upon them, pressing the young woman's hand affectionately or patting her cheek with her fan.

The specially-invited Uncle Hedley, sitting next to Vince, was being studiously ignored by that young man, intent upon discussing with his hostess his imminent trip to Vienna.

On Sir Hedley's other side, Superintendent McIntosh was enthusiastically following his host's dismemberment of cadavers while the Mad Bart looked bewildered and very glum indeed. Faro, after a few vain attempts to engage him in conversation across the wide table, gave up and regarded the scene thoughtfully.

Again he was struck by the ill-chosen assortment of dinner guests, puzzled by the reason for his inclusion. This first social invitation to the police surgeon's house was flattering but obscure, since they had little to say to one another, and before tonight he would have considered that their dislike was mutual.

He turned his attention to Vince and Eveline Shaw, clucked over in a nervous mother-hen fashion by Mabel Kellar. The thought sprang to his mind unbidden: had this dinner party been carefully planned as an occasion for matchmaking between the dearest friend and companion and his young stepson who was Mabel's confidant? Was that why the pleasure of his company had been required, to give approval and blessing? The thought was firmly rooted in reality, for matchmaking was the main creative hobby of Edinburgh matrons in Mabel Kellar's stratum of society. Faro imagined that just such a scene might be encountered at other Edinburgh dinner tables this evening, presided over by many an anxious mama, desperate to find a husband for a daughter no longer young, and whose face had never been her fortune.

As for Eveline Shaw herself, oblivious and indifferent to being the centre of her hostess's adulations, her attitude was one of sadness and patient bewilderment. She stared at her plate and spoke little apart from accepting or declining the food offered, her mourning dress serving only to enhance that young and lovely face.

Faro shook his head. No. Mrs Shaw wouldn't do at all for Vince. Small wonder he preferred his hostess. But what could have united these two women, so dissimilar, in friendship? The young widow, stricken and lost in the lachrymose stage of early bereavement, appeared to be scarcely older than Vince. Faro guessed that she had not been married long and was no doubt still deeply in love with her dead husband.

He knew all about losing one's beloved partner and sympathised silently with the countenance frozen in unhappiness across the table. Her expression suggested that she longed for the solitude of her own home, to be alone with her melancholy thoughts. Her silence and lack of spontaneity told a tale of bitter regret at having been persuaded to accept Mabel Kellar's thinly veiled invitation, and all its implications, to be jolly and meet 'the nice young doctor.'

Was her 'dearest friend and companion's' refusal to cooperate in the matchmaking activity, the plan that had gone awry, the reason for Mrs Kellar's distraught appearance? There was more in it than that. Faro had observed the fleeting glance of terror displayed earlier by Mrs Kellar. Mrs Shaw was also afraid.

Faro was to remember the significance of that moment when he endeavoured to deduce the sinister elements and motives lurking behind the masks worn by the guests at that very dull and chaotic dinner party.

His attention was drawn repeatedly to Sir Hedley. He

was not frightened but certainly appeared ill-at-ease. His attempts to engage Vince or the Superintendent in conversation had been rather discourteously ignored. What was his reason for being included? Surely more than an obligation to his niece and a fascination with crime had been required to persuade him out of that hermit's shell in Solomon's Tower?

Had he been invited out of thoughtful concern or simply to make up the sitting? Whatever the reason, the old man must have been concluding that it was all a dismal failure, thought Faro, turning his attention to Superintendent McIntosh.

A toady of the worst possible kind, McIntosh hung on every word Kellar uttered.

'A little bird tells me that there is a knighthood in the offing, Doctor. Let me be the first to offer my congratulations.'

Faro shuddered. Coyness sat ill upon the Superintendent's fleshy shoulders and Kellar's attempt at modest indifference also failed. He beamed.

'That is so. Word has newly reached me. But in the utmost confidence.' He put a finger to his lips. 'Not a word. I know I can rely on your discretion, Superintendent. Not one word.'

'You may rely on me utterly, Doctor. Utterly.'

Faro suppressed a smile. The forthcoming knighthood was common knowledge and he suspected that every policeman walking the High Street in Edinburgh was betting on its probability.

'How absolutely thrilling, Doctor Kellar,' put in Mrs McIntosh. 'And such an honour for your dear wife too.'

The dear wife alerted, looked momentarily more distraught as Mrs McIntosh endeavoured to gain her attention.

Faro had early decided that for Mrs McIntosh the evening would be memorable as a social triumph. True, she did not inhabit the same intellectual plane as her host but she shared his abominable snobbery, and was rosy with delight at finding herself dining with a Title and a Knight-To-Be. Her gushing attempts to converse with Sir Hedley had not met with much success, as the latter apparently failed to hear, or was deaf to the shrill remarks directed toward him.

Mrs McIntosh was two inches under five feet tall but she made up for her small stature by a massive temper, and her angry glances boded ill for her spouse who had twice interrupted her flow of eloquence on the one subject dear to her heart.

She understood, oh, how she understood and sympathised with dear Dr Kellar's outburst of passion on the subject of new housekeepers. She knew, oh, how she knew all about domestics and how hard they were to come by. And oh dear me, such low creatures they were these days, one would imagine they would be grateful for the chance to shelter under the same roof as their betters.

'You cannot get a good girl, a really good girl, cheap to live in anywhere these days. They actually demand wages in return for bed and board. Do you not find it so, Sir Hedley?'

The Mad Bart's eyes swivelled nervously in the direction of Vince and Mabel Kellar. With an exasperated sigh Mrs McIntosh turned to Faro. 'Now you must agree with me, Inspector. Servants must be of crucial importance for the smooth running of an Inspector's household.'

'I give the matter little attention, madam,' said Faro coldly.

'Of course, I understand you are fortunate in having that nice little Mrs Brook. We tried to get her to come to us – did you know that? – when her dear doctor, her former employer at Sheridan Place, died so suddenly . . . '

But Faro was no longer listening, thinking venomously of how he could remove that simpering glance with the information that his own dear Lizzie had been a domestic

26

servant who had an illegitimate son – Vince – as a result of being raped by one of the so-called gentry when she was fifteen years old.

Vince. He looked at his stepson fondly wondering, as he often did, if the boy had been his own child, whether he could have loved him better or found a more faithful and devoted son. Watching him animated and attentive to Mabel Kellar after rather rudely fending off Sir Hedley's attempts to be included in the conversation, Faro's qualms about the boy's happiness came again to the fore.

There was something too vulnerable about that bright head of curls, the gentle smile, a sensitive quality at odds with the grim medical task of assistant to the police surgeon. Somehow he could never imagine Vince ever acquiring the hard shell of Dr Kellar.

The clock seemed to have stopped on the mantelpiece as the meal dragged on to its weary conclusion and Mrs Kellar announced that the entertainment would now begin.

Entertainment, thought Faro. What a word to describe Mabel Kellar's monologue, 'A Sunday Afternoon Picnic', in which a whole family, celebrating Grandmama's birthday, took to the river and encountered many a storm, of the teacup variety. Mabel Kellar's change of voice for her bewilderingly large cast of characters left him stunned, his eyelids heavy. Later, he learned from Vince that this was her party piece. It seemed endless.

At last, she curtseyed delightedly to applause polite but feeble.

'Our dear Mrs Shaw will now play for us.'

Faro suppressed a bout of yawning and, with an irresistible desire to close his eyes, tried to focus his dwindling attention on the young woman as she sat down at the piano.

A few chords and he was wide awake, alert, his senses singing as he recognised Beethoven's Appassionata

27

brilliantly executed. One of his favourite pieces, he knew that this was no bungling amateur but a pianist whose rightful place was on the concert platform.

'Bravo, bravo,' he called as the final notes faded into silence. 'Encore, encore.'

The guests who did not share his knowledge of music or his enthusiasm looked mildly dazed by his reaction. Mrs Shaw regarded him gratefully, bowed modestly and then firmly closed the piano.

He went over to her side. 'That was superb, Mrs Shaw. Beethoven at his very best.'

'You are familiar with the piece, Inspector?'

'I am indeed. And you played it divinely.'

'Why, thank you. Thank you.' Animation transformed her face into sudden radiance and Faro saw fleetingly how captivating she must have been in the days before sadness engulfed her, swamping her young life.

And just when the evening had begun for him, Faro heard the doorbell. The carriages had arrived. As cloaks were gathered, Dr Kellar opened the front door to a moon gleaming fitfully and a gentle snowfall.

Mrs Kellar took an affectionate farewell of her dearest friend whom Vince handed into the carriage bound for Regent Crescent. Faro bowed gallantly over her hand. 'Thank you again for your exquisite playing, Mrs Shaw.'

A sweet smile, a kiss blown in her hostess's direction and she was gone. Faro observed that Mrs Kellar had taken Vince's arm and now kissed him, very tenderly, on both cheeks.

Sir Hedley, bound for Solomon's Tower, was disposed to linger. Watching Vince with that hooded intense look he said earnestly, 'Enjoyed meeting you, young fella. Drop into the Tower. Any time. Always welcome.'

'Thank you, sir. But I'm fearfully busy. You must excuse me.'

Faro noticed that Vince could barely conceal his distaste. He withdrew his hand from Sir Hedley's in a gesture almost

28

too hasty for politeness. Again struck by this unreasonable aversion to a sad lonely old man, so unlike his charitable stepson who was fond of everyone and was charming and popular, Faro frowned uneasily. He felt as if he was witnessing a resurrection of the spoilt ill-mannered small boy he had first encountered during his courtship of Vince's mother.

The absence of a carriage for Faro and Vince was another catastrophe for Mrs Kellar.

'We will enjoy the walk home.'

'But look at the snow. My dear, you must not catch a chill,' said Mrs Kellar, stroking Vince's arm anxiously. 'Do please accept Uncle Hedley's offer.'

'The exercise is good for us both, isn't it, lad?'

'It is indeed. Doctor's orders, Stepfather,' said Vince, with a look of gratitude. As they raised their hats to the departing carriages and set off down the drive, he said, 'I hope you don't mind, truly, Stepfather.'

'Not in the least.'

'The idea of sharing a carriage with that dreadful old man gives me the shivers. I absolutely loathe him.'

'That's a bit strong, lad.'

'So was the smell of cats. Don't tell me you didn't notice. I thought I'd succeeded in putting him in his place, when he kept trying so rudely to corner me with his wretched conversation. I was appalled at having to sit beside him. But tell me, what did you think of Eveline Shaw? Isn't she a stunner?'

Faro gave him a sharp look. Had he completely misread the signs? Was Vince about to confess devotion to the young widow?

'She's certainly lovely and such a talented musician.'

'Absolutely first class. I wonder where she learned to play like that?'

'How long has she been a widow?'

'Less than a year.'

'I thought so. She seemed so sad and detached.'

'Until she began to play, Stepfather. Then she was transformed.'

'You thought so too. What happened to the husband? Had she been married long?'

'Long enough to have a baby. There's a son and heir at least, a few months old, born after his soldier father was killed on the Indian frontier.'

Faro nodded sympathetically. 'Tragic. At least he left her comfortably off if she can afford a house in Regent Crescent.'

'Indeed. He was a Captain, and I gather there are very good family connections in the Highlands.'

'I'm glad to know that she'll be well provided for,' Faro hesitated and then added, 'although I doubt she will be a widow long. A wealthy widow, young and pretty too, should experience no difficulty in finding another husband.'

'Not in the least, if she is seeking one. And that I seriously doubt at the moment.' Vince laughed. 'I know you are looking very arch, Stepfather. Bless me, you are almost as bad as Mabel and I can read exactly the way your minds drift. Anyway, there were no signals in my direction, I can assure you. Not that I wanted any,' he added hastily. 'I don't see myself as a widow's consolation and I'm much too vain to play second fiddle to the dear departed.'

They walked for a while in silence then Vince said, 'There is something odd about her, didn't you think?'

'Mrs Shaw? Just lost and bewildered, lad, that's all. Isn't quite up to taking on the social round again, poor lass. Not interested in anything yet outside her own grief.'

'How perceptive of you, Stepfather. I'm relieved to hear that was the reason. You know I got a distinct impression that she didn't take to me at all, or any of us – except you.'

'Only because I appreciated her playing.'

30

'Oh, you do underestimate yourself, Stepfather. I despair of you sometimes, really I do.'

'Was that the first time you'd met?' asked Faro with a brisk change of subject.

'Yes. But I feel as if we're already well acquainted. Mabel talks constantly about her dear Eveline, calls her "my sister of the spirit". With no children of her own, she says the good Lord has compensated by giving her this one loving young friend.'

'Perhaps she should make it two now.'

'Two? How so?'

Faro smiled. 'Obviously Mrs Kellar regards you in the same fond light.'

'Dear Mabel. But everyone is important to her, servants, poor relatives. Fancy giving that dreadful mad old man house room. Fancy him actually being her uncle. Incredible.'

'Kellar has certainly kept very quiet about that particular skeleton in the family closet.'

'I don't suppose he's keen to have it made public, even if it is just a connection by marriage. However, it would have to come out some day. He was at great pains to tell everyone that Mabel is his heiress. There's no knowing what she'll inherit besides a multitude of cats,' Vince added. 'Solomon's Tower is fairly ruinous.'

'Yes, but don't forget, it's also on a valuable site for this upsurge of property developing in Newington area.'

As they reached the gates of Sheridan Place, Faro found himself haunted by a picture of Mabel Kellar standing on the front steps, blowing a kiss to Vince.

'Goodnight, Inspector. Goodnight, dear Vince, have a good holiday.'

A final wave as Dr Kellar drew her inside and closed the door.

And that, thought Faro, coming back to the present and his unwritten report, was the last time any of us saw the police surgeon's wife.

'Kellar is an absolute swine, treating her like that, in front of guests.' And with a chill feeling of disaster, he remembered Vince's concluding words: 'I could have snatched up one of those knives and plunged it into his black heart.'

But perhaps it was the warm-hearted Mabel who had been the victim of an assassin's carving knife.

Chapter Three

The house had seemed strangely empty without young Vince's presence. In the longest separation since they had come to live in Sheridan Place, Faro realised that this was a prelude to the future when, sooner or later, he must face the prospect of living alone.

Reasonably, he could hardly expect to have Vince with him for the rest of his life. Whatever his stepson's protestations, Faro had little doubt and fervently hoped that he would eventually fall in love and marry some suitable young lady. His wife, however, might be expected to produce excellent and convincing arguments against sharing their home with her husband's policeman stepfather.

Faro said as much to Mrs Brook who was also feeling bereft of Vince's bright presence and gentle teasing. She looked shocked.

'What an idea, Inspector sir. Why, there are your two wee girls growing up in Orkney. In a few years they will be ready to come to Edinburgh and do their duty by their papa.' And with one of her sly looks, she added coyly, 'That is, if there isn't a second Mrs Faro by then.'

Ignoring his gesture of impatient dismissal, she went on, 'I do hope and pray to the good Lord every night that you will meet a nice lady of your own age some day, that I do, Inspector sir.'

Faro's disapproving sniff was the answer she expected. Any argument that he put forward would be totally ignored. From long experience he knew that dignified silence was the only weapon against romantically inclined females of a certain age. They should have known better, but persisted in regarding marriage as the rose-strewn path to 'happy-ever-after-land'.

His mother and Mrs Brook were of one mind on the subject. But apart from occasional yearnings for a mate to share his bed and some of his dreams, Faro felt that the harmonious bachelor life had much to commend it and suited him well. The many daily hazards in a policeman's life made for poor husband material and he still suffered pangs of remorse recalling his neglect of poor Lizzie who had never once reproached him.

'As long as I have the bairns, dear, I am never lonely.' But the son they had both longed for after two daughters, had killed her.

At least Rose and Emily, with the resilience of childhood, were now settling happily and healthily with their grandmother while his stepson, after completing his year as Dr Kellar's assistant, would open the ground floor of 9 Sheridan Place as the surgery and consulting rooms of Dr Vincent Beaumarcher Laurie, general practitioner of medicine.

But without Vince's presence, Faro could hardly bear the Sunday afternoon ritual of tending the little grave in Greyfriars Kirkyard where Lizzie lay asleep with their baby at her side. He could still sob out loud at that bitter remembrance.

Once, unbearably alone, he had thought to love again and he carefully avoided the pathway by the willow tree, haunted by memories of his first meeting with the beautiful actress he had dreamed so passionately and so fleetingly, of making his wife.★

Never, never again, he swore. Let others fall in love and marry. It was not for him.

On the day he expected Vince's return from Vienna, Faro arrived at the Central Office as usual, to learn that

★ *Enter Second Murderer*

34

his presence was being eagerly sought by Superintendent McIntosh.

'Close the door and sit down, Faro. I have a rather delicate task for you, one which must be handled with the utmost confidence and care.' He shook his head sternly. 'Should information leak out of this office and the general public hear about it . . . '

'What is this task, sir?' asked Faro somewhat impatiently. McIntosh's normal instructions regarding his senior detective inspector's apprehension of criminals came down rather heavily on the side of brutal methods. Gentle persuasion was an art unknown to the tough Superintendent.

'Something very serious has happened. Something which, I need not tell you, might have the most serious repercussions on the reputation of our police establishment. It concerns Dr Kellar's wife.' McIntosh paused dramatically. 'She has disappeared.'

'Disappeared, sir? When did this happen?'

'About two weeks ago. They had a dinner party for a few friends.'

'Yes, Superintendent. I know. I was there.'

McIntosh's head shot up and he regarded Faro with some astonishment. 'Why, of course you were, of course. Well, well, that does help.'

'Help? In what way?'

'The very next morning it appears that Mrs Kellar left to go on a visit to her sister at North Berwick. Dr Kellar dropped her at Waverley railway station. She had sent a wire to her sister to expect her off the 12.45 train. When she didn't arrive, Mrs Findlay-Cupar wasn't unduly alarmed at first. She expected her the next day, but after two more days when Mrs Kellar still hadn't put in an appearance nor sent any explanation, her sister despatched a letter asking what had happened.

'As this was addressed to Mrs Kellar personally, the housekeeper, who is new, didn't regard it as urgent. Dr Kellar had told her the mistress was only away for a day or two, so she put it with other letters for Mrs Kellar on her writing desk, where it lay unread. An unfortunate set of circumstances, you'll agree. It was not until another week had passed without any word from Mrs Kellar indicating when she was returning home that Dr Kellar, glancing through her letters, opened the one from his sister-in-law. He immediately set out for North Berwick.'

Leaning back in his chair, McIntosh studied Faro's expression. 'Well, have you any explanation?'

Faro shrugged. Had he not been witness to the events at the Kellars' dinner party, his sense of danger would have been alerted and he would have viewed this disappearance with more alarm. He said as much to the Superintendent.

'You were present, sir.' Guessing at the unevenness of McIntosh's domestic bliss and harmony with The Tartar, he found it irresistible not to add, 'Surely the answer is obvious to a married man, sir?'

'Not to me, it isn't,' said McIntosh, eyeing him sternly.

'I would imagine that Mrs Kellar is teaching her husband a lesson.'

'A lesson, Inspector? What kind of lesson?'

'I think we'll discover that Mrs Kellar has left home and taken refuge with an understanding friend or relative, giving Dr Kellar time to regret his disagreeable conduct in front of their guests.'

'Yes, yes, Inspector. Maybe so. But where the devil is she?'

'She doubtless intends that to be kept secret meantime. Especially from her husband.'

'So that's what you believe?' Stroking his beard thoughtfully, McIntosh stared at Faro. 'All part of making Dr Kellar suffer, eh. I'm not saying I disagree with you entirely, but the doctor is a very worried man and expects us to do something about finding his missing wife. What you are suggesting has obviously never occurred to him.'

McIntosh added a sudden bark of laughter, as if the idea pleased him. 'Scandal, that's at the back of it. A breath

36

of scandal would ruin his chance of the knighthood. He insists that discreet enquiries begin immediately. I'm afraid that whatever the outcome, even if we all end up looking like idiots and Mrs Kellar walks in tomorrow, we'll have to humour him.'

'Very well, Superintendent. I'll proceed along the normal missing person lines and interview Dr Kellar first. I imagine he's checked the hospitals and so forth?'

'The first place he'd look, Faro,' said McIntosh sternly.

'Very well. I'll get confirmation of what he told you—'

'No need for that, Faro,' McIntosh interrupted hastily. 'He's told me all he knows and I've imparted the information to you. That's enough. He won't take kindly to being questioned again so you'd better talk to the servants. For heaven's sake, choose a time during the day when he's not at home. Then a visit to Mrs Findlay-Cupar.' He handed over a scrap of paper. 'Her address in North Berwick. Another person who might know something is the Mad – er, Sir Hedley.'

'I'd already thought of that. Solomon's Tower would be a good place to seek refuge.'

'As long as she likes cats. And what about that friend of hers, the young widow?'

'Mrs Shaw?'

'They seemed very friendly.'

'Very well. I'll try Regent Crescent.'

McIntosh frowned. 'But only see this Mrs Shaw if all other enquiries lead nowhere. Dr Kellar made quite a point about insisting on absolute discretion. So better keep it in the family.'

Taking the Superintendent's advice, Faro decided that Kellar was at this moment likely to be found giving his morning lecture at Surgeons Hall, demonstrating the arts of carving up corpses to a group of admiring students with strong stomachs.

Vince had told him that this ordeal was frequently too harrowing. Dazzling on the playing field, prepared

37

to carry their medical knowledge for Queen and country to battlefield or to darkest Africa, sturdy young men frequently dropped like ninepins and had to be gathered up from the floor and revived with smelling salts.

If Kellar suffered from a sense of humour, then it was of the macabre variety. He allocated to students with the weakest stomachs the most gruesome tasks related to the human corpse, relishing their discomfort and distress.

Faro left the horse-drawn omnibus which took him part of the way. It was a freezing day, and he walked rapidly in the direction of the police surgeon's house in the Grange. The snow by the roadside had melted and refrozen several times during the last week. It lay grey and pitted and his boots slipped ominously as he tried to avoid every passing vehicle which threw up a fountain of disagreeable brown slush.

The drive down to the Kellar house was hardly less hazardous under foot but mercifully without any traffic. At this hour servants should have been busily engaged in their household tasks but ten minutes later, as he waited on the front steps and the bell pealed through the house unattended, he wondered if his errand had been in vain.

His third summons brought forth a tiny housemaid who looked all of twelve years old, frail and undernourished, with what his Orkney mother called 'not a picking on her bones' and the hugest palest eyes he had ever seen.

'Detective Inspector Faro, to see Mrs Flynn, if you please.'

The girl's eyes grew wider, almost colourless, the pupils reduced to tiny black points. She regarded him with apprehension and he felt a desperate need to put this frightened child at her ease.

He gave her a warm and friendly smile. 'What's your name, lass?'

'Ina, sir.' The words were whispered with a slight shuddering movement away from him, as if the response to her name encouraged a violent reaction. She would see if Mrs Flynn was in.

Pitifully thin and frail, in a skirt several sizes too large for her, she seemed to float rather than scuttle across the hall to disappear in the direction of the downstairs kitchen. Her extreme youth was in keeping with Kellar's policy of employing child labour since it was cheap, thought Faro grimly. It was a disgrace. Thank God there were women like Mrs Kellar with her kind heart who allowed such lasses the privilege of returning to their homes at weekends.

Ina reappeared promptly and this time remembered to bob a respectful curtsey to the gentleman. 'Mrs Flynn will see you directly, sir.'

He followed her across the handsome panelled hall lit by many Gothic windows where a door disguised as an antique cupboard gave access down a steep flight of stairs into a gloomy basement, whose only light seemed to be reflected from whitewashed stone walls. Cold as the day was outside, he suspected sunshine seldom penetrated these dank nether regions. What a contrast from the handsome house above. These dismal stone-flagged floors and rough-hewn walled quarters, with every window barred, gave the illusion less of a house than a prison.

Faro knew all about such matters from Lizzie. She had told him that the reason for the barred windows was not only to keep intruders out, but equally important, to keep skittish and flighty maids and their followers from making easy exits and entrances at all hours. Once the master or the trusted housekeeper bearing her iron ring of keys had secured and bolted the doors at ten thirty each night, the servants were virtually prisoners until next day. Morning roll-call, as breakfast prayers were called in large houses, for those who had found themselves locked out the night before, brought retribution in the form of instant dismissal. For a servant girl innocently delayed, perhaps by visiting a sick relative, the future was bleak indeed, unless she was pretty enough to be taken on without references. If she was plain and had dependants, often the only answer to starvation was prostitution. Manservants fared somewhat better. In the ever-growing labouring class, cheap work and strong bodies were called for and no questions asked or references required.

Faro was not altogether surprised to find the housekeeper installed in a room poorly furnished and lit by the stumps of two feeble candles. She poked a few miserable coals into a lot of smoke without attendant fire and apologised that her bag of coal was finished. She was not due another until next week. Her bulky frame huddled in a thick shawl, the inevitable scarf about her neck, she grumbled hoarsely.

'If the mistress had been here she would have seen me right. But it's no good asking *him*. I keep out of *his* way as much as I can.'

Faro could well believe it as he nodded sympathetically and edged his chair closer to the fireplace. Really, the atmosphere was colder here indoors than it was outside, for this basement added a clammy dampness to the chill. He would have thought twice about keeping a pet dog or the Sheridan Place cat Rusty in such conditions and felt a surge of righteous indignation towards Kellar whose meanness bordered on cruelty to his servants.

Mrs Flynn managed to lower her chin back into the warm protection of the scarf.

'I trust your toothache—' Faro began.

'Better, sir. The gumboil burst. Only I got this awful sore throat,' she said, patting the scarf. 'Hurts to talk.'

'I'm sorry. Shall I come back?'

'No, no. I'll manage. Is it something urgent – about the mistress?' she asked eagerly.

'I wondered if you could help us with our enquiries, if you had any ideas where she might have gone. You know, friends and so forth.'

Mrs Flynn shook her head. 'She's left him. I'm sure of that.'

'So one would suppose.'

'Run away from him, that's what. And about time. And good luck to her. That's what I say,' she added defiantly.

'Yes, Mrs Flynn, but this is just speculation. Unless you have any proof? Did she tell you, or give any hint, that running away was her intention?'

'I'm not sure what you mean, sir?'

'Well, did she indicate that she might be gone for some time?'

'No.'

'She didn't leave you any instructions?'

'No, sir.'

'Wasn't that rather odd?'

'She probably didn't think it was worthwhile as I'm working my notice.' Mrs Flynn thought for a moment and then added, 'But I knew something was wrong. I saw how upset she was the night before, helping me in the kitchen. I tried not to notice, but she was crying her eyes out, the poor love.'

'Are you a married woman, Mrs Flynn?'

'A widow. For more than twenty years. I see what you're getting at, Inspector. All married folks quarrel a bit and don't I know it, as a housekeeper.' She laughed harshly. 'But Mrs Kellar was different. She doted on the master, anyone could see that with half an eye.'

She let this information sink in for a moment and then added, 'Besides she must have run away, otherwise she would have been at North Berwick, wouldn't she?'

'What happened exactly that last morning?'

'Ina came in early and took the wire from the mistress to the post office.'

'Did you see it?'

'Oh yes. It said, "Arriving today off 12.45 train from Edinburgh." I was making soup when the mistress shouted down that she was leaving. When I came upstairs, I saw the doctor handing her into the carriage.'

Mrs Flynn paused to lean over and retrieve a coal from the feeble fire. 'I opened the door and overheard

41

a bit of an argument. It was snowing quite hard and he was shouting at her: "Get in. Get in, woman. I'll take you there, the blasted station or all the way, if I have to."'

'You're quite sure that's what he said?'

'I'd swear to it in a court of law, Inspector,' said Mrs Flynn firmly. 'The blasted station or all the way,' she repeated, watching Faro make a note of the words.

'So he was driving her himself. No coachman?'

Mrs Flynn chuckled. 'There was not. Him? Waste money on a coachman? Oh, I hear that he sometimes gets a fellow from the hiring place down the road, but only for special occasions. Says he likes driving himself.'

'When did you see the doctor again that day?'

Mrs Flynn frowned. 'I didn't, sir.'

'He didn't return directly from the station?'

'I'm not sure but I don't think so.'

'What about meals? Didn't you serve him supper?'

The housekeeper shook her head. 'No, he hadn't left any note on the hall table that morning. That's the usual procedure. We have strict instructions, if there's no note saying what he wants to eat, then we are to presume he wishes to remain undisturbed or he's dining at his club.'

'When did you see him again, then?'

'Not until later that week at supper time. I can't remember which day it was.'

'He didn't seem anxious or upset in any way by Mrs Kellar's absence?'

'Of course not. Why should he? He had no idea that she had gone for good until he opened that letter from her sister.'

'And then, how did he behave?'

'Behave, sir?' Mrs Flynn thought for a moment. 'I didn't see him reading it. He just rang the bell for me and when I went upstairs he was sitting with a letter in his hand. "I have to go to North Berwick immediately." That was all he said.'

'Did he look shocked?'

'I couldn't say, sir. He had his back to me. Never looks at us, or speaks to us directly, if it can be avoided. So I guessed something serious had happened. I asked him if the mistress was ill and he snapped my head off. "None of your business, Flynn." I asked him if he was going to be away long, and reminded him that I was working my notice and would be leaving on Saturday. He said, did I have a situation to go to, and when I said no, he said then I'd better stay on meantime until the mistress came back.'

The housekeeper leaned back in her chair and sighed deeply, as if exhausted by the toll of this lengthy explanation on her sore throat.

Faro got to his feet. 'Thank you, Mrs Flynn, you have been most helpful. I wonder if I might ask you one other favour.'

Mrs Flynn stirred from her reverie. 'Yes, sir, of course.'

'You saw Mrs Kellar leaving? Did she take much luggage?'

'A leather travelling bag. Smallish. I carried it downstairs.'

'Did you help her pack?'

'No, I'm not a personal maid, sir. She wouldn't expect me to do that for her, although I did repair a petticoat hem that was torn, as an obligement.'

'What was she wearing, by the way?'

'Her lovely fur cloak, sable or something like that. Black with a shoulder cape. And a dark green costume with brown braid, a cream-coloured silk blouse. Looked a picture, she did. Is there anything else, sir?'

'I wonder if I could have a look at her room.'

'Her room, sir. Which one would you be meaning? Him and her both had their own bedrooms.'

'I'd like to see the room she occupied.'

'I don't see why not. Ina will show you.'

The housekeeper rang the handbell on her table and Faro asked, 'By the way, could you let me have a list of any callers Mrs Kellar received during the days before she left?'

'Callers?' Mrs Flynn frowned. 'You mean tradesmen and the like?'

'I was thinking of more personal callers.'

Mrs Flynn gave a throaty chuckle. 'Oh, you mean gentleman callers and such, do you, Inspector?'

Faro tried to look nonchalant. 'Something like that.'

'Only the young doctor, him that works for the master. He was with you at the dinner party. He calls on Mrs Kellar quite regularly. He looked in as she was packing. Went upstairs and stayed for . . . ' Mrs Flynn paused and thought, 'for twenty minutes or so. I expect his address will be in her book up on the writing desk, if you want it.'

She obviously had no idea that Vince was his stepson. A tap on the door announced Ina and, turning to leave, Faro said, 'One thing more, Mrs Flynn. Is there anything missing from the house that Mrs Kellar might have taken with her besides her personal possessions?'

Mrs Flynn gave him a puzzled look. 'I couldn't say, sir. I'm new to this house. It takes years to get to know one well.'

'Well, if you hear of anything missing, you will let me know.'

Glad to be out of the housekeeper's gloomy uncomfortable sitting-room, Faro thanked her for her help and followed Ina along the chilly corridor and into the hall, to gratefully breathe in the purer air of the house's upper regions.

As they climbed the stairs, he asked, 'Did you assist the mistress to pack?'

'No, sir. She didn't ask.'

Ina opened the door into a bedroom expensively furnished, but apart from the silver brushes, jewel box and toilette set on the dressing table, there were fewer mementoes than Faro would have expected to see. This characterless room gave no hints about Mrs Kellar's personality, but he realised that he could hardly, with decorum and in the presence of the maid, conduct a careful search of wardrobe and chest of drawers.

'Do you come into this room every day?'

'Yes, sir. I make up the bed and clear the ashes from the fire, re-lay it. I empty the slops and dust . . . '

'Good. Then you can tell me if anything has been moved since Mrs Kellar left.'

'Nothing, sir. Mrs Kellar is a very neat tidy lady, very thoughtful for everyone.'

'She didn't have a personal maid?'

'Oh no, sir. The master didn't think such expense was justified and Mrs Flynn told me that when the mistress's maid who had been with her for years took sick and left, he said a housekeeper and a maid should be enough.'

'Do you happen to know where Mrs Kellar's maid lives?'

'She died last year and Mrs Kellar went to her funeral. Such a kind lady, if it wasn't for her, he'd never get anyone to stay. Look at Mrs Flynn. She's only staying on as a favour – he had to fair beg her, I'll bet. And now she's working her notice, so to speak, she's very hoity-toity.'

Suspecting compassion from this nice policeman, Ina was no longer bashful or afraid. 'She does as little as possible, I can tell you. Says she's poorly with her toothache and her sore throat, gives me my orders, prepares the doctor's dinner and then retires to her room . . . '

Only half-listening to this tirade against Mrs Flynn, Faro was surveying the room very carefully, making mental pictures of the contents. When he left he would be able to write out an exact list of everything it contained. That was part of his job.

The writing desk by the window was a handsome davenport. He opened the lid and a cursory glance revealed the usual stationery and pens. There was no address book in evidence. It might have been pushed into a drawer but, in all probability, Mrs Kellar had taken it with her.

Looking around, he concluded there was not the slightest

45

indication in this peaceful, strangely impersonal room that Mabel Kellar had intended anything other than to spend a few days visiting her sister.

Where was she then? What had he overlooked?

His attention kept returning to that dressing table. He touched the silver brushes with a strange feeling that there was a lot more in Mabel Kellar's disappearance than he had first thought. Now he wondered whether the answer lay deeper and wider than a long-suffering wife teaching her ungrateful husband a lesson by leaving him to the tender mercies of incompetent servants.

'Will that be all, sir?'

Faro nodded and followed the maid on to the landing. He pointed to the drawing-room: 'May I?'

Crossing the floor, he opened the double doors leading into the dining-room. Sterile without the softening effects of candlelight, an atmosphere of melancholy pervaded the long table with chairs devoid of diners. He was not surprised to hear that Dr Kellar did not have his meals there.

'When the mistress isn't at home, he eats in his study across the way.'

Faro strode towards the study door. At present, Kellar's wife was merely missing from home and he had merely requested exhaustive enquiries to be made. He could imagine the doctor's righteous indignation, which would surely rebound on Detective Inspector Faro's head personally, should he return home unexpectedly. But the opportunity was too good to miss.

'Oh sir, you can't go in there. No one's allowed. He always keeps it locked.'

A pity. Kellar's study could well be the only room in the house where confidential information as to why his wife had left him might be found. But without authority, Faro was treading on very delicate ground. And without positive evidence that a crime had been committed he could hardly proceed to search the police surgeon's house.

'No matter. You have been most helpful, Ina.'

At the top of the stairs, the maid paused. 'There is something, sir.' Again she hesitated. 'I overheard you asking Mrs Flynn if there was anything missing.'

'Well, is there?'

Ina played nervously with the starched edge of her apron. 'I didn't want to mention it in front of Mrs Flynn, or I'll be blamed. You see, she hasn't noticed so far, but when the doctor finds out . . . ' She looked up at him with huge scared eyes. 'One of his precious carving knives has gone.'

'When did you discover this?'

'When I was washing up after the dinner party, that morning the mistress left. I was putting everything back and I suddenly noticed when I went upstairs to put the special silver back in the canteen that there was only one carving knife. I've searched for the other, but it's never turned up. I just can't find it anywhere.'

As she spoke she led the way back into the dining-room and walked over to the mahogany sideboard.

'There, sir.' She watched eagerly as Faro opened the elegant velvet-lined case, as if his action might miraculously restore the missing knife to its embossed silver-handled partner.

'Mrs Flynn will skin me alive when she finds out.'

'Oh come now, lass. I shouldn't worry too much. It'll turn up, you'll see. Probably put into the wrong drawer.'

But Ina was shaking her head. 'No, sir. It's not that. I know, I just know, that something – something wicked has happened to it.'

'Wicked?' Faro laughed uneasily.

'Yes, sir. Wicked.' The huge eyes turned on him again, almost tearfully this time. 'I see things, sir. People laugh at me, but I can't help it. There's something black, black and wicked going on in this house. I know it. Come the weekend, the master'll go mad. He'll never carve the roast . . . '

Faro was no longer listening. 'By the pricking of my

47

thumbs, something wicked this way comes.' Shakespeare, who belonged in a very different world to this simple maid, had been aware of the same devils. And so was Faro, his senses warning him of the enormity of the girl's words. Worse, he had a sudden inescapable vision of Vince saying, 'I could have snatched up one of those knives and plunged it into his black heart.'

Only this time, perhaps the missing knife had been plunged into everyone's favourite, Mabel Kellar.

Chapter Four

A great believer in the thought-clarifying powers of fresh air, on leaving the Kellar house Faro decided to walk around the extensive gardens. A gratifying burst of sunshine had temporarily demolished the leaden skies, turning untrodden snow and delicately frosted hedgerows into a semblance of winter fairyland. There was warmth on the sheltered paths and above his head birds twittered in a hopeful prelude to spring.

He breathed deeply, enjoying this blissful moment between the acts of winter's cruel drama, for he had little doubt that the heavy skies above the Pentland Hills foretold yet another snowfall was imminent.

How was Vince faring, he wondered, delighted that the lad would soon be home again. It had seemed a curious time to choose for a brief holiday at an asylum for consumptives in the Austrian Alps. One of the resident doctors had been Vince's close friend during University days and, Faro remembered, Walter had a very pretty sister.

He leaned against a tree in the sun and lit a pipe. Surrounded by so much beauty, the subtle varied shades of umber and heliotrope and rose, he could never understand why people thought of winter as being the drab dead time of year.

Looking across at the house, for the first time he envied the lot of those who could live in such comfort and enjoy splendid gardens of their own, akin to a small park. If he ever retired from the Police, or escaped the hazards of grievous bodily harm that threatened him almost daily, then he would crave a tiny house with a garden.

Suddenly the years ahead seemed very bleak. His ancestors had been Orkney crofters, perhaps their blood unsettled him from time to time. Why had he chosen this violent, unpredictable life of fighting criminals? Had it begun originally in order to avenge his policeman father who had been murdered for getting too close to the truth?★

Whatever his reason, it was too late to go back now and he was once more committed to solving yet another of those baffling mysteries that were his daily bread, of trying to get inside the criminal's head and walk around in his skin for a while, in an effort to piece together motives and opportunities. In this case, however, he suspected that there was no evidence of any kind beyond a domestic tiff.

The vital question remained. Was Kellar making too much of his missing wife? Had she merely absconded to teach her husband a lesson? Did he suspect that too?

Faro smiled grimly. Anyone less important than the police surgeon would have received a rude reception, told by Superintendent McIntosh not to be so daft and waste his precious time sending his senior Detective Inspector off on a wild goose chase. Walking towards the gates, he would have been inclined to agree except that his visit to the Kellar home had left some disquieting observations to mull over on his return to the Central Office.

First, the missing carving knife. Since cutlery had a habit of being mislaid or misappropriated in the best of houses, there was perhaps a perfectly innocent explanation. Mrs Flynn, uncertain of where everything was kept, had slipped it into the wrong drawer. But Ina, who was responsible for the washing up and stowing away of dishes had seemed so sure.

Faro would have liked to discuss the matter with Mrs Flynn but a tactful approach was needed, one that wouldn't involve getting Ina into trouble with her employer. Dr

★ *Blood Line*

Kellar's displeasure, rebounding on the housekeeper would, in the pecking order of such establishments, descend upon the hapless maid as everyone's scapegoat.

Why did that carving knife bother him? Was it because he kept on hearing Vince's words about plunging it into Kellar's black heart for his treatment of Mabel?

Faro was glad his stepson had been out of the country when she disappeared. He didn't care for the idea of Vince being associated, however remotely, with the police surgeon's absconding wife. In what must inevitably become known in Edinburgh circles as 'the Kellar scandal', even the innocent friendship of a very young man and a misunderstood middle-aged wife would be seized upon eagerly as a tantalising morsel of delicious gossip.

Yet even more disquieting than the missing carving knife was the picture that persisted of Mrs Kellar's bedroom and the feeling that there was something important he had overlooked. Deep in thought, Faro had almost reached the gates when a brougham approached. The familiar face of Dr Kellar leaned down from the driving seat, and Faro cursed under his breath, wishing he had made his escape two minutes earlier.

'Looking for me by any chance, Inspector?'

Pocketing his pipe, Faro nodded vaguely.

'I thought you might be paying me a visit, despite McIntosh being in possession of all the facts.' And tapping the Inspector's shoulder with his whip, Kellar said, 'No need to apologise. I haven't worked with the City Police for years without knowing all about the keen noses of detectives. In search of clues they could, and frequently do, put bloodhounds to shame. Have to visit the scene of the crime and all that sort of thing.'

'We don't know that a crime has been committed, sir,' said Faro sharply.

Kellar was unperturbed. 'A mere slip of the tongue – a figure of speech. I should have called it "the last known sighting".' His laugh was light hearted, causing

Faro to study him intently. If this was a guilty man, then he was behaving with considerably more aplomb than one might have presumed normal in the circumstances.

'Well, what are you waiting for, man?' Kellar indicated the seat alongside. 'Climb up. Come along to the house. Search the place to your heart's content.'

'At present we are merely investigating a disappearance, sir. Proceeding along the usual lines, beginning with relatives—'

'You are wasting your time. Her sister and her uncle know nothing,' Kellar interrupted.

'Then there are the hospitals.'

'Hospitals?'

'You will have already consulted their recent admissions lists?'

'Of course not. Why should I? What on earth for?' was the indignant reply.

Faro looked at him sternly. 'Suppose Mrs Kellar has been injured and has lost her memory. Or had an accident and was pushed from the train. Surely such possibilities have occurred to you?'

'What nonsense. Absolute rubbish,' roared Kellar.

Faro thought for a moment before replying. 'Then you believe that your wife is unharmed and that her disappearance is deliberate.' When Kellar stared at him blankly, he continued, 'If that is so, Dr Kellar, then you realise that you are putting a great strain on a police force already overburdened and that your action is hampering the investigation of serious crimes.'

'I am merely taking precautions I deem necessary, Inspector Faro,' shouted Kellar, pointing again to the carriage seat. 'Come along. Search my house. I have nothing to hide.'

Tempted, Faro hesitated and Kellar smiled grimly. 'Ah, I see I'm too late and that you've searched already. Find anything interesting that I should know about?'

'A search of the premises is hardly necessary. Or proper, sir. Not at the moment,' Faro reminded him.

'Not at the moment,' Kellar seized upon the words and repeated them slowly. 'Now that does sound ominous.'

Suddenly anxious, he leaned over staring down into Faro's face. 'Surely – surely to God, I'm not under suspicion. You can't think I – I – ?' Words failed him and observing with growing horror Faro's stern expression, he shouted, 'That is absolutely ludicrous, Inspector. I yelled at her, and in company, as you are aware. But then I do so frequently and she has never seized upon this as an excuse to leave me.'

When Faro didn't reply, he said angrily, 'I don't like your suspicious look, Inspector, indeed I do not. It offends me deeply.' And thumping the whip against the seat, 'My God, this is beyond a joke. I thought I had convinced McIntosh that there was a perfectly natural explanation for my wife behaving as she did and she will return home eventually.'

'Then why did you insist on an enquiry, sir?'

'Oh, I don't know. To teach her a lesson. I was confused and angry. I thought it was my duty to regard the matter as one that should be investigated – discreetly – just in case she had met with an accident – then my tardiness would pose a question in some quarters—'

'Then tell me, sir,' Faro interrupted. 'Why are you objecting to our enquiries? Had you some suspicions of your own regarding her whereabouts which you haven't imparted to Superintendent McIntosh?'

'What kind of suspicions?' Kellar demanded.

'Well, let us say, you suspected that your wife's destination was not North Berwick with her sister. That she perhaps had some other – well, assignation.'

Kellar stared at him. 'I haven't the least idea what you mean. What the devil are you implying, Faro?'

Faro sighed. 'To put it delicately, sir, was there any possibility that there was some other man involved.'

'You mean a lover. My Mabel?' Kellar's head shot back,

his mouth open in a roar of mirth. Then suddenly sober, he leaned over, his face inches away from Faro's. 'My wife worships the ground I walk on. There never was and never will be another man for her.'

And so, since time began, has every cuckolded husband believed, thought Faro grimly.

'Get this into your head, Faro. I've told you all the reasons why I mentioned her disappearance. But between ourselves, I haven't the slightest doubt that once she has come to her senses and realised that this is a joke in very poor taste, she will come back to me.'

So that was it and Faro felt sudden anger. A discreet private investigation, McIntosh had called it. None of the usual sources which would bring Kellar into the public gaze. Not out of natural caring and anxiety for his wife – oh no. Kellar probably didn't give a damn whether she had gone or not, but his lack of interest might be misinterpreted. A blot on his reputation as a devoted husband, a model citizen, and there might be second thoughts about the knighthood.

Faro regarded him with ill-concealed distaste. He had had quite enough of Dr Kellar. 'I trust your assumptions are correct, sir. Now if you'll excuse me.'

Back at the Central Office, Superintendent McIntosh was eagerly awaiting Faro's arrival.

Ushering him into the office, McIntosh closed the door. 'Look at this, Faro.' On a side table were the remains of a parcel of large dimensions, its brown paper wrapping disintegrating, sodden and wet.

Slowly the Superintendent drew out what appeared at first glance to be the limp remains of a dead animal, its fur sticky with mud. Watching Faro's face, he lifted it carefully and shook out the folds to reveal a fur cloak, a once-treasured possession, soft as a caress, cared for as the most exquisite and valuable garment in any well-to-do woman's wardrobe. The fur was sable with a black cape. Its ruin was not mud as Faro had first thought. A closer look was enough to reveal that it had been soaked in blood.

'Where . . . ?'

'Just brought in, Faro,' said McIntosh excitedly. 'Found beside the railway line near Longniddry Station. May have lain under the snow for a while. The railwayman who handed it in happened to notice that the melting snow had turned pink. He thought at first it was a dead cat.' Touching an area of the fur less bloodied, McIntosh added, 'Looks expensive, doesn't it. Not the sort of thing one would throw away without good reason. Any ideas, Faro?'

'One or two, sir. I think you'll find that it belongs to Mrs Kellar.'

'Mrs Kellar!' McIntosh gave a yelp of astonishment. 'Mrs Kellar! How do you know that?'

'Because I've just been to the Kellar house and this answers exactly the description of what she was wearing when she left the house for North Berwick.'

'You're sure?'

Faro examined the furrier's label. There weren't many who could afford such a couturier. 'Tracing the owner shouldn't present any difficulties and I think we'll find that was specially made for Mrs Kellar.'

McIntosh sat back in his chair and rubbed his hands together. 'Well now, if you're right, that's an extraordinary stroke of luck.'

Faro gave him a sharp glance, surprised by his insensitivity. Whoever had last worn this cloak – and if his assumptions were correct the last wearer had been Mrs Kellar – had run seriously out of luck.

'The railwayman thought it might have fallen out of a passing train.'

'More likely to have been thrown out,' said Faro.

'Well, whichever, it's been hidden by the snow.' McIntosh thought for a moment. 'If it belongs to Mrs Kellar then it could have lain there since she disappeared. Nice piece of fur. I suppose we were lucky to have it handed in at all.'

Faro was turning the cloak inside out. 'Extensive staining here too. Look at the lining.'

'No doubt that was the real reason for the person who found it not being keen to keep it.'

'All we need is the weapon . . . '

'Oh, I think we have that too,' said McIntosh with a grin, and from under the brown paper, with the air of a magician producing a rabbit from a hat, he dramatically withdrew a large knife. 'This was wrapped inside the fur.'

Faro held out his hand for the knife. Without a second's hesitation, he said, 'These are undoubtedly bloodstains.'

The information slowly dawned on the Superintendent. 'My God, Faro,' he whispered, 'you realise what you're saying. Someone murdered the police surgeon's wife. There'll be all hell to pay over this. If we can only find where this knife came from,' he added.

'Oh, I can tell you that too.'

'You can?'

Faro nodded. 'Yes. As a matter of fact, we've both seen the murder weapon before and fairly recently.'

McIntosh stared at him. 'We have?'

'Oh yes, and fairly recently. At Dr Kellar's dinner party the night before his wife vanished.'

Faro studied his superior's horrified expression with the grim satisfaction of knowing, without the least doubt, that what he held in his hand was one of a pair missing from the dining-room which had been used to more gruesome purpose than the carving of a ruined lamb roast.

Chapter Five

Superintendent McIntosh was put out of countenance by the enormity of the discovery of the fur cloak and the carving knife. Only a half-wit could now presume they were searching for an absconding wife when all the evidence pointed indisputably to the fact that Mabel Kellar had not only disappeared, but had been foully murdered.

Worse, suspicion might now be reasonably directed to the personal involvement in the crime of Edinburgh City Police's surgeon. Fearful repercussions were anticipated by the Superintendent when this disclosure was made public. Such circumstances demanded that Dr Kellar be confronted, on what McIntosh called neutral territory, to give a good account of himself, if that were humanly possible.

'Tactfully, you understand, Faro. Very tactfully. You can talk around it, you know the procedure well enough,' he said hurriedly, as was his way when he wished to rid himself of an unpleasant duty. 'See if he has any ideas about how his wife's bloodstained fur came to be found on the railway line.'

Faro smiled grimly at this somewhat naive method of approach. The evidence was overwhelming and had it been any other suspect than Kellar, doubtless policemen and the jail coach would already be bowling towards Surgeons Hall. Led by Detective Inspector Faro, the doctor would be questioned and if there were no satisfactory answers, then a warrant would be presented for apprehension on suspicion of murder. Considering the importance of the suspect and his unique role with Edinburgh City Police, Superintendent McIntosh seized his greatcoat and, more grim-faced than usual, decided to accompany his Inspector and be present at the interview.

A carriage bore both men rapidly towards Surgeons Hall. They travelled in silence as the thought hung unspoken and uneasily in their minds that they were already too late. Dr Kellar, aware of the damning discovery at Longniddry, might well have taken prudent flight.

It was almost with surprise that they met him emerging from the lecture hall. He did not seem in the least concerned at this unexpected visit.

'Is there somewhere we can talk, sir?' asked Faro.

'In private, if you please, doctor,' added McIntosh sternly.

Kellar nodded and opened the door into a rather dark study with all the comforting atmosphere of a bleak and draughty station waiting-room on a cold winter's day.

Motioning Faro and McIntosh towards two woefully uncomfortable wooden chairs, he perched on the edge of the table and for the first time he seemed to notice the parcel under Faro's arm, now re-wrapped in fresh brown paper. Sighing, he said heavily, 'Well, gentlemen, I suppose it's about Mabel, isn't it?'

Faro looked at him in amazement. Did he already know what the parcel contained and, if so, was he about to confess? If he did, this would be one of the most remarkable cases on record, with very little detection involved: confession upon confrontation before any accusation could be made. Such a situation was not unknown, especially in a case of crime passionel, but Faro had expected the police surgeon to be made of stronger stuff, to be wily and evasive.

Dr Kellar stabbed a finger in his direction. 'Go on, Faro, out with it.'

Faro noted the uncertainty. He had been mistaken about the confession and said, somewhat awkwardly, 'Thank you, sir.' This was not an interview that he relished.

'God knows what I expected,' he told Vince later. 'Sobs and screams of rage. When you consider how he could take on about a burnt roast and yet the same man could receive with complete aplomb the almost positive proof that his wife had, in all probability, been dismembered with the same carving knife he had used that Sunday evening.'

Faro was aware that the Superintendent was also watching Kellar's expression intently as he unwrapped the parcel and shook forth the bloodstained cloak and knife.

A faint groan hissed out of Kellar, his visible signs of discomfort were that his face paled, his knuckles whitening as he gripped the edge of the table.

He made no attempt to touch the stained fur which Faro spread before him. 'I want to see the label,' he demanded. When this was revealed, he nodded. 'Yes, there's no doubt about it. It belongs to Mabel. The knife?' He shook his head. 'It is not unique. I believe you would find one exactly like that, in my dining-room.'

'I'm afraid, sir, we have no option but to treat your wife's disappearance as a murder investigation,' said the Superintendent, clearing his throat in some embarrassment.

Kellar nodded rapidly, almost eagerly. 'Quite right, Superintendent. Quite right. If you will excuse me for a moment.' He put his hand to his mouth and gulped. 'I think I am about to be sick.'

He left the room hastily, while McIntosh and Faro exchanged uncomfortable glances. They avoided looking towards the revolting and incriminating evidence as each meditated on what the next move should be when Kellar returned.

'Perhaps you should have gone with him, Faro,' whispered McIntosh with a quick glance at the clock, and leaving the Inspector to wonder if at this moment Kellar was making a run for it.

Pretending to misunderstand, Faro said, 'I don't think

that would be strictly necessary.' Walking over to the fire-place empty of anything capable of ignition, he leaned on the stone mantel and concentrated on some particularly uninspired watercolours. 'A gentleman who is being sick prefers to be private.'

McIntosh came and stared curiously over Faro's shoulder as if he had discovered a lost Rembrandt. 'Interesting, eh?'

The door opened at that moment and thankfully they beheld Kellar, somewhat green about the gills, dabbing at his beard with a silk handkerchief. 'Please be seated, gentlemen.' He looked round the room, and said shakily, 'I should like to sit down myself, if you don't mind.'

Faro indicated the chair he had vacated.

'Thank you, Inspector. Ah, that's better. Now, perhaps we could all do with a dram. The cupboard over there, Faro, if you wouldn't mind doing the honours.'

The cupboard smelt of mould and mice but the glasses and decanter were a welcome sight and the whisky meas-ures were generously bestowed. The three men drank in silence, for no toast applicable to the occasion came to mind that would not have sounded flippant.

Watching him narrowly, Faro decided that Kellar was showing remarkable self-control and there was little doubt that he had purged his emotions with the physical act of vomiting.

Kellar nodded in the direction of the fur cloak. 'Where was that found?'

After Superintendent McIntosh had related the details of the discovery, there was a lengthy pause before Kellar said: 'I suppose I must have been the last person to see her, except for the passengers and the madman on the train who murdered her. Fancy choosing my poor silly Mabel as a victim. God knows why . . . '

'Tell me, sir, did you see her on to the train?'

Kellar shook his head. 'No, Inspector. I did not. As a matter of fact, it was snowing and I was already late for my midday lecture. I told her to get a porter, but she insisted that as she had so little luggage with her . . . '

'Did anyone see you return to the house?' asked Faro.

Kellar gave him a mocking look. 'What you mean is, have I an alibi?'

'Something of the sort, sir.' Faro heard McIntosh's shocked intake of breath. 'The maid or the housekeeper – were they in?'

'How the devil do I know whether the servants are in or out? It is one of my strict rules that they keep out of my way entirely, except when they are asked to serve food and so forth. My wife and I value our privacy, that is why we employ the absolute minimum of domestics.'

'Surely the housekeeper—'

'Her most of all. She's only in my house on sufferance – and on twice the salary she's worth – until Mabel gets back . . . '

And Kellar stopped suddenly, his eyes widened, as if this was the first time the full horror of the situation had struck him. 'My God,' he whispered and slumped forward, resting his head in his hands. 'My God – Mabel. She's never coming back – dear God. The poor stupid fool, she's dead, isn't she?'

The Superintendent and Faro exchanged glances and, with McIntosh murmuring platitudes, they withdrew and quietly closed the door behind them.

'Any theories?' asked the Superintendent.

Faro looked at the clock. 'If I hurry, I should just be in time to catch the North Berwick train, with luck the same one that Mrs Kellar travelled on. Since the murder probably took place between Edinburgh and Longniddry, and she would travel in a closed first-class compartment, it's unlikely that the upholstery escaped the murderous onslaught. There must have been blood spattered everywhere.'

'True. And as the evidence of the cloak suggests a struggle, a lot of it also went on to the murderer.'

'We're presuming, of course, that he left the train at Longniddry so perhaps a porter there might have noticed his bloodstained hands or clothes.'

At the door Faro hesitated. 'Might as well check on Dr Kellar's alibi while I'm here.'

'I was just going to suggest that, Faro,' said the Superintendent sternly. 'Find out, if he was late for his lecture that morning, and so forth. Discreet as possible, mind you. Better coming from you than from one of our lads. Think up some sort of excuse to see a timetable, make it sound feasible, will you? Leave you to it. No need to encourage any more gossip than necessary at this stage. There'll be more than enough when his students get wind of this. God help us all.'

Faro watched the Superintendent walk to the other side of the hall with an intense feeling of irritation at having been told how to do his job as if he was just being sent out on his first murder enquiry.

He found the registrar's clerk in his office.

''Morning, Inspector, what can we do for you?'

'We've lost our timetable of Dr Kellar's lectures,' he said casually. It was surprisingly easy. 'Have you a spare copy?'

'Certainly, Sir.'

Faro studied the paper set before him. 'I thought Dr Kellar had a Monday morning lecture.'

The clerk shook his head. 'Not this term, Inspector. Monday is his day off.'

The Superintendent joined him at the door and as they walked towards the Central Office, Faro repeated the clerk's statement.

'Why should Dr Kellar lie about being at his lecture?' said the Superintendent.

'Why indeed, when such matters are so easy to check?'

Things were beginning to look black indeed for the police surgeon, especially as Faro was inclined to disregard Kellar's hint that Mabel's assassin had been a madman on the train. If so, then where was her body?

Logically, it would have been expected to come to light as did the cloak when the snow melted, if it had been pushed out of the train. If not already dead, then appallingly injured and with such considerable loss of blood to be rendered incapable of travelling far. In all probability, she had lain undiscovered, hidden by the snow for the past two weeks.

Faro decided, without a great deal of hope, to examine the railway compartment. A struggle such as the dead woman must have put up would surely have been accompanied by screams for help and even if these had been ignored, it was unlikely that a heavily bloodstained compartment had not yet been reported to the police.

He was brooding on another theory that seriously incriminated Kellar. His wife had never boarded that train. Faro remembered the housekeeper had overheard Kellar shouting that he would take Mrs Kellar 'to the blasted station, or all the way'.

He was now giving serious consideration to the fact that Mrs Kellar had been driven in the brougham through East Lothian and in some lonely spot she had been murdered. Her fur cloak and the knife had then been disposed of on the railway embankment to make it look like a train murder.

As to the whereabouts of her body, no one enjoyed a more advantageous and unique position to commit murder and get away with it than the police surgeon. Dr Kellar was highly skilled at the disposal of corpses by the dissection and distribution of their limbs for anatomical study among his eager medical students.

Chapter Six

Faro soon discovered that there was little hope of asking porters if any of them recalled Mrs Kellar boarding the North Berwick train. He arrived on the platform in time to find that the services of all porters were keenly in demand by anxious passengers emerging from the train, wreathed in heavy clouds of steam.

'All change. All change.'

Seizing the opportunity, Faro sought the guard and introduced himself as investigating a suspected crime in Longniddry.

The guard, Wilson by name, whistled. 'Don't get many crimes in that area. Oh yes, sir, this is my regular train,' he added with a proud and affectionate look at the engine.

'Have I time to have a glance through the first-class carriages?'

'If you can do it quickly, Inspector. We move off again in five minutes.'

'That will be adequate. I wonder if you'd be so good as to accompany me.'

'Why, yes sir. Of course.'

Watching the Inspector's careful examination of the upholstery, Wilson said apologetically, 'The train's fairly new, only two years old, but the upholstery gets dirty quite quickly, as you can see, with all the smoke from the stack and so forth. These carriages are just about ready for a spring clean.'

Far from being pristine, indeed, but as Faro had already deduced, there was nothing resembling widespread blood-stains.

In reply to his question Wilson said, 'Oh yes, sir, we do this same journey back and forward between Edinburgh and Berwick four times each day.'

'Then you would be able to remember if it has been running as usual during the past two weeks.'

'Absolutely, sir.'

'There have been no breakdowns or replacement carriages?'

'Never, sir, without my knowledge. You can rely on that. This is my train,' he said proudly, 'a most reliable engine, never given us a moment's trouble.'

'Could you say definitely whether this train ran as usual at midday on Monday, January 16th?'

The guard grinned. 'It did, sir and I was on it. It was my daughter's first birthday and starting to snow heavily when we left Edinburgh. We were anxious about possible delays. Folks like to get home for their dinners and we have a lot of passengers joining and leaving the train at the intermittent stations.'

'Bearing in mind the snowfall, there were no blockages on the line, even just for a few minutes?'

Wilson thought. 'No, not that day, I'm certain. Everything went smoothly and we arrived in North Berwick on the dot of 12.45.'

'At the time you were checking the tickets, can you remember seeing anyone behaving in what you might consider an odd way?'

'Such as, sir?'

'Well, did you interrupt an argument, for instance?'

Wilson thought for a moment, pushed back his cap and scratched his head. 'No, sir, I can't honestly say that I saw anything at all out of the ordinary. All very normal, the gentlemen hiding behind their newspapers, as always. And the ladies reading or staring out of the window. Very well-behaved travellers, they are. Like their privacy, of course, and that day a lot of them travelled with the blinds drawn.'

'Surely that is unusual in daylight hours?'

'Not at all, sir. The sun is low at this time of year, and what with the glare of the snow, and the smoke, it can be trying on the passengers' eyes.'

'So you don't see much of what's happening inside the compartments.'

'Not a lot. I mind my own business, Inspector,' Wilson added sternly, 'leave them severely alone except when I have to examine the tickets.'

And so creating the perfect opportunity for a murderer, thought Faro hopefully.

'Were the first-class carriages crowded that day?'

Again the guard thought. 'No more than usual.'

'Were any of these compartments empty?'

'There might have been a couple.'

'Can you remember one being occupied by a lady and gentleman travelling together?'

Wilson grinned. 'Oh yes, that was the young honey-mooners, bless them. Got on at Musselburgh.'

'Tell me, do you remember a lady travelling that day in a very handsome fur cloak – sable, it was.'

'I wouldn't know sable from water rat, sir,' said Wilson ruefully, 'that's for sure. Besides most of our better-off lady passengers travelling first at this time of year wrap up well in their fur cloaks to keep warm. Was your lady young or old?'

'Middle-aged.'

The guard nodded. 'That's mostly the age that can afford the furs, sir.' He consulted his watch. 'Have to look sharp, sir. Time we were leaving.'

'I think I'll stay on. A ticket to Longniddry, if you please.'

As the train steamed out of Waverley Station, over-shadowed by Carlton Hill, Faro considered that the comfort of travelling in a first-class compartment was well worth the extra expense.

He enjoyed rail travel and regretted that it was a fairly

66

uncommon occurrence in his life. As he studied the passing landscape, reeling down the window to have a good
look at the three stations where the train halted before
Longniddry, he noted that the journey so far had taken
twenty minutes.

Twenty minutes would be more than enough time to
stab Mabel Kellar to death with the carving knife in a
compartment with the blinds drawn.

But if that was so, then there would have been blood
spattered everywhere, far more than could be contained in
the fur cloak. The murderer's clothing and hands must also
have been stained. Once his gruesome job was completed,
he would want to make a speedy exit from the scene of the
crime. Having disposed of the evidence he presumably got
out himself at Longniddry.

Faro shook his head. The explanation was plausible,
he could imagine the scene but one vital question still
remained unanswered. What did he do with the body?
All he had to do was open the compartment door and
push body, cloak and knife out on to the railway line.
Otherwise Wilson would have found the body when he
was collecting his tickets again after Longniddry and
the hue and cry would have been raised immediately.

The snow lay deep on both sides of the line covering
the banks. Here and there a shrub or hedgerow was
visible, but most of the landscape was hidden under a
heavy blanket of snow.

There was another possible explanation for the still missing body. Heavier than the cloak, had it rolled, gathered
momentum as it slid down an embankment? Was it still
lying entombed in a huge unmelted snowball somewhere
along the line?

As they approached Longniddry Station, a biting wind
and acrid smoke blew into Faro's face as he leaned out
of the window in search of places where a falling body
might have lodged. There were none immediately visible
and when the platform was in sight he beheld a band of

uniformed policemen carefully searching the area surrounding the railway line.

As the train slowed down, they recognised him and shouted, 'Nothing so far, sir. Nothing suspicious. No bloodstained corpse, but we keep hoping.'

Faro lingered, watching the station master collecting tickets. He seemed to know most of the passengers well enough to pass the time of day and greet them by name.

That was hopeful. This was a small station and the people who used it were probably regulars working in Edinburgh or Musselburgh. A stranger, particularly one wearing bloodstained clothes, would surely be remarked upon.

Station Master Andrews was more than willing to chat about this sensational occurrence which had put Longniddry on the map. But Faro was in for a disappointment to his hopes that he might remember a stranger carrying a large brown paper parcel.

'Two weeks, sir.' The man rubbed his forehead. 'That's rather a long time ago. This train's always busy – dinner time and a lot of coming and going between the local stations.'

To Faro's question, he shook his head. 'I think I would have noticed any stranger among the passengers, sir. I have a good memory for faces and it's mostly locals travelling on that train. Always a lot of our ladies with their maids returning from shopping expeditions in Edinburgh.'

He looked at Faro curiously. 'Word certainly does get around fast, Inspector. There was this reporter from the *Scotsman* wanting to know all the details . . . '

Faro groaned. This was the worst possible news. He must try to stop this sensational piece of information being made public, although at the moment there was nothing the press could do to tie it in with the missing Mabel Kellar. As far as everyone but the few Central Office officials knew, Mrs Kellar was still on holiday with her sister at North Berwick.

He just hoped that Ina and Mrs Flynn were not avid newspaper readers.

Trying to sound more casual than he felt, he said, 'He was off his mark very quickly, seeing that the cloak has just been discovered.'

'Yes, Inspector. It was a lucky day for him. He had been down here covering a society wedding in one of the big houses and was waiting for the Edinburgh train when Brown comes rushing down the track carrying the bundle and shouting. "Look at this. I reckon there's been a murder done." Those were his exact words and the reporter was on to it like a shot.'

'Where can I find Brown?'

'There he is now. Over there, crossing the line, just back from his dinner.'

Brown was young and eager. Yes, he found the parcel and took the liberty of unwrapping it, just in case. 'I could see straight away that there'd been foul play.' He paused looking at Faro's expressionless face. 'Been a murder, hasn't there, sir?'

When Faro said cautiously, 'Not necessarily,' Brown continued, 'But it's suspicious, wouldn't you say, sir? All that blood – and a carving knife.'

'But there's no body so far, so there might possibly be some other explanation. And that is what we have to find.'

Brown looked quite dejected.

'Now I'd like you to show me the exact spot where you found the parcel, if you please.'

Leading the way down the line, Brown sounded glum. 'But it is definitely foul play, isn't it, sir? I mean, the woman who wore it must have been stabbed to death, must have lost a lot of blood – and that knife too . . . ' Stopping, he rubbed his foot against the grassy slope. 'It was exactly here, sir. I put this mark against the telegraph pole.'

'Well done,' said Faro, thanking Brown and fending off his eager and curious questions. The lad seemed most reluctant to leave him and, finally watching him wander rather despondently back towards the station building, Faro thought wryly that Brown with his ghoulish relish for crime might have exactly the right brand of enthusiasm they hoped to find in new recruits for the City Police.

He carefully examined the place where the parcel had lain, two hundred yards away from the station on the same side of the line. The station side also gave direct access to the platform for first-class passengers. Close to the ticket barrier, the privileged passengers could leave with a minimum of effort, instead of having to walk along a corridor, the length of a carriage. A fact, decided Faro, imagining the hasty descent and hurried exit from the station, of considerable assistance to Mabel Kellar's murderer.

From where he stood the railway line stretched north and south between the snowy slope of winter fields on one side and on the station entrance side, the Edinburgh road.

Faro lit a pipe thoughtfully and was considering the discovery of the parcel when a uniformed policeman appeared and leaned over the fence.

'Afternoon, Inspector. I've spoken to the farmer over there,' he pointed to the fields. 'But he hasn't seen anyone behaving suspiciously on his property, or carrying a large brown paper parcel. He's a forbidding old man, sir, and I don't think he'd miss much. He also showed me a shotgun he keeps to warn off intruders.'

As Faro wandered back to the platform, he was in time to see Station Master Andrews chasing and capturing a youth of about fourteen. Holding him firmly by the coat collar, Andrews demanded, 'Travelling without paying your fare, eh? Is that your little game?'

Grumbling, red-faced, the youth took out a coin and handed it over.

'All right, I'll accept it this time. But try that again and we'll get the police to you.'

Andrews grinned at Faro. 'There's always one of these townies tries it. Manage to hide from the guard on the way down and then they jump off the train, lurking about in the waiting-room or the lavatory until they think they can slip through the barrier without paying.' A bell sounded shrilly inside. 'That's the Edinburgh train from Newcastle approaching now, sir. You'll have to get across the bridge, sharp as you can.'

As he settled back comfortably in the compartment and was carried to Edinburgh, Faro thought about the youth who had hidden in the waiting-room. If he'd managed to evade Station Master Andrew's sharp eyes, then what was to stop Mabel Kellar's murderer also washing the blood off his hands in the lavatory and then calmly crossing the bridge and boarding the Newcastle train back to Edinburgh as he had done?

When they reached Waverley, Faro made a mental note to have his constables carry out a routine check at the station. Meanwhile, on the off-chance that a porter might have remembered putting Mrs Kellar on the train or that the ticket collector, like Andrews, had a good memory for faces, he lingered at the barrier.

When the last passenger had departed, he described Mrs Kellar and asked, 'Do you recall any lady like that boarding the 12 o'clock North Berwick train?'

'A couple of weeks ago, sir? Now that's a poser. Fur cloak, you say, middle-aged? That's what most of the first-class ladies wear in this weather.'

As Faro was walking away, a porter who had been listening curiously and intently to this conversation came forward.

'Excuse me, sir, couldn't help overhearing. You say two weeks ago? Well, I remember there was a middle-aged lady, in a very fine fur cloak. She called for a porter at the station entrance, asked for the North Berwick train. She was very upset, poor soul, in tears.'

'Did she get out of a carriage?'

71

'Oh yes, sir, a brougham.'

If Mabel Kellar had travelled on the train alone then this information threw a completely new light on to the evidence and they were seeking a faceless murderer.

'The man who was driving the brougham? Can you remember what he was like?'

The porter shook his head. 'Not really, sir. But he was in a terrible temper. Shouting at her.'

'Shouting – like what? Do you remember?'

'Oh yes. Abuse, that's what. "Go to him and damn you both. Damn you both to hell."' The porter paused. 'I suppose that was her husband and she was going off with another man and taking the laddie with her.'

'Laddie? What laddie?'

'There was a wee chap with her, clinging to her hand. About nine or ten. And he was fair upset too.'

Thanking the porter, Faro walked away. So much for grand theories, advanced and demolished within minutes, he thought, making his way back to the Central Office.

Chapter Seven

Calling in at Sheridan Place to collect some papers from his study, Faro was delighted to find Vince had returned late that morning. Already well-cosseted and pampered by Mrs Brook, he looked up with a grin from reading the newspaper and greeted his stepfather.

'I have to rush out again, lad, but did you have a good holiday?'

'Superb. I'll tell you all about it at dinner. Bought a *Times* to read on the train. Have you seen this?'

A small paragraph read: 'Mysterious Discovery on Railway Line near Longniddry. The discovery of a woman's bloodstained fur cloak and a carving knife has led to an immediate investigation by Edinburgh City Police into the possibility of foul play.'

When Faro groaned, Vince said, 'Fame at last, eh? Is this one of your cases? Has all this happened since I've been away?'

'I'm just back from Longniddry.'

'Really? Tell me more.'

'Vince, lad,' Faro sat down heavily in the chair opposite and took his stepson's hands. 'I have to prepare you for a shock. We have reason to believe that the cloak belonged to Mabel Kellar.'

Vince laughed. 'How extraordinary. Then what on earth was it doing on the railway line. Stolen, was it?'

'We don't know. Vince, I warned you the news was bad. Mrs Kellar has been missing since the morning you went on holiday.'

'But she only went to her sister's at North Berwick.'

'She never got there.'

'But—'

'Vince. We think she's been murdered.'

'Murdered? Mabel? Oh dear God – no.'

And Faro was later to find some significance in the fact that Vince's cry of agony was considerably more heartfelt than Dr Kellar's reaction to the grim discovery that pointed to his wife's brutal murder.

'I have to go now, but I'll be back shortly.' He put his hand on Vince's shoulder. 'We'll talk about it then.'

Vince declined supper that evening. 'Mrs Brook fed me more than enough when I arrived home. I couldn't eat another bite, especially now – with all this about Mabel. Come on, Stepfather, tell me.'

As carefully as he could and without displaying any more emotion than he would have shown had the missing woman been unknown to either of them, Faro went carefully over the details, from Kellar informing Superintendent McIntosh that Mabel was missing to his own visit to Longniddry Station and the subsequent revelations.

Vince was silent, trying to take in all these crucial facts and at the same time trying not to link them with that dear woman who had befriended him. At last he spoke, wearily, as if the effort of remembering was too much for him.

'Did you know I called on her that – that very morning on my way to the station?'

'The housekeeper told me. Oh, I'm sorry, lad.'

'Don't be sorry for me, Stepfather. Be sorry for her murderer,' he said harshly. 'Because if the law doesn't get him and hang him, then I'll take the matter of justice into my own hands.'

Appalled at such a prospect, Faro said, 'I don't think that'll be necessary.'

'You know who did it then?'

'We have a good idea.'

74

'And you haven't arrested him yet? For God's sake, Stepfather, he might escape.'

'Be calm, lad, be calm. As you were almost the last person to see Mabel, anything you can tell us about that visit would be of enormous help.'

Vince stared out of the window at the snow-clad slope of Arthur's Seat. When at last he spoke, his voice was overcome with emotion. 'Thinking about it, I realise that she was trying to conceal how desperately upset she was that morning. There'd been that unholy row with Kellar after we left. Just one more but this time serious enough for her to be seeking refuge with her sister. Actually leaving her husband, as he rightly deserves. She should have done so long ago . . . '

'What was this row about? Did she tell you.'

'She spared me the exact details, hinted at a very unpleasant post-mortem on the culinary disasters of the dinner-party and that Kellar hadn't spared her. Anyway, I offered to escort her to the railway station as I was catching a train there myself. She refused. Said she wasn't ready to leave. Packing to complete, instructions for the housekeeper and so forth, very nervous and upset.'

Vince's words took on a sinister meaning. That had been his own impression of Mrs Kellar during the dinner. Of course, it might not indicate more than a nervous disposition heightened and upset by the new housekeeper's delay in preparing and serving the courses.

Faro rubbed his chin thoughtfully, as he remembered how the guests had stirred uncomfortably in their chairs, reluctant witnesses to their host's anger. That scene at least had survived the boredom of the evening.

'It would have made more sense if she'd taken the carving knife to him. There were moments when I felt like it, I can tell you,' said Vince.

'I distinctly remember you saying so, lad,' said Faro drily. 'It's a good job we're not dealing with a missing Dr Kellar or you might well be the chief suspect.'

75

Vince shrugged as if getting rid of Kellar might have been worth it. 'You remember, Stepfather, how frightful it all was.'

Faro nodded. 'If only we had paid more attention to the subtle undercurrents, for undercurrents there should have been that night. Some hint of the monstrous events to come, some plan in the mind of the murderer.'

'You mean the murderer was with us that evening? Surely not?'

'It has been my experience that when a murder is committed, one need look no further than the family circle to find the guilty party.'

'Not in this case,' said Vince firmly. 'And if you're hinting at Kellar himself, I think you're miles out. Never Kellar. Think again, Stepfather and you'll see I'm right. With so much to lose. I assure you his pride is far greater than his passion and he would never do anything to prejudice that knighthood in the offing.

'No,' – again Vince shook his head emphatically – 'you must be wrong this time, Stepfather. Kellar is much too emotionless to go for his wife with the carving knife. You have to love deeply to hate deeply and, quite frankly, I'd be prepared to bet that he hardly notices that Mabel exists. As for loving her, well, I imagine that part of their life was very brief and very long ago.'

He shuddered. 'I feel it is much more likely that she succumbed to the frenzy of some madman who boarded the train, found her alone and – and—' his voice broke into a sob.

'I know, lad. I know.' Faro patted his arm sympathetically. 'That is the answer one always hopes to find, the stranger on whom the bereaved family can vent their own grief and anger. Rarely, alas, is this the case. Besides,' he added in tones of consolation that he was far from feeling, 'the cloak and knife might appear to be damning evidence, but until the body is recovered we have no definite proof that murder had been committed.'

Even as he said the words, Faro had reached his own grim conclusions. If Kellar was indeed her murderer, then Mabel would never be found. Faro was not in the least doubt of that, with a horrific certainty of how her body had been disposed of. He must spare Vince from that knowledge as long as he could.

'The motive could have been robbery, Stepfather. She had a lot of very valuable jewellery. Inherited. Not from Kellar. He was too mean to spend money on frivolities. She was locking up her jewel case while I talked to her.'

'Can you describe it?'

'Yes. Red leather, with brass fastenings.'

And she hadn't taken it with her. Faro remembered it lying on the dressing table along with the silver brushes and toilette set.

'That's it, Stepfather. I've just remembered something. "People to see."'

'People to see?'

'Yes. Those were her exact words. "I have instructions to give to Mrs Flynn and people to see before I go." I wonder who they were.'

Faro sighed. 'Have you any theories about how her cloak came to be found on the railway line then?'

Vince formed the picture in his mind and closed his eyes against it. 'You say Kellar identified it as Mabel's. Surely if he were guilty . . .'

'Guilty or innocent, lad, what else could he have done? Since the housekeeper and the maid would no doubt also recognise the cloak, all he would have done was to have proved himself a liar. He even read the label inside and told us that was indeed Mrs Kellar's furrier and that it would be easy enough to check.'

'That doesn't sound like a guilty man to me,' said Vince.

'Unless he's also a very clever one,' Faro replied drily.

'Kellar is a beast but I still can't believe it was him,' Vince protested obstinately. 'Now if you were to suspect the Mad Bart . . .'

77

'Unfortunately we can't fix murders to suit our own prejudices,' said Faro sternly. 'I too hope you're right about Kellar being innocent for quite a different reason. Can you imagine the furore of public reaction when they learn that the Edinburgh City Police have a surgeon in their midst who has murdered his wife? McIntosh is afraid that, used by the wrong people, this could be the stepping stone for riot, for the breakdown of law and order. A bit drastic, but I see his point.'

'God help Kellar, guilty or innocent, Stepfather. Once the story gets abroad his reputation will be finished. You know how such muck clings to a man. I can't see him surviving such a scandal, either.'

'At this stage, all I am doing is piecing together, with some difficulty, the few facts we have to go on. Long experience has taught me to suspect anyone and everyone however remotely connected. And always to be ready for the unexpected.'

Faro paused before adding, 'It's no use you trying to be fair-minded and putting in a good word for him. I'm perfectly aware that you didn't care for him at all. And he's not popular with his students, either.'

He put a hand on Vince's shoulder. 'The first step in putting together the story of her last hours lies within the Kellar house and you, I'm afraid, are witness to that last hour. Her state of mind and so forth could be valuable evidence. We'll need a statement from you, of course.' Seeing Vince's still, stricken face, he added, 'I wish it was otherwise, lad, and that we could avoid having you dragged into this sorry business.'

'Don't worry about me, Stepfather. I'll be glad to say anything that will put a rope around her murderer's vile neck.'

Vince went to the sideboard and poured himself a whisky. After a moment he said, 'All I know is what I've told you. That she seemed extremely agitated and upset by the row with Kellar.'

'Yes, I know. But I keep going further back than that. To the beginning of it all. The dinner party.'

'The last straw, do you think?'

'I'm considering her distress that night. Are we being too hasty blaming it all on the burnt roast. Was there another cause? Could she have been afraid?'

'Of course she was afraid, Stepfather. Of her husband's brutal ill-humour.'

Faro shook his head. 'A storm in a teacup, lad. Hardly an uncommon occurrence, even in the most civilised of families. Situations regarding ruined food and the feeling that the wife is totally to blame for the servants' short-comings. Happens all the time, lad. The only difference was that Kellar didn't bother to restrain his wrath until the guests were gone.'

'They quarrelled, Stepfather. In front of all of us.'

'Not they – he quarrelled. The high words all came from Kellar. His wife uttered a few tearful protests. No, lad, quarrel is definitely a misnomer. Besides, all married couples bicker over domestic details.'

Vince regarded him steadily. 'Do they indeed? Then that makes me all the more eager to embrace permanent bachelordom.'

Faro laughed. 'If you do, then you will be throwing away an extremely valuable parcel unopened simply because the wrapping is slightly torn. You will never know the good things inside.'

'From what Mabel Kellar told me . . . ' Vince began darkly.

'My dear lad, I beg you not to read too much into the revelations of an aggrieved wife. They do tend to exaggerate.'

How to tactfully point out to his young stepson his invidious position – that women, especially childless women of a certain age and social standing, were too often bored with a busy husband's neglect and discreetly sought male attention elsewhere. And what better opportunity

79

for a gentle romance than a husband's handsome young assistant brought into their orbit? He looked at his stepson with compassion. This young and vulnerable lad still walking the cloudy dreams of chivalry, more than ready to be flattered by an older woman's interest, eager to lend a sympathetic ear and – perhaps a little too obviously – wear his heart on his sleeve.

Vince looked uncomfortable and growled. 'You know me too well, don't you.'

'Almost as well as I know married couples.' Faro laughed. 'An unholy row which sounds like pistols at fifteen paces to the embarrassed onlookers would be dismissed by the couple themselves as a harmless tiff, an almost everyday event which ends in a tearful reconciliation on the wife's part, with both firmly believing they have the victory. Such matters as a housekeeper's incompetence, lad, don't usually lead to murder.'

'If the shoe had been on the other foot, however. . . . '

'Mrs Kellar didn't strike me as a woman of such pride that she would want to commit murder because she had been made to look an idiot before their guests.'

'You forget one thing, Stepfather. She adores – adored him.' Vince closed his eyes tightly as if to shut off the realisation that he would never see her again. 'Incredible as it may seem and despite his abominable treatment, she would always go back for more. God alone knows why. And she would never look at another man.' Vince sighed heavily and added dramatically. 'I would have taken her away, you know, Stepfather. Protected her, worshipped her.'

'Then you would have been the world's greatest idiot,' said Faro furiously, thumping the table. 'Marriage with a woman more than twice your age.'

'I wasn't talking of marriage,' said Vince softly. 'Besides, age doesn't matter.'

'Not at twenty and forty, but what about in ten years', twenty years' time. When you are my age, and she is sixty. A mistress of sixty.' Faro laughed harshly. 'Chivalry is all very well. Be a knight in shining armour in theory but, I beg you, don't make me angry by talking absolute nonsense, lad.'

There was a moment's silence then Vince said contemptuously, 'Kellar is just the kind of man to marry for money, knowing she was the Mad Bart's heiress.'

'So that was the reason.'

'I know exactly what you're thinking,' was the defensive reply. 'Mabel isn't in the least pretty. But once you get to know her, you forget all about looks. She has such a divine nature, such a delicious sense of humour. So wise and warm-hearted. So different to all those silly giggling dolls, the simpering misses whom it's been my misfortune to meet up to now. If you'd ever known her, Stepfather, you'd know what I mean. No man could have resisted her.'

No man being Vince himself, thought Faro. Sadly one couldn't tell the lad that, given time, simpering misses of eighteen also learn wisdom – at least most do by the time they are forty – and that the wisdom and warm-heartedness and a sense of humour which he found so irresistible are time's compensation for growing older.

'Anyway,' continued Vince, 'a person's looks, like their age, mean nothing really. Not once you get to know them.'

Faro's eyebrows shot upwards in surprise. Here was a change indeed. How deadly accurate had been Cupid's arrows on this unfortunate lad who had been willing to lose his heart ever since boyhood to every pretty face.

'Surely you've noticed, Stepfather, how often handsome men choose quite plain wives. Like the peacock in all his radiant glory – and look at the poor peahen, without a fine feather to her name.'

'Nature has been most unfair in that respect.'

'Of course she has – but deuced clever too. Reason being that Nature's only reason for distribution of fine feathers – on all species – was intended for marvels of reproduction.

It was necessary to attract females in droves, the more the merrier, for a species to survive and multiply. After all, Nature never planned that males should take only one mate, that was man's mistake when he became civilised.'

Faro laughed. 'You do have some far-fetched theories, lad. And grand as all this is for your peahens, civilised humans behaving like barnyard fowls would have caused even more trouble in the world than we are in at present. And that was why the good Lord ordained that what was good for the animals going into the ark two by two was also good for his best creation, man.'

'Kellar didn't abide by that rule. He liked the ladies.'

'I rather suspected he might.'

The doorbell pealed.

'Expecting anyone?' asked Faro.

'Oh, I forgot. Rob said he would come round, to hear all about Walter and the Austrian visit. I could put him off. I don't really feel up to going out tonight.'

'You go. Do you good. Besides, I have a report to write. We'll talk about it when you get back.'

Chapter Eight

Faro did not see Vince again that evening. Finding his friend in very low spirits, Rob had suggested that there were places where sorrows might be effectively drowned in some of the more exciting howffs down Leith Walk.

Meanwhile Faro gathered together all his information on the case of Mabel Kellar, missing and now presumed murdered by person or persons unknown. That, he decided even as he began his preliminary report, wasn't quite true. Apart from the theory of the madman on the train, he was certain that her murderer would be found much nearer home.

Next morning, Vince came into the dining-room looking extremely weary and heavy-eyed, as if he had slept little. Seeing Faro about to depart for the Central Office Vince summoned a wan smile. 'If you can spare a minute, Stepfather, stay and talk to me while I have breakfast.' He pointed to the papers Faro was gathering together. 'I presume these relate to Mabel.'

Faro nodded. 'Just my findings so far. Possible suspects, motives and so forth.'

Vince held out his hand. 'May I?'

'Are you sure?'

'Yes, Stepfather. I've always tried to help in the past and this time, more than any other, I have a personal score to settle.'

'All right, lad. Read it if you like. It won't take long.'

Vince scanned the two pages. 'I think you can dismiss

the maid and housekeeper as possible suspects. Both are relative newcomers to the Kellar household and they have nothing but praise for Mabel. Besides they have no motive.'

He paused and shook his head. 'It would have made a lot more sense if Kellar had been the victim. I can just imagine him presenting an irresistible murder target for an ill-used domestic.'

'Does anything strike you as significant about this case, Vince?'

Vince thought for a moment. 'Yes. This is a man's crime. All the evidence points to a strong man, wielding the carving knife and,' he added with a grimace, 'disposing of the body. You agree?'

'My conclusions entirely.'

'So it would seem that the doctor is the prime suspect.'

'As yet, yes.'

Vince frowned. 'There is a possibility, of course, that there was no motive. That one of his fits of irritation with Mabel became uncontrollable, carried him across the threshold of normality and he suffered a brainstorm.'

'Aren't you forgetting the carving knife?'

'Yes, I am. Of course one hardly embarks on a peaceful journey to the railway station carrying a carving knife. I agree that has very sinister implications.'

'But if it had all been carefully planned – let us suppose that we are right and Kellar tricked his wife into believing he was driving her to North Berwick and then murdered her. Surely he disposed of that damning evidence in a remarkably clumsy fashion?'

'I agree, Stepfather, but again this is not beyond the bounds of possibility. In a medical study of the behaviour of wife-murderers, even the most fiendish and calculating have been known to give way to moments of blind panic.'

Faro tried to picture the scene: Kellar poised over his wife's dead body, in that terrible moment when the red murder light faded from his eyes. Horrified, sated with blood lust, had he seen the railway line as a hell-sent opportunity of diverting suspicion?

He glanced at his notes. 'The only other male employees, I gather, are a jobbing gardener.'

'I've met him. Had a word about roses – his passion. He's a harmless old lad who comes in twice a week in the summer and is never allowed to set foot inside the house. Not much for him to do this time of year.'

'There's also an occasional coachman.'

'He would be from a hiring firm Kellar and all the doctors use. Ambley's at Newington Road.'

'I'll have the constables make a routine check.'

'I doubt whether that'll reveal any motives for Mabel's murder.'

'Fragments, lad. That's what we're after. Minute pieces of information, observation. They are most often the pieces of the puzzle which seem quite irrelevant but when put together give us the face – and the motive – of our murderer.'

'I hardly think you need bother with exhaustive enquiries in this case. If Kellar did it, we only need to know why, where and how he disposed of – of her,' said Vince.

'Know anything about her sister, Mrs Findlay-Cupar? I shall have to go and see her in North Berwick.'

'I gather that they were very close, quite devoted. Mabel talked a lot about Tiz, that's her nickname. I think she could be ruled out of your list of suspects. What about her uncle? He's mad enough to do anything.'

Faro shook his head. 'I think we know that the Mad Bart's reputation is based on eccentricity, rather than dementia.'

'Well, as she's his heiress,' said Vince dubiously, 'I'd say he would bear some investigation.'

Faro smiled at his grim expression. 'Prejudice, lad. Prejudice.'

'Of course it isn't,' replied Vince crossly.

'All right. Item one, his hands are twisted with

85

rheumatism. As a doctor you must have noticed he has difficulty lighting a pipe so I don't imagine he'd be very deft with a carving knife. Item two, if Mabel was killed on the train, then we're looking for an agile man, strong, quick-witted, quick-moving. I think we can safely dismiss from our list of suspects an infirm old chap, who shambles along with the aid of a stick.'

'I suppose strong, quick-witted and quick-moving couldn't possibly include Mrs Eveline Shaw either,' said Vince. 'I see you put a tick against her name.'

'Not as a suspect. Only because as Mrs Kellar's dearest friend and companion – isn't that how she described her to us? – she might know something important.'

'In what way?'

'In the way of confidences. Something from the past that would shed an interesting light on an apparently blameless life.'

'I can assure you . . . '

But Vince's assurances went unuttered. The doorbell announced the arrival of yet another of his young doctor friends, who was calling for news about Walter.

Faro left the house very thoughtfully. His discussion with Vince had revealed only one true suspect. And that was, as it had always been, Kellar. Most damning of all was the absence of a body and although all the evidence so far silently accused Mabel's husband, as yet no motive for her murder was apparent.

He was not looking forward to confronting Kellar with his false alibi and demanding from him a satisfactory account of his movements that Monday, when he was not giving a lecture, as he had led them to believe. Here was another inconsistency in behaviour. Why had he told such a stupid lie when he must have known that it could be checked?

Even more important, Faro was aware of a nagging feeling of unease, insistent as a dull toothache, at the back of his mind. He knew what that meant. He had overlooked something vital, some very significant detail had not registered on that first visit to the house.

He decided that a vague excuse for another look around the house would be worthwhile, again choosing a time when, hopefully, the master was absent.

Considering that physical exercise was always beneficial in the process of mind-clearing, he walked the short distance to the Grange, having to take frequent refuge from the spray of unpleasantly brown slush sent flying by the wheels of passing coaches. He found that his concentration was needed less in agitating his powers of deduction than in keeping his feet as his boots slipped constantly on the treacherous expanses of frozen snow. He was glad indeed to reach the drive leading to the Kellar house although walking was still hazardous. At last he reached the front door and with his hand on the bell, he heard his name.

The maid Ina was approaching from the direction of the coach-house, slithering across the icy surface, hampered by a pail and scrubbing brush.

'Sorry to keep you waiting, Inspector,' she said breathlessly. 'I've been cleaning the master's carriage. Such a mess it's always in. He goes shooting on a Wednesday afternoon and then he complains to us that the upholstery was all stained.'

Faro was hardly listening. A bloodstained carriage. Was this what he had been expecting to find, that vital missing clue?

As if she had read his mind, Ina gave him a sideways glance and with a small shudder, whispered, 'I couldn't get it clean so when I showed it to Mrs Flynn, she said it looked like blood to her. I came over all queasy. But Mrs Flynn says what can we expect with the kind of work the master does.'

'Shooting game can make quite a mess,' said Faro in reassuring tones, so as not to alarm her.

She shook her head. 'He doesn't put them inside the brougham. Mrs Kellar would never allow that. Smelly stuff. Has a special box for his rabbits and birds at the back.'

Faro decided not to panic her by asking to inspect the carriage. He resolved to make a discreet and solitary visit to the coach-house a little later, after learning more about the stained upholstery from Mrs Flynn.

Leaving Ina in the hall, he found the housekeeper in her gloomy retreat below stairs. Almost dark, it was one of those winter days that is never really light and the hours designated daytime slide imperceptibly into night at about three in the afternoon. In the dim light from the high barred windows, Mrs Flynn was rolling pastry on the kitchen table. She stared at him over her spectacles and resumed her task without comment.

'Ina let me in. I met her coming from the coach-house. Seems she's been having problems cleaning the brougham.'

As he spoke to her, he wondered how on earth anyone managed to prepare food with little more than a feeble gas jet and the firelight from an indifferent blaze. Presumably domestic servants who live subterranean existences in large houses are like cats and of necessity have to develop their faculties for hunting in the dark.

'Oh yes, the master likes it cleaned every time he uses it, at least twice a week according to him, but being on notice, I forgot and I wasn't reminded by the mistress before she left.' Her cold, he noticed was worse, and her voice fainter than ever. 'I've had a lot to do, so it got left. The master complained the other day. Just like a man, never notice anything but what's wrong. Suddenly he was shouting about how dirty it was. I sent Ina out but she couldn't get it clean. The upholstery was badly marked.'

'Have you any idea what caused the marks?'

She shrugged. 'Couldn't really say, Inspector. I said to Ina when it wouldn't come out that it might be blood. She said she'd faint. But I said with his work, what can you expect? I told her salt's the thing that moves blood, works every time.'

So that piece of evidence which could have been damning might also have disappeared.

'Is there anything else I can do for you, sir?'

'I would like to have another look at Mrs Kellar's bedroom.'

She nodded. 'I'm sure that will be all right, Inspector. You know the way. I'll come up directly.'

He was glad of the chance to look around alone, but that quick inspection told him nothing. Everything was pristine, neat, as it had been the first time. He had a quick look in the wardrobe and the drawers opened without noise. He closed them almost hastily, with an apologetic feeling of guilt at the idea of examining all those elegant, lace-bedecked items of intimate feminine attire.

If Mrs Kellar was unhappy then it wasn't from the lack of worldly possessions and he thought of his dear Lizzie with sudden compassion. In all their married life she never possessed more than 'one for best, two for everyday'. The sad thing was that she felt that three of everything was a matter for pride, not deprivation.

Again he touched the silver brushes, toilette set and locked jewel case. Faro lifted it and it felt heavy. Perhaps that was the reason she had left it behind.

He stared at his own reflection in the mirror and saw Mrs Flynn watching him, her stout shape framed by the door.

'Everything all right, sir?'

'Seems to be.' He felt the statement needed further qualification and added, 'Always have to have a second look, you know.'

Waiting for him to leave, she closed the door and followed him downstairs. As Faro picked up his hat, she took from the hall table a newspaper, and opened it so as not to disturb the folds. 'I often have a quick glance, before the master sees it. I wonder if you can tell me what this is all about?'

She handed the folded paper to him and he read:

89

Gruesome Discovery on Railway Line

A railway worker Ian Brown of Longniddry today discovered a large parcel containing a woman's sable cloak of considerable value and a carving knife, lying by the side of the line at Longniddry Station. Both items which had lain under the snow for several days were heavily stained with blood and Edinburgh City Police have been called in to investigate this discovery.

Faro returned it to her and she said anxiously, 'The mistress was wearing her sable cloak, as you know, when she went to North Berwick. Has this anything to do with her disappearance?'

'We're looking into it, Mrs Flynn, that is all I can tell you at the moment.'

'Ina will have told you that one of the carving knives has gone.'

'Yes, she did.' Faro hoped his reply was unconcerned.

'Oh, well, I suppose that's all right then.'

She sounded relieved and Faro smiled. 'Carving knives aren't exactly unique, Mrs Flynn.'

He didn't want to scare the woman or Ina or let them get the impression that they were living in a house where the master had done in the mistress and, knowing his terrible temper, they might be next on the list.

Making sure that he was unobserved, Faro made a detour to the coach-house. The door was unlocked and the brougham was sparkling clean, the air redolent with the smell of cleaning fluid. He inspected the upholstery with its barely visible stains. There was no way of identifying the faint yellow marks now or testing out the new experiments Vince had told him about, of distinguishing human and animal blood.

Faro hailed a passing cab near the Grange. Unless Dr Kellar could produce a convincing alibi, things looked black indeed for him and as Faro was set down outside

Surgeons Hall, he had a feeling they weren't going to get any brighter for a very long time.

He did not relish the forthcoming interview. Kellar had deliberately misled them regarding his presence at a lecture on the morning his wife disappeared. If that was a sign of guilt, then he must be in a greater panic than they had realised.

There was also the matter of the bloodstained carriage. If this had been the result of Kellar's grisly murder of his wife, most likely on the way to North Berwick, then he was behaving in a remarkably naive fashion by drawing attention to it.

From his own experience with police procedure, Kellar must be perfectly aware that in a murder case, the victim's spouse is always the first, and most likely, suspect. Faro could only make the excuse of Kellar's notorious vanity, his assumption that his own connection with the Edinburgh City Police, a knighthood in the offing, rendered him beyond suspicion.

Chapter Nine

Faro's arrival coincided with Kellar emerging from the dissecting room, whose odours heavily disguised with antiseptic still clung to him, an unpleasant miasma. He did not look overjoyed at Faro's presence and walked briskly down the corridor. Without lessening his pace, he looked over his shoulder, demanded brusquely, 'Well, and what do you want?'

Faro groaned inwardly. This was hardly a promising start. 'Only a few facts to check, sir.' He tried in vain to sound nonchalant. 'If you will be so good as to spare me the time.'

'Very well,' said Kellar. 'Follow me. You know the way.' Ushered into the miserable room that served as office, Faro was not invited to be seated, an indication, he gathered, that this interview was unwelcome and was not to be prolonged a moment longer than necessary.

'What is it now, Inspector?' Kellar asked impatiently. 'As you can see, I'm a busy man.'

'I went to your house earlier today hoping to see you there.'

Kellar smiled grimly, seeing through this flimsy excuse. 'I am always at Surgeons Hall during the working week at this hour. You should know that, Inspector.'

'But not on Mondays apparently,' Faro reminded him.

'Mondays?' As if a new thought struck him, Kellar said, 'Mondays – no, as a matter of fact, I'm not.'

'So you weren't lecturing at all on the day you took your wife to the station to catch the North Berwick train.'

Kellar gave an impatient shrug. 'No. Obviously I wasn't.'

'Then why, sir, did you indicate—'

Kellar interrupted with an impatient gesture. 'Indicate? I indicated nothing. It was mere aberration, that's all. I forgot completely what day of the week it was.'

Faro tried not to look as disbelieving as he felt. Strange that a husband should forget the day of the week that his wife disappeared. One would imagine such information would be indelibly fixed.

'You let your wife believe that you were going to be late for a lecture.'

Kellar's head jerked up sharply. 'How do you know what I let my wife believe, Faro?'

'You were overheard outside your front door.'

'Overheard? By domestics, I suppose.' Kellar raised his eyes heavenward in a despairing gesture. 'Wasting time spying on their betters when they should be going about their business, which is what we pay them for. This is outrageous, Inspector.'

Faro ignored Kellar's growing anger. 'Perhaps you could remember where you spent the afternoon of Monday, 16th January. That would be of considerable help.'

'Help? Help, in what way?' Kellar sounded surprised and then seeing Faro's sternly guarded expression, he laughed softly. 'Oh, I see. I see. So what do you want me to tell you?'

'Anything that would account for your movements, sir.'

'An alibi, is that it?' Kellar sounded faintly amused.

'Yes, sir, as you know that is quite usual.'

'Usual, in what way usual?'

Kellar wasn't going to make it easy, thought Faro. Every move would have to be laboriously spelled out.

'Just so that you can be cleared—'

Kellar's eyebrows shot upwards. 'Cleared? Do I take it from that remark, you are hinting that I – I am under suspicion, that you seriously believe I had something to do with my wife's disappearance.'

When Faro could think of no suitable reply that evaded the truth, Kellar shouted, 'My God, man, how dare you make such a vile assumption. This is preposterous, do you hear? Preposterous.'

'So is murder, sir.' And in an effort to calm him, Faro added quickly, 'As a police surgeon you know that such enquiries are routine and that everyone connected with a murder victim, especially his or her own household, is under suspicion.'

'Aren't you presuming rather a lot, Inspector?'

'We'll only know that, sir, when we find your wife's murderer.'

'Or her body.'

Faro thought he detected a gleam of satisfaction in Kellar's eyes as he added, 'Don't let us forget the absence of that vital ingredient, the *corpus delicti*.'

'I don't think anyone, not even you, sir, could dispute the fact that the evidence up to now looks uncommonly like foul play.'

Kellar sobered at once. 'I see,' he said slowly and, thrusting out his upper lip, he gazed steadily at the ceiling as if words of inspiration might suddenly appear across its grimy expanse. 'I mostly spend Mondays doing work of my own, in my study. So I expect that is how I was occupied when I returned from the railway station.'

'Presumably Mrs Flynn or the housemaid would be able to confirm this, sir.'

'Of course they would not,' said Kellar irritably. 'It is my policy to assiduously avoid contact with domestics at all times.'

His tone of distaste made it sound like avoidance of lepers. 'When I go to my study and I am working on a paper or lecture notes, I am not to be disturbed. My instructions are very strict on that point. I may only be approached in direst necessity.'

'What about meal times, sir?'

Kellar stared at him as if the suggestion was mad or

highly improper. 'I communicate with domestics by leaving notes on the hall table.'

'Did you do so that day?'

Kellar looked at him narrowly. 'You know, Inspector, I really can't remember.' He paused and then added triumphantly. 'Oh yes, I can. Now it comes back to me. I didn't return home. I had an errand to do for my wife. Of course, of course.'

That was safe enough, thought Faro grimly. And difficult to confirm or deny in the prevailing circumstances. 'What kind of an errand would that be?' he asked.

'I was to take some garments across to her friend Mrs Shaw in Regent Crescent. The housekeeper had been given instructions to clear out the attic and while so doing had come across some infant garments.' He paused and added hurriedly, 'From the early years of our marriage when we had, er, anticipations. Mabel is very well disposed towards Mrs Shaw, and wished her to have these for her wee boy.'

A longer pause followed while Kellar smiled at Faro, as if inviting comment on such generosity. Then in his sudden burst of laughter, Faro thought he detected relief.

'Of course I had forgotten because it was all so unimportant. I had dismissed it from my mind entirely. After I set Mrs Kellar down at the station, I drove directly to Mrs Shaw's home. As a token of her gratitude, she was kind enough to offer me luncheon.'

Frowning, he thought for a moment. 'I found her greatly in need of fresh air, to cheer her spirits. So I took her and little Barnaby for a drive, well wrapped up, of course. We had to cut it short when the snow began to fall rather heavily again. I dined at the Surgeons' Club that evening. You can easily confirm this, if you wish.'

He looked across at Faro. 'Well, Inspector, are you satisfied?'

'It helps considerably, Dr Kellar.'

'No doubt you will wish to speak to Mrs Shaw. I am

sure she will remember the afternoon we spent together.'

Faro thanked him and left, resolving to interview Mrs Shaw immediately, before Kellar had a chance to communicate with her, on the unlikely chance that the two were in collusion.

He made his way on foot as swiftly as possible down the High Street, his progress impeded by the maze of luckenbooths. He had forgotten that this was market day. The din of stall-keepers yelling their wares, combined with smells of fish and vegetables and many less agreeable human odours made concentration impossible.

Walking in the direction of Regent Crescent, head down against the icy blast from the Firth of Forth, Faro saw the Palace and Abbey of Holyroodhouse stripped of all romance. Inadequately sheltered by skeletal trees whose feeble thin branches moaned back and forth in a pathetic protest against the sleet-like rain, the scene was one of direst misery, a monument of inescapable mourning for a Scotland lost for ever with the passing of the Stuarts.

With Mrs Shaw's house in view, Faro mentally rehearsed the forthcoming interview, bearing in mind the new turn of events. If Kellar had gone directly to Mrs Shaw's and spent most of the afternoon with her, then he could not possibly have murdered his wife.

And if not Kellar, then who? With an alibi for the main suspect, this would cease to be an open and shut case. The net must be opened wide to admit the usual exhaustive routine enquiries, for identity and possible motives of murderer or murderers, as well as her missing body. A bleak prospect indeed, Faro suspected, with a trail already cold as the snow which had so conveniently hidden the first evidence of possible murder.

Regent Crescent overlooked the grounds of Holyrood Palace and he soon identified the handsome Georgian house in which Mrs Eveline Shaw lived, by the grand piano in the window. Faro thought himself fortunate to have found her at home or, more correctly, encamped around a rather small fire. They made a pretty picture playing on the rug together, the lovely fair-haired young mother, the sturdy baby with his expressive velvet brown eyes, but they needed a gentler, less forbidding setting. Piano apart, the large drawing-room with its lofty ceiling could have accommodated a whole floor of Sheridan Place. Sparsely furnished, it suggested that the tenant had newly taken up residence.

There was none of the solid furniture, the family portraits, the photographs draped with mourning that he would have expected to find in the home of an affluent young widow whose officer husband had died recently fighting for Queen and country on the Indian frontier.

Mrs Shaw observed Faro's expression and in a wide gesture which indicated the rest of the house, said, 'It is really too big for me and Barnaby and the maid. We occupy only one floor.'

An unfortunate choice of establishment in her melancholy circumstances, thought Faro, needing a whole staff of servants to keep it warm and homely.

As if she read his mind she said, 'Perhaps I should find a tenant for the upper floor and the basement.' She paused to look hard at Faro, making him wonder if she was seeking his advice. 'I might wait until things sort themselves out. At the moment, I haven't the slightest idea what the future holds,' she added with a sigh.

The baby, neglected, issued a piercing yell of indignation and Mrs Shaw rushed to pick him up. 'This is Barnaby, Inspector. Say hello, Barnaby.'

Barnaby was a fine sturdy lad, six months old. Faro knelt down. The sight and warm smell of newly-bathed baby overcame him with the nostalgia for his own now distant fatherhood.

'Hello, young fellow.' But Barnaby wasn't in the mood to be friendly and tried to obliterate himself by burrowing into his mother's shoulder. Faro was disappointed. He was fond of babies, especially good-natured ones. He had loved his two wee girls at that age. Now they were growing up away from him in Orkney, ever faster every day.

When he said so, Mrs Shaw smiled sympathetically. 'You must miss them, Inspector. Barnaby is very good, but a little shy. He doesn't see many strangers.'

'I dare say you find it lonely here.'

'Lonely?' She stared at him.

'Without your husband.'

'Oh yes. Yes, I do. Very lonely.'

'What regiment was Captain Shaw with?'

'The Caithness Regiment.'

From his mother's arms, Barnaby lunged towards Faro's watch-chain. Faro grinned, grasping the tiny starfish hand firmly. 'Got you, young fellow. I get your little game. Snatch and grab, is that it?'

Barnaby gurgled and retreated again into his mother's shoulder.

'He's a fine lad. He must be a great comfort to you.'

'Oh yes,' agreed Mrs Shaw, studying the loose thread on the baby's petticoat. A tap on the door announced the maid. 'Off you go now. Bessie will give you some milk.' She paused to plant a kiss on his forehead, then they both waved as he was whisked away, gurgling happily, by the maid.

'What about your late husband's family?'

'What about them?' she asked sharply.

'Do they see much of Barnaby?'

'Hardly. They live up north.'

'Far away?'

'Caithness.'

'That is a long way.'

'Yes.'

'Do they come often to Edinburgh?'

'Why should they?' Again her voice sounded oddly sharp, as if the question irritated her.

'They must be pleased to have such a fine handsome grandson.'

Her face softened. 'Oh yes, they are.'

A long silence followed and Faro, looking at Mrs Shaw, decided this was going to be a difficult interview. Drawing conversation promised to be what was known in Orkney as 'hard as drawing hen's teeth'.

He was puzzled by the lovely face, which should have added up to a beautiful young woman, but his first impression returned. At the Kellar's dinner party, he had mistaken that rather vacant preoccupied stare for grief. Now he wasn't quite so sure about whatever emotions, if any, she had bottled up behind that spectacular façade. What had Vince called it: Like talking to a beautiful stone statue. He wondered about those Caithness in-laws, had they disapproved of the match?

'I am anxious for news of Mabel, Inspector.'

'I was hoping you might have heard from her.'

Mrs Shaw shook her head.

'You have had no communication from her?'

She seemed surprised by the question. 'None at all. I was very shocked when Dr Kellar called to tell me that she had never been to North Berwick.'

'When did he tell you that?'

'Oh, ages ago.' She shrugged. 'More than a week. Mabel is very fond of me and, naturally, this was the very first place he came to seek her.' She paused and then said, 'It doesn't seem a bit like her, you know. Such a considerate person, not the kind who would willingly cause anyone a moment's anxiety.' She frowned. 'I wonder where on earth she can be?'

Faro decided to say nothing of the cloak and the knife at this stage. Presumably she hadn't read the newspaper.

'You have no idea what has happened to her, Inspector?'

The idea that Faro had was now almost a certainty. But he dismissed it as much too cruel and brutal to put to Mrs Kellar's 'dearest friend and companion'. A man who shied away from womanly tears at the best of times, he did not care for the prospect of dealing with a hysterical woman whose best friend has been murdered.

'I came here in the hope that she might have confided in you sometime. Mentioned friends she could be visiting . . .'

'Without telling Dr Kellar?' Mrs Shaw sounded shocked. 'She told him everything. As for pretending to go to North Berwick and then going somewhere else and staying away and frightening everyone, as I've told you, Inspector, she wasn't that sort of woman at all.'

Faro sighed deeply. There was no way of shielding her from the unpleasant truth. 'I have to tell you that Mrs Kellar's disappearance is being regarded as a very serious matter by the City Police. And if, as a close friend of hers, you know of anything, no matter how insignificant, that might shed some light on her whereabouts, then I must prevail upon you to tell me.'

Mrs Shaw frowned. 'I cannot think of a single thing that would be of any help. You know as much as I do. I am so sorry, it has been rather a waste of your time coming to me.'

'Not at all. I came at Dr Kellar's suggestion.'

Mrs Shaw coloured slightly. Her expression was fleetingly angry. 'So he told you to come here—'

Her voice rising in indignation made Faro interrupt hastily, 'We have to take everything into account, no matter how seemingly obvious or trivial.' Preparing her for what followed, he paused before adding, 'I gather from Dr Kellar that he spent part of the day that Mrs Kellar disappeared here with you. A minor detail, I'm sure, but necessary for our information.'

Confusion had overtaken anger and she hung her head. 'Mabel sometimes sends messages by him if he is to be in this area.'

'And was it a message he brought that day?'

She looked embarrassed. 'Something of the sort. Yes.'

'Could you be a little more explicit, Mrs Shaw?'

'Mabel had sent me some baby clothes for Barnaby. She is very kind to us.'

'Did Dr Kellar stay long?'

She frowned. 'About an hour or so.'

'I understand you gave him lunch and then he took you and the baby for a drive that afternoon,' Faro reminded her gently.

Mrs Shaw looked as if she was trying hard to remember. 'Yes – yes, of course.' Her second affirmative was more convincing than the first. 'Why all these questions? I know nothing of Mabel's whereabouts. As for hiding her,' she continued, her colour heightening, 'the house is yours to search, Inspector. Please go and satisfy your curiosity. There are no locked doors, only a lot of very empty rooms.'

Her voice was pathetic suddenly and Faro said assuringly, 'Please, Mrs Shaw, there is no need to upset yourself. I believe you.'

'That's a relief. You see, Mrs Kellar has been very friendly towards me, but I cannot think of one good reason why she should want to leave her own very comfortable house and take refuge in mine. Just look around you, Inspector,' she added bitterly. 'You can see how little there is here for a woman of quality.'

'I'm sorry to have wasted your time, Mrs Shaw, but we have to speak to all her friends and acquaintances. Dr Kellar is very anxious that she should be found.'

He did not add that the main purpose of his visit to check Kellar's alibi, had been successful. As he was leaving, he paused by the grand piano with its sheaves of music. 'You are to be congratulated on your playing, Mrs Shaw. It was a great pleasure, most exciting to hear your rendering of the Beethoven. I wonder, have you ever performed in public?'

'You mean on the concert platform? Oh no. I did consider it at one time, but that is rather a long story and a long time ago.'

Unless she was much older than she looked it couldn't have been all that long ago, thought Faro, suddenly curious.

'Have you thought of taking in pupils?' he asked delicately.

'I might. When Barnaby is a little older.'

Faro detected little enthusiasm for that idea. As she was showing him out, he had one more question: 'By the way, did you happen to meet anyone who knew you – any friend or neighbour – when you and Dr Kellar were out driving together two weeks ago?'

Again she coloured, this time angrily. Her eyes widened in the dawn of a new and horrifying realisation. 'You surely – you can't – you don't imagine for a moment that Dr Kellar would – would – would harm dear Mabel? The idea is preposterous. He is your police surgeon.'

As she leaned weakly against the banister, Faro felt suddenly avuncular towards the pitifully young and helplessly inadequate woman. He patted her shoulder, murmured to her not to worry, it would be all sorted out and left as sharply as politeness allowed.

As he walked swiftly down the hill overlooking the ruined and ancient Abbey and the modern railway line, Faro had a feeling that there were some curious omissions from Mrs Shaw's statements.

Her shocked realisation that Dr Kellar was under suspicion seemed genuine enough. Obviously she had no idea yet that Mabel Kellar's disappearance was being treated as murder. Of that he was certain. But he was also left with a clear impression that Mrs Shaw was not as fond of Mabel Kellar as he had first thought, or as the latter had implied during the dinner party. Eveline Shaw did not reciprocate the older woman's affection or see her in the role of 'sister of the spirit'. Doubtless she encouraged that fond illusion for the benefits that might accrue in her present unhappy situation.

Her home troubled him deeply. The absence of any

mementoes implied that Mrs Shaw was very much on her own. Was this indicative that the marriage had been against the wishes of her husband's family? And had they turned their faces away from their son's young widow and their grandchild?

Although at present Faro was aware of no motive to connect Mrs Shaw with Mabel Kellar's disappearance, his natural curiosity suggested that her present circumstances might bear further investigation.

Leaving the house, he had observed several 'For Sale' boards and that they were being negotiated through the firm of Troup and Knowles. Alex Troup was an old friend. Where better to begin a few discreet enquiries about the enigmatic Mrs Shaw?

Chapter Ten

At the Central Office, he learned that Sergeant Danny McQuinn had been assigned to help him in the Kellar enquiry. McQuinn had fallen foul of a stray bullet in a dramatic chase across the Pentland Hills and an indulgent Superintendent McIntosh had sent him to County Kerry to recuperate among his numerous relatives.

Once upon a time, Faro would have prayed that the Kellar case would be over before McQuinn returned. But he found his past antipathy dwindling. They had brought to justice several fraud cases recently and although Faro often found McQuinn obnoxious, too eager for admiration from the ladies and for promotion at all costs, he had a grudging respect for McQuinn's efficiency and recognised a detective in the making.

Nevertheless the sight of the sergeant making himself very much at home in his office during his absence revived feelings of profound irritation. It was as if McQuinn, his junior by nearly twenty years, already saw himself ousting Faro as Senior Detective Inspector. What was worse, Faro suspected that the young officer was eagerly anticipating retired − or dead man's − shoes, whichever came first in the annals of daily crime with the Edinburgh City Police.

McQuinn looked up cheekily, tapped out his pipe, removed his feet from the desk, while a grunt of disapproval from his superior officer acknowledged the exaggeratedly smart salute.

'You've recovered, I see.'

'Yes, sir. Just a flesh wound. Nothing that good old

Kerry air couldn't cure. I reported for duty this morning. Superintendent told me about our police surgeon's wife and that you might need some help. Gave me all your notes to read. An extraordinarily interesting case, Inspector, not at all what we might have expected from Dr Kellar. What was it – a brainstorm? Seems to have possibilities of an early arrest.'

'Don't know about that,' said Faro shortly. 'But you can begin with a visit to the railway station—'

'I've already been down to Waverley, talked to the porters,' interrupted McQuinn. 'No sense in waiting until you got back.'

'Find out anything?' Again Faro felt unnecessary annoyance at having his orders forestalled.

'One porter thought that a woman answering Mrs Kellar's description took the North Berwick train that morning. Very upset, in tears, he thought.'

'I've already spoken to him. The woman in question was leaving her husband and had a wee lad with her.'

'Might not have been the same woman,' said McQuinn defensively.

'That's what you're expected to find out, McQuinn. The first question you should ask is: was she alone?'

McQuinn, obviously put out at being thwarted of his first useful contribution to the enquiry, ignored the implied reprimand. He stood up, stretched lazily, flexing his shoulders.

'I thought I'd take myself off to Longniddry and have a look round there.'

Faro was scribbling a few notes. 'You might begin with some routine enquiries here. You know the sort of thing we're after. Check the Surgeons' Club. See if anyone remembers seeing him that night.'

McQuinn scanned the notes and looked across at Faro. 'This Mrs Shaw? Is she to be regarded as a suspect?'

Faro shook his head. 'Not at this stage. But I'd like to know more about her husband's family. Also when the house in Regent Crescent was purchased.'

McQuinn grinned. 'And who by, eh? Just idle curiosity, sir?'

'You should know by now that my curiosity is never idle, McQuinn,' was the stern reply.

At the door McQuinn paused. 'I don't know about you, Inspector, but something tells me there's a lot of evidence in that report of yours and nothing that really adds up worth a damn. I feel the answer might still be down at Longniddry.'

Faro's homeward journey took him close by Solomon's Tower. It stood bleak and ruinous against the skyline, dramatised by the snow-clad Salisbury Crags and Arthur's Seat. Nearly as old as the Palace of Holyroodhouse itself, Faro noticed that, as usual, its dark towers were festooned with the ragged black shapes of crows, eternally circling. Corbies, the legendary birds of ill omen; there was an element of the sinister in their hovering. What strange vigil, its reason lost in time, brought them there? What fascination lay in that domain far below, occupied by one old man and his multitude of cats?

Fighting weariness, for it had been a long day and hard walking underfoot on the packed snow, Faro decided to save a further journey by calling on Sir Hedley.

At first he thought the door was to remain unopened. When at last he heard the old man's heavy footfalls, he realised that the off-chance of Mabel Kellar's flight having taken her to this inhospitable dwelling was well beyond the bounds of credibility. Mrs Shaw had pointed out the disadvantages of Regent Crescent as a refuge, but her house represented a paradise of luxury compared to Solomon's Tower.

As within keys were turned and bolts withdrawn, the thought of stepping inside almost defeated Faro. He lingered on the doorstep. Only someone in the most desperate straits, a criminal fleeing from justice, might have run to earth, seeking shelter behind these grim grey walls. The interior smelt worse than ever and he was engulfed in a wave of cats, scampering, jumping, sliding, all in a wild rush for the fresh air, they leaped from all directions as if to escape from the dreadful odours within.

Sir Hedley's broad smile at discovering his visitor's identity revealed gums long beyond memory of teeth. 'Come in, Inspector. Most welcome, most welcome. You'll take a dram.'

Ushered along the corridor and holding his breath, Faro followed the old man into the sitting-room, thinking wryly as he did so that there was, at that moment, nothing fitting the description of 'sitting-room' available. Each seat had a cat or cats already installed, curled up and sleeping. Apart from that peaceful feline scene of somnolence, the room looked as if it had been subjected to the tender mercies of burglars, carried off by an unexpected hurricane sweeping through the house.

Faro repressed a shudder. He was by nature inclined to tidiness, except in his own study, and now he tried to avert his eyes and his nose from matters which did not concern him. His main concern was for Sir Hedley. The old man seemed far from well. His creaky breathing sounded like the turning of rusty wheels, clearly audible across the room. Occasionally rusty wheels became a deep-seated cough which seemed to emanate from the soles of his ancient boots.

Handing over a whisky glass of finest crystal but sadly in need of washing, Sir Hedley apologised, patting his chest. 'A touch of the old trouble. Lungs bad, y'know.'

Faro decided that he looked very seedy indeed. He was perspiring freely and his face had a leaden appearance.

'You look as if you're running a fever, sir. You really should see a doctor,' he said sternly.

Sir Hedley frowned. 'Thinking the same thing. Have to see someone.' Again he patted his breastbone. 'Hate doctors, can't abide them. Have to keep going though. My cats, y'know. Rely on me,' he added pathetically and giving

107

Faro a speculative stare. 'Thinking of calling on your young fella for advice.'

Faro thought at first that this was a joke, but Sir Hedley was in earnest.

'Took a liking to the lad. Seemed genuine. Clever too. No larking about.' He paused. 'What do you think, Inspector?'

Faro could only reply somewhat lamely, 'Of course, sir. I'll get him to come by and take a look at you.'

Sir Hedley brightened. 'Will you? Extremely good of you. Bottle is all that's needed. Clear it up in no time.' Then he laid a hand on Faro's arm. 'Be a great favour to me. A great favour.' And lifting the glass, 'Slàinte!'

'Slàinte, sir!' They drank in silence.

'Suppose you're here about my niece,' said Sir Hedley.

When Faro said that was indeed the reason, the old man nodded. 'Thought so. Bad business. Bad business,' and shaking his head sadly, 'Haven't seen her since the party.'

So that was that. Faro didn't doubt for a moment that he spoke the truth. A few minutes' polite talk and then he could decently make his escape and breathe freely once more in the open air. He accepted another dram.

'When did you hear about Mrs Kellar?'

'Oh, Melville came by. Week ago. Demanding to know if I was hiding her.' His laugh changed into a deep cough. 'Used to look in sometimes. Brought me things. Food. Saw that I was all right. Kind gal.'

He stopped and gave Faro a long look. 'Can't imagine her coming here, can you? Can you?'

'Not really, sir,' said Faro uncomfortably.

'Of course not. Doesn't like cats,' added Sir Hedley in tones of righteous surprise and indignation.

'May I ask you something rather personal, sir? Did Mrs Kellar ever give you any hint that she wasn't happy?'

Sir Hedley thought about that. 'Sometimes had a feeling

that all wasn't well with Melville. Bit of a rascal, if you ask me.'

'In what way?'

'The way men are, Inspector. Women and so forth.'

'Did she confide something of the sort?'

Sir Hedley rubbed the end of his nose. 'No, never. Loyal as they come. As I said, just a feeling I had. Y'know, something wrong.'

When Faro reached home Vince was waiting for him. His first question: 'Well, any news of Mabel?'

'Nothing, lad.'

'She hasn't been to Eveline Shaw's?'

Vince listened anxiously as Faro outlined briefly his visit to Regent Crescent and his own reactions to the young widow.

'Now you understand why I found the relationship between Mabel and Eveline so extraordinary,' said Vince triumphantly. 'Your matchmaking idea was absolute nonsense.' Then, regarding his stepfather quizzically, 'Wait a minute – unless you were the lucky man?'

'You're not trying to say that Mabel was matchmaking Mrs Shaw with me. Come along, lad. Now who's talking nonsense.'

'I'm not, Stepfather. It's quite true. Now I realise how distant she was with me, how very uninterested. It's all coming back. You were the one she talked to most.'

'If that was most, it was very little. And only because I praised the Beethoven. Good Lord, Vince, I'm old enough to be her father. She's more your age than mine.'

Vince nodded and regarded Faro approvingly. 'And I hope I look as good as you do when I'm approaching forty.' When his stepfather snorted in disbelief, Vince continued sagely, 'It's true, and you know it. Be modest if you like, but you know and I know that a man who is attractive to the opposite sex is like a good wine – he only improves with the years. Besides when did age make any difference?'

'If I'm not mistaken, we seem to have had this conversation before and quite recently,' said Faro coldly.

Vince paused and grinned impishly. 'Oh yes, indeed. About a certain young miss from Canada.'*

'And we all know how that ended.'

'Well, it should have proved to you that some young ladies prefer older men.' A moment later, he asked, 'What was Eveline Shaw's late husband like, I wonder?'

'I have no idea.'

'No regimental photograph? Really, you surprise me. There's a great vogue these days for officers having a group photograph. And what about his lovely wife? Surely he would want to take her likeness on active service with him.'

'He may well have done so, but there were no mementoes of any kind. Nothing personal about the room at all, in fact. It was as if Mrs Shaw and her baby were living in a rather expensive but not very comfortable hotel.'

'How very curious. Nothing to remind her of the gallant Captain. I wonder if they had any contact or were even happy together in what must have been quite a brief marriage.'

'Considering the baby, who is a fine wee chap, they must have had contact at some time.'

'Yes, but I wonder if their communication existed outside the bedroom.' Vince thought for a moment and then asked, 'How did the stunning Mrs Shaw strike you on second meeting, Stepfather?'

'Not very much different from the first time, I'm afraid.'

'I suppose there are lots of females exactly like Eveline Shaw and perhaps some men are quite content with a beautiful package.'

'I'm sure that is the rule rather than the exception, lad.'

'I'm given to understand that we are now in danger of

* *Blood Line*

110

a new breed of womankind, who are no longer content to be treated as domestic slaves.'

'Aye, but most men, particularly of my generation, disapprove very strongly of such a preposterous idea. They consider that their hereditary rights, inherited from Adam, are being threatened.'

'I like the idea of this new woman, Stepfather, outrageous as it may seem. If I ever took a wife then I'd want more than a beautiful doll to undress and take to bed every night. I'd want more than begetting and procreation and stern reminders about conjugal rights.'

'Not all men are so demanding, Vince. Many just want that pretty doll who in time fulfils the functions of providing bed and board and a litter of sons and daughters.'

'Not for me, Stepfather. I believe that wives should be regarded as rather higher than breeding cattle. And if I ever find the right woman, I'd like to feel that we shared everything, the better and the worse. Especially on the intellectual plane, a sense of minds being united as well as bodies.'

'"Let me not to the marriage of true minds admit impediments",' quoted Faro.

'The Bard knew all about love, didn't he?'

'Yes, but I think the Moor of Venice probably tells us more about poor Mabel and Dr Kellar than the Sonnets.'

'True, Stepfather, sadly true. Mabel adored him and he treated her like the ground under his feet.' Vince looked thoughtful. 'Although I can't yet take in the idea of him murdering her. To me, it is still quite fantastic, beyond the bounds of belief, although I have a sneaking hope that he might be made to suffer a little bit. Teach the arrogant bastard a well-needed lesson.'

There was no way Faro could avoid telling Vince about the visit to the Kellar house and the implications of the bloodstained upholstery in the carriage.

'Oh my God,' whispered Vince, his face paling.

'It sounds bad, I know, lad. But let's not spring to

111

conclusions. It could have been from game he'd shot, or a rabbit, just like the maid said. If he was guilty in the way you are imagining, then don't you think he would have tried to remove the stains himself and not made a great fuss about the condition of the carriage.'

'True enough, except that he thinks of domestics as a sub-human species, incapable of the same feelings and presumably the same imagination as the rest of mortals.' Vince was silent before continuing: 'If only we could discover where those stains came from.'

'This German doctor you were telling me about? The one who is experimenting on blood types.'

'Doctor Landois. He was visiting Walter when I was in Vienna and we had a long chat. Of course, his experiments are still in the early stages, but he's quite convinced that he has made an important scientific discovery.'

Vince leaned across the table. 'When he heard that my stepfather was concerned with murder, he grew tremendously excited. Kept telling me how invaluable it would be some day in the detection of crimes. Insisted I should know what the procedure entailed. I have it written down somewhere.'

'That might come in very useful, lad, if you'd like to try it out. Not on the carriage upholstery. Too late for that but on the fur cloak.'

'I know it sounds very far-fetched, but if Landois's experiments are successful, he reckons that human blood also falls into several different groups and that it is completely different from the composition of animal blood.'

'If your doctor is right and blood differs from one human being to another, then this could open a new phase for the police,' said Faro excitedly.

'I've been thinking along life-giving lines rather than the hangman's rope,' said Vince drily. 'The transfusion of blood from one human to another could save a patient's life. Someone who has lost a lot of blood in an accident, or a woman in childbirth. We encounter this every day and

112

we just have to stand back and helplessly watch them just bleed to death.'

'It's a fascinating theory, Vince. Let's hope there's something in it.'

'Perhaps I could have a look at poor Mabel's cloak?'

'And the knife too. Although I'd better warn you, what we might call the evidence has been diluted by lying under the snow for a couple of weeks.'

'If they were wrapped up, as you say, then I think there'll be enough remaining to give some interesting results.'

'I hope you're right.'

'Do you realise, Stepfather, that in the normal way, this would become the province of the police surgeon.'

'In these circumstances,' said Faro hastily, 'I think it would be advisable to bypass the good doctor.'

'How did he react to the bloodstained brougham?'

'Too late to tackle him on that, but I dare say he'd have some glib explanation.'

'I've just remembered something, Stepfather. On two occasions when I had luncheon with Mabel, Kellar had been out shooting for the pot. She was very proud of his marksmanship. Didn't seem to regard it as a curious choice of leisure pursuit for a man who spends his time up to the elbows in blood almost every day.'

He gave a shudder of distaste. 'Frankly, though, I can't see Dr Kellar coming home in his carriage from Surgeons Hall dripping blood anyway. He always leaves well-scrubbed. Although some doctors are careless about such things and don't bother, Kellar is most meticulous. You wouldn't find him wearing his butcher's apron, as they call it, outside the dissecting room.'

As Mrs Brook came in with the supper, Faro reminded Vince about the Beethoven concert at the Assembly Rooms. 'It's Hallé conducting and the divine Neruda playing the Beethoven violin concerto.'

'Oh, Stepfather. I can't. It's Rob's twenty-first and there's a celebration arranged. I am sorry.'

113

'Oh, don't worry about it, lad. I dare say I'll find someone at the Central Office to accompany me.' But Faro doubted that. His taste in music was considered a little bizarre.

Instead of being content with promenading in Princes Street Gardens and listening, or rather only half-listening, above the constant chatter, to the military brass bands, Faro parted with a precious shilling for the luxury of sitting down in the Assembly Rooms and listening with rapt attention to a full orchestra. He knew that such activity caused much whispered comment among his colleagues. They regarded frequenting concert halls as a recreation belonging to the higher strata of Edinburgh society and, as such, not quite the thing for a detective inspector.

'How are the rest of your enquiries going, Stepfather? Where next?'

'I called in at Solomon's Tower.'

'Ah, my favourite suspect.' Vince's grimace warned Faro that he was not going to be greatly impressed at having to set foot in Solomon's Tower to examine Sir Hedley as a patient.

Faro was right and Vince swore.

'Sorry, lad, I let you in for it.'

'I suppose such a challenge is good for my soul. Having to remember the Hippocratic Oath and all that sort of thing. Even when wicked old devils are concerned.'

'Look, you make up a bottle of medicine for his cough and I'll hand it in, explaining that you're busy.'

'Oh no, you won't, Stepfather. It's good of you to offer but very soon seeing patients is going to be my daily bread. I can't afford to be choosy and whether I love them or hate them will be a matter of total indifference. All my concern will be trying to make a damned good job of curing them. I dare say I'll get many just as offensive – worse, although I doubt that's possible, than I find the Mad Bart.'

He grinned. 'This will be a good first lesson in humility and I might as well get used to it. Besides, I'd feel terrible, knowing he's ill, if he died and I hadn't had a look at him.'

Once again Faro found Vince's attitude to the old man, without rhyme or reason, very hard to understand.

'Just natural antipathy to the ruling classes. And the fact I can never forget or overlook that I am some nobleman's by-blow. The enormity of such injustice,' he continued bitterly, 'that I should have had aristocratic birth. Gates of privilege that were closed upon my mother and myself for ever. And what my poor mother suffered. I care more about her deprivation than my own.'

Faro didn't answer. Vince had never stopped to think whether his poor mother was fitted by her own humble upbringing to step into the role of a nobleman's wife. Lizzie hadn't often talked to Faro about the past after the early days of their marriage when she said, 'Once a servant, always a servant. I would never be able to enjoy myself, thinking about washing the dishes and clearing up after the guests had gone.'

'Come now, Stepfather, be honest. Wouldn't you feel the same if you were me?' Vince demanded.

'I don't know much about noble blood, lad. I'm of good solid farming stock as far back as any of the family can remember.'

'Only as far as Lord Robert Stuart and his Royal bastards.'

Faro laughed. 'Everyone in Orkney claims descent from Mary Queen of Scots' wicked half-brother. Rather too distant to get bitter about, don't you think? Just another romantic myth.'

'Myth or no, I'd much rather be a poor peasant and have some respectable humble ploughman for a father, or a man like you, Stepfather,' he added softly, 'who loved my mother and married her, even if she did have a bastard son. She was used so cruelly, not even allowed the romantic illusion of love. The brutal savagery of rape begot me, let us never forget that.'

Suddenly he stretched his hand across the table, smiled tenderly. 'I'm an ungrateful beast. All this prattle about an aristocratic life. We might both have been utterly miserable.

After all, Mother would never have met you and neither would I.'

He paused and smiled. 'And I have you to thank for giving us both such a truly happy home life, Stepfather. The fact that you could rise above regarding my mother as a scarlet woman, a social outcast. That was wonderful, but then, Stepfather, that's what you are.'

'Oh come, lad,' said Faro uncomfortably. 'It wasn't just one way, you know. You turned out to be a fine son.' He shook his head sadly. 'The best a father could have, thank God.'

And turning the subject on to a lighter vein, he added teasingly, 'I haven't noticed you exactly avoiding the rich life when it comes your way.'

'Not at all. Some of my best college friends are rich and bone idle and I number a couple of baronets among them. I have nothing against the rich life, if you're lucky enough to land in it. But as I'm doomed to be for ever on the other side of the fence, I intend to succeed, prove to the world that I can rise above my bastard birth.'

Chapter Eleven

Despite Vince's conjectures, the lack of any real motive for
Mabel Kellar's murder continued to trouble Faro. What had
Kellar to gain? He did not have long to wait for an answer.
Mrs Brook brought him up a card as he was about to leave
for the Central Office.

'A Mrs Findlay-Cupar wishes to see you, Inspector. I've
put her in the drawing-room.' The housekeeper's hushed
voice and deferential manner suggested that the Inspector
need have no fears. This was quality, a 'real' lady.

'Mrs Findlay-Cupar.' As Faro took the hand of Mabel
Kellar's sister, he realised the cruelty of fate that distributed
astonishing good looks to one sister and none at all to the
other. Laetitia Findlay-Cupar and Mabel Kellar were alike
as sisters, their features almost identical. And there all similarity ended, for poor Mabel's pale colouring, lacklustre
eyes and hair had been a faded watercolour, a mocking
travesty of the vividly attractive woman before him.

'Forgive me calling on you informally, Inspector. My
reason will be made clear directly. I won't beat about the
bush. I have received news that may have some bearing on
my sister's disappearance.'

Taking the seat he offered, she smiled. 'Mabel talked
a great deal about your stepson and he talked to her, I
understand, a great deal about you.'

'I had the pleasure of meeting your sister, ma'am. On
the night before she er, left, there was a dinner party at
the Grange.'

Mrs Findlay-Cupar brightened. 'Oh, that is such a help.

It makes the favour I have to ask so much easier.' Pausing, she searched his countenance anxiously and then taking a deep breath, said, 'Inspector Faro, I am taking the liberty of asking if you would personally take on this case.'

'I am already doing so, ma'am.'

Mrs Findlay-Cupar looked first relieved and then afraid. 'Dare I ask you to tell me then, quite frankly, if you have the least notion where she is or what has become of her?' Her voice dropped to a whisper. 'Is she still alive and well?'

'We are making exhaustive enquiries, ma'am.' Faro hoped he was succeeding in expressing those reassurances he was far from feeling. 'Dr Kellar asked us to investigate immediately and we are inclined to take cases of missing persons very seriously.'

Mabel's sister leaned back in her chair. 'Oh, so he asked you. That is interesting.' She sat up again hastily and withdrew an envelope from her reticule. Frowning indecisively, she tapped it against the chair's arm.

'I think you ought to know, Inspector, that all was not well with my sister, there was something troubling her deeply. When I spent a few days at the Grange recently she was very tearful.'

'How recent was this?'

'Between Christmas and New Year. At first I thought it was because she was having problems finding a new housekeeper. Dr Kellar had been very disagreeable and they had lost a very valued old servant.'

'Yes, there were some problems at the dinner party. I gather from the new housekeeper that Dr Kellar is not the easiest of employers,' said Faro.

This visit from Mabel's sister was most opportune, he thought, having already made a shrewd assessment of the woman before him. She was eager to talk and the more hooks he threw in her direction the bigger fish he might land.

'Dr Kellar has always been a very difficult man to live with but, amazingly, Mabel could find no fault in him. After twenty years of marriage, she still blindly adores him.'

Her mocking expression indicated that she found this astonishing. 'It is such a pity she never had a child. There was going to be a baby, but it came to nothing. I'm afraid that Dr Kellar disliked children intensely. He was not enamoured at the prospect of being a father and persuaded her that it would be in their best interests to remain childless . . . '

'May I ask you, was there good reason for his decision?'

'Good reason? You mean family traits, insanity and so forth.' She looked at him narrowly. 'Oh Inspector, I can see that you are thinking of our uncle. Well, his family have always had the reputation, well-earned alas, of being a fairly disreputable lot and Uncle Hedley disassociated himself with them long ago. I can assure you they have got all their wits about them. And Uncle Hedley too. But we are related only through marriage.'

She laughed. 'As for myself, I've had eight children and they are all fine in wind and limb. Mabel and I were the youngest of thirteen.' She sighed. 'No, it was nothing like that influenced Melville.'

'Could there have been something in his side of the family?'

'The Kellars have been respected in Edinburgh for many generations.' She smiled. 'I imagine your police are fully aware of their police surgeon's impeccable background. Besides people who love each other and want children desperately will always believe in God's goodness, that in their case the worst won't happen.'

There was a rather long silence as if Mrs Findlay-Cupar was reliving Mabel's unhappiness, before she resumed. 'Over the years, apart from the unhappy business over the baby, I have always found Mabel loyal and uncomplaining, quite content and happy in her life. She was a dutiful obedient wife and she readily came to terms with her husband's wishes in every respect, even to remaining childless.

'Yes, I would have said she was happy with Melville. Until very recently.' Again she looked away from him, cautious, hesitant. 'When I last saw her she was very upset, prone to tears on the least provocation. I had never seen her in such a state. It seemed, Inspector, that she had reason to believe that her beloved Melville was being unfaithful to her.'

And a pity it was that she had ever found out at all, thought Faro grimly. He was one of many at the Central Office who entertained shrewd suspicions that Kellar would not restrict his amorous activities to one rather plain prim wife.

Kellar was a handsome man who basked in female adulation and, like many professional men, found that opportunities for infidelity often came his way. He could afford extra-marital relations carried on with utmost discretion. Apparently this time he hadn't been clever or discreet enough.

As if she read Faro's thoughts, Mrs Findlay-Cupar continued, 'I tried to assure her that this was nonsense, and even if it wasn't nonsense, men like Melville do not risk scandal by leaving their wives for other women. I said all the things expected in the way of comfort from one sister to another. Bear with it, be patient, it will pass and so forth.'

She thrust the letter towards him almost reluctantly. 'This came from my sister. It was deposited with our family solicitor with instructions that unless he heard from her to the contrary this was to be delivered to me at North Berwick on February 4th. As February 5th is my fortieth birthday, and Mabel is always extremely generous, I presumed that this was some gift of bonds, a legacy of some kind. Please read it, Inspector.' She smiled wanly. 'Tiz is my pet name.'

My dearest Tiz: I write to you because I am at the end of my tether. I have found out something so awful I can hardly bring myself to believe it or put it into words. I was right – there is <u>another woman</u>.

Melville whom I love with all my heart, whom I have trusted with all my being, has a mistress. I have definite proof of this – they have been seen together. What is worse, I know her. Not only is she his mistress but <u>there is a child</u>. <u>His child</u>, whom he dotes upon.

Dearest Tiz, I am in agony. He has asked me to leave this house – my only home – as he no longer has any use for me. He no longer wants me for his wife. Our marriage is over but I am to say nothing, he says, until the knighthood is safe, <u>otherwise it will be the worse for me</u>. Dearest Tiz, what am I to do? I love him – love him – he is my whole life, but my life is in his hands and I fear that if I don't agree to his wishes that <u>he will do away with me</u>. Once he gets an idea <u>nothing</u> – nobody – is ever allowed to stand in his way.

What he really wants now is to marry this woman and legitimise their child. Everything is for the child, this <u>bastard</u> he worships. His only talk is about securing his son's future. I think I could share him with a mistress, bear with the ignominy as I know so many other wives do, if only he had <u>let me keep our baby</u>, then there would have been some comfort. But now I have nothing, no one to turn to.

I think if I do not agree then <u>he will kill me</u>. Do not laugh, dearest Tiz, he could dispose of me <u>so easily</u>, so cruelly and he has told me so many times, even laughing, <u>how easy murder</u> would be for a police surgeon. And I would rather he cut out my heart, the heart that is and always will be his, rather than live without him.

Your heartbroken sister, Mabel.

P.S.: You may never receive this letter. I trust not. On the other hand, it and I may arrive on your doorstep without warning and, knowing the state of mind I will be

121

in by then, I should like you to be in possession of a more articulate version of the true facts.

Faro laid it aside. A heartrending, moving letter, written in haste and desperation. Some words were almost illegible, blotted and smudged by her tears. But it was the words heavily underlined that troubled him most, with their appalling significance, as if Mabel Kellar had indeed a premonition of the dreadful fate that lay in store for her.

Mrs Findlay-Cupar declined to take it back. 'Keep it, Inspector. I know I can rely on your discretion. And if Dr Kellar has indeed put away my dearest sister, then I want him brought to justice. And if this letter will help to put a rope around his neck, then let it be done.'

'One thing puzzles me,' said Faro. 'The baby Mrs Kellar mentions, that she wasn't allowed to keep. I'm not sure that I understand.'

'I'm not sure that I do either,' said Mrs Findlay-Cupar hurriedly. 'I believe that Melville with his medical knowledge could have averted a threatened miscarriage, but declined to do so.'

'I see. Your sister's statement does rather imply that the baby was born alive and then put out for adoption.'

'You have my assurance, Inspector, there was no child.'

Faro saw her into her carriage. She thanked him for receiving her so informally and he promised to keep her in touch with any events relating to Mabel Kellar.

Vince was waiting for him. 'Well, what news of Mabel?'

Faro handed him the letter.

Vince could hardly control his emotion as he read, his face grew pale with horror. 'This is utterly appalling, Stepfather, appalling. The man is an absolute devil. This letter proves without a shadow of doubt that he planned to get rid of Mabel. It's all there in her own words, Stepfather. Why don't you go and arrest him?'

'It certainly provides a new and damning aspect of

the case against Kellar, lad, but without further evidence a court of law would dismiss it as the hysterical denunciations of a betrayed wife.'

'What about Mabel's bloodstained fur cloak, and the knife? What further proof do you need to put a rope around Kellar's neck?' demanded Vince angrily.

'A body,' said Faro shortly.

Vince shuddered and gave him an angry look. 'At least you are wrong about your motive this time, Stepfather. This hardly fits into your pet theory of gain.'

'That rather depends, lad. There are many aspects of gain and in this case it would appear that Kellar realised, almost too late, the benefits of fatherhood.'

'Of a bastard son,' said Vince bitterly. 'One that he wanted so desperately that he was prepared to go to any lengths, even murder, to legitimise.'

'Thereby following the desperate example of kings and nobles who set the pattern in ancient times and got rid of inconveniently barren wives.'

'Like Henry the Eighth?'

'If succession and a throne are in jeopardy then history is prepared to turn a blinder eye than Edinburgh society. I'm afraid as far as Kellar is concerned the scandal of divorce would have ruined him.'

Faro was silent, deep in thought. Have I been expecting something like this? Was this damning document written by a frightened wife the missing piece of the puzzle? Once you have that, the complete picture springs into view and leaves you wondering why on earth you hadn't seen the strikingly obvious.

'I wonder,' he said.

'You surely can't have any further doubts that Kellar is guilty after this. There were plenty of veiled hints among the students that the ladies pursued Kellar and that he wasn't averse to walking slowly.'

Faro smiled. Even the shrewd Sir Hedley Marsh had hinted that Melville was a womaniser.

While they were talking Faro had been mulling over the contents of the letter and had come to a rather obvious but very disturbing conclusion regarding the unknown woman's identity.

In reply to his question, Vince shook his head. 'No, Mabel never even hinted to me that she suspected Kellar of philandering. Misplaced loyalty, I suppose.'

'To whom?' demanded Faro sharply.

'Why, to her husband, of course.' He thought for a moment. 'I expect it was the kind of topic she considered too indelicate to discuss with a man. It never occurred to me to ask, but now that you mention it, she might well have confided in her best friend. Mrs Shaw, for instance.'

'Ah yes, Mrs Shaw. I've been thinking about her. A young woman with an infant. A son,' he added heavily. 'Does that not strike you as a remarkable coincidence?'

Vince stared at him indignantly. 'It strikes me as absolute sheer coincidence, Stepfather. And that's all. Mrs Shaw is a respectable widow. Why, Stepfather, I'm surprised at you even entertaining such a notion. You surely can't be seriously implying that Eveline Shaw would have an – an affair – with her best friend's husband? After all Mabel's kindness to her?'

'It has been known,' said Faro drily.

'But in this case, you should know better. You have the evidence of your own eyes. You saw them at the dinner party.'

One of Faro's lasting impressions had been Mrs Kellar's apparent devotion, her many smiles and anxiety that Mrs Shaw be included in every conversation, often staring uneasily at Kellar who was barely civil to the young woman.

'I'm just speaking my thoughts out loud,' said Faro. And tactfully changing the subject, 'When did you first become friendly with Mrs Kellar?'

'About three months ago, but it seems as if I've known her for a lifetime.'

'I'm curious about this baby she wasn't allowed to keep? Did she ever mention it to you?'

'Not on that occasion,' said Vince hurriedly. 'I was collecting some papers for Kellar and she asked for my advice on a quite minor affliction, some stiffness in her shoulder. As it turned out a pulled muscle, but she was worried that this might be the onset of rheumatism, common in her family.

'While I was examining her I observed a considerable amount of bruising. The nature and positions were curious and suggested that she had been physically beaten. She made several transparent excuses, but her reluctance became obvious.'

Vince fell silent and Faro said, 'Her assailant was none other than her own husband, was that it?'

Vince nodded. 'You guessed right, Stepfather. I was shocked and furious, although I knew Kellar to be a man quite capable of fits of sarcasm and even cold anger with his students. Anyway,' he continued, 'poor Mabel was full of blushing whispers and tears of embarrassment, trying to excuse her husband's ill-treatment. I was desperately sorry for her but, what was worse, I was quite helpless. Without betraying Mabel's confidence and making it a lot worse for her, I couldn't confront him with his beastly behaviour, tell him – my superior, my employer – to desist and that he was several kinds of swine.'

Vince banged down his glass on the table. 'Dear God. I shouldn't even be telling you all this, Stepfather, such matters between patient and doctor are utterly sacrosanct.'

'Quite so. Doctors are like priests in being the recipients of intimate confidences. I'm fully aware of that and you can rely on my discretion.'

'I am only telling you,' Vince continued desperately, 'because the matter is one of life – and I think, dear God, death too. And you, most of all, you must understand the sort of beast you are dealing with.'

Faro regarded his stepson with compassion. Vince might

be shocked by Mabel's revelations, but Faro could have reiterated many such tales of respectable middle-class men who allied Christian virtue with hypocrisy and abused their wives, treating them little better than animals once the bedroom door was closed. Faro knew of many husbands who could get no pleasure from normal lovemaking and sought satisfaction in outlandish and even brutish practices.

'His treatment of her was the first bond between us,' Vince whispered. 'I was, it seemed, as a doctor who was also a friend, the only person she could confide in.'

'What about Mrs Shaw?'

Vince gave him a sharp look. 'I think not. Mabel would have been too embarrassed and humiliated to confess such matters to another woman, especially one so much younger.'

Faro rubbed his chin thoughtfully. 'Has it ever occurred to you that as there were no children, you would be about the right age as a substitute for the son she had never had.'

Vince laughed. 'You imagine that that was the reason for us being drawn to each other.' He shook his head. 'Not so, Stepfather. You are wrong this time. Far from it. And her confessions, I assure you, were hardly the sort a mother would make to her son.'

'She told you the reason there were no children to the marriage?'

'She did indeed,' said Vince grimly.

Faro waited a moment and then said, 'Well, what were they?'

Vince looked doubtful, and regarded his stepfather uneasily. 'I don't know that I really ought to tell you, Stepfather. It is not a pretty story and one, I must warn you, which will only further prejudice you against Kellar.'

'I will have to take that chance.' When Vince hesitated, Faro continued, 'Come, come, lad. There is, and always has been, a tendency for husband to blame wife when the fault is not hers at all. You must know as a doctor, surely, that a man's pride suffers a mortal blow when he realises that his manhood is incapable of begetting a child.'

Vince remained silent and Faro said. 'You had better tell me. What was it? Syphilis? There couldn't be anything much worse.'

'Oh yes, there could. There could indeed.'

'Such as?'

'Aborting one's own wife.'

Faro stared at him. 'You don't mean . . . '

'I do mean. That the beast Kellar never wanted a child and refused to let his wife conceive. He took elaborate precautions, so she told me, and when by accident – or design, poor soul, since she yearned for a child – she became pregnant, he coldly insisted that the foetus be aborted.'

Faro shuddered. 'Dreadful. I can hardly believe that any husband would be so callous, so inhuman. There must have been some very good reason for such a terrible decision. A father-to-be often suffers qualms of conscience, such as fearing that he is too poor, or the world a too wicked place, to entrust another life into it.'

'Such reasoning could hardly be valid in Kellar's case, with so much to offer a child.'

'He might have feared taking second place in his wife's affections.'

Vince laughed derisively. 'An unlikely story. You've seen them together. You don't really believe that, do you?'

Faro remembered his own qualms when Rose was conceived within weeks of his marriage to Lizzie. He had felt dread and resentment of being plunged into fatherhood before they had a chance to get to know each other. 'There is always that other fear, that the mother may not survive childbirth.'

Such had been Lizzie Faro's fate with their third child. The two men, her husband and her beloved firstborn, exchanged stricken glances. Vince stretched over and put his hand on Faro's arm. 'You must not torment yourself, Stepfather. You were not to blame. Mother so wanted to give you a son.'

Faro patted his hand. 'I know, lad, I know. But nevertheless . . . ' Blinking away tears, he said, 'Oh, let's get back to Kellar. Presumably at that time he loved Mabel, so there must have been some other reason for his decision.'

'There was none. Only his detestation of children, which must have made Mabel's agony even harder to bear when she wrote to her sister.'

'This does indeed throw another light on her letter,' said Faro 'How appalling.'

'It was indeed. Can you imagine the feelings of a woman whose husband had put her through the depths of hell, both physically and mentally. That would be bad enough, except that when she is beyond child-bearing, he cheerfully gets his young mistress pregnant. And, worst of all, he dotes upon her child and wants to claim it as his own.'

Vince stared at him with stricken eyes. 'Dear God, don't you see how monstrous and inhuman Kellar is?'

'Aye, lad. I do. I'm shocked too. In the class Kellar belongs to, fathers need play little part in the upbringing beyond the begetting. Once property and inheritance are settled, the offspring can be safely left to the tender mercies of nurses and public schools.'

'Yes, however we look at it, an heir is often the only reason for marrying at all. As I fear it will be mine,' said Vince. 'But not until I am very old.'

Faro smiled. Vince's fierce determination to remain a bachelor was a constant source of discussion and friendly argument between them.

'Well, Stepfather, would you not say that this was the first indication of a black-hearted murderer?'

Faro shook his head. 'I can't believe that Kellar could have aborted his own child without extenuating circumstance, some powerful reason.'

'Some dread medical history in his wife's family which

he wanted to spare her, like insanity, is that what you are suggesting?' said Vince.

'We have her sister's assurances on that. From the standpoint of eight healthy children.'

'And the Mad Bart is only a relative by marriage, unfortunately,' said Vince.

'Aye, lad. And despite his nickname he's as sane as the next man. A recluse, with his own reasons for withdrawing from society.'

'Eccentric, crafty and wicked, I don't doubt, but sharp as a tack.' Vince jumped up from the table and strode over to the window, staring at the winter sunlight dying on Arthur's Seat.

'The story isn't quite over yet, Stepfather. Prepare yourself for something worse, much worse. And I doubt that even you will find excuses for Kellar's inhumanity.' Taking a deep breath he continued. 'Not only did this vile man remove the foetus conceived by himself upon his wife, he used it for experiments.'

Slamming his fists together, he turned to Faro. 'Experiments, Stepfather. You know what that means, cutting to pieces, coldly dissecting his own unborn daughter.'

'A daughter? It was so far advanced.'

'Yes. Mabel told me so. A female child. A female child who would have been about the same age as Eveline Shaw.'

Eveline Shaw.

Both men were silent and then Faro asked, 'Are there any other young women with babies in the Kellar circle?'

'They didn't have a social circle, Stepfather. I think I knew most of their acquaintances – yes, I'd call them that.'

'Considering that Mrs Kellar was so forthright about her husband's brutish treatment, I should have thought his infidelity would have been worth a mention. I'm surprised she gave no hint of it.'

'You're going too fast, Stepfather. You have the answer

129

there before you. Read her letter again. She had suffered the last fatal blow to that cherished illusion she had kept alive through their marriage. That Kellar still loved her in his fashion. Don't you see, a woman like Mabel had her pride. She could uncomplainingly endure and suffer physical ill-usage far more readily than her husband's adultery.'

Chapter Twelve

The revelations about Mabel Kellar's life with her husband were appalling, and although his stepson prided himself on being Mabel's confidant, Faro was in little doubt as to the identity of Kellar's mistress. He decided that an informal call on Mrs Shaw might prove worthwhile, especially as the bait he had to offer as excuse for the visit, was calculated to gain her confidence and promote further agreeable and sympathetic acquaintance.

When Vince asked if he had found a companion for the Neruda concert, Faro said, 'I've decided to ask Mrs Shaw to accompany me.'

'Mrs Shaw? Good heavens. Well, well.'

'As you're so fond of quoting, lad, music sounds ten times better when it is being shared by someone of a harmonious disposition. In this case who better than Mrs Shaw?' Watching his stepson's mocking expression, Faro's icy glare forbade the usual teasing.

'And I'll have none of your innuendos, if you please. The concert serves a double purpose since it provides an admirable opportunity of continuing my investigations. Discreetly, of course.'

'Of course, Stepfather.'

Vince's unchanging smile mocked him and he added angrily, 'Dammit, you know my feelings about her.'

'Ah yes, that is all very well, but do we know her feelings about you?'

'Listen to me,' said Faro heatedly, 'Even without the business about Mabel Kellar, I would still feel sorry for a young widow. Especially a talented pianist with possibly few chances to attend concerts or to hear the divine Neruda play. So it's a bit early in the day for you to start hearing wedding bells, I must say,' he added huffily.

'All right, Stepfather, I stand corrected and I apologise.' Vince's impudent grin was anything but apologetic, 'You're very sure of yourself where the ladies are concerned, so let's hope it stays that way and that one day I don't have to remind you with "I told you so".' He stretched out his hand, 'May I see that letter again?' And examining it carefully, 'You have observed that it is un-dated.'

Faro nodded. 'Irritating, isn't it?'

'But hardly surprising, considering poor Mabel's state of mind when it was written. Did Tiz leave you the envelope?'

'Here it is.'

'No postmark?'

'The answer is that the contents were too important to entrust to the mail or to any other person and Mrs Kellar most likely handed in to the solicitor's office personally.'

'When? Hardly on the way to the station without attracting Kellar's curiosity. Do you see what I'm getting at, Stepfather? The dinner party was on Sunday, so if Eveline Shaw was Kellar's mistress, Mabel already knew.' Vince jabbed a finger at him. 'Which makes absolute nonsense of your theory, doesn't it? You just have to remember her behaviour that evening,' he laughed. 'Mabel would need to be a far better actress than I credit her for to have sustained that elaborate exhibition of devotion to her dearest friend and companion. It has to be someone else, Stepfather. It can't be Eveline Shaw.'

The afternoon was bright and cheerful, with a cloudless frosty sky stretching to infinity. An azure glow hung over the Castle, a great sleeping stone monster dwarfing the ant-like creatures who scuttled back and forth along Princes Street enjoying the brief respite of springtime promise. Crouched among its own dark secrets, so the Castle had stood through centuries of winter snow and summer sunshine, a silent witness impervious to man's follies, his despairs and fleeting triumphs.

Faro's thoughts turned to the interview that lay ahead. Vince's argument failed to convince him, despite Mrs Kellar's display of affection to Mrs Shaw at the dinner party. Regardless of when that damning letter had been delivered to the solicitor's office, he had not the slightest doubt that Mrs Shaw was Kellar's mistress and that Barnaby was his son.

He saw that public façade of indifference and even dislike for what it was: a ruse, imperative if their association was to remain a closely-guarded secret. The whole evening must have been torture for them both, especially for Mrs Shaw. This theory interpreted her vaguely distressed manner, not as carrying a still inconsolable burden of grief for her dead husband but as constant terror that by word or glance her intimate relationship with Melville Kellar might be made apparent to Mabel.

Was it possible that Mrs Kellar had been naive enough to imagine that her sweet and caring behaviour would stir some pangs of conscience in the guilty pair and that Eveline Shaw, in particular, might decide to end the affair? If Mabel Kellar thought along such lines, Faro decided grimly, then she had a pitiful grasp of human nature or the fact that love, once dead, was seldom resurrected by self-sacrifice.

Faro was pleased with his astute observation that from Mrs Shaw's viewpoint the devoted friendship was somewhat one-sided. It did not take much imagination to realise that the young woman must be desperate to give Barnaby a father. And since Kellar was eager to bestow the benefits of parenthood on his bastard son, the presence of a legal wife was very inconvenient.

It was also the perfect motive for murder.

The day's pale warmth was deceptive and Faro reached Mrs Shaw's house half-frozen. Head down against the chill

133

wind blowing straight off the Firth of Forth, he almost cann-
oned into the young man who was dashing down her front
steps, having banged the door with shattering force behind
him. A lightly built young man of middle height, with the
darkly handsome looks of the Celtic Highlander, he was in
a high old temper. Face flushed and distorted with rage, he
swept past Faro, unseeing and without apology.

Behind him, the door that had been so forcefully closed
opened to reveal Mrs Shaw, breathless and distraught. Faro
realised that she must have rushed downstairs in the wake of
the departed visitor. Tear-stained, her expression of anticipation changed into deepest melancholy when she beheld
Detective Inspector Faro standing on her doorstep, instead
of the young man beseeching her forgiveness with abject
apologies.

Faro raised his hat, bowed. 'Good day to you, ma'am.'

Mrs Shaw summoned a smile, looking bleakly beyond
him down the now empty street.

I couldn't have chosen a less inauspicious moment to
call and invite her to a concert, thought Faro, expecting
an abrupt refusal.

But Mrs Shaw had regained her equilibrium and saw
his visit in quite another light. 'Is it about Mabel?' she
asked anxiously.

Faro had to confess, no, it wasn't.

Mrs Shaw frowned. 'I was hoping you had news of
her at last. Such a long time. I wonder where on earth
she can be?'

'I'm sure we'll find her,' said Faro smoothly, listening to
his own false tone offering consolation where he was certain there was none. 'It was quite another matter brought
me to your door this time.'

Her eyes, deeply violet, opened wide. Surprise became
her exceedingly well, he thought, a very pretty sight indeed.
'I wondered if you would like to go to the concert this evening. Neruda is playing the Beethoven Violin Concerto.'

Mrs Shaw didn't seem to hear him. 'I beg your pardon?'

He repeated the request and this time she stood very still. Her attitude of careful concentration and growing amazement suggested that a Detective Inspector was the last person from whom she expected such an invitation.

'My stepson usually accompanies me but he is engaged elsewhere,' Faro said, feeling that explanation was necessary. 'And knowing your interest in Beethoven . . . ' How lame it all sounded! He had wasted his time. He shouldn't have come, made a fool of himself.

But she was smiling. 'Oh, thank you. I would be delighted.' She clasped her hands together like an eager child given a particular treat. 'I would love that. Oh, I do thank you, Inspector.'

There was an awkward pause while she gazed at him, wondering what to say next while Faro considered whether he should take his leave before she changed her mind.

Smiling, as if she had come to a sudden decision, she opened the door a little wider. 'It's very cold standing on the doorstep. Barnaby is out with the girl, but they'll be back shortly. Would you care to come inside, take some refreshment?'

'Only if I could prevail upon you to play the Appassionata again,' said Faro wistfully.

Her answering smile was shy but happy. 'If that would give you pleasure, of course I will.'

He followed her up to the bare drawing-room and she sat down immediately at the piano. As she struck the first chords, again Faro had the feeling that he was listening to the true artist, the musician who was no longer conscious of him, of the room or, beyond the room, of time itself.

As he listened, rapt by her playing, he was no longer concerned that Eveline Shaw might be an accessory to murder. With her he too escaped into that boundless enchanted world of the senses. As the last liquid tones faded into silence, she sat with her fingers still on the keys, head downbent, unwilling to make that transition back into painful everyday existence with all its attendant cares.

135

Faro's applause, his whispered 'Bravo, bravo' seemed almost an intrusion and it coincided with jarring reality in the form of screams of rage. Growing ever nearer and more ear-piercing, they took form as a scarlet-faced, square-mouthed monster, hardly recognisable as the once genial baby Barnaby, was carried across the threshold by a frantic maid.

'Sorry, ma'am, I canna' be dealing wi' him today. Real naughty he is. Just had to bring him home.'

Mrs Shaw rushed to the rescue, seized those waving, clenched fists. 'Oh bad, bad Barnaby. Is it your teeth again, my precious?'

Faro found himself now examining the baby for likeness to Melville Kellar. Certainly the passion of rage before him struck a chord of familiarity. But the baby's continued screams put firmly at an end any immediate possibility of further conversation, or of putting into effect his own subtle methods of trapping suspects into betraying incriminating evidence.

His eardrums were sorely afflicted by the din, which threatened to be prolonged and immediate withdrawal seemed prudent. Indicating his intention, he called, 'Tonight at seven,' to which a harassed Mrs Shaw looked over her shoulder and shouted above the tumult, 'I will be ready. Thank you.' And to the maid, 'Please see the Inspector out.'

Faro gladly made his escape, the divine music of Beethoven and the baby's angry yells jostling each other in his head. Annoyed that the visit had been cut short without the least advantage to his enquiries, he was not the man to accept the frustrations of questions unanswered where such information could be readily obtained.

His way back to the Central Office took him past the rooms of Mrs Kellar's solicitors. Shown the envelope, the clerk at the desk looked through his register and shook his head. 'As this was marked private and personal, it would be taken directly to Mr Franklin and would not be entered.

I cannot give you any further details,' he added severely. 'You will need to approach Mr Franklin himself on the subject and he is in Court at Dundee today.'

Making a note to send McQuinn to interview Mr Franklin next day, Faro walked a little further along to Hanover Street and entered the office of Mr Alex Troup. He found that gentleman seated at his desk behind a mountain of documents. Always glad for a chat about hectic events the two had shared in Faro's earlier days with the City Police, he greeted his old friend warmly.

After a few solicitous enquiries on the well-being of Faro's mother and his two small daughters in Orkney, Alex Troup regarded him quizzically. 'I gather this isn't a social call, Jeremy. Is there something I can do for you?'

'There is indeed.'

When Faro explained that he wanted the name of the buyer of Mrs Shaw's house, Alex Troup regarded him sternly. 'You know, of course, that request is highly irregular. Such information is confidential but your visit implies that this is police business?'

'Yes. A murder investigation.'

Alex Troup went immediately to his files. A moment later he emerged, document in hand. 'Mrs Eveline Shaw. The house was purchased in the name of Dr Melville Kellar.'

Faro felt the glow of triumph. He had been right. 'And the date?'

'July of last year.'

'You've been a tremendous help, Alex.'

The date of purchase confirmed all he needed to know. This information was too significant to be written off as coincidence. Kellar had set up Eveline Shaw in the house in Regent Crescent when the son she had borne him was a few weeks old.

Returning to the Central Office, the report of a break-in at a Princes Street store and the round-up of suspected villains from the notorious Wormwoodhall was to command

137

Inspector Faro's full attention until early evening, driving out all thoughts of the evening ahead.

At last, he left matters in McQuinn's hands and hurried back to Sheridan Place. Vince had yet not arrived home for supper to be regaled with the new developments.

Fearing he would be late for the concert, he dressed hastily and declined all but Mrs Brook's excellent soup, much to that lady's displeasure. He was fastening his evening cape and rushing downstairs, when he heard Vince's key in the door.

'Can't talk now, lad.'

'I'll come with you to the cab stance.'

As they hurried along Sheridan Place and on to Minto Street, Faro gasped out the afternoon's events at the offices of Mr Franklin, ending with Alex Troup's revelations.

Vince halted in his tracks. 'So you were right. Eveline Shaw is Kellar's mistress. I can hardly believe it,' he added disgustedly. 'Poor Mabel. No wonder she was so desperately miserable, betrayed by her husband and her dearest friend and companion. I wonder why she didn't mention her name to Tiz.'

'I've no idea. Perhaps she didn't want to believe it.'

'That I can well imagine. She was the sort of person who would never believe evil of anyone. It makes my blood boil when I think of that dinner party. All that petting and cosseting – and all the time . . . How could she?'

'Yes, lad. I've been thinking along the same lines. This new evidence creates a bit of a poser. It doesn't take us anywhere, just creates a new puzzle. She never hinted anything to you? We know that she had her suspicions at Christmas.'

Vince shook his head. 'She did nothing but praise Eveline to me, what a wonderful friend. Her sister of the spirit, you know, the daughter she'd never had – all that sort of thing.'

'If she knew, then such an unworldly attitude, so saintly . . . '

138

Vince laughed softly. 'Oh, that was typical of her. Well, Stepfather, when are you going to arrest Kellar?'

'When we have a bit more evidence.'

'Haven't you got more than enough now?'

'Only circumstantial, I'm afraid. We still have to find the body.'

'It's too late, Stepfather. You must know that now from Mabel's letter. Kellar put the noose around his own neck. We have it in his own words when he bragged to her how easy it would be to dispose of a victim. The young vultures in the medical school will have reduced everything to indecipherable butcher's meat long since. Oh dear God, it's awful, awful,' Vince sobbed, leaning against the fence. 'She didn't deserve that.'

As Faro flagged down an approaching cab, Vince said bitterly, 'I hope you'll enjoy yourself. I'm glad it's not me. I'd hate to have to play the hypocrite and be nice to Eveline Shaw. She's as guilty as Kellar and I jolly well hope they both hang.'

Vince's words remained with Faro. He knew from earlier discussions about the disposal of bodies that even the head, unless required for demonstration purposes, could be dissolved in acid and nothing left but the skull. By the time he reached Regent Crescent he was so sunk in misery that he would have given a great deal to have had some other companion that evening.

But Mrs Shaw was awaiting him eagerly. Her happiness and excitement were so infectious that he resolved to firmly set aside for the evening the grim realisation that he might be in the company of a murderess. The lovely woman at his side had perhaps entreated and assisted her lover to get rid of the wife who stood in their way, but Faro soon found his self-confidence elated by stepping into the foyer of the Assembly Rooms escorting a lady whose youth and beauty turned every head in their direction.

Under the fur cloak Eveline Shaw wore a purple velvet gown, the fashionable bustle with its titillating glimpse of lilac lace petticoats showed off her tiny waist and exquisite figure to perfection.

Faro was charmed and flattered. Had she really blossomed out into half-mourning so splendidly on his account? He was heartily glad and relieved to have missed supper in order to change into evening dress, his top hat and opera cape and to take extra care over his own appearance.

Looking around in the interval, he was acutely conscious of the elegance of the concert-goers. Despite the fact that they and he wore the same correct attire for the occasion, there all likeness ended, for most were strangers to Faro's humble and often violent way of life. He lived daily with danger and sudden death. And here among the lawyers, judges, doctors, engineers, bankers and business men, was a stratum of Edinburgh life he rarely encountered socially and entered only from the professional viewpoint, often warrant in hand.

Some recognised him and moved away with a hasty backward glance, anxious not to be recognised. Faro smiled wryly. His contact with several of those concert-goers that evening was not one they would wish to acknowledge in public. And yet, listening to the buzz of talk around him, he realised that here they were all momentarily united in their love of music, discussing the programme and Hallé's powerful conducting of the orchestra in the Mendelssohn Hebrides Overture and his Third, 'Scottish', Symphony.

He found a corner seat and as Mrs Shaw gratefully sipped a glass of lemonade, he answered her question as to how it had all begun for him, this love of music.

'Many years ago, when I first came down from Orkney to join the police, I was sent here to arrest a Hungarian violinist who had been involved in a fraud case. Until that evening, all the music I had ever known was the Orkney fiddle, the fife, the drum, the clarsach. I had never heard so many instruments, wind, strings, all playing at the same time and making such heavenly sounds. Indeed, it was exactly what I expected of paradise. When I asked what they were playing, I was told it was Beethoven's Fifth Symphony. I was enthralled.'

'Did you catch your criminal?' Mrs Shaw asked gently.

'No. Not then. I was the one caught that night – caught by a passion for classical music that I have never lost.'

'Did you not have music round the piano at home?'

'Oh yes. But I had never appreciated that particular instrument until I heard it on the concert platform, in the hands of an expert.' He looked at her smiling. 'Divinely played, as it is when you play the Appassionata.'

'You are very kind.'

'Not at all. Just amazed that you are not up there yourself, on the concert platform. I feel certain that you did not reach such an amazingly high standard from taking piano lessons.'

She sighed. 'I was born into music. My parents were both musicians, the violin and the piano were their instruments. They had hopes that I too would become a professional and my childhood was dedicated to that high goal.'

Her face darkened and she shook her head sadly. 'Alas, they both died in a cholera epidemic and I was left on my own at sixteen. The aunt I was sent to in Caithness thought such ambitions far too grandiose for an orphan.' She stopped, frowning, as if reliving a particularly painful scene.

'A pity. Such a waste of talent,' said Faro.

'No, Inspector. It wasn't written for me, omitted from my chapter in the Book of Life, that's all. Anyway, it was very soon afterwards I met Barnaby's father . . . '

Ah, he thought, that careful and evasive phrasing gives nothing away. Before he could probe the subject further, the bell sounded marking the end of the interval.

Soon both he and Mrs Shaw were absorbed and captivated by Mme Neruda playing the Beethoven Violin Concerto in D. The thunderous applause and cries of 'Encore', were rewarded by a short virtuoso piece and at last the orchestra took their final bow.

The audience trooped out into the foyer to seek their carriages in the long waiting line extending down George Street and as Faro and Mrs Shaw stood under the brilliant lights from the candelabra, he was aware of admiring glances from young men and envious looks from their partners.

At his side, Mrs Shaw's eyes roamed constantly, and not in search of admiration, he realised as her hand tightened suddenly on his arm. Thinking she was about to bring someone to his attention, he turned and caught a glimpse of her expression. He was well aware of the miasma of fear after twenty years with the Edinburgh City Police. It was something so tangible, he could almost smell, see, and touch it.

Mrs Eveline Shaw was trembling and afraid.

A moment later, he saw the reason. The young man he had encountered at her front door was waiting on the steps. His eyes blazing in fury, left no doubt whom he was searching for. Mrs Shaw hesitated. He leaped up to her, hand upraised. The words he yelled were in Gaelic, but Faro was sufficiently familiar with the language to know that she was being cursed as a bitch and whore.

Outraged, Faro jumped forward, deflected the blow and was pushed aside.

'Keep out of this.'

Braver men than the one before him had lived to infinitely regret having laid hands on Detective Inspector Jeremy Faro. Now he raised his fists purposefully.

'Apologise to this lady, sir,' he threatened, 'or it will be the worse for you.'

Mrs Shaw dragged at his cape, adding her own entreaty. 'Keep out of this, Inspector. Please, for my sake.' And to the glowering young man, 'This is nothing to do with him. Please, Harry. He is just a friend of Mabel's. I beg you, please don't make a scene. Please.'

Suddenly the young man gazed down at her hand on his arm. Although he swept it aside, it had gentled him, like a wild stallion that feels the quieting caress of fond ownership.

He examined her face, looked deeply, beseechingly into her eyes, like one who searches for an answer.

'Harry, please listen, my dear,' she whispered.

But the momentary spell was broken and Harry threw off her hand again, this time violently. Turning, he quickly pushed his way through the crowd who had gathered silently, expecting a fight.

Ignoring stares and whispers, Faro tucked Mrs Shaw's trembling arm firmly into his own and led the way to the carriage that was awaiting them. She said nothing, crouched in the far corner like a hurt animal who wishes only to avoid all physical contact.

Once or twice on the journey back to Regent Crescent they stopped to give way to the traffic and, under the street lamps briefly illuminating the carriage, Faro saw her expression. Dazed and lost, that was how she now appeared, exactly as he remembered her from the Kellars' fateful dinner party.

She remained silent until her house was in sight. When the carriage stopped and Faro handed her down, she took his hand limply and said in a small exhausted voice, 'Thank you for this evening, Inspector. I am sorry, truly sorry, it had to end in such a way. Please accept my apologies.'

Running up the steps, she opened the door swiftly and hurried inside, as if afraid he might attempt to follow her.

But Faro was not prepared to depart without the explanation which he considered due to him. Afraid that Mrs Shaw was in danger from the violent young man, before taking his departure he required reassurances, and to offer his protection if necessary.

He raced up the steps. 'Wait. You have no need to apologise.'

She regarded him wide-eyed from behind the half-closed door. 'I find myself in a very difficult situation. Harry Shaw gets jealous . . . '

Shaw, thought Faro and said, 'He is related to you?'

Mrs Shaw seemed bewildered by the question. She shook her head, biting her lip.

'He is an acquaintance then?' Even as he said the words, Faro heard their echoing absurdity.

Mrs Shaw looked up into Faro's face sadly. 'Oh no, Inspector. He is more than that. Much more. He is my lover.'

Chapter Thirteen

Vince came down early next morning to join his step-father at breakfast, eager to hear about the concert with Mrs Shaw.

Faro described the scene outside the Assembly Rooms with Harry Shaw, the young man she claimed was her lover and whom he had met earlier that day, leaving her house in a temper.

Vince whistled. 'Now that is a surprise, Stepfather. Did Harry precede or succeed Captain Shaw? They must be related. Sounds as if she's got herself not only into a difficult situation but a right old pickle. And where does Dr Kellar fit into this new picture?'

Faro had much to occupy his thoughts as he walked down the Pleasance that morning and hurried towards the Central Office, where the mystery surrounding Mrs Shaw was beginning to unravel with considerably more speed than he had anticipated.

He was greeted by a triumphant and jubilant McQuinn. 'I've checked on the Caithness Regiment as you asked, sir. There isn't, and never has been, a Captain Shaw. He doesn't exist.'

So the late Captain Shaw who died fighting for Queen and country on the Indian frontier, leaving his grieving widow to bear him a posthumous child, had been a mere invention to appease convention. It raised some interesting speculations. Did this new piece of scandal, to be relished in due course by Edinburgh gossips, have any bearing on Mabel Kellar's murder?

But the most burning question of all remained unanswered. What part had Harry Shaw played in Mrs Kellar's disappearance? Kellar and Eveline Shaw had an alibi, they had spent that afternoon together. But was it, in fact, Harry Shaw who had been waiting for Mabel Kellar on the train where he had murdered her and helped dispose of her body?

A tap on the door and the constable on the desk duty gave him a note.

'Just found this, Inspector. It was handed in yesterday.'

Faro regarded him stony-faced. 'Yesterday! When yesterday, may I ask? There's no time stated.'

'It's a new young lad on the desk, sir. When you'd gone home, he probably thought it wasn't all that urgent.'

'He'll remember next time, that's for sure, if he hopes to stay in the police. Impress on your lad that this is an urgent missing persons case. McQuinn is my second and if he is unavailable, then I can be contacted at home.'

The note read: 'An errand lad brought a message from Dr Kellar's house. Mrs Flynn requires to see the Inspector only [the words were heavily underlined] as soon as possible.'

'Trouble, sir?' asked McQuinn, peering over his shoulder.

'You can come along and find out,' said Faro, handing him the note. 'This is something you could have dealt with.'

'But I wasn't— '

'Oh, never mind. Let's go.'

To the driver of the waiting police carriage he gave directions to the Kellar house where Ina opened the door, staring out at them with frightened eyes. 'It's to do with the mistress, sir.' She looked over her shoulder. 'I told you this was an evil house. I feel things.'

'What sort of things?'

'Presences,' she whispered.

She almost jumped into the air when the bell from the

housekeeper's room pealed through the hall. 'That's Mrs Flynn. She said I was to take you to her directly and not waste time gossiping.'

McQuinn made a grimace as Ina led the way downstairs. At the door of Mrs Flynn's gloomy apartments, Faro whispered, 'We'll talk to you later, Ina.'

'If you wish, sir.'

The housekeeper was lying on her bed. 'Ina?'

When the maid's scared face looked round the door, Mrs Flynn said, 'Here's the shopping list. Go as quick as you can. These things are needed for the master's supper.' And then to Faro, 'Excuse me not rising, Inspector. It's me veins. Bad they are just now.'

Faro decided the housekeeper was extremely unlucky in being so prone to indisposition. Every time he came he found her suffering from some new infliction. A sore throat, a bad leg and now she was back with the swathed jaw: presumably the toothache that had caused the initial disasters at the Kellar dinner table.

Following his gaze, she said. 'I'm nearly mad with that abscess again. Hardly closed my eyes last night.'

She certainly wouldn't last long in any employment at this rate, he thought, murmuring sympathy. 'But you really must do something about it, Mrs Flynn. The dentist can't be any worse than all this agony,' he said severely, and feeling no end of a hypocrite added encouragingly, 'It's all over in a minute, you know.'

The housekeeper shuddered. 'I'll have to think about it. I can't go on much longer like this.' Then, leaning forward, she whispered, 'I asked you to come because we found this in the chimney.'

From under the bed she withdrew a bundle.

'What is it?'

At first glance in the dim light, Faro thought he was seeing a bloodied, soot-streaked white seabird, which Mrs Flynn shook out to reveal a woman's petticoat. The bodice was heavily bloodstained.

'You say this was in the chimney, Mrs Flynn?'

'Yes, sir.'

'Tell me the whole story from the beginning, if you please.'

'It was just last week, sir, the chimney in the master's bedroom. He started complaining that it was smoking. Ina and I looked up but we couldn't see anything. It had been swept at Christmas so it couldn't be soot. He said to get a sweep. Well, that came down with the brushes.'

Spreading the garment on the table, even the bloodstains and the soot could not disguise that it was of fine-quality lawn and the lace was of exquisite workmanship.

'Do you recognise it?'

'Oh yes, Inspector. It belonged to the mistress. I ironed it the morning she left. She asked for it specially, one of her favourites.'

'You are absolutely sure this is the same garment she was wearing when she left?'

'Oh yes, sir. You see, as she was putting it on, she stepped on the lace and it tore. She asked me to sew it. If you'll hand it over – here, see – on the hem. I can recognise my own sewing,' she said proudly. 'I couldn't find the white cotton and as she was in a hurry I hoped she wouldn't notice that I used cream thread.'

Faro looked at the neat stitches. Cream against white, not particularly obvious, but the housekeeper's repair was further grim evidence that murder had been committed. The case against Dr Kellar was almost complete.

'If someone was trying to burn this garment, I don't understand why it was up the chimney?' At his side, McQuinn asked the logical question which had also been troubling Faro.

'I couldn't say, but it was rolled up in a tight ball,' said Mrs Flynn encouragingly. 'Inspector, may I ask you something?' When Faro nodded, she went on, 'The mistress – has she – is she – I mean, has she been done in by someone?'

'We don't know that, Mrs Flynn.'

'But, sir, what about the bloodstains in the coach? The fur cloak that the papers mentioned, and then there was the carving knife we missed from the kitchen. And now this . . . ' her voice grew shriller, as she pointed to the petticoat. 'What more do the police need to make an arrest, Inspector?'

'They need a body, Mrs Flynn.'

'A body, sir?'

'Yes, Mrs Flynn – a body.'

The housekeeper thought for a moment. 'Do you think the police will ever find her?'

'I expect so, if we're patient.'

Mrs Flynn shook her head. 'I don't think patience has much hope here. Not against him.'

'What do you mean?'

'Well, it's as plain as the nose on your face, Inspector. He spends his time cutting bodies up and, so I hear, giving bits to his students. Revolting, I call it, not even Christian burial, poor souls.'

As they were about to leave, taking the petticoat with them, Faro said, 'Perhaps we could have a word with the maid.'

'If she's back from the shops, yes. And she takes for ever. I'd better warn you, Inspector.' Mrs Flynn put a finger to the side of her head and twisted it significantly. 'She's not all there.'

'Simple, you mean?'

'That's right. Sees things. Ghosts and such rubbish. I've never felt or seen anything amiss in the house. I think she does it to make herself important.'

She struggled to rise from her bed. Putting her foot on the ground she gave an agonised gasp and Faro, bundling up the petticoat, said hurriedly, 'We'll see ourselves out.'

As they walked down the front steps, McQuinn said, 'Begging your pardon, Inspector, but this doesn't make sense to me. Everything points to Kellar having done his wife in, like the old housekeeper says. But if he put the petticoat up the chimney then he wouldn't have drawn attention to himself by complaining that it was smoking, would he? He could have burnt it, got rid of it somewhere else, couldn't he?'

'The only reason would be panic.'

'And from what I've seen and heard of that gentleman, he's a cool customer, sir.'

At that moment a hired carriage arrived, and the cool customer descended and paid his fare.

'We'll have the cab, sir. Wait a moment, if you please.'

Dr Kellar was looking decidedly flushed and ill. 'What do you want this time, Inspector?' he demanded irritably. 'Out with it quick, man. I've had to leave early. You must excuse me if I don't delay. Stomach cramps. There's a bit of drain fever about at Surgeons Hall – I think I must have caught a dose. Not helped of course by the vile cooking in my home these days. Well, what is it now?'

'We've solved the problem with your bedroom chimney.'

'Surely we didn't need to call in the police for that?'

'The sweep found this was causing the blockage,' said Faro pushing forward the petticoat.

'What's this? A woman's shift – what on earth?' Kellar sounded genuinely astonished.

'Do you recognise it?'

'No, should I?' When Faro didn't answer, Kellar said. 'Some damned servant girl larking around, I suppose.'

'I'm afraid not. We have reason to believe that it belongs to your wife.'

Kellar looked again and Faro thought he grew a shade paler. 'I've never seen it before.'

'Surely . . . ' Faro began.

'If you are asking me what my wife wore under her dresses, then I can only tell you I haven't the faintest idea.'

If they slept in separate rooms, thought Faro, then Dr Kellar was probably speaking the truth.

'So you wouldn't be prepared to identify it?' said Faro.

'No, I would not,' Kellar replied testily.

'You would agree then that the servants are better acquainted with your wife's undergarments.'

'Of course they are.'

'So what would you say if I told you that Mrs Flynn has identified it as belonging to Mrs Kellar, by a repair she did on the morning your wife disappeared?'

'I would only say, surely no one, not even you, would take the word of domestics against mine. Now I bid you good-day, gentlemen.'

Kellar hurried up the front steps and let himself into the house.

McQuinn looked at Faro as if expecting him to make some move to stop the doctor's hasty retreat. Faro shrugged and stepped into the waiting carriage.

'Waverley Station, if you please. I'm going back to Longniddry, McQuinn, see if there are any more developments. You stay here, try to be unobtrusive and talk to the maid when she gets back. Shouldn't be long,' he added, in response to McQuinn's sullen look.

When Faro stepped off the train at Longniddry, a railwayman standing at the far end of the platform waved frantically, as if he had been waiting for the Inspector.

'Thought I recognised you, sir. I'm Thomas. That was quick work, sir,' he added with a grin. 'I've just sent a message an hour ago, through one of your men working the line.'

'Another discovery?'

'No, just information, sir.'

'Good.'

Faro began to walk towards the barrier and Thomas put a hand on his arm and said, 'Do you think we could talk back here, Inspector? I don't particularly want Mr Andrews to see us together. Look, if we sit on the steps of the signal box there down the line.'

'I hope it won't take long,' said Faro, pulling up the collar of his coat against the bitter east wind.

'It's like this, sir. That afternoon when you asked the station master about ladies in fur cloaks. I was listening when he told you about the maids with their parcels helping their mistresses out of the station and into carriages and so forth. Well, I remembered something. I wasn't sure whether it was of any importance, but I've been thinking about it since . . . '

'Why didn't you speak up at the time?' demanded Faro crossly.

'Look, Inspector, when the station master, Mr Andrews, isn't on duty I'm in charge of collecting tickets. It's a punishable offence, a fine taken off my wages, if I let someone go without a ticket. So if I make a mistake, I keep quiet about it, see. It's happened a couple of times and I'm on my last warning. Next time it'll cost me my job. And I've got a wife and five wee ones . . . '

It was beginning to rain, rain that was turning into sleet.

'So,' said Faro trying not to sound urgent, 'what was it you remembered?'

'About ten minutes after the North Berwick train left that day, the one you were enquiring about, when all the passengers had gone and I was going to lock the gate, a maid came out of the waiting room. She was carrying a big parcel. I know all the lasses here but this one was a stranger and I said, '"You're lucky. Another minute and you'd have been locked in. Unless you're able to climb gates."

'She didn't say a word, searching for her ticket in her travelling bag. She was shivering and had no coat, just a shawl and it was snowing.'

'"Have you far to go, miss?" I asked her.

'"Just down the road."

'When she found the ticket I noticed it was all bloody. So were her fingers. "Cut yourself, miss?" I asked.

'She seemed put out. "Just a scratch. I was looking

152

for water to wash my hands and there is none on the train. None in the waiting room either."

"'Hold on, miss,' I said, "and I'll get you water from the station master's room. We keep emergency bandages and things there in case of accidents."

'But when I came back two minutes later, she was scurrying off down the road, fast as her legs would carry her.'

'What was she dressed like?'

'Like, sir?' Thomas laughed. 'Like a maid, of course.'

'Young, old?'

'Difficult to say, sir. Fiftyish, I'd reckon. Hair tucked into a maid's cap.'

A picture was forming in Faro's mind. 'Spectacles?'

Thomas screwed up his face trying to think. 'Couldn't say as I noticed that, sir. But I don't think so.'

'Well then, was she a big woman? Stout, a bit clumsy-looking?'

'Oh, no, Inspector. A right skinny one. Tallish, thin as a post, this one. Nifty on her feet, I can tell you, the way she made off down the road. I guess she'll be from these parts, with one of the big houses.'

'What makes you think that?'

Thomas laughed. 'That's easy, sir. She had a first-class ticket.'

'First class? Surely that's unusual for a servant.'

'Not hereabouts, sir. The quality ladies do like to keep their maids by them in the same compartment, especially if the train's crowded. If she'd been travelling on her own, of course, she'd have been in third class, that's for sure.'

Faro had much to occupy his mind on the train back to Edinburgh.

The case against Kellar seemed now cut and dried. The fact that there was no Captain Shaw, allied to the revelations in Mabel's letter to her sister, confirmed Faro's own deduction about what had happened on that fateful train journey.

If he had been in any further need of convincing, the revelations of Thomas were proof positive that Mabel Kellar's body was beyond recovery. Kellar had condemned himself in his own words, most diabolically, by boasting to his wife how easy it would be for a police surgeon with access to a mortuary and dissecting room to dispose of an unwanted corpse.

Eveline Shaw had certainly provided Kellar with an alibi. But he needed an accomplice. Now, from the assistant ticket collector at Longniddry, it appeared they had found someone, in the guise of a maid, who had helped them get away with murder.

Chapter Fourteen

It was already dark when Faro at last walked up the steps to the Central Office. McQuinn was writing at the desk in his office. As his superior came in the sergeant threw down the pen.

'I was preparing a report for you, sir, before I went off duty.'

'Yes?'

'I stayed around at the back door of the Kellar house until the maid came back from the shops. The girl believes that she sees things, feels presences, but when I asked her to be more precise, all she did was shake her head and look like bursting into tears. It seems that Mrs Flynn has scared the living daylights out of the lass, that she'll lose her job. She's more anxious about that than her ghosts, I can tell you. Seems she has a dying sister and an invalid mother. Poor wee lass.'

He paused and gave Faro a speculative glance. 'I could try talking to her again, but it would have to be away from the house. She'd likely be easier without feeling that Mrs Flynn was watching her.'

Apart from his natural gallantry towards the female species at all times, Faro felt that McQuinn had little interest in carrying this particular professional duty into the realms of pleasure.

'Tell me, McQuinn, did you think the girl was – well, genuine?'

'Oh, I did, sir. No doubt about that. She's seen something in that house that scares her all right. Apparitions, well, I'm doubtful. I was wondering if it could be – let's say a corpse.'

'You mean the missing Mrs Kellar.'

'I was thinking along those lines.'

'I think you're wrong about that, McQuinn.' And Faro proceeded to tell McQuinn about the development at Longniddry.

McQuinn pushed back his helmet, scratched his head. 'Well, sir, that is a poser, isn't it? Looks like the murder was committed on the train, early on, soon after leaving Edinburgh, I'd say, by this accomplice posing as her maid. Then her body was got off the train, don't ask me how,' he added hastily, seeing Faro's expression.

'If our suppositions are correct, then it was collected by Kellar in his carriage at some pre-arranged place along the line.'

'It couldn't have been at a station, sir. Even if your accomplice was carrying off an allegedly sick and injured woman, how would they account for all that blood.'

'She could have been murdered by strangulation or by a stab wound in some vital place which would not have bled profusely. Kellar would know all about that. Her body was taken to the mortuary by Kellar, while the bogus maid got off at the next stop – Longniddry – carrying the evidence which was then disposed of down the railway embankment?'

McQuinn brightened. 'That fits, sir.'

Faro shook his head. 'No, it doesn't. We haven't taken into account that vital factor of happenstance. However, it's well worth careful consideration. You might be on to something and we can check the stations en route, see if anyone was carried off the train.'

As praise from his superior was notably rare, McQuinn looked pleased. 'What shall I do next, sir?'

'Try and see the maid again. Use your charm on her, McQuinn.'

'Right, sir,' said McQuinn and saluted smartly.

Ever since Longniddry, Faro had begun to see a flicker of light, appropriately enough, at the end of the tunnel. Light that obstinately reflected a very different pattern from the one he had envisaged up till now.

As was his custom, he had been marshalling his facts together and when he wearily let himself into 9 Sheridan Place, he was pleased to find Vince at home, anxious for an account of his day's activities.

Regarding the revelations from the Caithness Regiment, Vince said disgustedly, 'Imagine there being no Captain Shaw and all this time we've been falling over ourselves to console the distraught young widow. What a cheat!'

'Do you think Mrs Kellar knew the truth?'

'Certainly not. She would never suspect a friend of telling her such a downright lie. What else did you find out?'

Vince listened eagerly to Faro's account of the interview with Thomas. 'This is great progress, Stepfather. All you need now is to trace the maid. What a piece of luck.'

'There's one thing more, lad.' Faro was reluctant to tell his stepson about the bloodstained petticoat. As he expected Vince was exceedingly upset.

'How can you sit there, Stepfather, so calm and doing nothing about arresting Kellar. In the face of such damning evidence,' Vince added, thumping the table angrily.

'Vince, lad. Listen. Please, I beg you, don't get carried away by emotions.'

'Emotions!' Vince exploded. 'My most dear friend has been murdered by her husband, aided and abetted by her false friend. And you ask me not to get carried away!'

'Vince. Listen to me. I need some clear concise thinking on this, the kind that you have so often provided in the past. I beg of you to forget for the moment that you are personally concerned. Pretend that Mabel Kellar is just one other murder victim and help me. Help me, lad, when I most need you.' He paused. 'Will you do that, lad?'

Vince sat back in his chair and said stiffly, 'All right,

Stepfather. But do try not to make it difficult for me by talking about my emotions.'

'Very well. I apologise for my lack of tact. It won't happen again. Now, let's consider all these latest developments I've told you about. I've come to only one conclusion and that is, all is not what it seems.'

'What is that supposed to mean?' asked Vince irritably. 'Why, it's all plain as the nose on your face to anyone with half an eye.'

Faro suppressed a smile. This was no time to tease his stepson about ill-chosen metaphors. 'It's meant to be, but you have my assurances, it is not. I must ask you to believe in my judgement. We are not nearly there yet.'

'I should have thought that Mabel's petticoat in the chimney would be enough, without her cloak and the knife, to prove that someone in the house, and Kellar is the most likely since he has the motive, has got rid of her body and is desperately trying to get rid of the evidence.'

Faro nodded. 'That is certainly the obvious conclusion. But I want you to concentrate your thoughts in quite another direction.'

Vince continued to look distraught and angry and Faro went on, 'Kellar denies putting the petticoat up the chimney, or to recognise it as belonging to his wife.'

Vince laughed harshly. 'That doesn't surprise me. I imagine the housekeeper and the maid are more familiar with his wife's laundry than Kellar, seeing that they live quite separate lives.'

'Indeed, and Mrs Flynn recognised the garment immediately.'

'So there you are.'

'The snag about this particular piece of evidence is that Kellar was the one to complain about the smoking chimney in the first place, and insist on getting the sweep. I find it extraordinary that a guilty man would want to draw attention to himself in this way.

'Let's assume for the moment that Kellar is speaking

the truth.' Faro ignored Vince's snort of disbelief and went on, 'Who do we have left who could have done away with Mabel? Bear in mind that we are also looking for someone with a motive.'

'And for someone who could wield a carving knife with good effect, and dispose of a body,' said Vince. 'There can't be many in this particular *dramatis personae*.'

'I agree. And we're discounting a possible madman on the train.'

'It lets out Mrs Shaw who would be physically incapable of the deed, although she was doubtless the motive for the murder.'

'Yes. In her way, she is as guilty as Kellar,' said Faro sadly.

'What about Sir Hedley Marsh?'

'We've covered that ground before. Why should he murder his heiress? Besides, the Mad Bart is too well kenned a figure about Edinburgh to murder anyone on a train, even if he was fit enough physically to drag a body around.'

'I suppose the old man who does the garden is similarly innocent.'

'We had a routine check on him. He was in bed all that week with a bad attack of pleurisy,' said Faro.

'And the maid Ina can be dismissed on physical grounds. She's hardly built for that kind of murder. What about Mrs Flynn?'

'She's stout and undoubtedly strong, if she ever gets rid of her toothache and bad veins.'

Vince shook his head. 'Remember the motive, Stepfather. She and Ina loved Mabel. They would have done anything for her, just like everyone else fortunate enough to know her.'

Looking across at Faro, he said, 'If it wasn't Kellar, then our best bet is Harry Shaw. I'm sure the same thought has occurred to you. From what your Longniddry fellow told you, I got a distinct picture that the maid he described could have been a man.'

Faro gave a sudden start. 'Disguised, of course.'

'What was this man Shaw like?'

'Tallish, but lightly built.'

'There you are, Stepfather. That's your answer, just as you speculated. Shaw was persuaded, or coerced into helping them out. You have Mrs Shaw's word and the evidence of your own eyes that he is a violent man.' He paused and gave his stepfather an enquiring look. 'Are you taking this in? Surely you've seen the significance?'

Faro turned to face him slowly. 'It's beginning to dawn very clearly, lad. Yes, that light at the end of the tunnel is growing distinctly brighter, quite illuminating, in fact.'

Vince gave his stepfather an exasperated stare. 'Well, I'm glad to have been of some help.'

Faro smiled. 'Oh you have, lad. You have indeed.'

'Good. Let's take our supposition a bit further. Harry Shaw helps out, as you surmised with the evidence, perhaps with the murder on the train.'

Faro didn't answer. He drained his teacup of contents that had gone cold long since.

'And now with the obstacle to her marriage out of the way,' Vince continued, 'free to marry Melville Kellar at last, Mrs Shaw sends her inconvenient lover packing. But he has other ideas. If she is as diabolic as we are beginning to suspect, I rather think the next corpse might be Harry Shaw.'

Faro sprang from his seat. 'Get your greatcoat, Vince, we're going out.'

'Out? Where?'

'We're going to pay a couple of unexpected calls. First of all, to the Kellar house.'

'Stepfather, it's nearly nine o'clock.'

'So?'

'You can't call on Kellar uninvited at this hour.'

'He won't be at home. I'm rather banking on it as I noticed in the newspaper that he is giving a lecture to a learned society.'

'Then what— '

'Don't argue. We're wasting valuable time.'

'Have you seen the weather?' protested Vince. 'It's been snowing since six.'

But Faro was already in the hall, donning his overshoes.

'Are you going to arrest Kellar when he arrives home? Is that it, Stepfather? Have I convinced you? Do we have to look sharp, call unexpectedly, in case he makes a run for it?'

Faro shook his head. 'The purpose of this visit is for you to see Mabel's room. You've got what they call a corbie's eye for detail. You see, I can't get it out of my mind that there was something I missed, something I should have seen but didn't on that first visit.'

Fortunately the snow had ceased and the evening was brightly moonlit. Faro, however, was impervious to the beauties of the night and Vince found himself indulging in a monologue.

As the cab carried them towards the Grange, he saw that his stepfather was unusually silent, huddled into a corner of the carriage, chin sunk into his collar, asleep or deep in thought.

At last they turned into the drive of Kellar's house where Faro sprang to life again and told the driver to set them down. 'We'll walk the rest of the way. Wait for us here.'

As the house came into view, there were no cracks of light visible behind the closed shutters. 'We're too late. Presumably they're all abed,' said Vince hoping this would dissuade his stepfather from proceeding any further.

'Then we'll have to wake them up,' said Faro cheerfully.

The doorbell pealed, once, twice. Vince shuffled his feet uncomfortably. 'Kellar will be furious if he catches us, Stepfather.'

'Listen. Someone's coming.'

'Who is it?' A woman's muffled voice.

Vince gave him a startled glance and whispered, 'Mrs Flynn?'

'Mrs Flynn, it's Inspector Faro.'

'What do you want? Master's not at home.'

'It is you I want a word with, Mrs Flynn. Or Ina.'

'Ina's away home.' There was a short silence. 'We're all poorly. Seem to have been poisoned with something bad we ate.'

'Poison, eh,' whispered Faro. He gave Vince a significant glance, his face unusually excited in the bright moonlight. 'Mrs Flynn?'

There was no reply and he rapped sharply on the door. 'Mrs Flynn. Open the door, please.'

'I'm in my nightgown, Inspector.'

'This is police business, Mrs Flynn. We have to see Mrs Kellar's room again.'

'At this time of night! Who's with you, sir?'

'Dr Laurie, Mrs Kellar's friend.'

'Come back tomorrow.'

'No. Open the door. We'll be as quiet as mice and it won't take more than two minutes.'

His wheedling tone succeeded in getting the door unlocked. As they set foot in the hall, Mrs Flynn retreated modestly.

'I've turned up the gas for you. I'm away back to my bed.'

Faro led the way upstairs and opened the door of Mabel's bedroom. 'All right, Vince lad, now you tell me what it was that I missed, because I'm damned if I know.'

Vince followed Faro round the room. Soon the room was brilliantly illuminated under the glare of gaslight. 'It's all exactly as I remember it the last time I was here. Nothing odd, certainly nothing out of place.'

Faro was standing by the dressing table. He lifted the silver-backed brushes as he had on that first visit.

'Exactly,' he whispered to Vince. 'And that is precisely what was wrong. What has been nagging at me all this

162

time. Look at these, lad. What do they say to you?'

Vince frowned. 'That they are exquisite, very valuable. Mabel was very proud of them.'

'Then, tell me, why did she leave them behind?'

Vince watching his stepfather's reflection in the mirror, looked puzzled. 'I have no idea. Mabel was very proud of her hair; brushing it was a bit of a ritual with her and that's why she mourned the loss of a personal maid.'

'So you would agree that these are intimate articles that no woman would be without on her travels.'

'Certainly Mabel wouldn't.'

And Faro knew he had the answer to what nagged him since that first visit.

'Don't you see what this means, Vince, lad? There was something far more sinister behind Mabel Kellar's departure than a mere domestic tiff with her husband.'

Vince continued to look puzzled and Faro went on solemnly, 'What you are seeing now is the very first clue.'

'Clue, Stepfather. I don't understand.'

'Yes, you do, lad. Think. The presence of those hair brushes when they should logically have been absent tells us something vital about this whole case.'

Leaving Vince still staring blankly at the silver brushes, Faro led the way downstairs. Once Vince stumbled and cursed.

In the hall, Faro paused. 'We'll have a word with Mrs Flynn before we go.'

'If Kellar arrives and finds us roaming about his house at the dead of night, there'll be hell to pay,' warned Vince.

'This won't take a moment.'

But they were out of luck. Faro went downstairs, tapped on the door of Mrs Flynn's room from which loud snores issued forth. He called her name several times, but the snoring seemed to have intensified. Turning the handle, he found the door firmly locked.

'What did you expect, Stepfather? With a madman still

163

at large, and a maid who sees things, she's not taking any chances. And neither should we,' he added with a shudder. 'Do let's go. This house is cold as a tomb and it's beginning to give me the creeps.'

Vince sighed with relief when he saw the cab driver's lights along the drive. 'Home again, Stepfather. I'll be glad of a dram, I can tell you.'

'Not quite yet, lad. In a wee while.' And, leaning forward, Faro gave Mrs Shaw's address.

Vince looked aghast. 'You can't be serious, Stepfather, calling on her at this hour.'

'The later the better. With luck we might also find Harry Shaw there. An unexpected pleasure you have in store, lad,' he added, ignoring Vince's grumbles as they boarded the carriage and headed towards Regent Crescent.

Chapter Fifteen

Edinburgh asleep under its heavy blanket of snow presented a scene of enchantment and delight for those inclined to romance. At this hour there were few people about to enjoy this spectacular backdrop and Faro's entreaty to his stepson to admire such unexpected beauty met with a somewhat disgruntled response.

'All in bed and missing it, are they? I wish I was too, or I wish that my feet were warm. I'm frozen.'

Faro suppressed a smile at Vince's return to the spoilt petulant child of former years. There was nothing to be done with him in this mood, his stepfather knew from experience, and instead stared out of the window, sighing deeply as if he could breathe in the moonbeams.

When at last they reached Regent Crescent, the fanlight showed illumination and their summons was answered with alacrity by Mrs Shaw. In a dressing gown with her hair unbound she presented a captivating sight. She did not seem perturbed by their late arrival and greeted them without surprise.

'As if gentlemen arriving on her doorstep at nearly eleven o'clock was a perfectly normal occurrence,' Vince murmured later in shocked tones. The significant look he gave his stepfather indicated that Mrs Shaw had slipped from the pedestal of unsullied virtue into the realms of scarlet womanhood.

'Do come in,' she said cutting short Faro's apologies for the lateness of the hour. 'How nice to see you again, Vince. Barnaby is teething and refuses to settle. I have had him up and down since teatime.' Ushering them into the drawing-room as she spoke, she stirred the embers of the fire into a welcome blaze. 'Now what can I do for you?'

Faro and Vince exchanged uncomfortable glances staring at the baby lying on the sofa, attacking a teething ring with cannibalistic venom. It wasn't going to be easy.

Mrs Shaw went over and, after kissing Barnaby, smiled at them. 'Let me guess the purpose of your visit. I suppose it's about the late Captain Shaw.'

Faro nodded, cleared his throat a little, while Vince shuffled his feet and tried to look unobtrusive. 'That is so.'

Again she smiled, sadly this time. 'I realised that the police enquiries would be very thorough if you were in charge, Inspector. It was bound to come out sooner or later that I did not in fact have a husband and have never had one.'

Barnaby uttered a yell of protest and she swept him up into her arms, laid one scarlet cheek against her cool one.

'Perhaps you would give us the whole story. That would help enormously and save a great deal of time.'

'There is not much to tell. I met Harry Shaw when I went to live in Caithness after my parents died. Harry asked me to marry him but his taste for adventure decided me against it. He wished to go to America and I wished to remain in Scotland. There seemed to be no solution. We quarrelled and I sent him away. A few weeks later Dr Kellar came on a shooting holiday and was very attentive.'

She coloured slightly at the memory. 'I am very ashamed of what happened next. I had discovered that I was carrying Harry's child. I was desperate. Harry had gone out of my life for ever. My relatives would show me the door when they found out. There was only one solution left and however despicable it must sound to you, I had to find a father for my baby.

'I need not elaborate on the rest of the story, Dr Kellar's

infatuation and our subsequent association. I knew he was married but I followed him to Edinburgh and allowed him to set me up in this house, believing, God forgive me, that Barnaby was his child.'

She smiled sadly. 'His eagerness to do so astounded me. He never questioned or doubted my word. And he loved Barnaby from the first moment he set eyes on him, so proud to be a father at last.'

'Did he say he would marry you, if he were free?'

'Of course, but we both knew that was quite impossible and a scandal would have ruined him, destroyed his career, his hopes for the future. For me there was another factor: as I got to know Mabel and she was eager to befriend me as a young widow, I could not bear to have her hurt.'

She paused, looking at them from one to the other. 'But perhaps my strongest reason of all was that, despite our relationship, I in no way responded to Melville's infatuation. I knew how foolish I had been to reject Harry. I had given my heart. I still loved him and would do so always, even if I never saw him in this world again.'

She let the words sink in before continuing. 'I was the happiest woman in the world the day that Harry Shaw walked into this house, told me he still loved me and met his son for the first time.' Her eyes filled with tears. 'Oh, what a joyous meeting that was. The answer to a miracle indeed.'

She spread her hands wide in a gesture of hopelessness. 'Until I remembered Melville Kellar and his demands upon my life. What was I to do? I decided there must be no more secrets between Harry and myself and, I must say, he took it all remarkably calmly. He said he forgave me, but that I must write to Kellar and tell him the true facts. I'm afraid I tried several times, but always my courage failed me. My rapturous joy over Harry's return was every day slipping further into the realms of nightmare as we began to quarrel

167

once again, for he thought my cowardice was lack of love for him.'

Barnaby began to whimper again as if in tune to his mother's sadness and she took him into her arms.

'It would be best, don't you see,' said Faro gently, 'if you were to write that letter.'

She looked up. 'But I have just done so. Harry posted it on the way to the station. I thought that was why you were here.'

'Where is Mr Shaw?' asked Faro.

'On his way to Yorkshire, for an interview with a firm of architects.'

'Then you are here alone?'

Mrs Shaw smiled at Faro's tone of alarm. 'I am used to being alone. I have my maid.'

'And yet you open the door to callers at this late hour?'

'I never gave it a second thought.'

'Then I urge you to do so.'

Her amused expression turned into a frown. 'Are you trying to warn me, Inspector. Am I in danger? I assure you I have no enemies.'

'All of us have enemies, whatever face they choose to wear.'

'You think Melville, when he finds out about Harry?' Her eyes widened in shocked surprise.

'I think nothing. I merely warn you to take extra care who you open your door to, especially at night.'

As they took their leave, bowing over her hand, Faro again urged her to be vigilant.

In the cab carrying them homeward at last, Vince mulled over the interview with Mrs Shaw. 'I still think of her as that.'

'And so she is under the Scottish law, Harry Shaw's wife "by habit and repute".'

'Of course. Well, this demolishes all our theories about the three of them conspiring to get rid of Mabel. I'm pleased about that.' He sighed. 'And if there were any reasons for joy in this miserable business I'm delighted that Melville Kellar has got his deserts and that Eveline Shaw's child isn't his after all.'

'It has a happier ending than perhaps she deserved.'

'The oldest trick in the world, Stepfather. Women have played that particular game since time began. And I have nothing but contempt for them. It is utterly vile, the ultimate unforgivable deception.'

'We must not let Mrs Shaw's revelations divert us from the main issue, lad.'

'I'm not forgetting, Stepfather. But you seemed remarkably worried, warning her about enemies and so forth, when she made it plain that she has none.'

'Oh yes, lad. She has one at least. I just hope to God that her letter arrived in time to avert yet another calamity and save her becoming the next victim.'

'Kellar, eh? I'd have liked to have been a fly on the wall when he read her letter of rejection,' said Vince with some relish. 'He must have been devastated, don't you agree?'

'I'm too tired to think straight any more, lad. What we both need is a dram and a good night's sleep. Everything will seem a lot clearer in the morning.'

But Faro, for once, was wrong.

He and Vince were indulging themselves with breakfast later than usual when the doorbell pealed shrilly through the house. They heard Mrs Brook come up from the kitchen, and by the time Faro had sprung from the table, Sergeant McQuinn was standing in the hall.

An unlikely figure to launch a thunderbolt set to reduce all Faro's new-found theories, his enlightened deductions to naught, he said, 'You're to come at once, sir, and bring the doctor along too. Kellar has shot himself.'

In the police carriage, McQuinn told them what had happened. He had been on his way to talk to the maid Ina before going on duty, when who should come along the drive, staggering through the snow but Kellar himself.

'Came out of the front gate, like a drunk man, wearing

169

nothing but his nightshirt. Then I saw the blood on the snow, dripping from his head it was. And when I went to help him, I could smell the gun smoke on him. I blew my whistle, got him into a passing cab and rustled up a couple of lads on the beat to take him across to the Royal Infirmary, quick as you like.'

He stopped. 'I was in a bit of a quandary, sir. I thought I'd best get back to the scene of the crime, so to speak.'

'You did quite right.'

McQuinn nodded. 'Went down that drive sharp as I could and there was Mrs Flynn standing at the door. Crying and wringing her hands. I could see she was in a terrible state.

'She'd been making breakfast when she heard a loud bang, that's how she described the pistol shot, coming from the master's bedroom. She went up to see what was wrong and there he was lying across the bed, with a bullet wound in his head, blood everywhere. At first she thought he was dead, then he groaned and moved. She realised he had tried to commit suicide. Here's the evidence, sir.'

He handed Faro a bloodstained note. Written in shaky capitals were the words: 'Goodbye, I killed her.'

'And here's the pistol I collected. There was this letter too, open on the bedside table. As it might be evidence, I took the liberty . . . '

The letter was from Mrs Shaw telling Kellar that she had deceived him, that Harry Shaw, who was Barnaby's father, had returned to Edinburgh and she was resolved to marry him.

'Did you read this, McQuinn?'

'Just a glance, sir. Evidence enough to prove that he got such a shock that his mind was temporarily unhinged. Mind you, he didn't strike me as the kind who would take his own life over any woman. Come ten a penny to a man like him.'

'Keep the contents to yourself, McQuinn, if you please.'

170

'Naturally, sir,' McQuinn sounded indignant. 'I suppose you'll need the servants to testify.'

Faro nodded rather absently, and the Sergeant gave him a curious look. The Inspector seemed almost as shocked as the housekeeper at the Grange had been.

'Mrs Flynn had a terrible fright. She told me when she saw he was still breathing, she rushed downstairs to get water to bathe his head – rushing around like a decapitated hen, I shouldn't wonder.' He grinned. 'Nothing as exciting as this had ever happened to her before. But when she got back to the bedroom, he had gone. Disappeared.'

As they boarded the carriage, Vince heard Faro giving McQuinn instructions about a locked cupboard he might expect to find. But no further explanation was offered to his bewildered stepson as they hurtled along towards the hospital as fast as the appalling condition of the snowy roads would allow.

Dr Kellar was occupying a private ward and, at first glance, Faro thought they had come too late. Kellar, with his head heavily bandaged, seemed to have a precarious grip on life.

'Looks pretty bad, doesn't he?'

Vince nodded. 'Can't really tell, until the doctors have had a chance to see how much damage was done by the bullet. I think I'll stay. This might take a little time.'

'Yes, yes, lad. I'll leave you to it. I'd better get back to the Grange and talk to Mrs Flynn and Ina.'

Vince looked at him frowning, seemed about to say something, then changed his mind and shook his head.

'What is it, lad?'

'Nothing, Stepfather. Just a thought. It'll keep.' And he turned his attention back to the doctors who were hurrying down the corridor to attend the injured man.

As the police carriage made its way through the melting snow taking Faro back towards the Grange, a sudden burst of sunshine, bringing with it unseasonal warmth, had set the birds singing an anthem to spring in the

171

skeletal trees. Faro shook his head. This time of hope, this suggestion of springtime was all wrong for sudden death.

McQuinn was waiting for him and when they ran up the steps to the front door it was opened a couple of inches by a scared-looking Ina.

At the sight of the Inspector, she became quite voluble, sobbing out all about the master and the pistol shot and how poor Mrs Flynn had been frightened out of her wits.

'Easy, lass. Easy now,' said McQuinn gently. 'No one's going to harm you. We're here to help you.'

Faro noted that once again the handsome young sergeant's charm proved effective and the girl smiled at him gratefully through her tears as if she had been offered manna from heaven.

'We're here to see Mrs Flynn. Downstairs, is she?'

Ina shook her head. 'No, sir. She's gone to the Infirmary. To see how the master is. So upset she was. Terrible bad fright she got. Thinking he was dead, and then him walking away like that. Said it was enough to give anyone a heart attack.'

'Ina showed me the cupboard,' McQuinn interrupted, removing a travelling bag from under the hall table. 'That's all there was. It isn't locked.'

Faro glanced inside, nodded with some satisfaction and said. 'Come along, McQuinn. Back to the infirmary.'

Ina seemed reluctant to lose them. She followed them down the steps to the waiting carriage.

'You take care of things, Ina. You're in charge until we get back,' said McQuinn, making her feel important.

'But— '

'You'll be all right. I'm leaving a couple of constables to look after you,' he added, making her feel safe too.

As they got into the carriage, she giggled slightly hysterically. 'Poor Mrs Flynn. That fright didn't do her any good, I can tell you. I've always thought of her as

172

such a big strong woman, but when I saw her hurrying down the drive, she didn't seem like herself at all. Dazed and scared-like. Isn't that amazing?'

Faro stared at her and slammed the door. 'Hurry, for God's sake. Fast as you can,' he told the driver.

The short journey to the Infirmary seemed endless and Faro drummed his fingers on the window-ledge, cursing the delays. What if they were already too late?

Reaching their destination, he leaped up the stairs to the ward, telling McQuinn to wait in the corridor.

'We may need you,' he added grimly. And to the nurse who approached. 'Has anyone been in to see Dr Kellar?'

'He is far too ill to receive visitors, Inspector,' was the shocked reply.

'That wasn't my question, Sister.'

'A Mrs Findlay-Cupar called a few moments ago.'

'Mrs Findlay-Cupar? Are you sure?'

'Yes, his sister-in-law.'

'Where is she now?'

'I sent her away, Inspector.'

'You sent her away?'

'Of course. My instructions are to admit no one. And that includes members of the family.'

In the ward, Faro was relieved to see Vince sitting at Kellar's bedside taking his pulse.

'Still alive, thank God.'

'I think he has a good chance,' said Vince cheerfully, 'Lucky for him, the bullet didn't strike any vital part. It grazed off the side of his head. He must have moved at the last moment. He's got a head as thick as a stone wall. Pity he'll only survive for the hangman's rope.'

The man on the bed groaned, opened his eyes, struggled to sit up and was restrained by Vince.

'Where am I?'

'The Infirmary, sir.'

Kellar blinked furiously. 'Thank God. Thank God, I can see. My head feels terrible. Am I going to die?'

It was a difficult question to answer in all honesty. Faro thought that 'Not just for the moment' would be inappropriate and rather unfeeling for the man's present condition.

'You're not seriously hurt, sir,' said Vince. 'The bullet deflected.'

'Ah, it's you, is it, Laurie, I hope you're remembering all I've taught you,' he said dazedly.

'Yes, sir.'

There was a short pause and then Kellar turned his head slowly towards them. 'All this is really happening. It isn't just a bad dream, is it?'

'No, sir. Unfortunately not.'

Kellar smiled wanly. 'I can see,' he repeated. 'I'm not blind or imagining things. So it was her.'

'Her? Who, sir?'

'Flynn.'

'When did you see her, sir?'

'She tried to kill me.'

'Mrs Flynn – the housekeeper – she tried to kill you?' said Vince and, looking across at Faro, whispered, 'His mind's wandering. He's having hallucinations.'

Kellar gave another groan and sank back on to the pillows. 'I'm telling you. She tried to kill me.'

Chapter Sixteen

Further questions were cut short by the arrival of the senior doctors. Faro was hustled into the tiny waiting-room by the grim-faced nurse, with Vince protesting furiously, 'How dare they treat me like a first-year medical student.'

Allowing his injured pride to be calmed down by his stepfather at last, he said, 'Kellar's mind must have been deranged. Or was it an attack of conscience?'

'An attack certainly,' said Faro, 'and by something much more substantial than conscience.'

'You mean, someone tried to kill him and make it look like suicide?'

'Exactly.'

'But the note— '

'I think we can dismiss the suicide note. The handwriting is not even a clever forgery.' Faro looked at the shaky capital letters. 'Look at the bloodstains. A man does not decide to shoot himself and write the note afterwards, although I imagine we are expected to make that account for the illegibility.'

'You're right, Stepfather. Kellar was no bungler. He was a highly efficient man and if he had been intending to kill himself it would have been done very tidily indeed.'

'Aren't you forgetting Mrs Shaw's letter of rejection?'

'A blow to his pride, but hardly enough to make him take his own life. Unless he realised that he had murdered Mabel for nothing. And talking of bloodstains, I'm working on the fur cloak. Using Dr Landois's experimental technique, I took a spot of blood from my finger and from Mrs Brook's. She was most impressed. However when I raided her pantry for raw beef, she was quite shocked, I can tell you. I've sent it off to Landois, although I'm not too hopeful of anything conclusive. As I told you, his experiments are in the early stages.'

'I think we'll hear that the bloodstains aren't human and that the blood doesn't correspond with either yours or Mrs Brook's. They most probably came from an ox heart or liver from the Kellar kitchen.'

'I don't understand. Why on earth should anyone counterfeit bloodstains?'

'The answer is easy. Dr Kellar was to be accused of his wife's murder.'

'Are you trying to tell me that there were to be two murders. The doctor and his wife?'

'No, I don't mean that at all. Kellar was always the intended victim, not Mabel. That was how it was planned, very carefully, right from the beginning.'

Ignoring his stepson's exclamation of disbelief, Faro continued, 'Right in fact from that fateful dinner party. That was all part of the plan too and the events of that evening are of vital importance. Nothing that happened that evening is too trivial to overlook, for it was all set out for us, like a play on a stage, a plot that had been worked out to the very last detail—'

'But I don't see how—' Vince interrupted.

'We were all invited for a definite purpose, with our parts to play. We were to be witnesses of certain happenings. I was puzzled, I have to admit. My first thought was that I was there as a parent to give his approval and blessing on a piece of matchmaking between his stepson and a pretty widow—'

Faro cut short Vince's protest. 'Hear me out, please. My role was as audience to a curtain raiser on a very clever crime, the death of Dr Melville Kellar.'

'And Mabel?'

Faro smiled. 'You're going too fast, lad. Let us return to our arrival at the Kellar house. I want you to remember, if you can, every detail of our reception from the moment we walked up the drive.'

'The door was opened by the housekeeper—'

'Too fast. We rang the bell—'

'We rang the bell,' said Vince impatiently. 'And we had rather a long wait—'

'Ah, yes. Why?' he added sharply.

Vince shrugged. 'Lack of servants.'

'Why?'

'Mrs Kellar had given the maid Ina the weekend off and she and Mrs Flynn were cooking dinner. They were both in the kitchen and I presume hadn't heard us ring the bell.'

'Can you remember which of them opened the door?'

'Mabel – no, Mrs Flynn.'

'Did you notice anything about her?'

Vince thought. 'She was very hot and flustered, dusting flour from her hands.'

'Good. Floury hands which indicated that she was indeed in the process of making pastry. Tell me, what were your impressions of Mrs Flynn?'

Again Vince shrugged. 'Mrs Flynn? Why, none at all. I doubt very much whether I'd know her again if I met her.'

'You can do better than that, lad, after all I've taught you. What did she look like?'

Vince shrugged. 'I don't know. Just like any other maid. I didn't pay particular attention to her appearance.'

'Ah!'

Vince stared at him. 'It's true. She made absolutely no impression. A middle-aged domestic. Let me think. Was her hair grey?'

'What could be seen under her cap – yes. Did you notice anything about her eyes, for instance?'

'You surely don't expect me to remember the colour

177

of her eyes, Stepfather,' Vince protested. 'I'm bad at that, even for my nearest and dearest. Wait a moment, was she wearing spectacles?' He looked at Faro for affirmation.

'Good. Do you remember anything odd about her face?'

'Odd? Let me think. Oh yes, of course, she was all muffled up, swollen with toothache.'

Faro smiled. 'Good. You're more observant than you thought. You have described Mrs Flynn more or less exactly.'

'That's a relief,' said Vince sarcastically, thinking that this dinner party step by step was going to be almost as long and boring to recall as it had been in reality. 'So we enter the house. We go upstairs and are ushered into the drawing-room, introduced to Mrs Shaw.'

'Not so fast, lad. We are in the hall. Mrs Flynn apologises for the delay due to the lack of servants. Then Dr Kellar appears— '

'On the landing outside the drawing-room and rages at the housekeeper for keeping us waiting. He tells her to summon her mistress immediately.'

'Splendid. So where was our hostess, anyway, and why wasn't she there to greet her guests?'

'That's easy. She was in the kitchen. Mrs Flynn said so and Mabel confirmed that later.'

'Very well. We have Mrs Flynn answering the door and Mrs Kellar in the kitchen, helping the stricken housekeeper with some very indifferent cooking, out of the kindness of her heart, as there was no other servant in the house that night. In fact, we realised she had been hard at work until the last minute before dressing, for when she appeared at the dinner table there was still distressing evidence of pastry making on her hands and nails.' He paused to let this information sink in.

'Hardly an auspicious beginning, was it? Chaos in the kitchen, a housekeeper with raging toothache and no other servant?'

Faro smiled and wagged an admonishing finger. 'Ah yes, but a most auspicious overture for a planned murder. Keep that information by you, Vince. What could be better for our murderer's purpose than comings and goings of a very furtive nature without witnesses?'

Vince looked slightly dazed.

'We went upstairs and the drawing-room was occupied by Dr Kellar and Mrs Shaw, presenting the appearance of polite strangers who have no interest whatever in each other.'

'Yes, it was odd, when you think about it, that Kellar made no attempt to introduce us. Rather rude, I thought.'

'Well, we have the answer to that part of the mystery. The assembled company were meant to see antipathy between Mrs Shaw and Dr Kellar in the little charade put on for our benefit.'

'Because they were lovers?'

'Had been lovers, Vince. But Kellar wasn't aware then that Mrs Shaw planned to reject him.'

'That accounts, I suppose, for her own rather distraught manner.'

'Indeed it does. She was wondering how to break the news and, more important, what his reaction would be. However, they weren't the only ones with a charade to present that evening. You were sitting next to Mrs Shaw and Mabel.'

Vince gave him an impish look. 'And the only time I saw a spark of animation was when she was chatting to you or playing the piano.'

'Ah, the entertainment. We mustn't forget that. Mrs Shaw's excellent playing and Mrs Kellar's long monologue.'

'I'd heard it before. I thought she was particularly good at all those changes of voice.'

'An excellent mimic.'

Vince looked hard at him. 'I didn't think you shared my enthusiasm. I'm afraid you were looking very bored and so was Mrs Shaw who seemed as embarrassed by her friend's performance as she was by her fulsome affection. We know why, now.'

'Bad enough being in the same room with Kellar, dining at the same table with his wife, the dearest friend she had also betrayed. But let us leave Mrs Shaw now.'

'Poor Mabel,' said Vince. 'I keep thinking how dreadful the realisation must have been for her, how shattering. If she'd had the least idea, I'm sure she would never have given Mrs Shaw houseroom.'

'I think she knew at Christmas.'

'Then when she wrote to her sister, why didn't she say so in as many words?'

'Ah, that letter, Vince. Revealing all, which was precisely what it was meant to do.'

Vince frowned. 'But even the most forgiving of women . . . Her behaviour doesn't make sense.'

'Oh yes, it does. Very good sense indeed. Think of the contents of that letter, Vince, and what they implied.'

'I am thinking.'

'Let's return to our charade of a dinner party. What else could Mabel Kellar do in the circumstances? Kellar has told her that Mrs Shaw is his mistress, she has borne him a child and he has set her up in a house in the New Town. What was to be gained by admitting that she knew? Divorce, or a scandal, would not bring her erring husband back to her. By ruining his chance of a knighthood, she also had a lot to lose, her social standing in society, for instance.'

'True enough, Stepfather. Many women endure such an existence. Even knowing that their husbands, respectable men holding high positions in society, are leading double lives with a mistress and often an illegitimate child, they are in a cleft stick. A respectable marriage bestows on a wife a desirable place in society and if her husband falls, then she falls with him.

'What must have made it worse, unbearable for Mabel,

was the knowledge that she had been deliberately deprived of finding solace in the comfort of motherhood, and by her own husband.'

'Exactly,' said Faro triumphantly. 'So now you tell me, who had the best motive for murder that evening?'

'Mabel, of course,' laughed Vince. 'If she'd been the murdering kind she'd have stuck the carving knife in Kellar. I've always said that.'

'So you have, so you have.'

But ignoring his stepfather's gratified expression, Vince continued, 'Ironic, isn't it. Poor Mabel. No wonder they wanted to get rid of her. Her continued devotion to them both must have been a source of embarrassment. Mabel, so gentle and loving. But murder, such a terrible step to take.'

'To many desperate people, murder is the last resort and only terrible if they are found out. Within the police we are fully aware that husbands constantly murder wives, and t'other way round in our community, mostly for gain of some kind. Although our suspicions are aroused, we can rarely raise enough evidence to prove that a crime has been committed.'

Vince nodded in agreement. 'I know from conversations I've had with other doctors that they often had strong suspicions that poison has been administered. The discreet and effective way of certain death, although alas, slow and often very painful, it can be diagnosed as food poisoning, or drain fever. But doctors are often hesitant and dare not bring a case against some respectable citizen, for fear of putting their own reputations into jeopardy.'

'Aye, and many a timorous spouse ill-treated by husband or wife would commit murder – they do so in their hearts every passing hour – if they knew they could get away with it. The one deterrent is the indisputable evidence in the shape of a dead body, that cannot be conveniently spirited away.'

'Not in Kellar's case. Who had better facilities for

disposing of a corpse than Melville Kellar? He had a hundred unknowing accessories all ready and willing to help him dispose of the body beneath eager dissecting scalpels at Surgeons Hall. No body, no murder. Dear God, it must have seemed so easy, so foolproof.'

'Ah now, Vince, I see you're thinking along the same lines as the murderer. So let's leave the dinner party now and consider what happened next morning. You visited Mrs Kellar and found her packing in readiness for a short visit to her sister at North Berwick.'

Vince nodded. 'Her behaviour was certainly agitated but not more so than might be expected in a wife who had decided to run away from her husband and had a train to catch,' he added wryly.

'And after you left, she was seen by Mrs Flynn leaving the house, having had an altercation with Dr Kellar who was to set her down at the railway station.'

'We know she never reached North Berwick,' said Vince.

'And the Doctor didn't hear for a week, until a letter from Mrs Findlay-Cupar was found on her desk. This apparently had not been handed to Kellar by Mrs Flynn. Quite normal behaviour in the circumstances. Mrs Flynn said she didn't recognise the writing and it was addressed to the mistress personally.'

Faro smiled at Vince. 'That was very convenient. All communication between housekeeper and master was limited to notes left on the hall table regarding menus. Our murderer made very good use of the fact that Dr Kellar hated servants and avoided them at all times,' he added thoughtfully.

'And then the clues to Mrs Kellar's murder began to appear. Her bloodstained fur cloak and the carving knife, which was reported missing to me by the maid Ina. This evidence would have appeared much sooner, of course, had it not been for the weather and the fact that they lay undetected under a heavy snowfall for longer than was intended.'

Vince thought for a moment. 'But she couldn't have been murdered on the train. There would have been far too much blood, commotion. Trains at that time are full of folk going home for dinner. No, no. That wouldn't work at all.'

'What is your theory then?'

'You know that perfectly well, Stepfather. It's the only logical solution. Kellar never put her on the train at all. He offered to drive her to her sister's, murdered her in the carriage— '

'Hence the bloodstained upholstery,' Faro interrupted, 'Reported to me by Ina, via Mrs Flynn, but conveniently obliterated – if it ever existed – before I arrived. Go on, so what happened to the body?'

'He carried her under cover of darkness to the mortuary, cut her into more convenient pieces for distribution among his students,' Vince added with a shudder.

'You're quite wrong there. Think again, Vince. Why should Kellar take the carving knife with him and murder his wife in his own carriage. Why should he use a knife at all, when he could have strangled her without difficulty and then disposed of her body in the dissecting room? The bloodstained cloak and knife were accessories to murder that we were meant to find, so was Mabel's bloodstained petticoat stuffed up the bedroom chimney. Think about that, Vince.'

'Presumably he put it there hoping it would burn.'

'And then he got very angry and complained to the servants when it smouldered and filled the room with smoke. Is that logical behaviour? The chimneys had been swept recently, the sweep was re-called and discovered the petticoat, exactly as he was meant to. Why should Kellar, knowing what was in the chimney and in his bedroom because he had put it there, deliberately bring attention to his own guilt?'

'The behaviour of a very scared man.'

'Or the deliberate action of a very clever murderer.'

Vince frowned. 'I agree. There is something wrong here. It doesn't add up to what we know of Kellar.'

'Correct. The answer is that he was speaking the truth. He hadn't the least idea of what was causing his chimney to smoke. As you've pointed out, there are too many inconsistencies here and I think, once again, we have to go back to that train journey.'

'That's it,' said Vince triumphantly. 'The maid with the parcel at Longniddry. Of course.'

Faro pointed to the travelling bag. 'There is the final clue, lad, to what happened. The secret of the locked cupboard, you might call it, in Mrs Flynn's kitchen.

'I don't know what you're talking about, Stepfather, but I'm suitably intrigued, although I doubt whether Mrs Flynn will be pleased.'

'You needn't concern yourself any further about Mrs Flynn.'

'But—'

'You have my assurances of one thing. We will never see Mrs Flynn again.'

'You mean – that she has been murdered too?' said Vince in horrified tones.

They were interrupted by a tap on the door and McQuinn looked in.

'The doctors have left now.'

'Very well. Come along, Vince.'

The nurse barred their way to the ward. 'You must wait. Dr Kellar already has a visitor. I've just shown her in.'

Faro sprang to his feet. 'Mrs Findlay-Cupar?'

'That is so.'

'Dear God, let's hope we're in time. Come along, McQuinn.'

And, pushing past the startled nurse, Faro ran along the corridor and threw open the door of the ward where Kellar lay.

The woman who stood looking down on the injured

man turned to face them. A woman who looked like a very faded watercolour of Mrs Findlay–Cupar. Faro heard Vince's horrified gasp from behind him.

'Mabel. Mabel! You're alive!'

Chapter Seventeen

Hearing her name, Mabel Kellar ran to Vince, who took her in his arms. Looking across at his stepfather, he made a gesture of helpless bewilderment and led her over to a chair.

Sobbing, she turned to Faro, 'I had to come – I had to come.'

'Mabel Kellar, I am taking you into custody for the attempted murder of your husband, Melville Kellar. Anything you say may be taken down and used in evidence,' said Faro sternly.

She looked at him wide-eyed. 'So you think it was me.'

'We know it was you.'

Suddenly she noticed the travelling bag. She gave a little cry as Faro slipped open the locks. At first glance the bundle he withdrew resembled a tailor's dummy, but closer inspection revealed a padded tunic.

Faro held it up triumphantly. 'Behold the earthly remains of Mrs Flynn.'

Mabel Kellar was suddenly calm. 'All right, I admit it. I wanted him dead. I wanted to punish them both. I could have forgiven him if he hadn't destroyed my baby. Then to give Eveline a child and to want to marry her. I wanted him to suffer as he'd made me suffer through the years. He even told me how easy it would be for him to commit murder and get away with it.

'I decided to beat him at his own game. It seemed so easy. Ever since Christmas I'd been planning my revenge in every detail and Melville played into my hands when he

186

dismissed the last housekeeper. I would pretend to engage a new one, Mrs Flynn. Melville hardly glanced at references and I knew he would never notice the new housekeeper or that he never saw us together. All I had to do was to appear a few times in the kitchen as Mrs Flynn, for Ina's benefit.

'I sent the letter to Tiz. I only intended being Mrs Flynn for a week or so, the longer I kept up the pretext the more dangerous it became, especially as I would have no excuse to remain in the house once Mrs Flynn had worked her notice.'

'All I had to do was disappear, leave some evidence indicating that I had been murdered and then Melville would be convicted and hanged for it.'

'How did you intend to return from the dead?'

'I'd wait a couple of years and pretend to have had a street accident in London and lost my memory. Something like that would work very well,' she said dismissively, while Faro and Vince exchanged helpless glances indicating her extraordinary naivety.

'I had you, Inspector Faro, to the house the night before so that you would be prepared for Mrs Flynn. All I needed were spectacles, a grey wig and a maid's cap. The toothache and swathing my face with scarves was a great help,' she added proudly and then with a sigh, 'No one will ever know how hard it was. I'm not a very good cook at the best of times but it was a nightmare trying to cook for a dinner party and have everything ready at the right time.

'But my plan was working. Next morning Melville took me to the North Berwick train and that was where everything went wrong.'

She stopped and stared miserably out of the window as Faro took up the story.

'When you boarded the train, you were fortunate enough to find an empty first-class compartment. Quickly you took off the fur cloak and became Mrs Flynn, but without the padded tunic because it hampered swift movement. You also had in the bag some raw butcher's meat which you intended to use for dabbing the fur cloak. However, you were unlucky. Another passenger got in. Correct?'

Mrs Kellar nodded dully. 'Yes, at Musselburgh. I decided I must get out at Longniddry and work in the waiting-room, praying that it would be empty. I didn't have a great deal of time if I was to catch the train back to Edinburgh.' She giggled. 'A few minutes, that's all I needed. And then— '

'And then you had your worst bit of luck. You were seen leaving and the man on duty thought you were trying to sneak out without a ticket. When he stopped you, he noticed blood on your hands. While he went for water, you disappeared down the road.'

She shook her head. 'I only went fifty yards, hid round a corner and doubled back and over the railway bridge in time for the Edinburgh train. As we left the station, I waited in the corridor and hurled out the cloak and the knife. If it hadn't been for the snow . . . I began watching the weather. It got worse and worse. And what if someone had decided to keep the cloak? Despite the stains it was valuable – and warm. What if they weren't discovered before Mrs Flynn had worked her notice.'

She paused and laughed bitterly. 'Notice? Melville never noticed me at all, living in the same house. Can you credit that? All he did was leave notes on the table for me. And I hadn't bargained for all that anxiety, those hours of terror when I thought my plan had failed. I couldn't believe that no one would arrest Melville after the cloak and the knife were handed in. It was then I decided on the petticoat.

'If that didn't work, then it would have to be poison. When the postman delivered Eveline's letter, it was like gift from heaven – or hell,' she added savagely. 'My troubles were over. I had been given the perfect reason for his suicide.

'That old pistol, he was very proud of it. I slipped into the bedroom and he was breathing deeply, still asleep, I thought. But as I fired, he opened his eyes, turned his head – oh dear God. He fell back against the pillow. But he wasn't dead.

'He was lying there bleeding to death. And in that moment, I knew how wicked I had been. I knew that I loved him and whatever he had done to me, I wanted him alive again. Especially now that Eveline didn't want him. He would need me again. I would be able to comfort him, prove what a wife's faithful love could be. He would never stray again, he would be so grateful to me for taking him back. And we would be happy,' she added with a wistful sigh and then the tears rolled down her cheeks.

'Oh dear God, what had I done. I had killed him for nothing, nothing,' she added pathetically.

'I must have been out of my mind. I rushed downstairs, got a basin and water – I think I fainted, because when I came to I was lying on the kitchen floor, the water spilt. I refilled it, ran upstairs – and he had gone, bleeding, terribly injured as he was, he had managed to get out of the house.'

She stopped. 'You know the rest.' She looked at Faro. 'I had some other awful moments, when you kept picking up my hair brushes. I was sure you guessed then and I thought Vince had recognised my voice last night.'

'I did – or thought I did,' said Vince.

With a sigh she stood up, 'I'm ready to go with you, but – but I just wanted to see him – just once more.'

She turned to Vince. 'I still love him, even though I wanted my revenge. When I saw him lying dying I knew then that I had only destroyed myself.' Staring across at the bed where Kellar lay, still and inert, she whispered, 'May I kiss him goodbye before I go with you?'

Over her head, Vince nodded eagerly to Faro.

'All right, Mrs Kellar.'

Kellar opened his eyes as she bent over him. 'Mabel – Mabel is that you . . . ?' His voice was faint, far-off. 'I thought you were Flynn.'

She fell sobbing at his bedside. 'Forgive me, forgive me – for loving you.'

Kellar, bewildered, put out a hand and stroked her hair. 'Mabel, you idiot,' he whispered.

Faro and Vince stood by the window watching the motionless couple, the weeping woman whispering at her husband's bedside, holding his hand, his white bandaged face staring straight ahead.

At last, she dried her tears and said, 'I'm ready to go now.'

'Where are you taking her?' asked Kellar weakly. 'Not jail. Oh, no, not until I've talked to Superintendent McIntosh. I've sent for him, he should be here directly.' And in a voice gathering strength, 'Please leave us alone, Faro.'

They joined McQuinn in the corridor and a few minutes later the Superintendent stormed along and, with a face like thunder, motioned Faro towards the waiting-room.

'Mind leaving us, Dr Laurie?' When the door closed, McIntosh sat down and said. 'All right, Faro. Now let's have your version of what all this is about.' He listened grimly and at the end said, 'I'm inclined to agree with your story. But Kellar tells me in confidence that he tried to commit suicide for personal reasons, especially since his wife had gone off and left him.'

It was Faro's turn to look amazed.

'For the record this will go down as an accident with an old pistol he was priming.'

'What about all the evidence, the cloak and the knife, for instance?'

'It will be filed away under mysteries unsolved.'

'And Mrs Flynn?'

'The housekeeper? Oh, she disappeared without leaving a forwarding address. Not unusual where a servant's working notice.'

Faro decided to say nothing of the contents of the travelling bag.

'As for that rather simple maid, we would never call her to give evidence.'

There was a short interval before Faro spoke. 'This is a miscarriage of justice, you understand that, sir, don't you,' he said severely. 'And you are contributing to it.'

McIntosh grinned. 'Of course. But we take our choice and frankly I'd rather distort the truth a little than have the scandal of the Kellar affair, his wife's imprisonment with the inevitable repercussions on the honour of the Edinburgh City Police, made public.'

McIntosh was unlucky. Kellar's accident found its way into the Sunday newspapers and so too did the scandal regarding Mrs Shaw. No one knew quite how or who to blame for 'Sensational story of police surgeon's secret amour. Disappearing wife returns home. After discovering awful truth about her husband's double life . . . '

There was no knighthood possible after that. Mabel could not have had a more perfect revenge since Melville was not only thwarted of honour but also of the woman he had loved and the son he craved, who went with his true father and mother to live in Yorkshire.

Kellar, released from hospital, went home to Mabel.

Vince, although sympathetic, considered it prudent to remain at a distance in future. 'She obviously hadn't even thought it through, had she? I mean, how could she possibly reappear and reclaim all her property without some very searching questions being asked?'

Faro shrugged. 'I don't think it would have ever got that far. The moment she knew Kellar had been convicted, she would never have let him hang. Not after that performance when he was only injured.'

'What would she have got, if he'd let her be taken? Not the death sentence, I hope,' said Vince.

'A few years for attempted murder.'

Vince sighed. 'Poor Mabel. Her sentence has already begun.'

'Yes, lad, it began by his bedside and I'm afraid it will continue for the rest of her life.'